Praise for CROWN OF FEATHERS

"Absolutely unforgettable. This is an instant favorite."
—KENDARE BLAKE, #1 *New York Times* bestselling author
of the Three Dark Crowns series

"A fierce and incendiary tale of warrior women,
sisterhood, and the choices that define us."
—LISA MAXWELL, *New York Times* bestselling author
of the Last Magician series

"A feast of magic, action, and romance."
—ELLY BLAKE, *New York Times* bestselling author of *Frostblood*

"Nicki Pau Preto is a bright new talent!"
—MORGAN RHODES, *New York Times* bestselling author
of the Falling Kingdoms series

ALSO BY NICKI PAU PRETO

Heart of Flames

CROWN OF FEATHERS

NICKI PAU PRETO

SIMON PULSE
New York   London   Toronto   Sydney   New Delhi

SIMON PULSE
An imprint of Simon & Schuster Children's Publishing Division
1230 Avenue of the Americas, New York, New York 10020
First Simon Pulse paperback edition December 2019
Text copyright © 2019 by Nicki Pau Preto
Cover illustration copyright © 2019 by Kekai Kotaki
Also available in a Simon Pulse hardcover edition.
All rights reserved, including the right of reproduction in whole or in part in any form.
SIMON PULSE and colophon are registered trademarks of Simon & Schuster, Inc.
For information about special discounts for bulk purchases, please contact
Simon & Schuster Special Sales at 1-866-506-1949 or business@simonandschuster.com.
The Simon & Schuster Speakers Bureau can bring authors to your live event.
For more information or to book an event contact the Simon & Schuster Speakers Bureau
at 1-866-248-3049 or visit our website at www.simonspeakers.com.
Cover designed by Sarah Creech
Interior designed by Mike Rosamilia
The text of this book was set in Adobe Garamond Pro.
Manufactured in the United States of America
2 4 6 8 10 9 7 5 3 1
The Library of Congress has cataloged the hardcover as follows:
Names: Pau Preto, Nicki, author.
Title: Crown of feathers / by Nicki Pau Preto.
Description: New York : Simon Pulse, [2019] | Summary: Veronyka, sixteen, leaves her controlling sister
and disguises herself as a boy to join a secret group of warriors who ride phoenixes into battle.
Identifiers: LCCN 2018013701 (print) | LCCN 2018020873 (eBook) |
ISBN 9781534424647 (eBook) | ISBN 9781534424623 (hardcover)
Subjects: | CYAC: Magic—Fiction. | Sex role—Fiction. | Secret societies—Fiction. |
Human-animal relationships—Fiction. | Phoenix (Mythical bird)—Fiction. | Sisters—Fiction. | Fantasy.
Classification: LCC PZ7.1.P384 (eBook) | LCC PZ7.1.P384 Cro 2019 (print) | DDC [Fic]—dc23
LC record available at https://lccn.loc.gov/2018013701
ISBN 9781534424630 (pbk)

TO MY MOTHER,

෴

a red-haired warrior queen who
taught me not only how to fly,
but also how to fight

What did the great heroes do
when the sun fell from the sky?

They leapt onto those wild flames
and learned how to fly.

—*Ancient Pyraean proverb*

*I had a sister once. If I had known then
what I know now, I might have chosen not
to love her. But is love ever truly a choice?*

- CHAPTER I -

VERONYKA

VERONYKA GATHERED THE BONES of the dead.

Joints of venison blackened and burned on the spit, and racks of ribs stewed so long that they were dry and brittle as driftwood. She dug through rotten lettuce and potato peelings for tiny, sharp-as-daggers fish bones and the hollow, delicate bones of birds.

The small owl perched on her shoulder hooted softly in distaste at her most recent discovery. Veronyka shushed him gently, piling the bird bones inside her basket with the rest and standing.

It was late evening, the cool night air threatening frost. The village streets were empty and quiet, with no one to notice the solitary girl digging through their garbage heaps. The clouds above glowed iron gray, obscuring the full moon and making it almost impossible to see in the darkness. That was why she'd called the owl to be her guide. His eyes were precise in the black of night, and with a nudge to her mind, he showed Veronyka the way over rocks and boulders and under low-hanging branches. In her haste, she tripped and stumbled anyway; Val had told her to hurry, and she knew better than to keep her sister waiting.

Excitement and anticipation crackled in her veins, tinged with no small amount of fear—would tonight *finally* be the night?

Veronyka's breath created clouds in front of her face as she made her way back to the cabin she and Val shared. It was small and had been deserted when they'd found it, the bright blue paint peeling on its front door and the shutters broken, probably used during the warmer months for hunting and then abandoned during the rainy winter season. The weather was getting drier and hotter with each passing day, so they wouldn't be able to stay much longer. Another home, come and gone.

As the cabin came into view, Veronyka's insides contracted. The thick column of smoke that had been billowing from the chimney when she left was nothing more than a thin stream of ghostly wisps. They were running out of time.

She ran the last few steps, the flimsy wooden door thwacking against the stone wall as she pushed her way into the single room. All was darkness, save for the orange flicker of the glowing embers. The smell of smoke was heavy in the air, the taste of ash bitter on her tongue.

Val stood in front of the round hearth in the middle of the cabin, turning at the sound of Veronyka's entrance. She wore an impatient, agitated expression as she snatched the basket from Veronyka's grip and stared in at its contents.

She snorted in disapproval. "If that's the best you can do . . . ," she said, tossing it carelessly aside, half the bones spilling onto the packed earthen floor.

"You said to hurry," Veronyka objected, looking around Val to see that the fire burned hot and low beneath a pile of new kindling. These weren't the boiled or spit-blackened bones of animals, though. These were large white bones.

Human-looking bones.

Val followed her line of sight and answered the unasked question. "And still you took too long, so I went looking on my own."

A shudder ran down Veronyka's spine despite the heat.

She tugged at the heavy wool cloak that was wrapped around her shoulders, and her owl guide, whom she'd completely forgotten about, ruffled his feathers.

The movement drew her sister's attention. Veronyka froze, her muscles tingling as she awaited her sister's reaction. Would she fly off the handle, like she often did, or would she let the animal's presence slide?

The owl twitched nervously, shifting from foot to foot under Val's gaze. Veronyka tried to soothe him, but her own anxiety was rippling across the surface of her skin. A moment later his clawed feet dug into Veronyka's shoulder, and he glided soundlessly out the still-open door.

Veronyka shut it behind him, taking her time before she faced her sister, dreading the argument that was sure to come. They were both animages—able to understand and communicate with animals—but they had very different views on what that meant. Val believed animals should be treated and used as tools. Compelled, controlled, dominated.

Veronyka, on the other hand, felt kinship with animals, not superiority over them.

"Loving them is weakness," Val warned, her back to Veronyka as she crouched before the hearth. She added some of the smaller bones from Veronyka's basket to the growing flames, piling them carefully around the sides of two smooth gray eggs, blackened and streaked with soot. They sat amid the glowing hot embers in a bed of bone and ash, tongues of fire licking up their sides.

Though Veronyka couldn't see Val's face, she could imagine the fervor in her eyes. Veronyka expelled a slow, somewhat exasperated breath. They'd had this conversation before.

"The Riders didn't treat their mounts like pets to be cuddled and fawned over, Veronyka. They were warriors, *phoenixaeres*, and their bond wasn't love. It was duty. Honor."

Phoenixaeres. Even with Val's scolding, excitement blazed in Veronyka's heart whenever her sister spoke about Phoenix Riders—animages who'd bonded with phoenixes. The literal translation of the ancient Pyraean word was "phoenix *masters*," something Val often reminded her of. Only animages could become Riders, because only through their magic could they hatch, communicate with, and ride the legendary creatures.

It was all Veronyka had ever wanted. To be a Phoenix Rider like the warrior queens of old.

She wanted to soar through the sky on phoenix-back, to be fierce and brave like Lyra the Defender or Avalkyra Ashfire, the Feather-Crowned Queen.

But it had been more than sixteen years since the last Phoenix Riders had graced the Golden Empire's skies. Most had died in the Blood War, when Avalkyra and her sister, Pheronia, were pitted against each other in a battle for the empire's throne. The rest had been labeled traitors for turning against the empire and were hunted down and executed afterward. Practicing animal magic without registering and paying heavy taxes had been made illegal, and animages like Veronyka and Val had to live in secrecy and squalor, hiding their abilities, in constant fear of being captured and forced into servitude.

During their glory days, the Phoenix Riders were guardians above all else, and for Veronyka, even the idea of them had been a shining beacon of hope when she was growing up. Her grandmother had always promised that one day the Phoenix Riders would return. One day it would be safe to be an animage again. And when her grandmother had died, Veronyka had vowed to become one herself. She wanted to be the light in the darkness for other poor, lonely animages living in hiding. She wanted the strength and the means to fight and protect others like her and Val. The strength she *hadn't* had to protect her grandmother.

Maybe the Phoenix Riders as a military order were gone, but you needed only two things if you wanted to be a *phoenixaeris*: animal magic and a phoenix.

Veronyka moved around Val to kneel next to the hearth. The phoenix eggs nestled there were roughly the size of her cupped hands, and their color and texture were so similar to that of natural stones that they could easily be overlooked. It was a defense mechanism, Val had said, so that phoenixes could lay their eggs in secret and leave them unguarded for years until they—or an animage—came to hatch them. The Riders often concealed eggs as well, placing secret caches inside statues and sacred spaces, but many had been destroyed by the empire during the war.

Veronyka and Val had been searching for phoenix eggs for years—in every run-down temple, abandoned Rider outpost, and forgotten building they could find. They'd traded meals for information, sold stolen goods for wagon rides, and made other transactions Val wouldn't let her see. After their grandmother had died, Val had been determined to get them out of Aura Nova, the capital of the empire, and into Pyra—but it hadn't been easy. Travel outside the empire after the war had been closely monitored, as many of Avalkyra Ashfire's allies had tried to get into Pyra to avoid perse-cution. In the years since, with the threat of bondage or poverty under the magetax, many animages had tried to do the same. Pyra had once been a province of the empire, but it had declared its autonomy under Avalkyra Ashfire's leadership. With the death of its Feather-Crowned Queen, it had become a lawless, somewhat dangerous place—but it was still safer for animages than the empire.

Without proper identification, Veronyka and Val hadn't been able to cross the border. *Plus*, they were animages—if their magic had been dis-covered, they would have been put into bondage. So they'd been forced to travel within the empire, Val leading, Veronyka following. They'd slept in ditches, on rooftops, in the pouring rain and the sweltering heat. Val would disappear—sometimes for days—then return with blood on her shirt and a coin purse in her hands.

Those had been hard times, but they'd finally bribed their way onto a merchant caravan and been smuggled into Pyra, their parents' homeland. Veronyka had been certain that, finally, their luck would change. And after several long months, it had.

Val had found two perfect phoenix eggs hidden in a crumbling temple deep in the wilderness of Pyra. One for each of them.

Just thinking about that day brought a prickle of tears to Veronyka's eyes, a surge of emotion that she fought to keep in check. Whenever Val caught sight of Veronyka's euphoric smile at the prospect of what they were doing, she'd meet it with cold, hard truths: Sometimes eggs didn't hatch. Sometimes the phoenix inside chose not to bond or died during the incubation process.

Even now, Val didn't smile or take joy in the sight of the eggs in the hearth. Their incubation was as somber as a funeral pyre.

A bone snapped in the hearth, and a cloud of ash rose up. Veronyka held her breath so she wouldn't inhale the dead, drawing a circle on her forehead.

"Stop that," Val snapped, seeing Veronyka's hand and swatting it aside. Her beautiful face was a severe mask, her warm brown skin painted with black shadows and swathes of red and orange from the firelight. "Axura's Eye should not be called for some silly superstition. That's for peasants and fishermen, not you."

Val was never much for religion, but Axura was the god most sacred to Pyraeans—and Phoenix Riders—so she usually let Veronyka say prayers or give thanks. Still, she hated the small superstitions, turning up her nose and pretending she and Veronyka were somehow above the local villagers and working-class people they'd lived among all their lives. They hadn't had a proper home since they were children, and even that was a hovel in the Narrows, the poorest district of Aura Nova. Right now they were squatting on the floor of another person's cottage. Who were they, if not peasants?

"Have you eaten?" Veronyka asked, changing the subject. Val wore that fanatical look on her face again, and heavy bags sat under her eyes. Val was only seventeen, but in her exhaustion she appeared much older. Quietly Veronyka moved away from the fire to dig through their box of food stores, which were getting dangerously low.

"I had some of the salt fish," Val answered, her voice taking on the familiar distant tenor that came over her after too much time fire gazing.

"Val, we ran out of the fish two days ago."

She shrugged, a jerking twitch of the shoulder, and Veronyka sighed. Val hadn't eaten since she'd found the eggs. For all her intelligence and cunning, she often lost track of the mundane activities that made up daily life. Veronyka was the one who cooked their meals and mended their clothes, who worried about sleep and nutrition and a clean home. Val's mind was always elsewhere—on people and places long gone, or on distant dreams and future possibilities.

As she continued to search through their stores, Veronyka unearthed an almost-empty sack of rice. They'd have to find something worth trading in the village the next day, or they'd go hungry.

"You know we won't," Val said, speaking into the flames.

Immediately realizing her mistake, Veronyka closed her eyes. She'd been projecting her thoughts and concerns into the open air, where anyone— where *Val*—could snatch them up. While their shared ability to speak into the minds of animals was fairly common—one in ten people, Val said, though it was higher in Pyra—their ability to speak into *human* minds was as rare as a phoenix egg. Shadowmages, they were called, and for two sisters to have the gift was even rarer. Unlike animal magic, shadow magic wasn't hereditary, and as far as Veronyka knew, most people thought it was a myth. It existed only in old stories and epic poems, a magical ability belonging to ancient Pyraean queens and long-dead heroes.

While they had to be careful with their animal magic since it had been outlawed in the empire, they had to be extra cautious when it came to shadow magic. People in Pyra would often let animages be, but if anyone were to catch Veronyka and Val using shadow magic, they would almost certainly be turned in. For every legend of a powerful Phoenix Rider queen with an uncanny ability to tell truths from lies, there was also a cautionary tale about a dark witch who corrupted souls and controlled minds. It was mostly nonsense, Veronyka suspected, but people often rejected and distrusted things they didn't understand. She and Val were safest if they kept their shadow magic to themselves.

Of course, that didn't stop Val from using it on Veronyka whenever she pleased.

Guard your mind, Val said, speaking the words inside Veronyka's head rather than out loud. Like speaking to animals, shadow magic could be used to communicate, or it could be used to influence a person's will: to order and command. Val often used the latter to get them food or clothes or shelter, but she only ever turned shadow magic on Veronyka to communicate. As far as Veronyka knew. Still, she could see Val was tempted sometimes, when Veronyka disobeyed and refused to listen, and she could understand the danger of such a powerful ability.

"I'm making dinner," Veronyka announced, drawing her thoughts and feelings inward and putting up mental walls to surround and protect them, just like Val had taught her. She was usually better at keeping her mind guarded, but they'd been tending the fire for two days, and in her exhaustion, her emotions were raw and close to the surface. Cooking some food would help distract her from the alternating surges of fluttering anticipation and aching dread that were in constant flux inside her. The closer they got to the moment of hatching, the more terrified she became that it would go wrong, that it would all be for nothing.

Everything rested upon those two round rocks in the fire.

Veronyka lifted their heavy clay pot and hoisted it over to the edge of the hearth, the bag of rice tucked under her arm. "We've still got some onions and dried meat to make broth, and . . . Val?"

Veronyka caught the scent of singed fabric. Val crouched so near the flames that the hem of her tunic was smoking, but she was still as a statue, oblivious to the heat, a steady stream of tears making tracks down her soot-smeared cheeks.

Veronyka's heart constricted, and she looked into the flames, expecting to see cause for concern. Instead the nearest egg twitched and rattled. Veronyka held her breath. The gentle sound of hollow scraping punctuated the hiss and pop of the flames.

A font of purest, powerful hope welled up inside her chest.

She looked back at Val, asking the question—begging for the affirmation.

Val nodded, her answer barely louder than a whisper. "It's time."

In the beginning, there was light and dark, sun and moon—Axura and her sister, Nox.

Axura ruled the day, Nox ruled the night, and together there was balance.

But Nox, ever hungry, wanted more. She began sneaking into the sky during the day, unleashing her children, the strixes, to spread shadows over the world.

To combat Nox's devouring ways, Axura's own children, the phoenixes, joined the fray. Only light can defeat darkness, and so they did, beating back the strixes again and again.

The war lasted centuries, and the world suffered under such a regime. But Axura was wise, and in humankind she saw not beings to rule over, but allies to fight alongside.

Atop Pyrmont's highest peak, Axura took her phoenix form and made contact with the Pyraean tribes who lived there.

"Who among you is brave and fearless?" she asked.

"There is no bravery without fear," said Nefyra, leader of her tribe.

Axura was pleased with this answer and offered a trial for Nefyra to prove her worth. As a test of faith, Axura lit a fire as tall as the trees and asked Nefyra to enter the flames.

Nefyra did so, and burned alive. But her death was not the end.

She went into the fire a tribal leader and emerged as an animage, a shadowmage, and the First Rider Queen.

—"Nefyra and the First Riders," from *The Pyraean Epics*, Volume 1, circa 460 BE

I am a daughter of death. I killed my mother
when I was pulled from her womb; from the ashes
I rose, like a phoenix from the pyre.

- CHAPTER 2 -
VERONYKA

ON THEIR KNEES IN front of the fire, Veronyka and Val watched as a tiny crack appeared on the egg, growing and spreading, as complex as a spider's web, until the bits of shell were held together by only a thin membrane. The egg expanded and contracted, pulsing like a heartbeat, glimpses of scarlet plumage visible in the jagged openings. There was a shudder, and then a small golden beak poked through.

A thrill surged into Veronyka's limbs—she wanted to clap, to cheer—but she fought the sensation, remaining rigidly, unnaturally still. She was afraid to breathe, to blink, determined not to miss a single glorious moment. There was a roaring in her ears, a rushing sound that turned everything in the world except her and this egg into empty, white nothingness.

Veronyka didn't know how long they watched, but hours—or maybe minutes—later, the egg finally cracked open, and a phoenix fell sideways onto the burning embers. It was a brilliant, vivid red—a color Veronyka had never seen in all her life, brighter than a jewel, more exquisite than dyed silk.

She stared at the creature, the jubilation brimming inside her tinged with complete and utter astonishment—they'd actually done it. After all this time, they'd actually hatched a phoenix.

As the bird struggled to its feet, its damp down hissed and smoked, making contact with the charcoal beneath it.

Forgetting that this was a firebird, that heat couldn't harm a creature born from ash and flame, Veronyka gasped and reached forward. Val blocked her outstretched hand, giving Veronyka a moment for her brain to catch up with her body.

The phoenix stumbled over the bits of broken shell, impervious to the heat, until at last it steadied itself and shuffled around to face them. It looked like any ordinary newly hatched chick—wobbly and unstable—with barely there wings and a narrow, spindly neck that could hardly hold up its head. But its eyes . . . They were wide and large and alert.

And they latched on to Veronyka.

She exhaled, a last breath of air that marked the end of an old life—one that was small in scope and purpose. When Veronyka drew air again, it was the start of something new—a life that promised wind-tossed hair and endless blue skies and fire that burned hotter than the sun. Her fingers tingled, her senses sharpened, and the world was alive in a way that it had never been before. Her magic buzzed inside her, drumming like a second heartbeat—or maybe that was this creature's pulse beating in time with her own.

In that instant Veronyka knew Val had been right about the bond between animage and phoenix. It wasn't love—such a small word couldn't begin to encompass the feelings of respect and devotion, of trust and codependence that existed between human and beast. The bond was a unity that was written in the stars, older than the empire and the valley and the mountains, older than the gods, a connection that not even death could shake. Endless, limitless, and somehow timeless, Veronyka's fate was tied to this creature, and they would always be together.

They were bondmates.

A cool breeze slipped across her skin, and Veronyka broke eye contact. The cabin was glowing with pale dawn light, the front door wide open.

Val was nowhere in sight.

～ ～ ～

She returned some time later. Wearing a mask of indifference, she carried a new sack of rice, some cornmeal, salt fish and dried deer meat, a small ceramic jar of honey, and a bag of dates. The dates were a rare treat—expensive and grown only in the province of Stel. Even corn was hard to come by in the mountains, though some farmers worked the crop on the lower rim.

Veronyka got to her feet, leaving her phoenix on the ground and wiping sweaty palms against her trousers. Val often stormed off when she was upset, disappearing for hours—or days—with little by way of explanation. If Veronyka was lucky, the time would allow Val to cool off and forget her anger. If Veronyka was *unlucky*, Val's rage would ripen and rot, becoming all the more potent in their time apart.

Sometimes Veronyka would have no idea what had set Val off—but this time she thought she knew. The first phoenix should have been Val's—she was the eldest, and she'd been the one to find the eggs. Guilt nagged at Veronyka, but she fought hard not to let it spoil this sweet, shining moment. Val would be fine. They simply had to wait for the second egg to hatch.

The phoenix chirruped softly as it pecked around the edge of the fire. The warmth had turned its fiery red down into a soft puff, and its beak and feet were as golden as the phoenix statues Veronyka had seen as a child in the gods' plaza in Aura Nova—before they'd been taken down. Once guardians and defenders of the empire, the Phoenix Riders had abandoned their posts and sworn their loyalty to Avalkyra Ashfire instead. This made them traitors, and phoenixes along with them. While Avalkyra was the true heir to the throne, she'd committed treason and been labeled a criminal before she was old enough to be crowned, and had been chased from the empire. The governors threw their support behind the nonmagical sister, Pheronia, instead, while Avalkyra set herself up in Pyra. She and her supporters had soon been deemed "rebels," refusing to abide by empire law or answer for their supposed crimes. In the years following her death, the empire had destroyed anything that could be construed as supportive of her and her legacy—phoenix imagery most of all.

It was no easy task, as phoenixes had been a part of empire history from the very beginning. They were symbols of the royal line and sacred to the empire's highest god, Axura—translated to "Azurec" in the Trader's Tongue, the common language of the empire. One by one temple statues were removed and sacred prayers altered. Axura—who had always been depicted as a phoenix—was anthropomorphized, and even songs, poems, and plays that featured phoenixes were forbidden.

Though they had begun this process during the Blood War, it had taken the Council of Governors years to finish the job. Veronyka had caught small glimpses of the phoenixes' continued presence up until her last days in the empire several months ago: faded frescoes peeking out from under a peeling coat of paint or crumbling concrete revealing glass mosaics underneath.

Veronyka would often daydream about returning to those places on phoenix-back, scraping the paint clean or cracking the sidewalk in half to reveal the truth beneath.

With a jolt, she realized that this daydream now had the potential to become reality.

Veronyka watched her sister warily; first Val put away the food stores, then she tore open the bag of cornmeal with her teeth, pouring some into a small bowl and stirring in dollops of honey, producing a fine, grainy paste.

"For the bird," she said at last, nodding her head in the direction of the phoenix. "Later it will be ready for dates and fresh fruit, if we can get them."

Val knew everything there was to know about phoenixes, thanks to their *maiora*, who had been a Phoenix Rider back in her day—one of the few who had escaped the empire's notice, at least for a time. Their grandmother loved to tell stories, and while Veronyka had been interested in epic battles and romances, Val had wanted to know more practical things.

Veronyka took the bowl from Val, who refused to meet her gaze, and placed it on the ground next to the phoenix. The bird inspected the mixture for a moment before dipping its beak into the sticky-sweet concoction. "The other one's gonna hatch soon, right, Val?"

Val looked at the rocklike egg, sitting among the burning coals.

"Going to," she said, avoiding the question and closing the shutters with a loud *clack.*

The phoenix's head popped up at the sound, but it quickly returned to its meal. The broken shutters blocked out most of the late-morning sunlight, leaving the cabin in near darkness, save for the warm glow of the fire.

Strange that there were three of them now, when it had just been Veronyka and Val for most of their lives. Their parents had died in the Blood War, and their grandmother, who had raised them for a time, had been beaten to death by an angry mob almost ten years later.

While the immediate aftermath of the war was apparently the worst, there had been many incidents throughout the years—trials of famous Riders discovered in hiding, small groups of rebels and dissidents rounded up and executed—that had caused new fervor to ripple through the empire. The council—the ruling body of the empire, made up of the four provincial governors as well as lawmakers, bankers, landowners, and other important political leaders—made an example of anyone who didn't fall in line, doling out punishments that were swift and severe. Animages grew more fearful and went deeper into hiding, while those who'd grown to hate them thanks to the war became eager to hunt them down and ferret them out again.

It was one such riot that had taken their grandmother. It began outside the courthouses after a trial and spread toward the Narrows, where many animages lived in secret.

When their *maiora* heard the mob coming, she'd told Veronyka and Val to flee and leave her behind. The girls were small and fast and could slip out windows and slink through alleys that she could not.

Veronyka had refused and held fast to her grandmother's old, withered hand. When their door had burst open, her grandmother turned to her, as calm and reassuring as the eye of the storm.

"Protect each other," she'd whispered in Veronyka's ear before being wrenched from her grasp and dragged toward the door.

Val had wrapped an arm around Veronyka's middle, hauling her away, but Veronyka had refused to go quietly. She'd kicked and screamed and bit

Val's arm, but her fighting was useless. She'd been forced to stare, wild-eyed and panicked, as her *maiora* was swallowed by the seething crowd. Veronyka didn't know how they'd found her grandmother or what had given her away, but the mob was too worked up to be reasoned with.

Val pulled Veronyka out the small window, only just evading the grasping, clawing hands of the crowd.

As they fled from the chaos, her grandmother's whispered words echoed in Veronyka's mind. *Protect each other.*

At the time she'd taken the words to mean that she and Val must look out for each other, but the longer she thought about it, she suspected that her grandmother had meant more than that. In the face of hatred and fear and death, her *maiora* had spoken about love and protection.

That was what being a Phoenix Rider meant to Veronyka. Riders were guardians and protectors, and that was what Veronyka wanted to be as well. It was how she'd keep her grandmother's memory alive.

Still, Veronyka had hated Val in that moment, resenting the ease with which she'd left their *maiora* behind. Veronyka had fought, no matter how fruitless, but Val had not.

With time and perspective, Veronyka realized that Val had been what she'd needed to be for them to survive. Veronyka's tears and panic helped nothing. It was Val's determination and levelheadedness that had gotten them through. She was only eleven when their *maiora* died—just a year older than Veronyka—and had shouldered the burden of caring for them both ever since.

As Val lay down on their pallet against the wall, a pang of guilt throbbed low in the pit of Veronyka's stomach. Val had done so much for her, had given her more than Veronyka could ever repay. Now Val had given her a bondmate—the greatest gift of all.

After a moment's hesitation, Veronyka left the phoenix—the simple act of putting distance between them was like a physical pull on her heart—and joined her sister. They always slept together out of necessity, for warmth or because of limited space. Val would never admit it, but Veronyka knew they slept side by side for comfort, too.

As she settled in next to her sister, the knot of unease that had tightened inside her after Val's disappearance loosened somewhat. *Protect each other.* No matter what, that was what they did—what they would always do. Val was difficult. She had the capacity for dismissiveness and cold cruelty. But she was also Veronyka's sister, the person Veronyka loved and respected— and yes, feared—most. They would get through this, just like they'd gotten through everything in their lives: together.

Val faced the wall, and Veronyka stared at the back of her head. Her sister's long dark-red hair pooled on the mat between them, the color rare and particularly unique among brown-skinned Pyraeans. The light of the fire made the strands glow, glinting off beads and brightly colored thread woven into dozens of braids. The plaited hairstyle had been a Pyraean tradition since before the Golden Empire, during the Reign of Queens, when Pyra was ruled by a succession of fierce female sovereigns—Phoenix Riders every one. Both men and women would adorn their hair, using valuable gemstones or found keepsakes to commemorate important events and milestones.

Even after Pyra became a part of the empire, Phoenix Riders would wear phoenix feathers and bits of obsidian, marking them as part of the elite class of warriors. Each piece of volcanic glass, often used for spears and arrowheads in the old days, represented a victory in battle, a token of pride and a mark of experience. It was said that Avalkyra Ashfire had so many knotted into her hair that they scraped and sliced her bare skin, leaving a mantle of blood about her shoulders.

Braids had become increasingly rare in the valley, where the decorations could be seen as a mark of loyalty to Phoenix Riders and Avalkyra Ashfire—and *disloyalty* to the empire's governors. Val had refused to give up the tradition, so the sisters had worn headscarves for most of their childhood. It was a common accessory in the empire, helping them blend in and hide the evidence of who they truly were.

Veronyka ran her hands absently through Val's silky red hair, which was in desperate need of care. Knots and tangles had formed among the loose strands, and many of her braids were sloppy and growing out. They had to be periodically redone, so that the heavy beads and keepsakes didn't fall out, and since Pyrean hair was straight and shiny, treated with wax or oil for better grip. Unless Veronyka did it for her—and even that was something Val barely tolerated—her sister was completely uninterested in washing, brushing, and caring for her hair.

While Val's deep red shade was prized among their people, like the fiery plumage of the sacred phoenix, Veronyka's hair was common black. It was a bit shorter than her sister's, but dressed similarly with plaits accessorized with charms and colored thread. They even had a few matching braids, and sometimes Veronyka liked to seek them out, to remind herself of all they had shared, despite their differences.

She found the pearlescent shells from the time both girls had learned to swim with their *maiora* in the Fingers, the network of rivers that split from the Palm and snaked past the capital city. The entire system of rivers was called the Godshand, fed by the River Aurys, which began atop Pyrmont and split in the valley to spread across most of the empire. Their grandmother said that all Pyraeans should learn to swim in the Aurys, the river of their homeland, and that the water of the Fingers was as close as they were going to get.

After weeks of practice, young hearts full of determination, both Veronyka and Val swam to the opposite bank of the fattest Finger, collected a shell from the pebbled shore, then swam back. Val had been fastest, of course, but for once she hadn't made Veronyka feel lesser because of it. They'd both sat on the riverbank afterward, faces glowing and teeth chattering, while their *maiora* braided the shells into their hair.

With a wistful sigh, Veronyka put the shell-capped braids aside and located the wooden beads they'd carved and painted by hand during their first night spent in Pyra, and next to those, the strips of cotton they'd twined into their hair, dipped in ink and ash to commemorate their grandmother's death.

Each braid marked a memory of their lives together, woven in a living tapestry, forever binding them.

When Val's breathing turned steady, Veronyka released her hair, sat up, and crept toward the fire. Quietly she picked through the embers at the edge of the hearth, the phoenix watching curiously. Veronyka saw flickers of its mind through their bond—a series of sights, sounds, and sensations—that made the world around her feel brighter and more interesting. The phoenix was too young to form any real thoughts or reflections, but already its presence was reassuring to her.

When she found what she was looking for—parts of curving, jagged phoenix shell—Veronyka carefully selected a piece that wasn't too sharp. Setting it aside, she found the small box of thread and wax that she used to maintain her and her sister's hair. There was a wooden comb inside as well, plus twine, needles, a file, and other small tools. Veronyka unearthed the file, carefully wearing down the sharp edges of the eggshell, which was a good deal thicker than regular bird shells. Then she used a needle to carefully twist a hole through the thickest part, as she'd seen her grandmother do with the delicate river shells from the Fingers.

Finally, she pulled forth a chunk of loose hair from the nape of her neck. She wasn't hiding it, exactly, but she didn't want the braid to be too noticeable in case it made Val angry. Surely she wouldn't appreciate the reminder that Veronyka had a bondmate and she did not.

For now.

According to Val, the bonding process began before the phoenix even hatched, which was why it was important to remain close during the entire incubation period. Each phoenix chose their bondmate before they entered the world, making a magical connection before a physical one. And for some reason the first phoenix had chosen her.

Veronyka worked hand-warmed wax through her hair before she began braiding, the familiar twisting motions soothing some of her remorse.

Val would forgive her—she always did. Soon the second egg would hatch, and everything would be right again. They'd raise their phoenixes together and become Riders just as their parents—and their grandmother—had been.

The thought lit a fire in Veronyka's belly.

With phoenixes, she and Val would be able to travel all over the empire with ease. They'd have to be careful, of course, but soon they'd find others like them—*phoenixaeres* in hiding. The empire couldn't have killed and captured them all. There had been hundreds once. And there would be hundreds again. Together, the Riders would be stronger, strong enough to help others, and they wouldn't have to live in fear anymore.

And this time, if someone dared to knock Veronyka and Val's door down and come after their loved ones, Veronyka would have the power to fight. What happened to their grandmother wouldn't happen to anyone she cared about ever again.

Reaching the end of her hair, Veronyka tied off the braid with some twine, then carefully threaded the piece of shell into place with several more knots. She looked down at it, then at the phoenix pecking the ground next to her. Not just any phoenix, but *her* phoenix.

Smiling, Veronyka scooped up her bondmate and crawled back in next to Val. The phoenix brought more than just physical comfort; calmness settled over Veronyka like a warm blanket, and sleep descended at last.

She sat in a sunny room decorated with plush carpets, fine wooden furniture, and carved stone niches filled with scrolls. A library. Veronyka had never been in a library, or seen any room so fine, but in the dream she knew where she was; it felt like home.

Across from her was a girl. Veronyka didn't know her, but she was familiar— she'd seen her in dreams before. Her dark hair was braided with finely made beads and sparkling jewels, and she frowned down at the table between them, her lips twisted in concentration as she stumbled through a scroll.

Dream-Veronyka loved her—affection swelled in her chest, amusement and fondness bubbling up from somewhere deep inside her, some well of emotion that wasn't her own. This was someone else's life she was seeing, someone else's body she was inhabiting.

"*What is* 'phoenovo'?" *the girl asked exasperatedly.* "*It almost looks like* 'phoenix,' *but it has different letters on the end.*"

"*Remember your root words,*" *Veronyka found herself saying, her voice only slightly chiding—and definitely female.* "*If half the word looks like* 'phoenix,' *what does the other half look like?*"

The girl paused for a moment, biting her bottom lip. "*Ovo . . . ovo—egg!*" *she whispered, face alight with triumph.* "*So it's a . . . phoenix egg?*"

Veronyka nodded, her dream-self pleased with the girl. "*They're extremely rare and difficult to hatch. They symbolize life, but also death—it's a cycle. That's how they're able to be reborn. . . . Death gives them life. If not carefully incubated in the ashes of the dead, they will draw life from elsewhere, including their own brothers or sisters, if necessary.*"

"*They kill one another?*" *the girl asked.* "*Their own siblings?*" *Her triumphant expression turned darker, warier, and the room around them grew colder.*

Veronyka shrugged, but she had the sense that they were talking about more than just phoenixes. "*They cancel each other out. A death for a life. It's called balance, xe xie,*" *Veronyka said.*

"*Xe xie*" *was a Pyraean term of endearment translating to* "*sweet*" *or* "*precious one.*" *Its use made Veronyka think that these girls were probably family. Sisters, maybe.*

Footsteps echoed in the dream hallway, and both girls looked toward the door. Their afternoon together was coming to a close. . . .

The dream faded away, and Veronyka woke up in the dark, cold cabin, dread pitted in her stomach.

Visions had plagued her all her life. It was a symptom of shadow magic, Val said, which was why she must constantly guard her mind, even while sleeping. People's thoughts and emotions floated through the air like dandelion spores, waiting to stick to unwary minds like hers—or be snatched up by sharper ones like Val's. For Veronyka, who had a hard time keeping her mind locked at night, these stray thoughts and emotions twisted themselves into strange dreams.

It had been worse in Aura Nova, when there were so many people nearby. Things had been quieter in the mountains, with only Val for company—but her sister explained that minds were cavernous places and that thoughts and memories could linger there for years, only to surface later. Veronyka supposed that was why she'd sometimes see the same people over and over again in her dreams, as if they'd wormed their way into her consciousness and refused to leave.

But this dream, wherever it had come from, chilled her to her core.

Val had often spoken to her about balance. A phoenix couldn't be born from nothing—it either died, turning its own body into ash from which it could be reborn, or as an egg, it had to be incubated in the ashes of another. In the wild, mothers had to die in order to give life to their young, and only birthed a single egg at a time. It was the early animages atop Pyrmont who learned how to burn the bones of dead people and animals to achieve the same effect, allowing the phoenixes to live longer and thrive in larger numbers than they ever had before.

When Veronyka had asked what would happen if she and her sister tried to incubate a phoenix egg in a regular fire, with no bones to feed it, Val had given a single answer: "Death."

And suddenly Veronyka knew why the second egg hadn't hatched yet. What's worse, Val knew it too. They hadn't gathered enough bones for both phoenixes, which meant that Veronyka's bondmate had had to draw life from elsewhere . . . from the other phoenix egg.

Heart tight with worry, Veronyka moved to get up—and noticed Val standing over her, an ax dangling from her left hand.

The sight of it brought Veronyka back to their first night traveling outside of the empire, concealed within a wagon. They'd stopped at a border inn for the night, and Veronyka and Val had had to sleep in the woodshed. When a drunken villager lurched into the building, leering over them, Val had hoisted up an ax in their defense.

The man had staggered back, fleeing out the open door, but Val had followed him.

When she'd returned, it had been dark, but Veronyka had seen her wipe the ax on an apron hanging from a peg. The next morning the apron and the ax were gone, and Veronyka had wondered if she'd imagined it all— except that Val had a shiny new pocketknife and a handful of coins they'd not had the day before. Val had purchased them a hot breakfast from the inn, and then they had used her new knife to carve wooden beads from real Pyraean trees.

Looking back, Veronyka had to wonder what those beads were truly commemorating.

The ax Val held now was closer to a hatchet, but its edge was no less sharp, gleaming in the darkness. The fire had gone out inside the cabin, leaving the room as cold and gray as the second egg, still among the ashes. Veronyka searched for something to say, but Val had already turned away from her. Before Veronyka realized what was happening, Val brought the ax down upon the egg, cracking it in two.

Veronyka's sharp inhalation of breath was lost in the crunch and splinter, and her bondmate's head popped up in surprise.

Veronyka couldn't help but peer around Val's legs with icy trepidation. She didn't know what she expected to see—perhaps the charred remains of a bird?—but what she saw instead was as dense and unremarkable as the inside of a cracked rock. Had it ever been anything more than stone?

Val stood in front of her once more. She nodded her chin at the phoenix next to Veronyka, though she refused to look directly at it.

"You must name it," she said.

"She's female," Veronyka said. She didn't know *how* she suddenly knew, but her instincts told her it was the truth.

The phoenix chirruped softly next to her, and a deluge of ideas and pictures flooded their connection. It seemed that overnight the phoenix's mind had grown and developed tenfold, thanks to the bond magic. The phoenix's thoughts weren't yet the fully structured concepts of a human mind, but they weren't the moment-to-moment impressions typical of most animals either. Though animages could only bond with phoenixes, they tended to have an impact on the minds of regular animals they frequently communicated with too. Horses or working animals that were managed by animages often became smarter in the human sense and much easier to train.

"Unsurprising," Val said. "Female phoenixes are generally drawn to the female spirit, and the other way around. They usually adopt their gender during the incubation process, based on their chosen bondmate."

Veronyka nodded, her thumb stroking the phoenix's soft head. "I think I'll name her Xephyra."

Val's eyes narrowed. She stared at Veronyka for a long time, before crossing her arms and looking up thoughtfully. "'*Pyr*' means 'fire' or 'flame' in Pyraean. Coupled with '*xe*' . . ."

"Sweet Flame," Veronyka said, still running her fingers along her drowsy bondmate's silky feathers.

"Or Flame Sister," Val corrected, given that the prefix could also mean "brother" or "sister," based on the gender of the name. Val had taught her all about language, how to read and write, and about the stars and the seasons and history.

Everything Veronyka was, she owed to Val.

She held her breath a moment, afraid that the suggestion that this new intruder was as close to her as a sister would make Val angry.

Finally Val spoke. "That is a name worthy of a Pyraean queen." Her eyes glittered as if the words were the highest praise.

Veronyka felt a surge of pride at having pleased her sister, and yet she feared what Val said might be true, that she and her bondmate could meet the same fate as the Pyraean queens: fire, glory—and death.

After all, while animages across the valley and beyond might rejoice to see flaming phoenix tracks across the sky once more, not everyone wanted the Phoenix Riders to return.

In Pyra, death was celebrated as much as life.
Only through endings could there be beginnings.
That was the lesson of the phoenix, and it was
the lesson of my life as well.

- CHAPTER 3 -

SEV

SEV KEPT HIS EYES on his feet.

It was a survival tactic, a defense mechanism—and a way to avoid stepping in another steaming pile of llama crap.

For the past six months, Sev had adjusted rather poorly to his new life as a Golden Empire soldier. He'd not chosen this path, after all, and resented being lined up alongside a ragtag mix of petty thieves, murderers, and poor children with no other options.

They reminded him of exactly what *he* was: a poor, thieving murderer.

If possible, he enjoyed his proximity to the empire bondservants even less. They reminded him not of his worst self, but of his best—the part he'd sworn to leave behind. The part he'd had to stifle and suffocate until only the smoking wick remained. Sev might be an animage, the same as them, but that didn't mean he had to live like one—an unpaid servant for the rest of his life.

And he didn't have to die like one either, leaving people who needed him behind. Like his parents had done to him.

Of course, no one needed Sev. He'd made sure of that. It had seemed like a good idea as a child, when his world had collapsed around him. Love no one, and let no one love you. Less pain that way. Sev could die tomorrow, and not a soul would miss him.

Sometimes it was hard to remember why he'd thought that was a good thing.

Sev continued to trudge on, but when the feet in front of him slowed, he risked a glance up. He and the rest of his unit—ten soldiers in total, not including nearly a dozen bondservants—were escorting thirty llamas they'd purchased from a breeder in the backwoods of the lower rim of Pyrmont, the mountain that held the majority of Pyra's settlements.

It was painful to be here again, so close and yet so far from home. He'd longed for a chance to return, to leave the empire behind, but he'd never imagined he'd return like this—as a soldier serving the very empire he hated.

It was thanks to the empire that Pyra was now a cursed land with cursed people. Their fight for independence had ended in thousands of deaths— the deaths of the Phoenix Riders, in all their fiery glory. The deaths of Avalkyra Ashfire, their would-be queen, and the sister who challenged her.

The deaths of Sev's mother and father.

Now Pyra was the home of exiles and people who'd fought against the empire in the Blood War, or animages who wanted to avoid the registry and use their magic in peace. There were no governors stationed here, no laws or taxes or even soldiers to defend this place. Raids were common near the border, which was why Sev and his fellow soldiers were dressed in rags and mismatched gear. They wanted to blend in.

They were part of a much larger force, which was camped well away from the Pilgrimage Road, the main thoroughfare through Pyra. Sev and this small splinter unit had been tasked with exchanging their wagons— useless on the steep off-road paths they intended to take—for the sure-footed llamas, who were docile and mild-mannered beasts of burden, excess excrement aside. Their unit was meant to return to the rest of their regiment before nightfall, and they were cutting it close as it was.

So why were they stopping?

Sev craned his neck and took a step forward, but before he could figure out what was happening, his heel sank into a warm, slippery heap.

"Teyke," he muttered. Only the god of tricksters could manage to constantly put piles of feces underfoot.

Unearthing his boot with a squelch, Sev caught sight of the bondservant next to him, watching Sev's struggle with a frown on his face. The bondservant was familiar. Not because Sev knew him, but because he always seemed to be watching Sev—especially when Sev did something stupid. This happened often, and so the bondservant watched him often. He was about Sev's age, tall and broad-shouldered, with golden-brown skin and black hair cropped close to the scalp. He had a chain around his neck—a requirement for all bondservants—from which dangled a plain pendant, stamped with his name, crime, and the duration of his sentence.

The bondservant seemed curious rather than hostile, as if Sev were a puzzle he couldn't quite figure out, but whenever Sev met his gaze, his expression would turn wary.

Hatred for animages was rife in the military, carried over from the Blood War. It began with the higher-ups, who'd spent years fighting against Phoenix Riders—with all the gruesome wounds and burn scars to prove it—and then trickled down to the lower ranks. Many of the younger soldiers had been orphaned by the war or had grown up hearing their parents disparage the rebel animages and the Pyraean separatists. The two were often lumped together: Not all animages were Pyraean, and likewise, not all Pyraeans were animages. But after the war, when animages found their magic outlawed and their lives in danger, many fled the empire altogether into the relative safety of Pyra.

Most soldiers were spiteful toward the animage bondservants, lording what status they had over them and treating them like lesser servants. Like criminals. After all, they *were* criminals, and whether their crime was serving Avalkyra Ashfire in the Blood War, avoiding the register, or using their magic in secret, the animages in the empire had been rounded up and either taxed into poverty or, if they couldn't pay, forced to serve their debt to the empire as a bondservant. Half of the soldiers were criminals too, but their crimes were forgiven upon enlisting. Like Sev's had been.

Of course, the hatred went both ways. Animages had been treated like traitors—even if they'd had nothing to do with Avalkyra Ashfire's rebellion—and had suffered at the hands of the empire.

Sev was stuck somewhere in the middle, having as much in common with the bondservants as he did with the soldiers.

On the one hand, his parents had been Phoenix Riders, and he carried that same animal magic in his veins. The threat of the empire had forced him to keep it hidden for most of his life, and the fear of soldiers discovering his secret had often haunted his dreams. They didn't know he was an animage in hiding, just trying to make it through another day.

No one did. And they couldn't.

If anyone found out Sev was an animage, he'd have a chain on his neck too, and given his criminal past, a life sentence to go with it.

Of course, on the other hand, Sev *was* a soldier, despite hating and fearing soldiers for as long as he could remember. The Phoenix Riders had stolen his parents, ruined his life, and left him orphaned on the streets of Aura Nova. He couldn't help but dislike them, too.

Sev belonged nowhere, a sheep without a flock.

Staring down at his boot, he gave the bondservant a rueful smile before trying to scrape the mess off on a nearby patch of grass. The bondservant shook his head, looking away. Sev continued to struggle, and the bondservant finally looked back and tapped his belt exasperatedly—as if trying to show Sev something. Sev frowned in confusion, staring somewhat awkwardly at the bondservant's empty belt, before realizing he meant for Sev to look at his own. There hung a waterskin, perfect for removing animal dung. Face heating, Sev nodded his thanks before pulling out the stopper and making quick work of the cleanup.

Once finished, Sev squinted through a gap in the trees. The soldiers had come up to a sun-drenched clearing, and visible in the middle of it was a small cabin with a blue door.

The cabin was round in shape with a domed roof, a popular style in Pyra, and was probably a single-room hunting cottage or the dwelling of some old hermit, tucked away here in the middle of nowhere.

They'd had two orders from Captain Belden when they'd left camp that morning. Return before sundown, and don't be seen. As empire soldiers, they were unwelcome in Pyra, and Sev didn't think their raider costumes would hold up under close inspection. And besides, it wasn't like the locals would welcome raiders, either.

There was a commotion somewhere up the line, and it seemed they were moving out once more. Sev expected they were diverting around the clearing in case anybody was inside the cabin. It looked empty, but not abandoned. Firewood was stacked against the back wall, the pathway was cleared of overgrown grass and weeds, and ghostly wisps of smoke slipped from its chimney.

"Boy!" came a sharp voice, drawing Sev back to his immediate surroundings. Up ahead, Ott was making his way down the convoy. Short and round and puffing from exertion, he reminded Sev of the Fool from one of the Arborian Comedies. Even his patchwork tunic added to the effect; all he needed was a pointed hat and bells on his shoes. Ott's usually sallow skin was ruddy with splotchy sunburns, and sweat trickled down his temples from his thinning hair.

"Sir," Sev said, straightening his spine when Ott reached him and standing at attention. He made sure he moved slowly—never too quick of mind or foot. That kind of thing will get you noticed, after all, and that was the last thing Sev wanted. Most of the other soldiers thought Sev was as dull as an unsharpened blade, and Sev did his best to encourage that assessment. He was just good enough at his work to go unnoticed and just bad enough that they didn't ask too much of him.

"Stay here," Ott said, actually pointing to the ground, as if Sev could possibly misunderstand the instructions. "The animals will move on, but you're gonna be our eyes," he added, pointing to his own with two fat fingers. "Make sure no one sneaks up on us. Me and Jotham are checkin' things out."

Ott hitched up his trousers, as if preparing for the real work to begin. Jotham was his usual partner in crime—in this case, literally—and stood just behind Ott as the line of llamas started to move past them.

Sev knew what "checkin' things out" meant. The empire might have forgiven their felonies so they could serve in the military, but Jotham and Ott were career criminals. They didn't break the law to survive. They did it because they enjoyed it—and because it allowed them to fill their purses above and beyond a soldier's meager salary. They were "innocent" men now, their criminal records expunged and their previous misdeeds forgotten. There were dozens like them in the military, and as long as they didn't steal from their commanding officers and fellow soldiers, no one seemed to care what they did. Jotham and Ott often chose a green soldier like Sev to act as a look-out or an accomplice because they thought young, untried soldiers were too stupid to understand what they were doing.

Sev enjoyed a good theft as much as any poor street rat, but it was one thing to cut a rich merchant's purse and quite another to steal from a run-down cottage with broken shutters. These weren't the kind of people who had excess anything.

And what if the cabin wasn't empty, as they expected?

Sev knew what.

Violence.

"You, mageslave," Ott barked, directing his words at the nearest bondservant—the one who'd seen Sev's heel skid through llama dung. The term "mageslave" was a disrespectful slur, and the sound of it made Sev cringe. He glanced at the bondservant, but the boy didn't react to the insult—save for a tightening in his shoulders. "Bring up the rear. I don't want any stragglers."

Jotham joined Ott, and the two men disappeared through the trees.

Sev hesitated, looking at the bondservant again. "Sorry about him," he muttered.

"Excuse me?" the bondservant said. Sev had never heard him speak before; his voice was a low rumble, as if it came from deep inside his chest.

"It's just . . . They shouldn't use that word."

The bondservant stared at Sev for several silent heartbeats, as if trying to determine the tone of Sev's apology—if it was mocking or genuine. Most soldiers didn't bother speaking to bondservants, and certainly none of them would dream of saying sorry.

At last the bondservant snorted, almost in disbelief, chin falling to his chest as he shook his head. "The word's not the problem, soldier. It doesn't matter if he called me 'slave' or 'sir.' What I *am* is the problem."

He was right, of course. The only difference between Sev and this bondservant was that he had been caught using his magic and Sev had not. Magic had always been a part of the empire—for some people it was like breathing. How was it okay to make *existing* illegal? It wasn't, and as a soldier, Sev was complicit in the injustice.

Sev didn't know what to say, and remembering Ott's order, he stifled his guilt and stepped through the line of trees, leaving the bondservant behind. He took up a position at the edge of the clearing, around the side of the house and away from the front door. He didn't want to see what happened inside.

The full heat of the sun pounded down on him, and the faint smell of woodsmoke—tainted with something bitter and unsettling—flavored the air. A bead of sweat trickled down Sev's forehead, and his leather-padded tunic stuck to his dampened back.

As Jotham and Ott walked closer and closer to the cottage, the silence pressed in, like the forest held its breath while it marked their passing. It was unnatural. Ever since they'd crossed the border of the empire a week back, Sev had been overwhelmed by the sound of the wilderness. He was used to the noise of Aura Nova, where his senses were overloaded with shouts and cries and rolling wagon wheels. But here in Pyra—the Freelands, the Pyraeans liked to call it—the noise wasn't noise at all. It was music, lyrical and lilting and somehow falling into a rhythm that set his mind at ease and soothed his weary soul. The sounds reminded him of his childhood on the farm, when life was small and simple and safe.

How he longed for it.

Something brushed against Sev's fingers, and he whirled around to find one of the llamas next to him, butting its head against his hand in a comforting sort of way. There were two others lingering nearby, along with the bondservant, who had apparently chosen to follow Sev into the clearing rather than keep up with the convoy, as he was supposed to.

Sev pushed the llama aside, more gruffly than he wanted to, but he had to keep up the appearance that he was disinterested in animals. Even regular human affection might be mistaken as magic these days, and Sev couldn't afford to give himself away.

The bondservant's eyes narrowed. Had he sensed Sev's magic just then? Sometimes it got away from him, when he was distracted or upset, and the next thing he knew, a bird or cat would sidle up to him, called there by accident.

"What are you doing here?" Sev asked.

The bondservant's nostrils flared. "What are *you* doing here?" he demanded, his dark eyes fixing at a point over Sev's shoulder, where Ott and Jotham approached the cabin door on quiet feet. "Don't apologize to me for a soldier's harsh words and then stand aside while that same soldier robs innocent people, leaving nothing behind but their corpses."

Sev scowled. "They won't listen to me," he said, gesturing toward Ott and Jotham. "And I hate to break it to you, but they'll do a lot worse before we leave this mountain." The empire hadn't disguised a two-hundred-person regiment and snuck them into the Freelands to undergo treaty negotiations. Sev didn't know exactly what they were here for, but whatever it was, it wasn't about peace.

The bondservant gave him a look of open disgust. "And you're okay with that, are you?"

Sev stared at him, at the challenge on the bondservant's face. It wasn't that Sev was unused to being challenged, but since he'd been a soldier, no bondservant had dared to even speak to him. Yet this one did so without hesitation or fear.

"It doesn't matter what I'm okay with," Sev said. "I have no choice."

The bondservant's lip curled, as if Sev were lower than the dung on his boots and not his superior. "There is always a choice."

Lies.

Sev hadn't *chosen* to be abandoned by his parents at age four or to live in the overcrowded war orphanages, where sickness and hunger were rampant and hiding his animage ability was the difference between freedom and bondage. When Sev had accidentally killed a soldier, he hadn't *chosen* to take the soldier's place, joining the very people he'd hidden from all his life. Choice was an illusion, a fork in the road in an adventure story. Choice wasn't real life—at least, not without desperate consequences.

If Sev was going to make one choice in his life, it would be to run *away* from death and the people who dealt it, not *toward* it.

If the forest was silent before, now not even the wind rustled the leaves.

Then, like thunder out of a clear blue sky, Jotham kicked down the door.

The death of our father marked the end
of a dynasty a thousand years in the making.
But it was not the end of us.

- CHAPTER 4 -
VERONYKA

VERONYKA'S FINGERS WERE GRITTY with soil, the knees of her trousers damp as she knelt in the cool grass. With a sharp tug, she gripped the onion's base and unearthed it by the roots. She tossed it into her basket, and as she reached for another, a bristle of awareness tickled the back of her neck.

She heard something—no, she sensed it, the sound reverberating through her magic, not her ears.

Unease tightening her chest, Veronyka whirled—and came face-to-face with Xephyra. Veronyka smiled, her heart soaring at the sight of her bond-mate, despite the fact that Xephyra wasn't supposed to be out in the open.

"I told you to stay in the cabin," Veronyka chided, though the words were unnecessary given their bond. *You could have been seen.* Xephyra blinked at her, all innocence and curiosity, before snapping at a moth that flitted by.

Veronyka sighed. Even though they were in Pyra, supposedly out of the empire's reach, it was still dangerous for an animage to be seen. And for a phoenix, it was life or death. They weren't too far from the Foothills, where it was common for raiders to strike nearby settlements. If they were caught, Veronyka would be forced into bondage, and Xephyra would be executed.

At least Val wasn't with them. She'd left first thing in the morning to "barter" at the Runnet market and replenish their stores, which for Val meant using shadow magic to convince unsuspecting sellers to give her their wares for free. Wanting to be useful, Veronyka had left soon after to gather bulbs of wild onion, garlic, and edible roots, and Xephyra was supposed to remain safely behind.

Since the moment Xephyra had taken her first flight two weeks ago, Val had forbidden her from ever leaving the cabin unless Val herself was present to keep a lookout, and even those opportunities were rare. Just as she'd turned her nose up at Veronyka's other animal friends, Val's distaste for Veronyka's bondmate grew more obvious every day. Veronyka knew it was jealousy, that Val felt hurt and left out, but the more Veronyka tried to bridge the gap that had grown between them, the surlier Val became. For every affectionate croon or indulgent praise Veronyka gave the young phoenix, Val spat out a dozen rules and warnings about their dangerous magical relationship.

Veronyka mustn't coddle Xephyra, or the bird would grow pathetic and complacent.

She mustn't let Xephyra misbehave, for that showed weakness and Veronyka would lose control over her.

She must maintain the power dynamic: Veronyka was the master, Xephyra the servant. They were not family—not like her and Val—and Veronyka's insistence upon treating Xephyra as a friend and an equal would be their undoing.

Veronyka tried to listen to Val, but she had been close with animals all her life, and she'd always gotten what she wanted or needed with a request—not a demand. Sometimes Val's words seemed like the highest wisdom; at other times they sounded like convenient trumped-up excuses to put a wedge between Veronyka and her bondmate.

Whenever Veronyka openly disagreed with Val, she'd lash out. It had always been that way.

"It's just your sister's nature," her grandmother used to say whenever Val would be cruel or controlling. "She's like fire—she devours."

"What am I like, *Maiora*?" Veronyka would ask.

"You're like fire too—you light the way."

Thinking of her grandmother made Veronyka smile, no matter how desperately she missed her—especially since Xephyra had been born. Veronyka was certain that her *maiora's* advice would counterbalance Val's and help make peace between them again. To Val, their differences were something to fix—a problem that required a solution. And of course, Veronyka was the one who should change, never Val. But their grandmother had a way of highlighting their similarities—like the fire analogy—helping them see that they were simply two sides of the same coin; opposites, but ever connected.

It was okay to be different from Val, and the sooner her sister accepted it, the better off they'd both be.

But Veronyka's determination to stand up for herself wavered the closer she got to the cabin. Things had been so tense between them lately, and she didn't want to have another unnecessary fight. Her patience with Val's surliness was wearing thin. If Veronyka and Xephyra beat her sister back to the cabin, they could avoid a confrontation altogether.

Xephyra soared ahead as they cut through the thick forest, flitting from branch to branch, poking her beak at worms and grubs, and chirruping at other birds that crossed their path. She was like a precocious child—intelligent, curious, and sometimes impulsive, but still lacking a certain maturity and understanding of the world. Their communication had grown in the weeks since her birth, shifting from images and impressions to more developed thoughts and even the odd word or sentence, though it would be months until Xephyra had the vocabulary and language comprehension to have a full conversation. They'd begun to anticipate each other's movements and thoughts, doing daily chores as if attached by an invisible string.

Much as Xephyra was changing, Veronyka found her own mind expanding with all the sensory information her bondmate gave her. Smells and sounds and sights that had always gone unnoticed by Veronyka became bright spots of interest for the phoenix. Veronyka's magic was affected too. Ever since they'd bonded, the strength and reach of her animal magic had almost doubled, bringing the world to life around her more vividly than ever before.

Already Xephyra was the size of a large eagle, her down replaced with silky, iridescent feathers, longer and darker on her tail, matching the beginnings of a crest growing atop her head. Females had deep purple crowns and tail feathers, while the males' accents were golden yellow. Val had said Xephyra was large for her age, and by two months she could be ready to ride. Though the timing varied, most phoenixes were considered fully grown between three and six months.

Phoenixes developed quickly, physically and mentally, their accelerated growth cycle giving them lightning-fast healing times and sharp intelligence. Xephyra was thirsty for knowledge, which was why it was so difficult to get her to remain indoors. The other reason was her deep-rooted interest in finding other phoenixes—"brothers and sisters of fire," she called them in her mind. Phoenixes weren't solitary; they mated for life, and they usually lived in groups, gathering food and defending territory together.

Veronyka knew it was only a matter of time before Xephyra would insist on leaving to seek others like them. She would need the guidance of other phoenixes, and Veronyka would definitely need the help of other Riders. The thought of striking out together was impossibly exciting, an adventure Veronyka hardly dared to imagine. It was the logical next step, but it was so much more than that. The idea of being welcomed by other animages and their phoenixes, of making friends and finding a place to belong was an intoxicating dream. But there were so many uncertainties, not least of which was the question of whether any such place—or any such people—existed.

There was also the question of whether or not Val would come. If she even *could* come. She didn't have a phoenix, after all.

Absorbed in her thoughts and distracted by Xephyra's contemplation of a cobweb, Veronyka actually jumped when a loud *crack* echoed through the forest, coming from the direction of the cabin.

She swallowed, a hot spasm of fear lancing through her stomach. It had sounded like a door being kicked in.

Val.

She must have returned home early.

Veronyka quickened her pace, telling Xephyra to do the same. If they hurried, she might get within view of the cabin before Val saw their approach, and Veronyka could convince her sister that they'd never journeyed beyond the isolated safety of the small clearing.

Fixing the story in her mind, Veronyka ducked under a heavy bough, sticky bits of sap clinging to her fingers and hair. She released the branch with a swish, and the cabin came into view, bathed in the hazy, brass-colored sunlight of late afternoon.

It was peaceful-looking. Idyllic. Like a wise *maiora*'s cottage in an old folktale.

Except there was no kindly old woman before her, offering sweets and a story.

There wasn't even Val, with arms crossed and nostrils flared.

Instead there was a raider. And he was staring right at her.

We clung to each other in our grief.
Her suffering was my suffering.
Her pain was my pain.

- CHAPTER 5 -
SEV

SEV'S HAND DROPPED REFLEXIVELY to the knife strapped to his belt. He was surprised such an instinct existed in him. He supposed the months of combat training were finally starting to pay off.

Only, he'd never trained against an unarmed girl bursting forth from the trees like a startled animal. Her eyes lit on him, then darted to the cabin. This must be her home, and here he was, armed and blocking her from returning to it.

The girl was young—not much younger than Sev himself, but something about her seemed childlike. Her rich golden-brown skin glowed like bronze in the sun, and her black hair was twisted with braids, thick and thin, some capped with beads and shining objects, others woven with thread. Her feet were bare, and that willful vulnerability told Sev that she'd thought she was safe here, safe enough to leave her home without fear of never returning again. Perhaps it was that certainty of survival, that sense of invincibility, that made her seem young to him. It had been a long time since Sev had enjoyed that feeling of safety.

As soon as she saw the knife in his hand, she became abruptly, unnaturally still—like prey sensing a predator.

Sev swallowed, his throat as dry as sunbaked sand. What was he supposed to do now? If Jotham and Ott saw her, they'd want her silenced.

The sound of breaking glass echoed from the cabin behind him, shattering the frozen moment. The girl's head whipped in the direction of the noise, and the realization that there were more raiders, that Sev was not alone, dawned on her face.

"Empty," came Jotham's voice, loud and impossibly close-sounding. Sev's heartbeat spiked painfully, but when he glanced behind him, both Jotham and Ott were still inside the cabin. "Not a damn thing worth stealing, either," Ott added.

Panic sang through Sev's veins. If there was nothing worth stealing, they'd be outside again at any moment.

He turned back to the girl. "Get out of here," he whispered, waving his hand toward the trees.

The girl frowned, clearly confused. Why was a raider who'd drawn his knife on her now telling her to run away? She must suspect some kind of trick, and when her eyes roved the trees around them—and settled on the bondservant, lurking in the shadows behind Sev—she stepped away from them, deeper into the clearing. Wrong direction.

"No, wait. I, we . . . ," Sev began, gesturing toward the bondservant, "mean you no harm." He sheathed his dagger. "But they"—he pointed toward the cabin—"*do*."

She wavered, her gaze flicking from Sev and the bondservant to the cabin, as more sounds drifted out to them: the clatter of items being carelessly tossed around, followed by indiscernible mutters and curses.

Before any of them could make another move, something drew Sev's attention to the forest behind her. A ripple of energy or movement. He thought it might be an animal, but before he could figure it out, the branches to the right of the girl shook and creaked, and something fluttered forward to land protectively on her shoulder.

It *was* an animal—a bird, bright red, with long tail feathers and the beginnings of a spiky crown atop its head. It stood out like fire in the darkness, like the moon on a cloudless night. This was no ordinary animal; this was a creature of magic, its presence pure and powerful and tingling against Sev's skin.

A phoenix.

The bondservant shoved Sev roughly aside, gaze fixed on the firebird. The girl's muscles tensed, but this was no attack. The bondservant stopped and pressed a hand to his chest, a gesture of reverence and respect, and bowed his head. The girl looked up at him, at the chain hanging heavy on his neck, and it seemed that she knew what he was. An unspoken understanding passed between them. They were both animages—only someone with animal magic could hatch and bond with a phoenix, and only animages were forced into bondage in the empire—and that seemed to unify them in a way that left Sev feeling cold and disconnected despite his own magic, standing in the shadows cast by their warm glow.

She gently stroked the phoenix, perched on her shoulder, and a hesitant glance seemed to invite the bondservant to do the same. He took a halting step forward, hand outstretched, when the loud smack of the door against the frame brought them all sharply back to reality.

"Captain'll have our hides if we don't get moving . . . ," Ott was saying, as a second smack of the door told Sev that Jotham was following just behind, as usual. They'd round the side of the cabin at any moment.

Sev's brain rang with alarm bells, and he couldn't seem to untangle his thoughts and form words. "Bushes," he managed, gesturing frantically for the girl and her phoenix to take cover in the trees. His sudden movement caused the phoenix to squawk and spread its wings in a defensive stance, but luckily, Ott chose that exact moment to speak.

"Kid?" he called, heavy footfalls crunching on dried leaves. "Where are you?"

The girl glanced at the bondservant, clearly trusting one of her own kind over Sev, and after the bondservant's reassuring nod, she dove into the cover of the leaves, her phoenix flapping behind her. After making sure both were hidden from view, Sev whirled around.

The two soldiers approached, Jotham as stoic as ever, while Ott's round-cheeked, pockmarked face scrunched in disapproval. "What's this one still doing here?" he demanded, speaking to Sev about the bondservant as if he weren't even there, gesturing carelessly at him with his crossbow.

Sev's mind was still ringing, his hammering heart making it difficult to focus. "He . . ."

"I was looking for this," the bondservant said, stepping forward. In his palm was a bent piece of metal that looked like it belonged on a buckle or strap. "From one of the saddles."

Ott's eyes narrowed, before shifting to stare into the trees behind them. Had he seen the girl, or was he searching for the end of the llama train?

"Listen, mageslave," Ott spat, stepping into the bondservant's personal space, though all this did was highlight the considerable height difference between them. "We're the soldiers"—he gestured to Sev and Jotham—"and you're the servant. Got it? Next time do exactly as I tell you, else I'll fill you full of bolts and leave you for the crows."

The bondservant lowered his hand in acquiescence, but Sev could feel the hatred radiating from him. Ott smiled at his subservient posture, too convinced of his own authority to notice.

"Now get outta here—and make sure that broken saddle gets fixed," he ordered, before returning his attention to Sev. As soon as Ott's back was turned, the bondservant met Sev's eyes for an instant before staring meaningfully at the place where the girl and her phoenix hid. Then he left.

It was all up to Sev now.

"They'll never respect your authority if you don't exercise it every now and again," Ott was saying in his oily voice, slinging an arm around Sev's shoulders conspiratorially. Sev held his breath to avoid the stench of sweat and unwashed skin. "And if they don't respect you, they best fear you. Eh, Joth?"

Jotham nodded placidly, his attention focused on picking his grimy fingernails. Then Ott shoved Sev roughly aside, laughing loudly as his gaze swept the area.

Sev remained perfectly still as Ott looked about, as if his own stillness could help the girl in the trees achieve the same. They were very nearly in the clear. . . .

"What's this, then?" Ott demanded, squinting at a point just behind Sev's shoulder.

Sev kept his features as blank as possible as he turned, though his gut clenched in dread.

Ott pushed past him to pick up a woven basket from where it lay on the ground, a collection of bulbous vegetables scattered around his feet. The girl must have dropped it when she'd first arrived.

As Ott held the basket up expectantly, awaiting an answer, Sev did the only thing he could do. He shrugged. While he was a decent liar, sometimes it was better to just say nothing at all. Stupidity—feigned or otherwise—could explain away any number of strange occurrences.

Ott peered around them, then back into the basket. He snorted.

"Some lookout," he said, tossing the basket back onto the ground in disgust. "Wouldn't notice a swarm of wasps until one stung him on the ass."

"Time to leave," Jotham said, his tone bored. For every ten words Ott spoke, Jotham said two. If Ott was the Fool, short and round and blustering, Jotham was the Scarecrow, his silent, lanky counterpart. Jotham's gaunt face and long greasy hair added to the effect, while his leathery brown skin was crisscrossed with a maze of jagged, poorly healed scars.

The Fool and the Crow had been one of Sev's favorite shows as a child, along with *Princess Pearl* and *The Conman's Bluff*. Sev would squeeze through the legs of the crowds outside the theater on Mummer's Lane and watch from between people's knees as the actors performed. While most of the Arborian Comedies were still allowed, the Epics and Tragedies had been banned. They were popular and, since the war, controversial, featuring many famous warriors and notable figures from Phoenix Rider history—and that was exactly why they were forbidden. Rumor had it that some of the underground theaters and gambling halls in Aura Nova paid extra for the players to perform them in secret for the after-hours crowds, charging twice as much admission to make up for the risk.

As Jotham stalked away, Ott considered Sev.

"Since you're no good as a lookout, you can make yourself useful and carry this," he barked, dropping his crossbow into the dirt before grinning smugly and sauntering away.

Sev watched him and Jotham leave, not daring to breathe until the sound of their departure was swallowed by the forest.

He took a shaky breath, unsure what to do or say, when the girl stood up. She had surely overheard them and knew that he was no regular raider, but a soldier. The phoenix remained somewhere out of sight, and now that the danger had passed, Sev's mind was free to face the knowledge of its existence for the first time.

They were supposed to be things of the past, snuffed out just like the rebellion they had symbolized. Once the war was over, the empire's governors had deemed the creatures too dangerous to remain and too loyal to animages to be trusted. Phoenixes had been hunted into extinction within the borders of the empire, and in the early years following the war, poachers had tracked them into Pyra as well. While the empire's laws didn't exist in the Freelands, with the fall of Avalkyra Ashfire, there was no one in the now-independent country to defend them or their lands. No government, no soldiers or infrastructure remained. Each village governed itself and didn't have the population or resources to unite with the others under a common banner or purpose. Pyra's people might be free of the empire's laws, but they were free of its protections, too.

Sev had often wondered why the empire didn't march into Pyra with its full army and retake the lost province, but according to what he'd overheard, the answer was simple: It wasn't worth it. The land was too wild and vast to easily reclaim and would require spreading the empire's forces thin. Besides, Pyra wasn't a rich country—its economy had all but collapsed during the war, when travel and trade became dangerous—and the cost of rebuilding would be too high.

But then Sev had to wonder—if there was nothing in Pyra the empire wanted, what were he and the other soldiers doing here?

He looked at the girl again. Maybe the Riders weren't gone after all. Maybe *this* was why they had come.

"Is that . . . ? Are you a Phoenix Rider?" he asked, his voice soft. He hadn't spoken the words "Phoenix Rider" in a long, long time. Since his mother and father had died. What if this girl was part of some new rebellion?

The girl crossed her arms, her expression stony. He might have saved her from detection, but he was still a soldier standing between her and her home.

The phoenix chirruped from somewhere behind her, and her harsh features softened somewhat. She crouched down and scooped up one of the tubers from her upturned basket and tossed it into the trees. There was a great crunch and a crackle and an erratic stirring of leaves as the phoenix devoured the treat.

The girl grinned—and Sev smiled too.

There was a moment of camaraderie between them, a heartbeat of relaxed tension, before her breath hitched and her dark eyes widened in alarm.

Sev understood a second later when the air stirred behind him, cooling the sweat that dotted the back of his neck. Before he could react, there was pressure at his hip, a barely audible *snick*, and then a rough hand jerked his chin to the side while another pressed the blade of his own knife against the exposed flesh of his throat.

I promised her the throne would
not come between us. Nothing would.
How I long for the foolishness of youth.

- CHAPTER 6 -

VERONYKA

VAL HELD THE KNIFE in a steady hand, a savage smile on her lips and murder in her eyes.

With her long red hair blowing in the breeze, she looked like a death-maiden, one of Nox's guides into the dark realms, and this poor soldier had been ensnared like a lost soul on a battlefield.

"Val, no—wait!" Veronyka shouted, her hand outstretched. "Stop."

Val stayed her hand, though she didn't remove the blade. She breathed deeply, and the boy shuddered. "He smells of the empire."

"He saved my life!" Veronyka blurted, stepping closer again. The gravity of the situation hit home when she realized that Xephyra was still about, somewhere in the trees. If Val was mad *now*, she'd be a raging volcano if she knew Veronyka's phoenix was out in the open . . . if she knew that this soldier—and that bondservant—had seen the phoenix.

If Val used her shadow magic to interrogate this soldier, she would learn the full truth, and he wouldn't make it out of here alive. Even though he was an empire soldier, Veronyka didn't want to see him die because of her.

She had to keep her sister distracted.

"He was here with three others," Veronyka said, speaking fast, playing her advantage. Val was probably exhausted after a long day in the village, overusing her magic and pushing herself to her limits. If Veronyka stuck *mostly* to the truth and made sure to hide incriminating details deep down in the corners of her mind, Val might just take her words at face value. Veronyka was capable of lying to her sister if she worked hard at it, but it required intense focus. Val usually found her out eventually, but if she kept her wits about her, she could save this boy's life.

"They were armed and came here looking to steal from us," Veronyka continued. "He helped me hide in the bushes and didn't give me up to the others. He saved my life," she said again.

Val considered. "He also robbed us."

"You know there's not a damn thing worth stealing," Veronyka said, using the other soldier's words. The boy darted a glance in her direction, but Veronyka kept her focus on Val.

She considered the boy. "I can sense the coward in you," Val murmured, her body shifting, her movements liquid as she moved the edge of the blade along his neck, almost like a caress. The boy's throat bobbed in a tense swallow, and the tip of the knife bit into his skin. "She's a sweet young thing," she said, eyes flicking to Veronyka. "All alone in the forest, where no one could hear her scream . . ."

Veronyka almost groaned, realizing that her words had somehow become twisted in Val's dark mind. She was inventing trouble now, looking for any excuse to hurt this soldier.

"Val, the others," Veronyka said hastily. "They're waiting for him. If you kill him, they'll come looking—who knows how many. They'll come back, and you can't fight them all."

"I can try," Val said. But Veronyka saw a frown crease her forehead, and her face lost some of the fierce intensity that had come over it.

"He didn't hurt me, never even touched me. He means us no harm—do you?" Veronyka asked, turning her question to the boy.

He was wild-eyed and panicked, and his olive-brown skin had lost its color like painted shutters in the sun. When Val loosened her grip, he slowly shook his head.

She looked bored all of a sudden, as if the joy had gone from the day. She removed the knife and gave the soldier a hard shove in the back. He stumbled and turned around, rubbing a hand across his neck, smearing blood from the small wound Val had opened there.

Smiling her most beautiful, most terrifying smile, Val raised the dagger and pointed it at him. "If I see you again, empire rat, there won't be words between us. Only this knife. And just like this time, you won't see it coming. Not even a sweet story from my sister will save you. That's a promise."

The boy bowed slightly as he nodded his head, then stumbled, looking around for the crossbow his companion had abandoned. He held it out, showing his finger was far from the trigger, before backing into the trees. His footfalls were heavy, uneven things, as if he tried to run forward and look backward at the same time.

After several tense moments, the forest became quiet again.

Val slid the boy's knife into her belt.

The cabin looked much the same as they'd left it, except that their box of food stores was open, their sleeping pallet turned over, and their ceramic cooking pot was laying on its side, a crack running from the rim to the chipped handle. The soldiers were right: There was nothing of value here.

Val began storing the supplies she'd gotten from her day in Runnet. The village was a few hours south at the edge of the Foothills, a popular stop for valley traders. Veronyka stood in the doorway, her basket of garlic and potatoes in hand, uncertain of what would happen next. The events of the afternoon were finally catching up to her, and her hands shook. The rapid succession of emotions—shock, fear, panic—had now receded, leaving her body an empty, quaking shell, and she had the horrible feeling that the worst of it was yet to come.

Surely Val was angry—surely she had something to say, some reprimand or warning. But her sister only poked at the smoking embers of the fire, placing several pieces of wood on top from the basket near the hearth, and then settled the chipped pot on the edge.

"Close the door, Veronyka," she said without looking her sister's way. The words were simple, direct—and yet the hairs on the back of Veronyka's neck rose.

She took her time, mentally calling Xephyra in from outside, hoping that Val's preoccupation would allow her bondmate to return without notice. As Xephyra flew through the door, some of the anxiety that filled Veronyka's chest eased. Her sense of safety had been shattered, but as long as she and her bondmate were together, everything would be all right.

Veronyka closed the door behind her as Xephyra fluttered to the ground, poking her curious beak into the contents of their food stores before flitting off again.

Val watched the phoenix, expression unreadable. Then she drew the soldier's knife from her belt and held it out to Veronyka.

Veronyka frowned, uncertain. Then Val nodded down at the basket of vegetables she'd gathered.

"Careful," Val said when Veronyka wrapped her fingers around the hilt. "It's sharp."

Veronyka didn't know if it was the lasting tension from the confrontation outside, but the words sounded closer to a threat than a caution. She looked down at the shining blade, its edge catching the waning evening sunlight that filtered through the shutters. She was startled to discover it was stamped with the crossed-dagger symbol that marked it as Ferronese steel, the finest blade money could buy and rare in the mountains. All the best metalworkers came from the province of Ferro, where the iron ore used for steel was mined. The weapon was more suited to a ranking officer than a lowly foot soldier, and it was strange using the instrument of war to cut up vegetables. It was like using a shovel to stir soup.

They prepared their meal in silence. They'd have to talk about the soldier at some point, but Veronyka was in no hurry to broach the topic. It would mean addressing the fact that she—and Xephyra—had left the cabin against Val's wishes, and it was a fight Veronyka knew she would lose. They might be sisters—equals, in theory—but Val was always in charge. Veronyka was always meant to fall in line behind her, no matter how much Veronyka resented it.

Still, the silence made her uneasy. The only time her sister was ever truly still was when she was plotting.

"I'm going away for a couple of days," Val announced, stirring the contents of the pot, causing great tufts of steam to swirl about her face.

Going away?

"Where?" Veronyka asked, putting down the knife and scooping up handfuls of vegetables to toss inside. Next to her, Xephyra nibbled at a potato skin, lifting the oversize piece into the air, only to shake her head, spit it out, and try another one.

"To look for another egg. There's an outpost just outside Vayle; it hasn't been in use since the Reign of Wisdom, when they relocated to Hightower across the river."

"But . . . Wise Queen Malka ruled almost a hundred years ago. Do you really think there'll be eggs there?"

Val shrugged. "Only one way to find out."

"We should go with you," Veronyka said, her heart fluttering at the idea of going on a journey, however short.

"*You* can come," Val said, "but your phoenix cannot. I won't compromise our safety as cavalierly as you do."

Veronyka stared at her hands. They had come to it, her and Xephyra's disobedience. Rather than await Val's tirade, Veronyka jumped in and changed the subject.

"Maybe it's time we moved on anyway," she said carefully. She might defer to Val, let her make the majority of their decisions, but Veronyka had a brain too—she had opinions and ideas of her own and plans she wanted to make. Veronyka had always wanted to seek out other animages once she and her sister were in Pyra, to try to find friends and allies. Now that they had a phoenix to protect, Veronyka and Val needed those friendships more than ever. "The owner of this cabin could be back at any moment," Veronyka continued. "Xephyra's still small, but she's only going to get bigger. And those soldiers . . . We're not safe here."

"I will protect us," Val said. "I always have, haven't I?" Her jaw jutted out, as if daring Veronyka to claim otherwise.

"Even if you're not here?"

Val's nostrils flared. "If you'd done what I told you to do and stayed inside—"

"I'd probably be dead," Veronyka snapped. They stared at each other, but Val made no reply. "We don't have to do this alone," Veronyka whispered, trying to keep her voice reasonable. "We could look for other animages. We could look for Phoenix Riders."

"Phoenix Riders?" Val repeated flatly. "There are no Phoenix Riders, Veronyka. The empire slaughtered them all."

"The Riders maybe, but not the animages. If *we* can hunt down lost eggs and hatch them, who's to say that others haven't done the same? We should travel higher up Pyrmont. The farther we get from the empire, the better."

"The empire is everywhere, not just on the lower rim. We can't trust anyone but ourselves."

Veronyka bit her lip. All their lives it had been like this. Veronyka was never allowed to make friends, to attend festivals or walk the city alone. It had gotten worse after their grandmother's death, but her loss made Veronyka yearn for connection all the more. Val pretended it was about safety, blindly threatening to kill any stranger who crossed her path, but Veronyka knew it was more about control—and she was tired of constantly bowing to Val's whims.

Yes, the empire was everywhere—they'd just seen the evidence. But just because someone was from the empire didn't mean they were bad. Veronyka and Val had both been born in the empire, no matter their Pyraean roots, and so had their *maiora*. She had told them to protect each other—but that didn't mean living in seclusion and never trusting anyone else ever again.

Trusting that empire soldier had saved her life. If she'd been like Val, blindly threatening to kill any stranger who crossed her path, she'd probably be dead.

There was strength in trust, in unity. They needed to find a place where people like them could be safe and protected. If such a place didn't exist, they'd have to make it for themselves.

"Call her off," Val said, interrupting Veronyka's thoughts. She jerked her chin down at Xephyra, who was picking her way across the floor, burrowing her beak in a pile of shavings.

"What—why? They're garbage anyway."

"That's not the point," Val snapped, picking up the knife from where it lay on the cutting stone. The air in the cabin stilled, as if all the oxygen had been siphoned from the room.

"She followed you today, left the cabin when you told her not to."

"Val, nothing happened!" Veronyka lied, her throat tight with dread. She tried to think of what to say, how to talk Val down from her simmering rage, but her mind was a blank haze. "She's still young. She's curious, and—"

"She's almost ready to *ride*, Veronyka! She's no fresh hatchling. It's been weeks since we built that pyre. Look how fast she grows, how much stronger she gets each day. You must rein her in. There may come a time when Xephyra's obedience is the difference between life and death. You can't *ask* her then. You will have to tell her—and she must listen."

With the knife gripped in one hand, Val drew a pitted date from her pocket with the other, holding it in the center of her palm. Xephyra's head popped up, drawn to Val's movement, her eyes fixed on the fruit in the girl's outstretched hand. Dates were her favorite.

"Val," Veronyka said sharply, her muscles stiffening as she prepared to stand up. Val took a step backward, putting distance between her and Veronyka, and Xephyra followed.

Powerlessness seized Veronyka, turning her body to lead. Xephyra was just out of reach, yet she might as well have been on the other side of the valley. The phoenix's attention was turned toward Val, but she soon felt Veronyka's distress. Xephyra's black eyes glittered as she swiveled her head, looking from her bondmate to the treat, and then back to Veronyka.

"Just call her off," Val said calmly, stooping low to offer the date to

Xephyra. Veronyka couldn't take her eyes off the knife in Val's hand. Dark, dangerous memories flashed before her eyes: Val dragging the dead body of their landlord into the alleyway after they'd missed several months of rent; Val defending them against three men who wanted more than their money, her face exultant and her hands dripping with blood.

"I'm *trying*," Veronyka said in a strangled voice, blocking out the haunting images and turning her focus to Xephyra. She slowed her breathing, trying to calm herself and convey meaning to her bondmate, to explain the concept of danger. Xephyra's response was to send her bright-eyed reassurance: She'd had dates before. They were sweet and delicious, and Val was a familiar sight and sound and smell. Xephyra didn't understand.

"Don't *explain* it to her," Val said, while Xephyra took another step forward. "*Tell her.* Command her to step back. Command her to go to you."

Terror had sunk its teeth into Veronyka, and she tried—but she knew she did it wrong. She was desperate now, afraid and on the verge of tears. She didn't command; she begged. She pleaded. And all her wild emotions managed to do was cause her phoenix to tilt her head in confusion before edging nearer to Val.

"I can't!" Veronyka cried out, losing her faith that Val would never do anything to hurt her. "Please, Val—I can't. I—"

"*Order her!*" Val yelled.

The words weren't just words—they were power. Val had used shadow magic on her, the magic she'd never turned on her sister before. For a moment Veronyka thought her body might bend to Val's will. But the next thing she knew, she was on her knees, reaching, sobbing, tears streaming down her face.

Val straightened up, no longer trying to lure the phoenix toward her. She sighed, her dark eyes filled with disappointment. She tossed the knife onto the cutting stone and dropped the date onto the ground at her feet. Xephyra leapt the last few paces between them and began pecking at it eagerly.

Relief flooded Veronyka's chest, loosening the tight knot twisted there.

"Val—" she began, but she was interrupted by a retching, spluttering sound. A second later panic seared through the bond, intruding upon her thoughts.

She knocked the cutting stone aside and leapt for Xephyra, but Val got there first, slamming into Veronyka and pushing her backward. Xephyra gagged, opening and closing her beak as she tried to bring up the date. Her feelings were so wild and insistent that Veronyka couldn't tell which thoughts were hers and which belonged to the phoenix. As Veronyka struggled against Val, sorting through her clouded mind, she finally made sense of what was happening. Xephyra wasn't *choking* on the date; it wasn't lodged in her throat, obstructing her airway. She'd already swallowed it. So why was she struggling to breathe?

"You poisoned her," Veronyka gasped, unable to believe it even as she knew it must be true. She stared wide-eyed at Val—the person who'd helped raise her, Veronyka's sister and protector and friend.

"*Xe* Nyka," she said, using the Pyraean nickname for "Veronyka." Val's voice was sweeter in Pyraean, the long *e* sound of *Nyka* softer, gentler— almost soothing. But if it wasn't a denial Val intended to speak, Veronyka didn't want to hear it. She shoved her sister, hard, and Val toppled backward into the cabin wall.

Veronyka didn't hesitate, but flung herself onto the ground next to her bondmate. Xephyra's bulging eyes met hers, but they couldn't focus. Pain gnawed at Xephyra's stomach, pulsing through the bond, while her thoughts, her emotions . . . they were ebbing away, like water through cupped hands.

Veronyka reached out for her, mentally and physically, but then Val was there again, dragging her backward. Veronyka fought her—more savagely than ever before, more than she'd fought even for her *maiora*—but Val's grip was unrelenting. Veronyka could do no more than watch in horror as, with a stagger and one last chirrup, Xephyra fell to the ground, unmoving.

Veronyka's mind went silent.

Their bond, their connection—just like that, it was gone.

Phoenixes are the reason magic exists. Azurec's flaming warriors of light needed to be able to communicate with humankind, and vice versa, and so Nefyra and the First Riders were gifted with animal magic.

Because the First Riders were Pyraean, some people believe that the people of Pyra are the source of magic and that all magic in the valley was brought with them when Elysia made her conquest. But, of course, Elysia didn't come alone—she came with phoenixes.

Therefore, Azurec is the source of magic, and phoenixes are its bearers, spreading magic across the land and bringing it to life where it lay dormant in humans all over the valley.

Of course, if phoenixes were ever to disappear from the empire, magic would soon follow.

—"Origins of Magic," from *Solstice Day Sermons* by Friya, High Priestess of Azurec, published 111 AE

There was rot inside the empire,
taking root in secret, unchecked places.
I knew I could not unplant the seeds, but
I could raze the crop to the ground.

- CHAPTER 7 -
SEV

SEV RETURNED TO THE campsite in a stupor.

He kept seeing the girl and her phoenix, kept feeling the phantom press of cold steel against his throat. Sev rubbed the wound, the cut a superficial, stinging reminder of how close he'd been to death.

But it wasn't the brush with death that had him rattled—he'd been there many times before.

No, it was that gods-cursed phoenix.

What was he supposed to do now? Sev had known he wasn't cut out for life as a soldier, but now he knew it beyond any shadow of a doubt. He couldn't stomach the thought that they might run into more like her and that things might turn out very differently. He had been lucky today—both he and the girl had—but next time he might not be.

Next time Sev might find himself with an innocent animage's blood on his hands.

He had to find a way out of this mess.

When he rejoined Jotham and Ott, he kept his distance, not wanting to draw notice to himself or the fresh cut on his throat. It was growing dark by the time they passed the perimeter guard, and soon a low rumble of conversation, followed by shadowy figures moving through the trees, told him they'd arrived at camp. They'd set up in a thick copse of trees, and though the darkness was growing deeper with every step, there wasn't a single torch or fire to light the way. Secrecy was paramount, and any fires after nightfall were prohibited.

The soldiers tended to their weapons and set up their tents and bedrolls, while the bondservants fed the newly arrived pack animals and cared for the messenger pigeons. The cooks and attendants were already preparing the evening meal, slicing up cured meats and slathering honey on cold barley cakes. Just the sight of the hard, round disks made Sev want to gag. He'd been starving most of his life, but even he struggled with the bland, starchy food, a staple in the empire's military diet.

Better barley than black stew, he thought. It was a common saying among the soldiers he'd met who had, like him, gotten their start in the poorest parts of the empire, lining up for hours in the Narrows or the Forgotten District for a ladleful of the dark sludge-like gruel served by the acolytes of Miseriya—goddess of the poor and hopeless.

Up ahead Ott's angry voice floated above the sounds of the camp. "What d'you mean the captain's gone?" he demanded. "What'd we rush back for, then?"

"You rushed back because your captain ordered you to," came the curt reply.

It was Officer Yara, Captain Belden's second-in-command. She was a veteran of the Blood War, her face and hands pocked with scars and burn marks. She was one of the few women in their party, a relic from the time before the war, when female enrollment in the military was encouraged. It was Phoenix Rider tradition for both men and women to fight, but after the Riders defected and betrayed the empire, the governors did everything they could to erase their influence—from destroying statues and banning songs to changing laws and customs. As far as Sev knew, women were still allowed to join the army, but it wasn't common practice.

Officer Yara was also Pyraean, but she was no animage, and so had remained loyal to the empire. She had earned her position during the war and fought hard for the respect of her peers. She was strict and no-nonsense, overseeing the daily operations of their company with a firm hand.

"He has gone on an urgent errand," she continued, "and you will report to me in his stead."

After some dark muttering, Ott proceeded to recount the day's events, conveniently leaving out their stop at the cabin.

Sev barely listened, his mind racing with what Officer Yara had said. The captain had gone on an urgent errand. That meant a change in routine. That meant possibility.

Sev closed his eyes and flashed back to the duty roster he'd seen just that morning. He had a gift for memory, and he usually put his overactive brain to use, studying people and things and ordering them in his mind. It was a habit he'd picked up on the streets of Aura Nova. Just as he knew where to beg for coins and where to beg for a roll, he also knew which alleys were off-limits, thanks to gangs and street lords, and the best shortcuts to make an easy escape.

He'd had to start all over again in the army, learning who to avoid— like Jotham and Ott—and who might show a kind hand. Sev had memorized people's schedules and preferences, as well as their skills and liabilities. Most of it was useless, but sometimes it came in handy.

Like today.

Captain Belden had two personal guards, both of whom usually worked a night watch shift. But with Captain Belden gone from camp—and them with him—their shifts would have to be covered by two others. It was a small thing, but it might just be the advantage Sev needed, the twist of fate that he'd been waiting for.

He had wanted a way out ever since he'd been made a soldier, but it hadn't taken long to realize that desertion was next to impossible inside the empire's heavily guarded training facilities and walled compounds. But then he'd been sent on his first mission, *outside* the empire. Sev had figured his work was half-done and had been on the lookout for his chance ever since.

Dragging his feet, Sev lumbered forward. "'Scuse me, Officer Yara?" he said as Jotham and Ott were dismissed.

She peered down her nose at him, and Sev guessed she was trying to remember his name. "Yes . . . soldier?"

"D'you know if Garret is already at his post? He said it was my duty to bring 'round dinner to him and Arro, and—"

Yara's lips pursed. She knew full well that it wasn't Sev's duty to bring dinner to his fellow soldiers, and no doubt assumed this was some form of hazing that the younger recruits often endured at the hands of the older— like the crossbow Ott had ordered Sev to carry on his behalf.

"Garret and Arro are currently accompanying Captain Belden on his errand. Rian and Heller have taken their places, but I assure you, you need not bring them dinner."

Sev nodded gratefully and bowed his head before departing, trying to hide the smile that lit his face as he delivered Ott's crossbow to the weapons master. Rian was as good a soldier as any, but while Heller was experienced, he wasn't terribly spry. Old injuries plagued him, and though he did his best to hide it, Sev knew he was going deaf in his left ear. He'd first noticed it weeks back, the way Heller always tilted his head when someone spoke to him, and then Sev had tested his theory several times, sidling up to Heller's left-hand side and trying to catch him off guard. It had earned Sev a smack to the side of the head, but it had been worth it.

It wasn't much by way of an advantage, but it might be enough.

The watch would change once more before they broke camp at dawn, so Sev would have to make his move before then.

Exhilaration swelled inside him as the soldiers settled in for the night. Sev performed his usual routine of wandering the edges of the clearing, outwardly looking for a spot for his bedroll but in actuality refreshing his knowledge of the names, faces, and habits of his fellow soldiers.

Confirming that no eyes followed him and that any problematic soldiers were occupied with sleep or liquor, Sev clutched his bedroll tighter— concealing the fact that he wore a travel pack stocked with water and food supplies—and drifted deeper into the shadows before turning his back and slipping between the trees.

The darkness pressed against his eyes, and Sev had to take careful steps to ensure he didn't trip over roots or get caught in brambles. The perimeter watch always maintained a certain formation, and from his memory of the day's duty roster, Sev knew that Garret and Arro had been assigned to the southwest points, so that's where Rian and Heller would be.

Tiptoeing in that direction now, Sev smiled when the stooped figure of Heller became visible between the trees. Limbs tingling with anticipation, Sev paused to gather himself. He had only one shot at this, and if he was caught, he had no reason for being this far from camp. Reaching into his travel pack, he took a hasty swig from a bottle of liquor he'd stolen from Ott, reasoning that if all else failed, he could pretend to be drunk.

Clenching his jaw, Sev closed his eyes and cast his awareness wide, searching. . . .

Finally, he had it—a cluster of bats perched on a branch nearby. Perfect. While he sent the creatures right, distracting Heller, Sev would slip left.

Once he got away, no one would think to look for him until morning. By then Sev would have several hours' head start. He'd continue south, into the Foothills, and ask around until he found his way to his parents' old farm—or what was left of it.

It had been a beautiful place to live once. Sev's family had been sheep-herders, and to this day, when he closed his eyes at night, he saw rolling green fields and wide-open skies.

When the war broke out, the Pyraean border became the front lines, and animages had fled to the mountains in droves. People like Sev's parents were recruited, given secondhand weapons and phoenix eggs, and expected to fight to keep the empire foot soldiers back.

They never complained, never lamented their fates. It was an honor to serve a Rider queen, they'd said, and Avalkyra Ashfire had the rightful claim to the throne. Her mother was queen at the time of Avalkyra's birth, which made her the trueborn heir, while her sister was made legitimate after the fact.

Sev's parents were proud to don their armor, and with every victorious battle, they braided pieces of obsidian into their hair. The sight of his mother and father flying out to meet empire soldiers had filled Sev with blistering, blinding pride.

Foolish pride.

He'd thought his parents were invincible, but of course they weren't. Nobody was.

Sometimes Sev hated them for dying and leaving him behind, but it had taught him a valuable lesson about survival. He wouldn't make the same mistakes as them.

As soon as he got away from camp tonight, he'd disappear. No more Jotham and Ott, no more scowling bondservants and vengeful girls with sharp knives and extinct phoenixes. He wanted none of it, had chosen none of it. It was time he took his life into his own hands.

With a forceful, somewhat clumsy command, Sev directed the bats away from Heller.

They resisted. Sev was a passable animage at best—too many years of hiding his abilities had left them weak and unimpressive—and the creatures merely chittered and shifted in agitation.

Heller glanced up at the tree, and a cold sweat broke out over Sev's neck. With a desperate surge of his magic, Sev pushed hard, and the bats took flight, darting through the leaves in a burst of shifting, flapping shadows.

Heller cursed and lurched to his feet, squinting into the darkness toward the sound of the chattering bats.

This is it.

"I'd be more careful if I were you," said a voice just behind him. Sev's heart leapt into his throat. He whipped around to see a small figure standing mere inches behind him.

It was a withered old bondservant whose pale, wrinkled face was topped with a cap of wispy white hair, which caught the barest gleam of the moonlight above like a tuft of cotton on the end of a stalk. He'd noticed her before, laughing darkly all by herself and muttering constantly in her sleep. The links of her chain gleamed, casting reflected light onto her face.

"Careful?" Sev asked, turning back around, seeking Heller through the shadows. "Get out of here, old woman," he whispered angrily, preparing to make a run for it, noise be damned.

"You know," she said loudly—too loudly—leaning comfortably against the tree. "If you were smart, you'd do exactly as I tell you, before it's too late."

Sev wanted to wring her spindly neck. He'd completely lost track of Heller, the bats were still putting up a racket, and even as he resolved to throw caution to the wind and make a break for it, a voice called out through the darkness.

"Heller, you there?"

It was Rian, wandering over from his position farther south. Had the noise from the bats been that loud, or did they often visit each other during lookout shifts?

Sev was still hidden from view, but he wouldn't be for long. He looked desperately at the old woman.

"Up, in the tree," she said, pointing to the heavy, low-hanging boughs. It was definitely climbable. Not pausing to think about why she was helping him—or how she would explain her own presence at the edges of camp in the middle of the night—Sev took hold of the nearest branch and hoisted himself up.

He was just crouching into position on a wide branch when the old bondservant began screeching from somewhere below.

"Help, help!" she cried into the night, and Sev nearly dropped from his perch. What in Noct's name was she doing? "Over here!"

Rian found her at once, blade drawn. The tree cover was thinner out here, and Sev could make out the man's scowl in the dappled light of the moon.

"Oh, thank the gods and their servants," the woman said breathlessly as Heller joined them as well.

"You'll have the whole camp up in arms with your incessant trilling, woman," Heller barked, wheezing as he caught his breath. "What are you on about?"

Sev was utterly still. Even his lungs didn't move—though he silently begged them to.

"I . . . that is to say, *we* . . . need your help." And to Sev's horror, she pointed at him, squatted above in the tree like an overgrown bird.

"What in blazes are you doing up there?" asked Rian, sidling next to her and bringing Sev into his sights.

"One of my pigeons has taken ill," the woman said hastily. "Took off when I tried to tend to him and wound up in this tree. Refuses to come down, no matter how I beg and cajole. You know how the pigeons get. Their brains are a bit addled—see, there it goes."

A warm *something* splatted on top of Sev's head, and he suspected he knew what it was. Looking up, he was unsurprised—though no less chagrined—to spot a pigeon cooing meekly after emptying his bowels on top of Sev. He had dealt with entirely too much crap today.

"This lad was helping me retrieve the poor fellow, but alas, he's not much of a climber and can't seem to get down again."

Sev shot daggers at the old woman, who only looked up at him with wide-eyed concern. After taking a deep breath and fighting the urge to call out her ludicrous lies, Sev did as Rian and Heller instructed and held the pigeon in his hands while Rian scaled the branches to help him.

It was mortifying, having the man half carry him down the tree like a child who'd climbed too high and gotten scared.

Standing before them at last, with a pigeon clutched to his chest and bird droppings in his hair, Sev couldn't quell the growing suspicion that the woman was having rather a good time. She was certainly smiling widely enough.

Rian and Heller told them to head back to camp, and Sev walked alongside her, trying to decide whether he should thank her or throttle her.

She *had* helped him, in an extremely roundabout way. If she hadn't stopped him, he'd likely have barreled into Rian as he tried to run away.

Even if he hadn't, the bats had made such a fuss that Rian and Heller probably would have come poking around anyway. Sev could've tried his drunk routine, but he knew that was a less-than-foolproof strategy.

Once they were out of earshot of the perimeter guards, Sev cast the woman a sidelong glance.

"You're welcome," she said graciously, and Sev scowled.

"For what? For making a fool out of me?" he snapped.

"Oh, I think you were doing a fine job of that on your own. I saw your, uh, *trick*, with the bats. Do you want them to know what you are, boy?" she asked. "They'll tag and chain you faster than you can say 'phoenix.'"

Sev's mouth went dry. She had caught him using his magic.

While at first glance the woman seemed frail and grandmotherly, Sev sensed she was anything but. Even as she stood there in her loosely hanging tunic, with bits of her cotton hair standing in all directions, her eyes glittered with keen intelligence.

Sev opened his mouth to speak, cleared his throat, then shrugged as nonchalantly as he could manage while still holding the pigeon. He pushed it into her hands. "Don't know what you're talkin' about."

Best to play dumb. Sev was very good at it.

"Oh, I think you do," she said as she took the pigeon. "An animage living and working among the empire's soldiers. Such a terrible secret to bear."

She bowed her head to the pigeon in her hands, murmuring in a low voice, and then released it. The bird soared away as gracefully as an eagle on an updraft. Sev frowned. The pigeon wasn't even sick. Had the whole thing been some kind of trap?

"Perhaps it was that burden that drove you to sneak off in the dead of night with a packed bag and purseful of stolen gold," she said with a weary sigh, as if the entire thing were some terrible tragedy.

Sev gaped at her, unsurprised that she'd gleaned he'd been trying to escape but confused about her last comment. "Gold? What—"

She gestured for him to check his pack, a smug smile on her face. Frowning, Sev dug within its depths, drawing out a coin purse—one he most certainly had not packed—embroidered with Captain Belden's initials in golden thread. When had she planted it on him? He'd never felt so much as a tug or brush against him.

"What did you . . . ? I never—how—" he blathered. She only smirked, snatching it from his hand in a lightning-fast move and making it disappear again.

"It would be a terrible thing to have to report you," she said, her tone still heavy with feigned sorrow.

"No one would believe you," he said faintly.

That had to be true. Sev was a soldier, one of the empire's most celebrated servants—no matter how low he was on the food chain. This woman was a bondservant, a criminal.

It seemed she was following his train of thought. "Whether they believed my word or not, the facts would be stacked against you, boy. Stealing from the captain's own personal stores, your fondness for poor sick animals stuck in trees. . . ."

Tingling, crackling fury was creeping up Sev's neck.

"And that's not to mention the way the other animals flock to you."

"The animals don't flock to me," he said automatically, though he thought he already caught her meaning.

"Not yet they don't."

Sev stopped walking. He was truly and completely foxed.

"Why are you doing this?" he asked.

"I propose a deal: You give me what I want, and I give you what you want—an escape."

"There you are," came a low voice from the darkness of the camp. Sev blinked in surprise when the bondservant from earlier emerged. When he spotted Sev, he scowled. "What's he doing here? And what's . . . ?" he trailed off, eyeing the mess in Sev's hair.

"We were talking," Sev said shortly, tugging a rag from his pack and wiping angrily at his hair. "Me and . . . uh . . ."

"The soldiers and servants call me Thya," she said, filling in the silence.

"But I grow weary of it. I'd like something with more *oomph*, you know? More pizzazz."

There was a pause. Sev was certain she was going to keep speaking, but she didn't.

"Like what?" he prompted.

She pursed her lips. "I'm not sure yet. There's so much in a name. . . . What's yours again, boy? Seb?"

"Sev," he corrected.

"*Sev*. A unique name. Ferronese, isn't it? Short for Sevro?"

His brows rose. "Sevro" wasn't so much a *unique* name as it was a rare one, even in Ferro where it originated—and where his father was from. People rarely guessed his Ferronese background, as he'd taken both the straight hair and warm brown skin from his mother's Pyraean side. He did grow a bit paler in the winter months, though, and it was only just spring.

He nodded in confirmation, and she grinned. "Yes. Thought so— you've got hints of that olive-toned *Ferronese glow* about you. And those eyes are as golden-green as Teyke's cat. He's quite handsome for a soldier, isn't he, Kade?"

Kade scowled, and Sev's face grew hot under the attention of their stares. He jumped in before the bondservant could answer.

"Look, I don't care what you want to be called," he began, trying to get the conversation off his looks and back on point. "Just tell me—"

"Trix," she announced, and Sev faltered.

"Uh, okay, fine. Trix—"

"Or Trixie? No, no, I take it back. Too silly. Trix is best."

"Enough of this," Kade growled, as fed up as Sev. He turned to Trix. "I need to talk to you."

"So do I," Sev cut in, stepping forward.

Kade glared at him, straightening his spine and filling the space between them with his broad chest. Sev might outrank him—just barely—but that meant nothing when they were standing alone in the dark with no commanding officers to keep order. Kade knew Sev was a green soldier, easier to stand up to and bully than someone like Ott, but Sev wasn't going to be intimidated. This woman had just offered him an ultimatum—or maybe it was a threat—and he needed to understand what he'd gotten himself into.

"Well, now, an old lady could get used to this," Trix said, eyes twinkling. "Come on, boys, let's take a walk through the moonlight."

She made for the darker cover of the forest thicket, away from the sleeping figures in the camp but still a good distance from the perimeter guard. The moonlight she supposedly sought was nowhere to be found in the dense trees.

"It's about the girl," Kade said under his breath, trying to exclude Sev from the conversation, though they were walking mere feet apart.

"What girl? The one by the cabin?" Sev asked.

"What's it to you, soldier?"

Trix sighed, coming to a stop next to a massive gnarled tree and taking a seat on a thick root. "Enough, Kade. He's working with us now."

"I am?" Sev asked at the exact same moment Kade said, "He is?"

"Aren't you, soldier boy?" she asked, carefully adjusting the folds of her threadbare tunic, all dignity and polite innocence. *You give me what I want, and I give you what you want.* But working with them, what could that possibly mean? Did they want help with their bondservant duties?

Kade frowned between them. "I don't have time for your little games, Thya."

"Trix. I'd like to be called Trix."

"The captain has left camp," Kade practically growled, his voice rumbling. "This will be our only shot. She's little more than a girl, and she's in danger."

Trix's expression turned thoughtful. "Safer as a girl, I think, than as a woman. Besides, she'll be in more danger if you go back there."

"It *is* the girl by the cabin you're talking about, isn't it?" Sev asked. "The one with the—"

"Watch your mouth, soldier," Kade hissed, glancing quickly around.

After several heartbeats' silence, he turned back to Trix. "Now is the perfect opportunity. We have to help her."

"*How* can we help her, Kade? Better to leave her behind than to lead her onward . . . into peril."

"But she's defenseless."

"She's not," Sev said quietly, thinking of her sister's ease with a blade.

"Did she do that to your neck?" Kade asked, rounding on Sev again. When had he seen the knife wound on Sev's throat? Surely he couldn't see it now, when Sev could barely see the bondservant's face. "What did you do to her after I left?"

"Kade," Trix said sharply, and to Sev's surprise, he backed down at once.

"I didn't do anything to her except save her life."

Trix smiled at this, but Kade remained stony.

"She's fine, I swear it," Sev added softly, but there was no reply.

"See? No need to fret," Trix said brightly, though her voice turned severe as she continued. "I will not sacrifice our mission, and the fate of the Phoenix Riders, for one mountain girl."

Sev felt like the ground had disappeared beneath his feet. "Phoenix Riders?" he whispered hoarsely.

While he gaped at Trix in shock, Kade was glowering at her in outrage. He obviously hadn't taken kindly to her shutting down his idea, and Sev didn't know what was more confusing—that she had the audacity to give him orders, or that Kade apparently followed them.

"Oh yes, soldier. Your captain would have you march up this mountain and wipe out the last remnants of the Phoenix Riders. He's off right now, meeting with his sneak of an informant."

Sev felt nauseated. He should have known—did know, somewhere deep inside. Maybe that was why the girl had spooked him so badly today. Maybe that was why he'd been so desperate to make his escape.

"The tree cover," he muttered, waving over their heads, "the 'no fire' rule. He's not worried about us exposing ourselves to the local villagers. . . . He's worried about exposing us to the sky. To the Riders."

Sev couldn't deny that a part of his heart soared at the idea that there were still Phoenix Riders out there in hiding, but the rest of him quickly stomped down the feeling. What was there to be happy about? They didn't stand a chance against the empire before, when there were hundreds of them and they had a fiery warrior queen to lead them. But now, with no heir in sight and their numbers reduced to the brink of extinction, what chance did they have?

Trix positively beamed at him. "Told you he was brighter than he seemed," she said to Kade.

It appeared Sev's reputation of mild-mannered stupidity preceded him—even if this woman had seen through the ruse. Kade was looking at him with unflattering surprise, as if he'd truly thought Sev were some kind of simpleton.

"What's it to you if I'm smart or not? What do you want from me?" Sev asked Trix.

She twisted her lips thoughtfully. "I could make good use of a soldier."

Sev gritted his teeth, the events of the night starting to catch up with him. "For *what*? What *use* is a soldier to a bondservant?"

"There are places a bondservant cannot go and things a bondservant cannot *access*."

Sev frowned at her. "Like?"

"Like duty rosters, supply lists, weapons . . . ," she clarified with an airy wave of the hand.

"What if I refuse?"

"Give us a moment, won't you, Kade?" she said sweetly, and after a breath of hesitation, Kade stomped off into the darkness.

"I thought I made myself clear, soldier," she said conversationally, turning back to Sev. "Whether you're an animage or not, I can certainly make you look like one. Cross me, and you'll have every critter in this forest on your heels. I could make those llamas *purr* if I wanted to—and they'd do it just for you. They're a superstitious lot, soldiers are, and you'd hardly be the first person thrown into bondage without proper proof. And when they come for you, I'll make sure you're caught with the captain's gold, silver, and silks, too—just to be certain."

Sev clenched his fists, his heart thumping in his ears.

"Besides," she added softly, all hint of threat gone, "you want a way out, and I'm your best chance. Help me, and I'll help you—that's a promise, Sevro."

Sev's pulse fluttered as he replayed her words. He knew Trix could do all she'd promised—she'd shown him that tonight. Worse, soldiers were the type to act first, think later—and if they suspected he was an animage for even a second, there'd be no going back for him. Add stealing from the captain into the mix . . .

Sev *did* want a way out. He felt no love or loyalty to the empire or their cause, but he still wasn't exactly sure how she could be the one to set him free. Unless . . .

"Help you with what?" Sev asked, unease building inside his chest. "What's your goal?"

Trix smiled warmly at him. "To bring these filthy empire assassins down from the inside, of course."

*It was the death of her mother that
ended us. Let me be more specific. It was the death
of that regicide-committing, whorehouse-dwelling
usurper queen regent that ended us.*

- CHAPTER 8 -
VERONYKA

VERONYKA WENT LIMP IN Val's arms.

Xephyra was dead.

"I did it for your own good," Val was saying, panting slightly from the effort of holding Veronyka away from Xephyra. "We'll start over. We'll get two new eggs and do this *together*, so I can guide you properly. You weren't ready—it's not your fault this happened."

Veronyka stepped back from her, the silence of the severed bond echoing in her mind. The spot in her heart where Xephyra had burned bright was now a cold, hard lump. With every breath she took, the knot in her chest grew tighter, heavier, until she thought she might suffocate under it.

"You're right," Veronyka said, her voice utterly lifeless. Like Xephyra.

Val visibly relaxed, opening her mouth to speak, but Veronyka continued. "It's not my fault—it's your fault. You did this. You *murdered* her!" she finished with a scream. The words ripped from her throat, leaving a raw track of fiery agony in their wake. Her face crumpled, and she had to force breath in and out of her lungs. *Xephyra is dead. Xephyra is dead.*

And Val had killed her.

"I will never," she continued raggedly, throat tight with unshed tears, "*ever*," she added, needing stronger, better words, but unable to find them in the maelstrom of her mind, "forgive you for this."

Her hands were shaking. She wanted to hit Val, to make her *hurt*, but what she did instead was turn away and heave onto the dirt floor at her feet. Painful spasms racked her body, but she hadn't eaten much that day, and nothing came out except acid regret.

The next thing she knew, Val's arm was against her back, rubbing circles there. *Comforting* her.

"Phoenixes died all the time in ancient Pyra, Veronyka," she said soothingly. "In training, in war, in sacrificial fire dives that set cities ablaze. It's the animage, the *Rider*, that matters. Xephyra was just an animal."

Just an animal. Veronyka wanted to turn around and spit in her face, but she couldn't make her body move. Xephyra had been more than "just an animal"—more than just a bondmate. She had been Veronyka's future, her whole world, shattered in an instant.

The last time her sister had tried to "comfort" her had been in the wake of their *maiora*'s murder.

They'd been running across tenement rooftops and down narrow alleys, until the screams and shouts of the mob faded into distant background noise and then into nothing. Veronyka had finally jerked her arm out of Val's grip.

"Where are they taking her?"

"To the stars," Val had said, looking up at the blue sky, where nothing but sunlight shone. It was strange for Veronyka to hear those words from Val when it was her *maiora* who had taught her that after death the soul rose up into the sky to live among the stars, to be Axura's light in the darkness of night, where she could not shine.

"Does that mean . . . ? Is she . . . ? Is she . . . ?" Veronyka had faltered, not wanting to know the truth, but needing to hear it all the same.

"She is dead, *xe* Nyka."

"Are you *sure*?" Veronyka whispered, tears blurring her vision at the realization that she'd abandoned her grandmother to that fate. When Val didn't answer, she'd taken it as an affirmation. "But who will burn her body?"

Val had knelt in front of her then. "Do not cry for the dead," she'd said, stoic as ever as she'd mopped her sister's wet face. "Cry for the living—cry for us. Things will be harder from here on out."

"But . . ."

"Soldiers die all the time, Nyka, and no matter how much she liked to play nursemaid, your *maiora* was a soldier. *We* survived. That's what matters. It's what she would have wanted."

Now, in this cold cabin, rage reared up inside Veronyka. Val knew the motions, understood the gestures and the words that were expected, but she performed them like a poor player reciting an epic poem—the moves studied and unnatural.

Val had never shed a tear, said a prayer, or even spoken fondly of their grandmother. Sometimes Veronyka wondered if it was because she wasn't technically related to them. Their "grandmother" had been their mother's mentor and dearest friend, and as the war had grown desperate, she had sworn to protect Val and Veronyka if the worst should happen. It had—both of their parents had died during the Last Battle of the Blood War.

Other times Veronyka convinced herself that Val was cut off and distant not because of a lack of feelings, but rather because she hid them, forcing the emotions down as a survival technique.

But that was wishful, childish thinking. Val was every callous word spoken and cruel action undertaken. Val was colder than the River Aurys and more hollow than a solstice festival bell. It was no wonder the second egg didn't hatch, no wonder that Xephyra had chosen to bond with Veronyka. Val was an empty shell and had nothing in her heart to give.

And now, for the first time, Veronyka was seeing her sister clearly.

She shoved Val aside and lurched toward the door. She couldn't bear to look at Val or to even glance in the direction of the body. Just the thought of it was enough to leave her dizzy and weak. And she couldn't be weak—not now.

Val followed her as she rounded the side of the cabin. "Veronyka," she said, her voice wavering slightly. "Veronyka, stop. What are you—" But as Veronyka started piling firewood in her arms from the stack against the wall, Val's mouth snapped shut.

Veronyka pushed past her, back the way she'd come, her footsteps slowing as she approached the door. Her jaw trembled, but she clenched it tight and forced one foot in front of the other.

Her vision blurred with unshed tears, but she could still see the body.

Xephyra.

She was as brightly colored as always, vivid red feathers and autumn-gold beak, yet somehow smaller in death than in life.

Veronyka stepped around her bondmate and threw the wood onto the hearth. Showers of sparks and clouds of ash billowed up, and Veronyka breathed deeply.

This is not the end.

Movement sounded behind Veronyka as she stoked the flames, but she ignored Val completely, urging the wood to burn hotter, faster.

Like many things, her *maiora* had taught Veronyka about phoenix resurrection. She'd explained how phoenixes could live forever if not mortally wounded, but if they had grown weary with the world, they might ignite and choose death—or resurrection—instead.

Her *maiora* had said the eldest female phoenix in existence had been at least two hundred years old.

"Maybe even older!" she had exclaimed. "The phoenix just turned up one day, mind closed tight as a trapdoor, with no hint of her name or her bondmate. She had the longest tail feathers ever recorded, so putting an exact age on her was near impossible—though she was certainly older than the empire. Imagine all she'd lived through, all she'd seen. Maybe she even remembered the Dark Days, before the queendom, before time itself, when Azurec summoned the first phoenixes to defeat Noct and his endless night and bring light into the world."

"*Axura* and *Nox*," Val had corrected. She'd risen from her place in a darkened corner of the room and joined them by the fire. Their *maiora*'s stories had always come at night, when the rowdy Narrows neighborhood around them had grown quiet. Their grandmother had had some training as a healer, so in the daytime, people were always coming and going from the back door, sharing gossip or paying for salves and tinctures.

"Your peasant upbringing betrays you, old woman," Val had continued, her voice dripping with disdain. "These valley nobles claimed our goddesses and made them into men to suit them. Axura is the sun in the sky; she is light and life, wings and fire, and phoenixes are her earthbound children." Val had snatched a pitcher of water from the ledge and emptied it into the hearth with a smoking hiss, plunging them into darkness. "Nox is more than just night and shadow. . . . She is a void; she is death—she is the end of everything."

"What happened to her?" Veronyka had whispered after Val stormed off to brood alone. "The old phoenix?"

Though her grandmother had gone stiff and silent in Val's presence, the light in her eyes had flickered back to life at Veronyka's question. "Her bondmate died young, some said, and so she loved the hatchlings best. When the Blood War broke out, many of her charges were slaughtered. She fought for them, with beak and talon and flame, but could not save them all. After that she disappeared, and no one ever saw her again."

"Dead?" Veronyka had said, disappointed at how the phoenix's story had ended.

"Or reborn?" her *maiora* had asked, an enigmatic look on her old, wrinkled face. "Where there is will, there is possibility, Veronyka. Remember that."

Possibility.

Most of what Veronyka knew about rebirth had been in the form of myths and stories, like the old phoenix who loved hatchlings, but no matter the tale, the resurrections all went the same: Phoenixes were born from fire and ash, and phoenixes were *re*born from fire and ash. Veronyka understood the basic principle, the concept of balance that had so recently haunted her dreams. *A death for a life.*

Phoenixes could resurrect by using their own deaths to fuel their funeral pyres—and their new lives. However, the phoenixes were usually alive when they did this. With Xephyra already gone . . .

This is not the end.

Veronyka would have to start the fire herself and keep it burning through the night. During incubation, you needed to keep a fire blazing hot for twelve hours per egg. Veronyka could only hope the same would apply with a pyre.

After putting all their wood into the hearth, Veronyka cast around for more to burn. She added her woven basket, their rolled-up pallet, and even the window shutters. She hauled the heavy stewpot outside and upended it onto the ground next to their door, the soggy chunks of vegetables sloshing across the packed earth. She picked out the joint of meat Val had boiled for the flavor, her fingertips burning as she carried it back inside and wedged it into the heart of the flames. She added the rest of the bones she'd gathered the night of Xephyra's hatching, the ones Val had deemed unworthy of their fire, and the broken shells of the egg that did not hatch, the phoenix that never was. Val had ordered her to get rid of them, but in a fit of sentimentality, Veronyka had wrapped them in cloth and hidden them on the windowsill, behind the broken shutters. Her face grew hot as she worked, her hair plastered to her neck with sweat.

Lifting the heavy strands, Veronyka unearthed her newest braid. Feeling Val's eyes on her, Veronyka took up the soldier's knife and cut the braid with a savage jerk. Then she tossed it into the fire, the last bit of shell she had left.

The last bit of life.

Veronyka feared it wasn't enough, even though logic told her Xephyra's body alone should suffice. *A death for a life.* They had burned dozens of bones for Xephyra's incubation, though, and only one egg had hatched. Still, she worried time was a greater concern, that the longer her phoenix's body was allowed to sit, cold and unmoving, the lesser the chances this would work.

And it had to work.

Putting Xephyra's empty, lifeless body onto the flames was almost more than Veronyka could bear. She flashed back to the moment of the phoenix's birth, when Xephyra had stood upon hot coals without so much as a scorch mark. Now her body went up instantly, like dry paper. The flames licked across her spread wings, her curled feet, and Veronyka thought she might choke from the desperation inside her.

This was her bondmate. Xephyra's pain should be *her* pain, but Veronyka knew the blistering anguish inside was entirely her own.

Val had been standing against the wall the entire time. She didn't speak a word, didn't ask questions or point out mistakes. Good. Veronyka had had enough of Val's advice.

She settled on her knees and stared into the flames.

This is not the end.

The sun set.

Dawn came.

Went.

Shadows moved across the ground, and the bright sky outside their window bruised with the coming twilight.

She had kept the fire burning for twelve hours. Then twenty-four, using every scrap of wood from the stack outside.

But just as the fire dwindled, so too did Veronyka's hope.

She was cold. Bone-chillingly cold. The steady heat that had warmed her all night and all day was gone, the fire nothing but a pile of ashes, softly stirred by the evening breeze.

Her tears had stopped, her eyes so dry that Veronyka didn't know if she'd ever be able to cry again. They were itchy and swollen and heavy with sleep, but Veronyka continued to watch.

She watched until the last flickering ember went out. It echoed something inside her, some lost piece of herself that Veronyka knew she'd never get back.

Is this what the end feels like?

As intently as Veronyka had watched the flames, so Val had watched her.

Now she put a hand on Veronyka's shoulder and opened her mouth to speak.

Veronyka jerked away and gathered her belongings. She felt stiff and disconnected from the world, numb in a way that had nothing to do with the cold outside and everything to do with the cold inside.

"Veronyka," Val said, her tone measured. "Talk to me."

Veronyka ignored her, tugging on her warm leather boots and grabbing her cloak from the hook by the door.

"*Xe* Nyka—you need me. Don't do anything stupid."

"I do not need you," Veronyka snapped, her voice raw from the smoke.

Val bristled. "Oh, yes you do. This cabin, that food—the clothes on your back. All of that comes from me."

Veronyka glared at her. Despite Val's sharp tone, her eyes were glistening with unshed tears. The sight made Veronyka's fists clench. Val had no right to sadness, not in the face of what she'd done.

"Fine," Veronyka said, kicking off the boots and flinging the cloak onto the dusty ground, leaving behind anything Val had given her. She stood in nothing but the threadbare, undyed tunic and pants she'd been wearing since the previous day—clothes she had made herself. Val called them "farmer's dreck" and hated the practical worker's attire. She preferred scraps of expensive silk and faded embroidery, no matter how old, dirty, and worn-out.

"Veronyka, you'll freeze."

"No I won't," she said, marching over to the edge of the cold hearth and picking up the soldier's knife from the dirt. "This," she said, holding it outward and causing Val to stop in her tracks, "does not belong to you."

"You don't know what you're doing!" Val shouted to her retreating back, following Veronyka as she marched out the door.

"Yes I do," Veronyka said, whirling around. Val stood on the threshold of their home, looking strangely small and forlorn. Veronyka was repulsed by the sight of her. "I'm getting away from you. As far and as fast as my feet will carry me. I would rather die than stay here one second longer."

Val's face twisted with rage. "Where will you go? Off searching for Phoenix Riders?" she sneered. "They are gone, Veronyka, and not even your foolish hope will change that."

"Nothing about hope is foolish," Veronyka said, turning her back on her sister once more. Val was a determined person, almost to the point of obsession, but one thing she'd always lacked was imagination.

Veronyka couldn't see the end of the long winding path before her, but she could see the first step. The rest she'd make up as she went along.

"If it's eggs you're after, you won't find any without me," Val called out, almost desperately, as if searching for some way to slow Veronyka down or make her turn around.

You're wrong, Veronyka thought, her mind locked tight as she pressed on. *About everything.*

First she would go to Vayle and Wise Queen Malka's abandoned outpost. If Val didn't want her to be able to find an egg on her own, she shouldn't have told her exactly where to find one.

After that . . . she didn't know where, and she didn't know how, but Veronyka would find other Phoenix Riders if it was the last thing she ever did.

That was the day her loss became
my victory, and everything changed between us.

- CHAPTER 9 -
TRISTAN

TRISTAN PERCHED ON THE edge of the rocky cliff, staring down at the steep, jagged drop. The sky was vast above him, with barely a cloud to break the endless blue, and below, his phoenix's scarlet feathers were the only pop of color among a sea of gray stone.

The other Apprentice Riders, along with their instructor, stood behind him, awaiting their turn.

Tristan took a deep breath, steeling himself. It was no small thing to leap blindly into the abyss, timing his jump *just* right so he landed on the back of his phoenix as he soared far below.

But this, believe it or not, was the easy part. The hard part? Rex, his bondmate, was supposed to be in *full flame* when Tristan landed.

It didn't get much worse than being a Phoenix Rider who was afraid of fire.

Maybe, Tristan thought darkly, fighting to keep his legs from trembling, *being afraid of heights would be worse. Maybe.*

Logically, Tristan knew that, at least when it came to his bondmate's fire, he couldn't be harmed—their bond protected him. An animage bonded to a phoenix had a higher tolerance to all fire, though Tristan had yet to test the theory. Would never *ever* test the theory.

He squeezed his eyes shut. *Focus.*

Rex's fire couldn't harm him—that was what mattered. When an animage and a phoenix bonded, their magic intertwined, and their beings became inextricably linked. Emotions and internal sensations were shared, so that when Tristan felt angry or scared, Rex did too. The same was true of certain abilities. Rex's immunity to fire extended to Tristan, and likewise, Tristan's use of language and communication expanded the phoenix's mind beyond what it would become on its own.

Tristan repeated the reassurances over and over in his head, trying to bury his fear in facts and centuries-old knowledge, but it never worked. Fear, he'd learned, didn't leave room for logic. It didn't leave room for much of anything, except mistakes.

Fear is a luxury.

It was one of his father's favorite maxims, lifted from some ancient bit of Pyraean poetry. When Tristan thought about luxury, he imagined fine silks, expensive Arborian honey wine, and gilded furniture. Not a ridiculous fear of fire. But he supposed that while he couldn't afford those luxuries—not anymore—he could afford his fear even less.

Rex would try to help, of course, but while their bond would make it easier to time the landing, Rex couldn't very well stop in midair if Tristan's muscles refused to make the leap. All their bond would do then was allow Rex to feel Tristan's terror before he plummeted to his death.

Calm as the mountain, he told himself, repeating one of the phrases his mother used when he was angry or sullen as a child. She would tell him to look up at Pyrmont and imagine himself as stone, still and quiet and unchanging. He tried it now, pressing his feet into the steady, solid ground beneath him.

"Whenever you're ready, Tristan," prompted Fallon, their instructor, his voice seeming to come from very far away. He was the youngest of the Master Riders to survive the war and something of a hero to a lot of the apprentices. Fallon had both youth and experience—even if he'd been too young to actually fight in the Blood War—and Tristan hated the idea of embarrassing himself in front of him.

No one knew about Tristan's fear. They probably thought he was delaying for dramatic effect or trying to one-up Fallon's demonstration. That was not who Tristan was, but with a Master Rider father who was confident and fearless—and who held the rest of them, particularly his only son, to an impossible standard—many thought Tristan was the same. A hardheaded perfectionist. Serious to a fault.

"While we're still young and pretty, Tristan!" shouted Anders from somewhere behind him.

"When were you ever pretty?" asked Latham, and laughter broke out.

Tristan clenched his fists. He knew they were only messing around, that they didn't have any clue what he was dealing with—but their teasing didn't help things.

Tristan squared his shoulders, staring at the expanse below, though his vision blurred and slipped out of focus.

It doesn't even hurt, he told himself firmly, sensing as Rex swooped back around, leveling out his flight and building his heat to prepare for Tristan's jump. Even when Rex was blisteringly hot, fire rippling across his feathers, it felt like nothing more than a tingling sensation—like pins and needles, strange and a bit uncomfortable at times, but not painful.

So what was Tristan afraid of?

Rex was making his final approach, his focus and determination helping to break up the building terror in Tristan's mind. His bondmate knew he could do it, and so he knew it too.

Only, he didn't.

It happened the way it did in his dreams sometimes, when he'd see himself in the middle of a battle. The fear would take hold of him, and he'd freeze, unable to move, even to save his own life. His muscles would lock, his heart would stutter, and he'd stand there, immobile, as the world burned around him.

Rex sensed Tristan's faltering resolve, throwing his wings out wide to slow his pace, but it was no use. As if time itself had seized, Tristan watched in slow motion as his bondmate floated past while he remained still as a statue on the cliff above.

A gentle wind disrupted the stillness, ruffling Tristan's hair and bringing with it the scent of smoke, ash, and defeat.

Heart heavy with disappointment, Tristan slowly faced the others, pretending not to notice as the other apprentices whispered and muttered behind their hands. Fallon clapped encouragingly, telling him he'd get it the next time—but Tristan barely noticed.

His father was there, standing next to Fallon, in the space that had been empty moments before. His arms were crossed over his chest, his expression utterly unreadable.

Tristan's stomach dropped.

His father must have arrived while Tristan's back had been turned; he had seen his son's failure firsthand.

And failure—like fear—was something the Phoenix Riders simply couldn't afford.

They had been struggling to rebuild for years. After the war, those who weren't killed or captured had gone into hiding, and even after his father reunited with other survivors, they'd had to scout locations, find resources and funds, and recruit new Riders, all without drawing notice from the empire. It had taken more than a decade to get them where they were now—fewer than two dozen Riders hidden in the wilds of Pyrmont—and they still had so far to go.

Too far, Tristan thought desperately. Only with a strong Rider force could they hope to defend their lands and protect their people. Tristan *had* to do better.

As the next apprentice stepped up, Tristan walked to the back of the group. He tore off his armguard and threw it to the ground. Next came his other armguard and the straps across his chest. One piece after another, Tristan shed the fireproof armor he hadn't needed because he hadn't jumped.

He slouched onto the ground and stared at his clenched fists.

There wasn't some devastating story, some horrible event that had led to Tristan's phobia. It was a little thing, a memory from when he was a child. He'd been quite young—maybe five or six—and playing in his father's library. He wasn't allowed in there, of course; the room was like a museum, stuffed with rare art, draped in fine fabrics, and populated with expensive furniture. While playing with a carved onyx figurine of Damian, first King Consort of the Golden Empire—and Tristan's distant ancestor—he'd accidentally knocked over a candle. It had landed on a rug, and in seconds the small flame had spread, tearing hungrily through the fabric.

He'd known a singular moment of terror as the flames leapt toward him—fear for himself, but also for the rug, for the books and scrolls stacked three deep in the fine wooden shelves. He wasn't supposed to be in this room, and in the space of a few breaths, he'd imagined the whole place burning up with him still inside.

But it hadn't. One of the servants had come running, lifted him out of danger, and easily stamped out the rug. It was rolled up, replaced, and never mentioned again.

Tristan and his father had left that house—a country cottage on the outskirts of Ferro—soon after, all their properties confiscated as they were banished from the empire following his mother's death. That burning candle was Tristan's last clear memory of his life *before*, when things still made sense. After that, his father had become even more distant, always locked away or gone on business, and Tristan had spent more and more time alone with the servants.

Somehow that moment in his father's library had become embedded in his mind, laced with a terrible fear—of the burning rug beneath his feet, of his father's wrath, and of that crawling, spreading, devouring flame.

He was fine with fireplaces and lanterns and candlesticks. He could even shoot flaming arrows—but there was always a breath of hesitation, a stutter where his body refused to obey his mind. And when that fire leapt free, skittering over dry brush in a forest fire or licking across the scarlet feathers of his bondmate? Something shook loose in him, something he'd not yet been able to fix.

Rex tried to comfort Tristan as he circled back around, coming to perch next to the rest of the apprentice mounts on an outcrop nearby, but Tristan was in no mood to be comforted. How could Rex possibly understand his struggle? Rex was a *firebird*. For him, heat and flames were a part of his personality. Whenever Rex was angry or excited, he would grow hot, the same way a human might flush or feel their pulse pounding in their veins. Fire was a phoenix's lifeblood, and it was their greatest weapon.

And for Tristan? It was his greatest liability.

He glanced at his father, hoping for some encouragement or reassurance after his dismal performance, but his father seemed to have forgotten he was there.

Tristan sighed, watching from the back of the crowd as another apprentice started the exercise.

Maybe fear of fire wasn't the problem. Maybe fear of his father was.

She had changed, but I had
changed too. Bloody vengeance and righteous
murder will do that to a person.

- CHAPTER 10 -
VERONYKA

THE PROMISE OF FINDING another egg was all that sustained Veronyka during the long, dark walk. She tried not to think of Xephyra, but every now and then her body would wilt, folding in on itself, and a gasp of sorrow would work its way out of her throat. There was a hollowness, a gaping chasm inside her, and it seemed only to grow as the night wore on. The place where Xephyra had been felt oddly numb, and Veronyka's mind was filled with terrible, ringing silence. Her bondmate had become a part of the way she lived and experienced the world, and now she felt blind, cut off, and vulnerable. She knew she should probably call an owl or night creature to help guide her, but she couldn't muster the strength or the magic.

The idea of starting over, of seeking a new bondmate when her first had only just died, made Veronyka's stomach churn. But it was all she had, the one thing in her life she could cling to. Without it Veronyka feared she would lie down in a ditch and never get up.

But then she'd think of her *maiora's* words and keep on moving.

Where there is will, there is possibility.

Veronyka wanted—*needed*—to be a Phoenix Rider, but not a Rider on her own, isolated and shut away, as Val would have had her. She would be a

Rider in a flock, one of dozens, maybe even hundreds, soaring through the sky on flaming wings. Together they would make right the wrongs that had plagued their people since the war. She couldn't undo what had happened to her *maiora* and countless others, but she could be a part of the change that made the world safe for them once more.

Veronyka crossed the bridge into Vayle just before dawn, her legs aching and her throat dry. Villagers were out and about already, fishermen readying nets and boats for a day on the water, while lights glimmered inside the bakery.

Though Veronyka longed for sleep and the sweet oblivion it would provide, she couldn't waste her head start. Eventually Val would realize where she had gone and come after her. Veronyka kept looking over her shoulder, expecting to see Val burst from the bushes to drag her home or to berate her for her foolishness. The shadows moved, the trees whispered, but there was no sign of her sister.

Vayle grew gradually brighter as Veronyka wandered its quiet streets, individual buildings distinguishing themselves with every step she took. Outposts were always on the highest ground available, and Vayle was a village perched atop stony bluffs and rocky hills, each street stacked above the other. The sound of the river helped Veronyka keep her sense of direction through the winding alleys, and by the time she reached the high street, she could actually see the water below, rushing underneath the arching bridge and disappearing down the mountainside.

Veronyka looked around as she caught her breath after the steady climb. She had a decent view of the surrounding landscape, but of course, most of Pyrmont was rock or tree and not much else. Was she imagining it, or could she see the clearing where the cabin was, just barely out of sight?

Veronyka turned resolutely around. She didn't need to look back and down. She needed to look forward—and up. Ahead of her was a row of fine houses, larger than most village cottages, their window boxes bursting with flowers and their shutters coated with fresh paint. Everything looked bluegray in the predawn, but Veronyka knew the houses would glow in bright pastel shades in the daylight. Behind the houses was a copse of trees rising higher than all the land around it. Veronyka squinted, looking for a stone tower, but the forest was dense.

The sun was breaking free of the jagged mountain skyline by the time Veronyka crested the hill, practically dragging her leaden legs. Dusty white beams of light sliced the countryside, and she came to a stop in front of Malka's outpost.

Or at least what remained of it.

There was nothing left but a circle of crumbling stones marking the base of the once-tower, with tall shoots of grass and skinny saplings poking up between the ruins. Part of a spiral staircase lay on its side, while other bits of wall or broken statuary dotted the ground.

"No," Veronyka whispered, her voice faint with exhaustion. *"No."*

She fell to her knees and squeezed her eyes shut, forcing herself to think. This wasn't destruction from war or raiders—no major battles were fought this high up Pyrmont, and no bandits or thieves had the machinery required to bring down stone buildings. This must have been deliberately dismantled for materials or because the crumbling tower was no longer safe. Eggs were usually hidden at the highest point of the structure, preferably somewhere reachable only by phoenix. This meant any eggs that *might* have been here were long gone.

Veronyka searched anyway.

She rolled heavy stones and dug through dirt. She hacked at mortar and scraped fingernails into every crack and crevice.

Despair welled up inside her, crowding her throat. She didn't remember when she'd started crying, but soon she was so blinded by tears that she was forced to stop her search and sag against a piece of cold granite wall.

She couldn't stand it, this gnawing ache. It wasn't just Xephyra that was missing. It was the part of Veronyka that had bonded with the phoenix, the part she'd willingly given—gone forever.

Veronyka embraced the emptiness, let it surround and consume her.

The exhaustion she'd been fighting off since she'd left the cabin washed over her, and she slumped down onto the grass.

She was asleep before her head hit the ground.

When Veronyka woke, the late-afternoon sunlight was hot against her cheeks—and there was a cool obsidian blade pressed against her neck.

She fought the instinct to jerk away and blinked furiously against the blazing sun, her gaze traveling along the rough shaft of a spear and coming to rest on a young girl. Veronyka relaxed slightly—she'd expected it to be Val—until the girl slid the flat edge of the weapon along her jawline, expertly applying pressure that forced Veronyka up off her back and onto her hands and knees.

"What you doin'?" the girl asked. Her voice was surprisingly husky, yet her tone was blunt with the kind of self-assuredness that comes only with youth.

"Sleeping," Veronyka said, unable to keep her irritation from leaking through.

The girl cocked her head, not looking directly at Veronyka, but instead focused somewhere in the middle distance. "In the toilet?"

Veronyka reared back, horrified. Her gaze flicked around, but there were only indistinct lumps of stone and nothing to suggest that this particular patch of grass was used as a latrine.

"I don't . . . It's not . . . ," Veronyka stammered, and the girl grinned.

Her smile was impish, making her seem young again, though Veronyka suspected that only a few years separated them. Her hair was a tangle of honey blond in the warm sunlight, and though tiny objects were visible among the strands, Veronyka was quite certain these items had gotten stuck there by accident and had not been braided in on purpose. Her suspicions were confirmed when she spotted a skein of cobwebs tangled near the girl's right ear and a live sparrow perched by her left. She must be an animage.

The girl lowered the spear and straightened from her aggressive stance, letting the weapon dangle carelessly from her hand. "Not a toilet no more," she said with a shrug. "Still a strange place for a snooze."

She jerked her chin in the direction of the stone wall directly behind Veronyka. She hesitated a moment, wary of the girl's weapon, before turning. The bit of wall behind her had a face carved into it, just barely visible beneath climbing vines and decades of dirt. Veronyka had noted it during her desperate search of the ruins but hadn't paid much attention to the details. Now she saw that it was a woman's face, upturned, and in her arms was a round bowl. It was a water deity, Veronyka suspected—they were usually depicted carrying bowls, jugs, and other vessels that held liquid. The inscription was obliterated, but bits of colored glass protruded from the dirt beneath Veronyka's hands, suggesting the kind of tiled floors common in bathhouses. It must have been a part of the outpost complex.

Turning back around, Veronyka stood. The girl was a head shorter than Veronyka, dirty and thin, and her cool sand-colored skin was freckled on her cheeks and bare shoulders from too much time in the sun. She'd clearly made her own spear, the shaft a knotted branch that wasn't quite straight and the obsidian tip fastened with a length of oiled leather rope. Still, it looked sharp.

"Won't hurt you," the girl said, smirking in amusement, as if Veronyka were being suspicious and overcautious—and hadn't just been awoken with that very weapon pressed to her throat. The bird in the girl's hair twittered, and she nodded, as if reminded of something.

"What's your name?" the girl asked.

Veronyka hesitated, fearing that the word alone would somehow draw Val down upon her. "Veronyka," she whispered.

The girl pointed at herself. "Sparrow, and this is Chirp."

The bird chirped obligingly, and Veronyka knew her suspicion that Sparrow was an animage was true. It wasn't uncommon for animages to have loyal pets, almost as near and dear to them as Riders and their phoenixes but without the magical bond.

Veronyka held a hand out to her in greeting. The girl continued to stare somewhere slightly off to Veronyka's left, until the silence caused her to frown. She blinked, tilted her head, then Chirp dislodged himself from her hair and fluttered onto Veronyka's outstretched arm.

Sparrow's frown smoothed out, and she took Veronyka's hand.

She can't see, Veronyka realized, as Chirp hopped up Veronyka's arm to land on her shoulder, his black eyes gleaming as he studied her. The sparrow must act as her guide, much in the same way Veronyka used owls and other night creatures to help her see in the darkness.

Tentatively, Veronyka reached out to Chirp. Before she'd more than brushed the bird's mind, Sparrow gasped in pleasure.

"You're an animage!" she said, cheeks flushing with delight. Chirp left Veronyka's shoulder and took up a perch on Sparrow's instead. They cocked their heads at Veronyka in unison before Sparrow scanned the area around them—not with her eyes, with her magic. "But you're alone."

Val had never let Veronyka keep a pet. Even the creatures that helped her every now and again suffered her sister's scorn and contempt. Only a phoenix was worthy of them, Val would say, and animages who kept cats and dogs by their sides deluded themselves with a pale imitation of what a true bond was.

Veronyka nodded in response to Sparrow's observation, then, remembering that the girl couldn't see, added, "Yes, I'm alone." The words caused Veronyka's throat to tighten. Barely a day had passed, and she'd lost both a bondmate and a sister. Xephyra's loss was like a fresh knife wound, raw and stinging, but she refused to feel hurt over Val. Her sister had *chosen* this schism. She had willingly destroyed the most precious thing in Veronyka's world, ruthlessly and without remorse. "For now," she added.

"For now," Sparrow repeated, nodding, as if Veronyka's words were the highest wisdom. "Sometimes we have to be alone. But not always. And look, now you're with me. Not alone no more."

Veronyka expelled a breath, relieved that the tension of this confrontation had defused. She looked around the clearing again, a frown creasing her forehead. Did Val know this place was in ruins? Had she deliberately sent Veronyka here or lied about where she actually intended to go to make sure Veronyka couldn't follow?

"Sparrow, I—" Before Veronyka could finish, the girl had her by the arm and was yanking her down behind part of the wall with the water goddess.

Veronyka staggered after her, confused, until faint voices drifted through the trees, followed by the steady roll of a wagon's wheels.

Her mind immediately went to raiders, then to the soldiers she'd found outside her door. But when Veronyka peered around the edge of the wall, she could see the approaching people through the trees.

There was an older man, past middle age, and a teenage boy, both sitting at the front of a wagon pulled by a pair of sturdy mountain horses. They were dressed simply, like many of the local villagers, in short tunics and cropped pants, though Veronyka spotted knife hilts on both of their belts. It was common enough to carry a weapon while traveling, but the younger of the two had a bow across his back as well. While the older man looked like a local, the boy had coloring similar to Sparrow's, his light-brown hair shining gold in the sun.

When the older of the two spoke in a low, barely audible rumble, Sparrow visibly relaxed.

"It's just the steward," she said, though she made no move to pop up and say hello. That was probably for the best, given the boy's bow and wary expression. Maybe he was the man's personal guard?

"Steward for what?" Veronyka asked, still watching their slow progression. As far as she knew, stewards ran households for rich lords and merchants in places like Marble Row, where the empire's wealthiest lived. Veronyka remembered seeing the stewards and their attendants at the local markets, purchasing all the best food, wine, and finery for their employers. The concept of a manor household filled with staff wasn't something that had ever taken hold in Pyra—even the wealthiest of Pyraean merchants, farmers, and tradespeople employed only a bare-bones staff: a cook, an animage or animal keeper, and maybe a household attendant to clean and maintain the home.

Sparrow had turned away, leaning her back against the wall as she picked at a bit of twine on her spear. "For that exiled governor's house. They say he's an old hermit, walled inside his country estate, and he sends his steward to the villages every month or two. Sometimes they come looking for stablehands or . . ."

Veronyka stopped listening to Sparrow. The steward's voice was growing louder, and she was shocked to hear the man speaking ancient Pyraean. It hadn't been an official spoken language in at least a hundred years, slowly phased out in favor of the Trader's Tongue.

But Veronyka knew it. It was still part of upper-class education, and so her *maiora* had learned it, thanks to her status as a Phoenix Rider. She had been common born, just like Val and Veronyka, but being a Rider elevated you to the highest echelons of society. Or at least it used to.

It took a moment for Veronyka to understand what they were saying— she hadn't spoken it much since her grandmother was taken from her.

But there was one word she would never forget—one that Val made sure she always remembered.

Phoenixaeres.

Phoenix Riders.

Veronyka lurched to her feet, seeking out their faces, hoping to better hear their conversation. They continued to speak in Pyraean, but seeing their lips move helped Veronyka puzzle through it.

". . . enough for everyone, including the underwings. We ran out last month."

Veronyka's heart was beating very fast now. Underwings were Apprentice Riders. These travelers were here on behalf of Phoenix Riders.

The lane twisted away before she could hear any more, and they soon passed out of sight.

"He always goes to the Vayle market," Sparrow said, getting to her feet.

"The market . . . ," Veronyka muttered, turning on the spot and looking back down the hillside. "Where—"

"Come on, I'll show you," Sparrow said, and Chirp agreed, trilling loudly before zipping forward to lead the way.

ↇ ↇ ↇ

Sparrow didn't bother with the road. She cut directly through the trees, down the sloping ground like water over a riverbed, swift and smooth, either very well connected to the bird who flew just in front of her, or so familiar with her surroundings that she didn't need guidance. She used her spear like a walking stick, poking aside brambles and stepping over rotten logs.

Veronyka did her best to keep up, stumbling over gnarled roots and getting her hair snagged on branches, her mind whirling.

The steward's arrival provided Veronyka with some much-needed hope— and focus. The outpost had been a bust, but all was not lost. He'd mentioned both Phoenix Riders and underwings—surely that meant whatever exiled lord he served had been a Phoenix Rider. Still was. And they had Apprentice Riders with them as well.

Maybe they would take her with them when they returned to the Riders' estate. The thought lightened her heavy spirit, filled her with a sense of opportunity . . . and yet there must be a reason they were speaking ancient Pyraean to each other and claiming to simply work at a country estate.

They didn't want people to know they were Riders.

It was wise, especially on the lower rim, so close to the border to the empire. But if Veronyka told them she'd overheard their secret, would they welcome her or be angry with her for eavesdropping?

"What was it you said about stablehands, Sparrow?" she asked, thinking back on their earlier conversation.

"Most of the time the steward comes for food—bags of dates and casks of honey wine," she said, "but other times he needs extra help with horses and hounds and the like, so he brings workers back with him."

"Animages?" Veronyka asked. Surely "stablehands" was code, their way of recruiting without drawing unwanted notice.

Sparrow nodded. "Only boys, though."

"What—why?" Veronyka asked, her theory unraveling. There had been male and female Phoenix Riders since the dawn of time. The First Riders were all women, chosen by Azurec—*Axura,* she corrected herself, then immediately thought of Val. Hot anger burned through her body, but she pushed it down, refusing to let her sister take hold. In the early Pyraean tribes, women were the hunters and fighters, and so Axura chose them to help fight the darkness and bring balance back to the world. It wasn't until the next generation that daughters *and* sons rode, and even during the height of the Phoenix Riders in the empire, the women outnumbered the men.

Maybe they really did need help in the stables. *Not that girls can't do that, too,* Veronyka thought irritably.

"Something about sleeping bunks," Sparrow continued skeptically. "As if boys and girls can't sleep side by side without trying to stab each other."

Veronyka cast Sparrow a sidelong glance, unsure if the girl was trying to speak in innuendo and messing up the subtleties, or if she really thought it was fighting the steward might be worried about.

Still, the idea nagged at her. Could it be true? Could Veronyka have found Phoenix Riders regrouping on Pyrmont only to discover that she couldn't join them anyway?

It must be a mistake. She would talk to them, *convince* them that she belonged.

As they stepped onto the road, Sparrow began pointing to houses and shops, indicating who lived where and what they sold. She knew about their families and their friends, old grudges and new romances, and if ever she were uncertain of who she was seeing or where they were, all she needed was a quiet tweet from Chirp to get her back on track.

The buildings were mostly made of large local stones, except for their roofs and shutters, which were made of woven slats of wood, painted in sun-bleached shades of blue, yellow, and red. Tinkling wind chimes and bright flowers added more color to the stony village.

Despite the fact that Pyra had been a part of the empire for almost two hundred years, the countless gods of the empire's pantheon never really took root there. Some would pray to Teyke the trickster for luck or to Miseriya for her mercy, but those gods had come from the valley, and their worship was seen more as superstition than true piety. Technically the Pyraeans had two gods, Axura and Nox, but you didn't really worship the goddess of death and darkness. Smoking incense was burned at funerals, and black veils were worn in mourning. Otherwise, Pyra was Axura's domain. Circular Eyes of Axura were painted on thresholds and entryways—protection against lost spirits of the dead—and woven phoenix idols made with red-dyed dove feathers dangled in open windows.

Though Sparrow seemed to know the villagers inside and out, Veronyka was surprised at their cool treatment of her. They regarded her as somewhat of a pest, like a buzzing fly they wanted to swat away. Did she not have family or friends here? Was she even *from* Vayle? She had the look of someone from Stel or Arboria South, but there were plenty of people living—or hiding—in Pyra these days who weren't Pyraean. The fact that she might be alone made Veronyka feel new kinship with her, and she remained close to the girl's side as they wended their way through the busy Vayle streets.

When at last they caught up to the steward, the market was too crowded for Veronyka to hear any more, and she was anxious to approach him. But if the steward and the boy were speaking Pyraean to keep their affairs secret, they certainly wouldn't appreciate Veronyka approaching them in the middle of the bustling market.

"You're staring at them," Sparrow said. It wasn't phrased like a question. Her brow was furrowed and her head was tilted slightly, as if trying to make sense of the noise all around.

"Uh, yes, I guess I am," Veronyka muttered, turning around and pretending to shop at a stall of headscarves. The proprietor gave her and Sparrow dubious looks—both were barefooted and dirty—and when Sparrow began feeling the fabrics enthusiastically, the saleswoman slapped her hand away.

"Why?" Sparrow asked Veronyka, unperturbed by the chastisement. She turned away from the stall and twirled her spear in front of her with a haphazard flick of the wrist, causing everybody they passed to gasp and scuttle out of the way.

Veronyka glanced around, but Sparrow's spear made sure everyone gave them a wide berth. "I think they might be Phoenix Riders."

Veronyka didn't know why she trusted Sparrow with this information, but she figured she could use all the help she could get.

"Oh, *Phoenix Riders*," Sparrow breathed, eyes alight. Her hands stilled, and the butt of her spear landed on the ground with a soft *thud.* "Lyra the Defender. Wise Queen Malka and Thrax. Aurelya, the Golden Queen."

"Have you heard anything about them recently, Sparrow? Anything to do with the steward?"

The girl shook her head. "I will listen harder."

Then, without another word, she darted in the direction of the steward's wagon.

"Sparrow!" Veronyka hissed. She chased after the girl, leaping back from a horse-drawn cart and dodging the flailing arms of a fishmonger promising the freshest catch of the day, before finally catching up to her next to the wagon.

Veronyka opened her mouth to insist that they leave at once, afraid they would be seen eavesdropping, when Sparrow clapped small, clammy fingers against Veronyka's lips.

"Rooms are booked," the steward said, his voice drifting over to them from the opposite side of the wagon. The words were followed by the grunt and shift of heavy items being loaded inside. "We'll leave just before dawn. Then it's Rushlea and a hard push to Petratec. You off to see her?"

"If that's all right, Master Beryk," the boy answered, his voice tight with worry. *Master* Beryk, as in *Master Rider*, the designation for a fully trained Phoenix Rider? While anyone who rode a phoenix could be called a "phoenix rider," when referring to Phoenix Riders in the military sense, there were two specific subgroups: masters and apprentices.

"Remember, no formalities here, Elliot."

"Of course—I'm sorry, sir."

"You've plenty of time for a visit, so long as you're back before daybreak."

"I will be."

Beryk sighed. "If only the commander weren't so strict . . . you might have brought her back with you. Your sister's an animage, yes?"

"Everyone is in my family. She'd have come when I did, if he would have let her." His voice wavered slightly, as if fighting to hide his bitterness. "She desperately wants to be a Rider."

Beryk cleared his throat, and Veronyka feared he could hear her heart skip a beat on the other side of the wagon. "Well, lucky she's visiting relatives so close to Vayle and that you get to see her now, at any rate."

"Yes, sir. I'll go now, then."

Veronyka had a split second to realize that the scraping footsteps were heading in their direction before she straightened up, trying to pull Sparrow back with her.

The young boy, Elliot, rounded the wagon and spotted them lurking near the edge of the canvas flap that covered their supplies.

"Hey!" he shouted, eyes landing first on Sparrow. Like the scarf seller, Elliot had taken one look at her wild hair and dirty clothes and had decided she was no good. "Get away from there, thief!"

He lunged forward, waving an arm as if he meant to scare her off, and Veronyka instinctually leapt between them. She didn't want to see Sparrow harmed and was fed up with the careless way people treated her.

"She's no thief," Veronyka snapped, keeping a hand on Sparrow, pleased to hear that her voice sounded braver than she felt. Chirp started twittering away, zooming in wide circles around all three of them, and it seemed their combined efforts were enough to stop Elliot short.

He stared at the bird, then at Veronyka, and she knew she looked hardly better than Sparrow.

"What's this, now?" said Beryk, rounding the side of the wagon. Veronyka froze. She hadn't thought this through. She'd only meant to protect Sparrow—the last thing she wanted was to be seen as a thief or a troublemaker by the man who might be able to make her dreams come true.

Without another word, Veronyka pulled Sparrow's arm and marched her through the crowd, Chirp following behind. She glanced over her shoulder, but they weren't pursued. It was probably obvious by their lack of possessions that they hadn't actually stolen anything. Still, Veronyka's insides twisted. Had she just ruined her chance with the steward?

"You stood up for me," Sparrow said as they came to a stop in the outskirts of the market. She reached absently for Chirp, who landed in her palm. She gazed down at him, patting his head, her brow furrowed. "No one ever stands up for Sparrow and Chirp."

"Oh," Veronyka said, her thoughts still on her next move. The girl's words were so frank and earnest that a pang pierced Veronyka's chest. "It was nothing. You've been really nice and helpful. Chirp, too," she added, and Sparrow beamed.

"The steward's staying at the cookhouse for the night," she said, clearly determined to continue being helpful. She pointed over Veronyka's shoulder, where Beryk was delivering the wagon to the hostler at the attached inn. Elliot had already disappeared to visit his sister and the relatives she was staying with. "Want me to get you into his rooms? I know the servant passages."

"No," Veronyka said sharply, afraid Sparrow would run off and get them into more trouble. She didn't need to accost the man while he ate, or barge into his private room, as Sparrow suggested. The steward said he was leaving at dawn, and Veronyka would just have to be there when he did. She wouldn't let him leave this village without getting some answers. "I'll just wait out here until morning."

To Veronyka's surprise, Sparrow stayed with her.

When the market closed and the sun began to set, Sparrow begged a free dinner for both of them at the cookhouse back door. The endless tendrils of smoke issuing from the domed roof reminded Veronyka unpleasantly of Xephyra's pyre, and just like that, the memories pressed in on her, sudden and suffocating. The dark, malignant glint in Val's eyes, the dense smell of boiling vegetables, and the choked sound of Xephyra's last labored breaths. The stillness of her body and how quickly it had gone up in flames.

Thinking of her bondmate was like being punched in the stomach, and Veronyka took a great shuddering breath. She couldn't afford to go to pieces every time Xephyra popped into her mind. Val thought Veronyka was incapable of moving forward—incapable of *surviving*—without her help, and Veronyka refused to prove her sister right.

She knew what she had to do, even if it felt like betrayal to do so. Veronyka swallowed, her throat thick. Mere hours ago, Xephyra had been a source of strength, a part of her very being. Now her bondmate was a source of despair. How could Veronyka move forward if she carried the weight of the dead with her?

Veronyka closed her eyes and steadied her breath. She could never forget Xephyra, not truly, but she could make her memory harder to find. She'd learned the technique from Val, or rather, *because of* Val. It was hard to keep secrets from a sister like her, but Veronyka had figured out a few tricks.

There was a way of walling things off in her mind—hiding them from conscious thought, so that people like Val, who had shadow magic, couldn't easily find them. Veronyka had never tried to hide things from *herself*, but it was worth a shot.

She visualized an empty, dusty corner of her mind—far in the back, out of sight, and easily forgotten. There she would hide Xephyra away.

Just for now, she told herself, hating the cold necessity of it and the way it reminded her of Val. *Just for now.*

Carefully, like a collector with her most delicate and prized possessions, Veronyka gathered every fond memory and happy feeling she had of her bondmate: Xephyra's hatching, her first wobbly flight, and the comforting warmth of her feathers. Veronyka experienced each moment of joy one last time, then put them inside that dark corner. She thought of it like a mental safe house, tucked away and concealed, but not truly gone. Xephyra was still a part of her. She always would be.

As her bondmate slowly disappeared from her thoughts, the weight in Veronyka's chest lifted. Instead of a chasm left behind after a catastrophe, her mind was an empty field. Soothing. Peaceful—no matter the turmoil just below the surface.

Later, when she had her life sorted out, she could take the time to properly grieve for Xephyra.

ↀ   ↀ   ↀ

"You gonna go with them if they let you?" Sparrow asked, several hours after dinner. "Become a famous warrior, like Avalkyra Ashfire?" She was playing with a moth, catching and releasing it over and over again, while murmuring encouragement and cooing words of praise. Insects were nearly impossible to communicate with, their minds too small and foreign for most animages to grasp—usually. It wouldn't have surprised Veronyka to know Sparrow had managed to make contact with some of them.

Veronyka smiled. "I hope so. What will you do?" She didn't know anything about the girl, where she came from or where she was going. Maybe Sparrow didn't know either.

"We haven't been to Runnet in a while," she said with a sigh, letting her moth friend fly away. "Maybe we'll go there next." Her sparrow cheeped his assent, making it clear who the "we" was in that sentence.

Sparrow was soon snoring, but Veronyka only dozed lightly, afraid to miss the steward's departure. She saw the fishermen leave for their boats and smelled the baker's first bread. Elliot returned just before dawn, shoulders hunched against the cold—or maybe it was the idea of leaving his family that dragged him down.

When the wagon rolled out of the stable yard into the golden morning sunshine, Veronyka was waiting by the gate.

"Excuse me," she said, startling Beryk as he shuffled through some papers. Elliot was just out of earshot, adjusting the wagon's canvas cover, though he frowned at her in recognition.

"Yes?" the steward asked. While Elliot seemed to remember her, Beryk's expression was vaguely polite.

Veronyka swallowed. "I heard—I know that you're . . . *phoenixaeres*," she said, keeping her voice low.

Beryk had leaned in to hear her, but he straightened abruptly when she spoke in Pyraean. "I'm sorry, lass," he said sharply, "but I don't speak ancient Pyraean."

"Please," Veronyka said, stepping in front of him as he moved to walk away. He glanced at her, and she must have truly looked pathetic, because he stopped. "I want to go with you. I'm an animage, and—"

"You must be confused. I manage a country estate, and this here is my assistant."

"Your *underwing*?" Veronyka asked stubbornly.

Beryk smiled tightly, and when Elliot wandered over, he waved for the boy to get onto the wagon. "Listen, lass, and listen closely," he said in a rapid whisper. "Whatever you think you heard, you'd best forget it. For your own sake. Even if I were recruiting—which I'm not—and even if that recruitment were for animages—which it isn't—I'm afraid you'd not fit our requirements."

"Because I'm not a boy?" Veronyka asked.

The man wore a heavy, regretful expression, as if this weren't the first time he'd had to reject a girl and he didn't enjoy it. "I know it seems unfair, but he has his reasons."

He, this commander that Beryk had mentioned the previous day. Before Veronyka could argue further, he gave her arm a bracing pat, then hopped onto the wagon.

She watched them go, a riot of emotions inside her chest. She was disappointed, yes, but he'd basically admitted that he was a Rider. The existence of even one Phoenix Rider on Pyrmont was cause for celebration.

"What'd he say?"

Veronyka jumped, surprised to find Sparrow standing right next to her. She'd been lurking in the shadows outside the inn, but once Beryk left, she had sidled up to Veronyka on silent feet.

"It's like you said; they only want boys," Veronyka muttered, still trying to understand their exchange and what it meant. Were the Phoenix Riders of the future going to be men alone?

Sparrow shrugged. "Then be a boy."

Veronyka's breath caught, and she looked up at Sparrow in surprise.

Be a boy.

It was simple. It was brilliant.

It was exactly what Veronyka would do.

Aura, the original capital of the Queendom of Pyra, sat atop Pyrmont's highest peak. It was built around the Everlasting Flame, a massive pit filled with the same god-made flames that had tested Nefyra a thousand years ago. It continued to burn long after her trial, constantly fueled by gases leaking from holes in the mountain.

Stone filled with veins of precious metals surrounded the Everlasting Flame, and the Pyraeans slowly excavated temples and statues from the living rock. Fissures of gold reflected the firelight, gilding every surface, leading to the name "Aura," the Golden City.

The Pyraeans slowly spread over the highest peaks of the mountain, able to live and build in places where only those with phoenixes could ever reach. It wasn't until the Everlasting Flame went out that the Riders went in search of new lands and new prosperity. Many saw the extinction of the Everlasting Flame as a sign that Axura was displeased with them and that they had fallen out of favor. Every phoenix ever hatched until that time had been incubated in the Everlasting Flame, and it was an integral part of everyday life for the ancient Phoenix Riders. In that divine fire, lives were birthed and dead bodies burned; festivals and celebrations, weddings and ceremonies, all were done in the light of the Everlasting Flame.

Newly crowned Queen Elysia knew her people needed more than a new home. . . . They needed a new start. After years of maintaining and defending Pyra's borders—which had grown to encompass all of Pyrmont and the surrounding Foothills—Elysia set her sights on expansion and exploration. She maintained that was their true purpose—to spread Axura's light into all corners of the world.

There were battles and alliances, treaties and new boundaries, and soon Pyraean queens married valley kings and established the Auran—more commonly called Golden—Empire, never returning to the highest reaches of their mountain home.

—*Myths and Legends of the Golden Empire and Beyond,* a compilation of stories and accounts, the Morian Archives, 101 AE

She called it betrayal. I called it justice.
A poisoned cup for a poisoned cup, a death
for a death. A queen for a king.

- CHAPTER II -
SEV

SEV SOON CAME TO regret his deal with Trix—if it could even be called a deal. Blackmail, more like. He thought often of reporting her, but he didn't doubt she'd make good on her threats. He hadn't built up any amount of clout or goodwill with the other soldiers, and he knew from experience that Trix could be very persuasive.

The fact of the matter was, the woman was smarter than him, and he couldn't afford to cross her. Trix knew about his little escape attempt and would probably keep an eye on him at night to ensure he didn't make another run for it. If Sev refused to help her, well, she'd reveal his secret—and frame him for any number of other things as well—and he'd find himself in bondage, or worse. Being an animage in hiding was one thing, but being an animage hiding among the empire's precious ranks of soldiers was something else. Most bondservants were forced to serve until they'd "paid back their debt to the empire," which really just meant paying back lost taxes. That usually resulted in a term of at least ten years, depending on how old the animage was and what exactly they'd been caught doing. If they were running a booming business thanks to their magic—breeding Stellan horses or training expensive hunting falcons—without paying the magetax, the empire would have lost out on piles of gold, so their term as a bondservant would be much longer. Children and poor folk tended to serve shorter terms, but their families usually suffered without them. And once they were released from their bondage, they were taxed twice as heavily for the rest of their lives.

Traitors who were captured after the Blood War—animages who supported Avalkyra Ashfire—served for life or were deemed too dangerous to live and were executed. Sev expected to be lumped in with the traitors if he were discovered, but he wasn't sure if his crime would be considered bad enough to get him killed. The empire took its military seriously, and Captain Belden was not an understanding man. Plus, Sev had been a convicted murderer before he enlisted—in the face of his treachery, they might decide to unforgive that crime, take his head, and be done with it.

He was stuck; Sev knew it, and Trix knew it too. For better or worse, he was a part of her scheme. Since her plans would get him out of his life as a soldier, their goals aligned for the time being.

Still, joining her, trying to "bring these filthy empire assassins down from the inside," went against everything Sev had learned about survival. Heroics were for fools, and what was more heroic—or more foolish—than a handful of servants trying to bring down two hundred soldiers?

She'd already been at the task for weeks, and Sev was just one of many moving pieces. Trix's role as a bondservant was to manage the messenger pigeons, and Sev had no doubt she read the captain's letters. She had the cooks and the craftsmen, the young runners and the old washerwomen—people from every facet of camp life—reporting to her, including Captain Belden's personal attendant. They gave Trix every scrap of information they had, and she weaved them all together like Anyanke, goddess of fate, spinning her tangled webs. Everyone in the camp was caught up in it, including Sev.

"What makes you think you can even pull this off?" he asked her several days after Trix had first recruited him.

The only time Sev could really talk to the woman was late at night, when everyone's duties were done and most of the soldiers were either passed out or so deep into their cups that they didn't notice a soldier fraternizing with a bondservant.

Fires were still forbidden, but the bondservants had set up an area to sit and work, with logs ranged in a rough circle in the barest scraps of moonlight filtering through the trees. Trix was seated there, humming to herself, and Kade was next to her, mending a bit of broken harness. Though his hands were large, they were graceful, too, and capable of delicate work. His head was bent over the strap, a tool held between his teeth as he carefully took the buckle apart.

Despite Kade's apparent focus, he snorted at Sev's question.

"What makes you think I can't?" Trix asked, grinning slightly. Sev gave her a sidelong look, taking in every inch of her bent, gray, and less-than-intimidating form. Sure, she was a good gossip, but gathering information was one thing, and acting on that information was something else.

Trix was calm as she patted the log next to her, inviting Sev to take a seat. "Not all battles are fought with ax and arrow. Some say the war ended sixteen years ago, when the sister queens died. Not me. I've been fighting this war every day since. This," she said, pressing a hand against the metal chain dangling from her throat, "is my armor, and this"—she swept an arm over the quiet campsite—"is my battlefield."

A shiver ran down Sev's spine. He cast his gaze over the prone soldiers, imagining them not as sleepers, but as corpses.

"You've been a bondservant all this time?" Sev asked. "For sixteen years?"

"Six," she said. An icy chill emanated from her, so Sev decided not to ask her what she'd been doing before that. Living life on the run? Blackmailing other careless empire soldiers? He supposed it didn't matter. Whatever Trix had done, no one deserved bondage. No one.

"Did you fight in the war?" he asked. "As a warrior? A Phoenix Rider?" He couldn't help the way his words sped up at talk of the Riders, the way they tumbled from his mouth in excitement or fear—he couldn't be sure which one.

"Does that surprise you? Not all of us were fit to grace palace frescoes and temple mosaics like Avalkyra Ashfire, with her crown of feathers. Some of us were best suited for the shadows."

"Did you know her, Avalkyra Ashfire?"

"We were acquainted," she said offhandedly.

Sev's eyes widened, and he stared at her with newfound respect. To actually have met the queen meant that Trix was no lowly conscript like his parents had been. "Does that mean . . . were you a part of her patrol? Were you a famous Phoenix Rider too?"

"If I were, that would have quite defeated the point," she said dryly.

Sev frowned. "The point of what?"

"No more questions, soldier," Kade interrupted, but Trix quieted him with a hand on his shoulder.

"I was an *adviser*, of sorts."

"An adviser to Avalkyra Ashfire?" Sev asked incredulously. It was one thing to fight alongside her as a soldier, and quite another to give her council. He lowered his voice. "How did one of the Feather-Crowned Queen's own advisers wind up here, in service to Captain Belden, who's been charged with the destruction of whatever is left of the Phoenix Riders?"

"That's none of your—" Kade began, but Trix cut him off.

"They have no idea what I did or didn't do in the war," she said disdainfully, jerking her chin in the direction of the captain's tent. "To them I am an old animage woman past my prime, meek, slightly mad—and nothing more."

"That still doesn't explain how you wound up on this mission. Dumb luck? A happy coincidence?" asked Sev.

"You're nosy, boy," Trix said, her tone thoughtful, and Kade nodded, clearly anticipating a reprimand, until— "Which is exactly why I need you."

"For what?" he asked, latching on to the change in subject.

Whatever it was she needed from him, Sev wanted to know. He had no intention of getting roped into rebellions and stupid heroics. That was how people wound up dead. "Please, just tell me what you need, so I can do it and be free of this arrangement."

Kade stared at him, a frown creasing his brow. It almost looked like disappointment, but Sev shook the odd sinking feeling it gave him.

He wasn't joining their little revolt because he wanted to. . . . He was doing it because Trix was forcing him. What he really wanted was to escape, and the sooner he did whatever she needed, the sooner that would happen.

"I need you to sign up for pack animal duty," she announced.

"I . . . What?" Sev asked, his gaze flicking to Kade. He was one of a dozen bondservants who were responsible for the newly purchased llamas' care, and if Sev signed up for pack animal duty, they'd be stationed together.

"Why?" Kade demanded, getting to his feet. "I don't need him."

"I never said you did."

"For how long?" Sev asked.

"Until I say so."

"What? Why can't you just tell me?" Sev demanded.

"Some things are best kept secret," Trix said. Both Sev and Kade continued to scowl at her, but she seemed wholly unperturbed.

"Secret?" Sev repeated blankly. "Okay . . . well, what do I need to *do* while stationed there? Surely more than my regular duties."

Trix only smiled. "Consider yourself on a need-to-know basis, boy. And right now you do not need to know. So, for the time being, that information . . ."

"Let me guess," Sev asked resignedly, "also a secret?"

"That's the thing with secrets," she said. "They never really die. Just when one bursts into flames, another rises up to take its place."

*She knew my darkness better than anyone,
and always, she had forgiven me. Always, she had
seen the good in me. Until the day she didn't.*

- CHAPTER 12 -
TRISTAN

TRISTAN'S FAVORITE PLACE WAS soaring through the sky on the back of his phoenix. His not-flaming phoenix, of course.

The pump of Rex's powerful wings beneath him, the gusts of warm air that floated up from the rocky earth below, and the vistas that showed him mountains and rivers and endless trees as far as the eye could see—that was, when his eye wasn't fixed on the back of his bondmate's head.

Unlike usual, Tristan didn't scan the ground below for danger, as he was supposed to do, or gaze into the distance, where mountain ranges enclosed the valley like a sturdy rock palisade. He didn't even try to see his old home in Ferro—an impossible feat from this distance and angle, but something he did almost every time he rode.

No, Tristan hunched in the stirrups of his saddle, muscles rigid and hands clenched tight on the reins, as if riding a stampeding horse, not floating above the ground in wide, elegant arcs. He refused to enjoy his late-afternoon flight, preferring to scowl at Rex's feathers and stew in silence.

Rex tossed his head, taking Tristan's irritation and making it his own— one of the negative effects of the bond. The phoenix dipped suddenly, beating his wings with an impatient flap and jolting Tristan out of his distracted thoughts. He realized his stiff, awkward riding position was as uncomfortable for his bondmate as it was for him.

"Sorry, Rex," Tristan murmured, settling more comfortably in the saddle. With a heavy sigh and a twist of his neck to work out the kinks, Tristan took in the familiar landscape that unfolded below them, running a gentle hand down the silken feathers of Rex's bright red neck, warmth bleeding through his gloves.

Tristan was dressed in his full Rider regalia—leather gloves and armguards, fitted tunic, a thick woven breastplate, and padded riding pants tucked into boots, all coated with a fire-resistant resin. The layers made Tristan hot and uncomfortable, and he much preferred to fly without them—but today's ride wasn't for leisure. Today he and several of the more senior apprentices were participating in the local patrols along with the Master Riders.

It should have made him happy—and it did at first. Tristan had begged and pleaded for the chance, and at last the order had come through. Finally, after months of asking, he'd get the opportunity to prove to all the Master Riders—including his father—that he was ready to become one of them, that he belonged among their ranks.

Tristan should have known better.

He'd been assigned the easiest, tamest area to watch, a segment of the surrounding land that was so safe, they usually didn't patrol it at all. The opportunity he'd so longed for immediately became an insult.

It was a useless post, and Tristan knew his father was behind it.

Ever since that day on the bluffs two weeks ago when he'd failed to make the jump, Tristan had been waiting for his father to bring it up, to use it against him in some way. Never mind that Tristan had since completed the exercise correctly nearly a dozen times; he'd known that one slipup would come back to haunt him.

And here it was.

Tristan had seen the look on the other apprentices' faces when his patrol was announced: Several clearly pitied him, while others smirked at what they saw as a deflation of Tristan's overlarge ego. The reaction of the Master Riders was worst of all: They stared openly at Tristan and his father, seeing it as an example of favoritism. Like his father was trying to give him an easy path.

It only proved how little they knew him.

Tristan pushed the thoughts from his mind, imagining them floating away on the wind that whipped across his skin. He tried to focus on his patrol, urging Rex to fly in the crisscrossing pattern they'd been taught, but there was nothing to see.

As a rule, they stuck to the air above the very upper reaches of Pyrmont, not wanting to draw attention from the empire or the villages on the lower rim. They flew only one daylight patrol, soaring so high up that they appeared as no more than distant specks—perhaps a particularly large eagle or falcon—to anyone on the ground. The rest of their patrols were at night, which allowed them to fly lower, but of course the landscape was more difficult to see in the darkness, no matter how superior a phoenix's eyesight. This left them blind to a lot of what was happening in Pyra, and in the empire beyond.

This was why Tristan had pushed for more horse-mounted patrols. He had also pushed to accelerate the apprentice program, so they could put together a third patrol group. He had been rebuffed at both turns.

And now, just when he'd thought things were happening for him, he'd been sent to float above the Pilgrimage Road like a kite in an Azurec's Day parade.

With an unspoken command, Rex banked hard, and together they set their sights to the east. Tristan had long since memorized their patrol grid and knew where there were gaps in their surveillance. The road didn't need watching; the wilderness did.

The moment Tristan deviated from his orders, a bubble of exhilaration inflated inside his chest. Rex flew faster, and they surged up and down with every powerful thrust of his wings. This was the land of Tristan's Pyraean ancestors, and right now he felt as if he claimed it for himself. He wanted to discover its secrets, to know the mountain better even than those who were born here. As he soared through the sky, he wasn't the son of an exiled governor; he was a *Phoenix Rider*, like the legendary warriors of old.

He identified familiar landmarks as he flew: the domed houses of Montascent, the last still-occupied village before the thrust of rock that led to the ruins of Aura; the serpentine twist of the River Aurys, snaking down the mountainside; the staggered row of carved phoenix statues that lined the path on the way to the village of Petratec—and the lone figure, cutting through the long grasses between the village and the river, making their way toward the bridge that led to the Phoenix Riders' hidden base.

Tristan almost fell from his saddle.

While Rex tucked his wings and dove for the skulking traveler, Tristan fumbled for his horn. The ringing sound drew the person's gaze, but they didn't run or wave; they simply froze, openmouthed and gaping, neck craned toward the sky.

The instant Rex landed, Tristan leapt from his back, drawing his spear and leveling it at the intruder. They locked eyes—and Tristan's heart sank.

It was just a boy, some kid barely into adolescence, scrawny and dressed in rags.

He was definitely Pyraean, with large, deep-set eyes and dark brows. His mess of straight black hair was cut in a jagged cap around his head, and his brown skin was smudged with dust and dirt.

They stood in awkward silence until the thump of beating wings echoed from above. Tristan squeezed his eyes shut. The nearest Rider patrol had answered his call and were about to discover that he'd raised the alarm over this child—and of course, the nearest patrol just happened to include the commander. Dreading what would come next, Tristan fixed his gaze on the boy as the Riders—including Ronyn and Elliot, the other apprentices chosen for patrol—descended, kicking up grass and leaves in a gust of warm wind.

Rex shook his wings and edged closer to Tristan, puffing out his chest in an attempt to assert dominance as phoenixes landed all around them. There were eight new Riders in total: a full patrol, plus the two apprentices and everyone's mounts. The phoenixes retained their flight formation, feathers bristling and heads tossing as they stood in a rough V shape, and every single Rider had a bow or spear drawn. They scanned the area, ready for a threat, and it took them several moments to notice the boy Tristan held captive.

Cassian, patrol leader and commander of the Phoenix Riders, pursed his lips, then made a quick gesture for the rest of his Riders to stand down. Weapons were put away and arrows returned to quivers as the entire patrol— except for the commander—dismounted. Even the phoenixes relaxed their postures and quelled their battle fever.

At last Commander Cassian turned his attention to Tristan.

"Sir," Tristan said, bowing his head slightly.

The commander's face was expressionless, yet there was a rigidity to his features that told Tristan he was much angrier than he looked. Tristan tried to square his shoulders and stand his ground, but he had difficulty meeting the commander's eyes.

Yes, he had disobeyed orders, but he had also found a strange traveler dangerously close to their hidden base, proving those orders were flawed. The intruder was a small, unarmed boy, but it was better to be overcautious than caught off guard.

He hoped.

"You've found a child," the commander announced from astride his phoenix, turning his imperious gaze toward Tristan's captive.

"He's an unknown traveler," Tristan said, feeling slightly foolish for being the only one with his weapon out, as if he were afraid of the boy. He lowered it slightly. "I was only following protocol."

"Protocol?" the commander repeated, his voice cracking like a whip. "If you were truly following protocol, you'd still be patrolling the ninth quadrant, where you were assigned, and not raising the alarm for an underfed, unarmed child."

Low murmurs rippled through the group of Riders, who stood in a semicircle around the boy, their mounts looming behind them. The boy cowered slightly, and Tristan let the butt of his spear hit the ground.

"I blew the horn before I landed, so I didn't know . . ."

"You. Didn't. Know," the commander said, emphasizing each word and loosing them like well-placed arrows into Tristan's already wounded pride. "You didn't know, and yet still you acted. If we blew a horn every time we saw a traveler, our patrols would never sleep."

Tristan's face flushed, and Rex snapped irritably at a nearby phoenix. The rest of the patrol studied their boots or the straps on their saddles, avoiding Tristan's chastisement.

The commander dismounted, and as he walked past Tristan, he spoke in a low voice. "Secrecy is our greatest weapon—and our greatest defense. You undermine both by calling us here."

Before Tristan could answer—and truly, he had no idea what to say—Commander Cassian's steward and second-in-command, Beryk, moved to the front of the group, a frown on his face.

"We've met before, haven't we?" he asked, staring at the boy before them.

"In Vayle, sir," Elliot interjected, straight-backed and serious. He was training to become steward one day, and so he was usually lurking somewhere in Beryk's shadow. He'd never gotten particularly close to the other apprentices, always busy running errands or attending Beryk in meetings, and had a reputation for being a bit stuck-up. Tristan didn't mind, though. His father had been pushing *him* to become steward, apparently more than happy to let Tristan remain safely buried in papers for the rest of his days. Luckily, Elliot had practically begged for the opportunity, relieving Tristan of a future stuck mostly behind a desk. The idea that his father thought he was better suited to a position as an administrator rather than a soldier was a painful blow.

"You know him, Beryk?" the commander asked in surprise.

"I-I think it was my sister, sir," the boy said, his high voice confirming his youth—and complete lack of threat. "You met her outside the inn, about a week ago?"

"Yes, that's right," Beryk said, nodding, though he still seemed troubled. "You're a long way from home, lad."

"What is your name?" the commander asked, cutting into the conversation.

"Nyk," the boy answered, his voice quaking slightly. He seemed . . . not scared, exactly, but distracted by the group around them. Obviously the boy had never seen phoenixes before, never mind so many all at once.

"Where are you heading, Nyk?" the commander asked. "Montascent is farther north, and Petratec's behind you."

"I came to find you, sir—to find Beryk and the master he served. I came to find the Phoenix Riders."

Ringing silence greeted his words.

The commander glanced at Beryk, who raised his hands helplessly. "His sister came asking . . . wanting to serve us, heard us speaking Pyraean. I turned her away as best I could, but . . ." He shrugged.

The commander sighed. Secrecy might have been their greatest defense when they'd first set up, but word traveled down the mountain, no matter how careful they were. Beryk needed to purchase supplies, and even if he didn't, people turned up occasionally—lost travelers or traders—and of course they had servants and guards working for them. There were too many loose strings, too many variables to constantly monitor and keep track of. It was only a matter of time before the entire mountain knew they were here, and the empire wouldn't be far behind. They'd want the Phoenix Riders, the so-called rebels, snuffed out for good. With them gone, there would be no one to challenge the governors' rule or to put an end to the magetax and the persecution of their people.

This was why they needed more patrols. They were essentially sitting ducks.

"I don't know what your sister told you, what she might have guessed or overheard, but we are not the Phoenix Riders your parents told you about. I am a private citizen, and these Riders are my personal guard. This is not a government-funded military order."

"But . . . ," Nyk said, taking hold of the commander's arm as he turned to go. "What if I paid for my own supplies and training, and—"

The rest of the Riders stiffened, as if preparing for possible danger for the first time. Tristan didn't understand their concern at first—until he saw the glint of steel. The boy had drawn a knife. Apparently he was armed after all.

Realizing his mistake, Nyk released the commander's arm and stepped backward, holding the knife in the palm of his hand. It was a dagger, small but finely wrought. "I only meant . . . Maybe I can trade this for enough gold to join?"

Everyone in the group stared at the blade. It wasn't just steel; it was *Ferronese* steel, stamped to mark its origin and authenticity. It was quite valuable, though it would hardly be enough to fully fund a new Rider. Still, it wasn't the value of the object that was the trouble; it was the fact that this humble Pyraean child possessed it. Where had he gotten such a weapon? Was he a thief? An escaped bondservant or an empire spy?

"Search him," Commander Cassian ordered.

After taking the knife and handing it to the commander to inspect more closely, Beryk took hold of the small bundle slung over Nyk's back, while Elliot strode forward to check the boy's body for more concealed weapons. Nyk's jaw clenched during the search, but it was over quickly, and his pack's contents were laid out for the commander to examine.

There was nothing more of value or interest: a small collection of roots and berries, some dried meat, and a tin pot.

Rather than waylaying their concerns, the boy's modest belongings only drove home just how curious his possession of the dagger really was.

"How did you come by this weapon?" the commander asked, glancing at the bottom of the hilt before handing it back to Beryk. He was looking for a maker's mark, to link the weapon to a specific metalsmith, or perhaps other signs of personal ownership.

Nyk hesitated. He must have stolen it, Tristan guessed, or he was lying about being from Vayle. Even on the lower rim, where trade was more common, no mountain-born kid without two coins to rub together could afford a weapon such as that.

"I found it . . . ," he said, though he sounded uncertain. Tristan was torn between an odd sense of anxiety for the boy and his own self-satisfaction: He had been right to blow the horn, even if he hadn't known it at first.

"His sister tried to steal from us," Elliot piped in, looking triumphant. "They're probably a team: One distracts while the other—"

"My sister wouldn't steal," the boy snapped. "And neither would I."

The commander glanced up at the darkening sky, then down at Nyk. He frowned. "Take him to Morra," he said to Beryk, and mounted up.

"But, sir—Commander Cassian!" Tristan called before the commander could fly away. "Can . . . shouldn't I escort the prisoner, since I was the one who discovered him?"

"Since you shouldn't have been patrolling here in the first place, I think I'd do better with a Rider who follows orders, rather than an *apprentice* who does whatever he pleases."

Day 12, Second Moon, 169 AE

My sweet Pheronia,

I hated to leave without saying goodbye, but I was chased from my bed in the dead of night. Perhaps you know this already. Perhaps it is upon your orders that I was hunted down.

You should also know that I am not sorry for what I have done, but I am sorry for your pain.

It has taken me some time to get settled, but I am safe now. I am ready. Let's put this behind us.

We've an empire to rule.

Your sister, Avalkyra

*The winner in any contest is
the person who's willing to go the furthest,
to do whatever it takes to succeed.
That person is me.*

- CHAPTER 13 -
VERONYKA

PRISONER.

The word fell like the final spark from a flint stone, setting the dormant fears in Veronyka's heart ablaze.

The first flicker had been the horn call; the second, the young Rider's gleaming spear. Everything had happened so quickly after that, the terror building inside her chest, waiting for release. The looming crowd of indifferent faces, dressed more like military foot soldiers than Phoenix Riders. The commander's brusque questions and easy dismissal. The dagger. The rough, searching hands that threatened to accidentally discover her bound breasts at any moment. All the while, Veronyka held her breath, afraid her hitching chest might stoke the flames of her emotions or draw attention to the smallest of swells beneath the fabric. The presence of the phoenixes with their wild hearts and fiery minds had made it all worse, but somehow her secret remained her own. For now.

It had never occurred to Veronyka that a simple knife could arouse such suspicion. Then again, coupled with her vague account of being the brother of the girl who had eavesdropped on Beryk in Vayle—and Elliot's accusations that her sister was a thief—she supposed her story was far from perfect. She hadn't expected to be interrogated, and that small moment of hesitation when she was deciding what she should and shouldn't say was all it took to condemn her in their eyes. Now she was being escorted to their compound as a prisoner. It felt like some kind of irrevocable sentence; it felt like failure.

A lead weight settled into the pit of her stomach as the majority of the Riders took off into the sky, leaving Beryk and Elliot behind. The boy who'd found her was last to leave, his scowling face telling her she'd made an enemy already, though she wasn't entirely sure how. When he'd first landed before her, swooping in on phoenix-back with his drawn spear flashing in the setting sun, he'd looked like a hero out of a Pyraean Epic. Then he'd dismounted and pointed the weapon at *her*, and the fantasy had shattered.

Lost in thought, Veronyka was startled when Beryk sidled up to her again. "Twins?" he asked curiously. His voice was gruff but not unkind— still, Veronyka jumped as if he'd shouted at her.

"P-pardon?"

"You and your sister. Are you twins?"

"No, sir," Veronyka said, avoiding his eyes and running a self-conscious hand over her cropped hair once his back was turned.

It had hurt at first, hacking away the long braids she'd worn all her life—but Veronyka wouldn't let a little thing like being a girl stop her from becoming a Rider. While plenty of Pyraean boys wore their hair long and braided, Veronyka hadn't failed to notice that Beryk—whose deep brown skin surely marked Pyraean heritage—did not.

Her *maiora* had told her that it was tradition for Phoenix Riders to cut their hair short when they began training, symbolizing a new start. It also created a camaraderie with the other empire military orders, who wore short hair as well. Braids became a status symbol, something earned and possible only after years of training allowed freshly shorn hair to grow long again.

When Sparrow suggested Veronyka become a boy, it was the first thing she'd thought of. If she were going to transform herself and start over, why not fully embrace it? Besides, anything she could do to be more like the others could only help her in blending in. The short hair did make her look more masculine, highlighting her sharp jaw and cheekbones, and when she used a scrap of fabric to flatten her breasts, the simple transformation was complete.

While the hair itself was meaningless to her, the beads and sentimental embellishments she'd added over the years were priceless. Veronyka had salvaged what she could and stuffed the mess into a secret pocket inside her trousers. She had stitched it in years ago in order to hide coins and other valuables from pickpockets and thieves—and, in this case, random body searches.

As long as she didn't let her voice get too high, she'd be fine. She was Nyk now, and Veronyka was just another part of her past she'd have to leave behind.

"Well, we'd best be off," Beryk said. "It's a short walk, so the mounts'll meet us there," he continued as the last two phoenixes took to the sky, leaving their Riders behind.

Beryk took the lead, keeping Veronyka's knife and small bundle of supplies in hand, while Elliot walked behind. He seemed tense and wary, as if he expected her to make a run for it, and it almost made Veronyka laugh—she could barely put one foot in front of the other, never mind attempt an escape.

It was a strange relief to surrender herself to her captors' control after almost a week of hard travel, worrying about getting lost and struggling to keep herself from going hungry or becoming dehydrated.

By the time she'd gotten her disguise in place in Vayle, Beryk's wagon had long since disappeared over the hills. Veronyka had been ready to run after them when she realized that time might be her friend. If she'd caught up to Beryk that night, surely he would have been suspicious and would have remembered the girl's face from that morning a little bit too clearly. But if she crossed paths with them at Rushlea or Petratec—the places he'd mentioned visiting next—she had a better shot at presenting herself as a boy recruit and fooling them. She knew he might still spot similarities between Veronyka's two personas, which was why she'd thought up the sister lie. She did have a sister, much as she loathed to remember it, so it felt easier to pass off as a truth.

As Veronyka had prepared for several days of travel, Sparrow had been worth her weight in gold. She'd helped gather provisions for the journey, begging stale bread from the baker, scraps of salt trout from the fishmonger, and several packs of dried venison from a hunter passing through town.

When she was young, Veronyka had struggled with the concept of eating animals. It had seemed cannibalistic in some way, as if she were eating her friends. But over time, after connecting with animal after animal, she began to understand that *they* didn't see it that way. Humans were predators, and eating prey was where they fit on the food chain. Hunting was still difficult for her to imagine, though animages did it all the time, tracing back to the First Riders, who were famed hunters. They would never use their magic to lure prey, though, because they considered that an abuse of Axura's gift.

The nonmagical folk in the empire, however, felt differently. They were more than happy to force their bondservants to keep livestock docile before they were slaughtered or to ensnare a stag on a hunting party. It was a cruel use of their gift; animages deserved better than that, and the animals under their charge did too.

After the food stores were taken care of, Sparrow had given Veronyka a small satchel and an old tin pot from her personal supply of hoarded items that she kept hidden in a tree. When Veronyka mentioned her Ferronese steel blade, Sparrow's mouth had fallen open.

"Would fetch a pretty penny if you wanted to part with it. Then you could make your own, like me," she added, indicating her spear.

"I think I ought to keep it," Veronyka had said, adjusting the knife where it stuck out of her belt. "In case of emergency."

She remembered her grandmother mentioning private Phoenix Rider tutors. They were usually retired Riders paid for by wealthy valley lords to teach their animage children, making them top-notch recruits by the time they joined the military and ensuring they gained a spot among the elite ranks. Her *maiora* saw it as disgraceful cheating and claimed that no

Rider should have to pay out of pocket for their training. But this wasn't the empire's well-funded military. Whatever this was, Veronyka needed to be prepared, and if she had to pay to join them, she'd best keep the most valuable item she had.

"Thanks, Sparrow, for everything," Veronyka had said as they'd parted ways at the edge of the river. Though she'd been anxious to get going—it was a two-day walk to Rushlea, and she had a lot of ground to make up— the prospect of being alone again made her dawdle. "I hope I see you again."

Sparrow had looked confused for a moment, as if unfamiliar with those kinds of pleasantries. Then she'd smiled widely. "Good luck tricking the steward. Maybe I'll try to trick him next time he comes to town."

And with that she walked away, disappearing from Veronyka's life as abruptly as she'd arrived. Veronyka thought of Val, the way she used her shadow magic to force and manipulate people into helping her. But as Sparrow strolled away, twirling her spear and chatting animatedly to Chirp, Veronyka reveled in the knowledge that you didn't need to control someone in order for them to help you.

Sometimes you didn't even have to ask.

Unfortunately, it wasn't long until Veronyka's plans went to pieces. The journey took far longer than she'd thought, thanks to her tired muscles and the fact that she'd barely slept in two nights. She missed Beryk and his wagon at Rushlea, and she got lost twice on her way to Petratec. In truth, that Rider boy spotting her from the sky had felt more like rescue than capture, and now, finally, she was on her way to their hideout.

Before long they came to the edge of the River Aurys and crossed it by a rickety rope bridge that dangled over the foamy water like a damp cobweb. Though full dark had fallen, it was brighter in the open space surrounding the river, the moonlight coloring the mountainside in shades of charcoal and ash. Water beaded in Veronyka's short hair, and the steady rush muffled all other sounds.

When they reached the far side, a wide path—the Pilgrimage Road— came into view, slicing across a rolling plain of tall grasses. It led directly to a series of lantern-lit buildings tucked into the side of a soaring cliff face, the looming spear of rock a solid black mass against the star-encrusted expanse of the sky. There was a stable, a stone well, and a larger building Veronyka assumed was an inn and cookhouse—a way station for weary travelers. As they drew nearer, she could make out a steep, narrow stair cut into the living rock of the escarpment, zigzagging to the top of the precipice and out of sight.

Realization dawned on Veronyka. This was the *end* of the Pilgrimage Road, which meant they were standing on the Field of Feathers. This was where Queen Lyra the Defender rallied the Phoenix Riders during the Lowland Invasion. There had been a tribe of people living in the Foothills hundreds of years ago who'd tried to conquer Pyrmont. Queen Lyra's Riders, often called the "Red Horde," represented the first-ever gathering of the entirety of Pyra's Phoenix Riders. Traditionally the Riders lived in scattered settlements on the higher reaches of Pyrmont, villages and cities accessible only on phoenix-back. It was after Queen Lyra successfully beat back the Lowlanders that the Riders expanded farther down the mountain into the rest of the lower rim and Foothills, establishing the boundaries of Pyra still in place today.

Veronyka wasn't going to some exiled governor's country estate. If this was the Field of Feathers, then those stairs must lead to . . .

"Azurec's Eyrie," Beryk said, following her line of sight and pointing to the rocky bluff that loomed above them.

There was nothing to see from this angle—but that was the point. After Queen Lyra defeated the Lowlanders, the buildings atop this bluff—given the name "Azurec's Eyrie" centuries later—became one of the largest military outposts built during the Reign of Queens, encompassing a temple to Axura, living quarters, and training facilities. The temple at the Eyrie was supposedly located in the exact place that Axura's phoenixes won their first battle against Nox, commemorating the victory.

When Pyra became a part of the empire, most training facilities were moved to the valley, and this location fell into disuse. It was during the reign of Pious King Justyn that the compound was transformed into a religious site and construction of the Pilgrimage Road began. The project had taken most of King Justyn's reign to complete, but the resulting trade and tourism helped Pyra's economy flourish and encouraged travel throughout the mountain region. When Avalkyra Ashfire moved to have Pyra separate from the empire, all that commerce was lost, and Pyra hadn't recovered since. All the inns and cookhouses that had serviced the pilgrims had closed down, and religious sites like the Eyrie were left untended and abandoned, with no funding or leaders remaining to see it restored.

Until now, apparently.

High as Azurec's Eyrie was, Pyrmont's upper reaches loomed farther in the distance, rising steeply to disappear into the night sky. No road cut a path through that wilderness. Those that had dwelt there rode phoenixes and had no need for such conveyances.

Veronyka's escorts led her past the way station and straight for the staircase, pausing just long enough to adjust their packs before starting the climb. She worried her legs might give out beneath her, but she refused to ask for a break. Instead she focused on counting the number of stairs to the summit.

Veronyka passed under hanging vines and into the cover of twisting, gravity-defying trees, before the stair switched back and there was nothing but wide, open air between her and the ground below. During one of these open stretches, Veronyka chanced a look back down the mountainside. She felt incredibly small, the mountain stretching endlessly beneath her. Many of the peaks that surrounded the valley were lower than she was now, their jagged tops ringed with wisps of clouds. She couldn't see any of the villages that lined the road, but for a moment she swore she could feel the distance between herself and where she'd started.

Between herself and Val.

The air became thin and sparse in her lungs, and she forced herself to look at the steps directly beneath her feet. What kind of would-be Rider got silly when it came to heights?

Two hundred and twenty-one steps later, gasping, Veronyka crested the top of the staircase. While Beryk and Elliot murmured about reporting to the commander, Veronyka took the opportunity to plunk herself on the ground and catch her breath.

They were on the edge of a gently rolling plain, enclosed by rocky spears of stone on all sides, making the plateau invisible to anyone below. It was like a little slice of soft Pyraean countryside, wedged into this hard, jagged landscape. Long grass swished in the breeze, and the sky above was vast and star strewn. At the far end of the field was a small stone village, tiered gardens of carefully tended crops butting up against the walls that enclosed it. Rising above the village was another set of walls, taller and thicker than the first, surrounding a fortified stronghold. The walls were dotted with flickering lanterns, casting the buildings and the people who walked among them into dancing shadows and silhouettes.

A magnificent temple rose behind the fortress walls, at least ten stories high and topped with a carved golden phoenix, wings spread as if about to take flight.

Veronyka remained on her hands and knees—it seemed fitting, to lie as supplicant to a sight such as this. All her life, the glory and power of the Phoenix Riders were a long-lost story, a whispered history. Now it was alive before her. She was here with her people at last, and she was ready.

Veronyka was led through the courtyard of the stronghold, past the stables, kitchens, and dining hall and around the towering temple. Behind it were a series of stone buildings, including smaller wooden structures like storage sheds.

At the farthest point in the yard, a wide set of stairs led to a carved arch. Veronyka couldn't see anything through the doorway in the darkness, but she sensed the stir of magic beyond.

Phoenixes.

They must live and roost there, out of sight of the rest of the stronghold. Veronyka's body crackled with a surge of warm, tingling energy, her exhaustion completely forgotten. The archway called to her, and she yearned to follow.

"This way," said Beryk, steering her toward the largest of the stone buildings. It had the same hard gray exterior as the rest of the stronghold, nondescript and unadorned, but the inside was another matter entirely.

They were greeted by a servant and led through richly carpeted halls hung with colorful tapestries and populated with the kinds of carved wooden tables and shelves of scrolls that Veronyka saw only in her dreams.

At last they were directed into a large chamber, the imposing stone walls brightened by sconces casting pools of molten light. Taking up the majority of the space was a long table made from a single slab of wood. Veronyka had never seen anything so fine, the light from the lanterns high-lighting the contrasting wood grain and the delicately carved details along the corners and legs. It was surely Arborian-made; the province was famous for its massive trees and talented woodworkers. A dozen matching chairs surrounded the table, though only one was occupied.

The commander sat at his leisure, and the rest of the Riders from the clearing stood behind their leader, including the boy who'd caught her. He was stiff and scowling, and as she entered the room, he turned his bitter gaze in her direction.

Veronyka stared at her feet, trying not to slump or fidget as Beryk briefed the commander on the journey back. Her tiredness had resurfaced, yet her growing nerves buzzed like wasps inside her mind.

"He needs some sleep, Commander Cassian, and a proper meal. I can call Morra in the morn—"

"We'll deal with this now," the commander said, cutting off the end of Beryk's sentence. He turned to Veronyka. "You'll answer our questions now, and you'll be truthful. Depending on how you do, you will either sleep in a guest room or in a cell—do you understand?"

"Yes, Commander, sir," Veronyka said.

"It will do you no good to lie, so I'd advise against it," he added, and something in the tone of his voice made a finger of dread slip down her spine.

Following Beryk's lead, the others in the room left, except for Veronyka, the commander, and the boy. He projected his anger and frustration, so potent that it bumped distractingly against Veronyka's mental defenses. Was this how Val had felt when Veronyka was careless with her emotions?

The room was silent, and Veronyka didn't know where to look or what to do with her hands. The commander had a way of filling the space, of making Veronyka feel crowded and small. He was a large man—well over six feet, she would guess—with big hands and wide shoulders, but it was his attitude that was imposing. He radiated superiority and power, but it came across as elegant rather than brutish. He was olive-skinned, his wavy, salted brown hair receding slightly from his proud forehead. He had changed from his armor into a magnificent embroidered tunic, patterned with a Ferronese crossed-dagger motif picked out in silver thread, and several golden rings glimmered on his hands as he knit them together. He looked every bit an empire governor, exiled or not, and reminded Veronyka of the wealthy merchants and noblemen she'd seen in Aura Nova being carried through the narrow city streets on palanquins.

The boy, on the other hand, had his arms crossed over his chest and his feet spread wide, as if bracing himself. While his posture was rigid and unmoving, his gaze flicked restlessly around the room. He had the look of someone with at least a bit of Pyraean ancestry, though his hair was a soft, curling brown, and his golden skin had olive undertones.

Veronyka couldn't figure out if he'd chosen to be there during her questioning or if he was being made to stay now as punishment. Maybe he wanted to make sure she was proven guilty to redeem himself in some way. The result of this interrogation would affect him almost as much as her, after all. If she truly was a threat, his apparent disobedience from earlier would be forgiven. If she turned out to be harmless—which she was—he'd look all the more foolish. *Her* success would mean *his* failure, and the dichotomy left her feeling like there was no way to really win.

Veronyka was oddly relieved when the woman named Morra arrived. She wasn't what Veronyka was expecting—some wealthy lady with fine clothes and a noble look, like the commander. Instead she was short and stocky, with strong arms and a plain, no-nonsense kind of face, and she brought with her the warm, comforting scent of fried bread and spices. Her hands were calloused and blistered, and her forearms bore scars that certainly hadn't come from the kitchens. She was Pyraean, her braided hair tied into a knot at the back of her head, the strands thick with adornments that clinked and jingled as she limped into the room. There were feathers there too, more than one, along with several gleaming chunks of obsidian.

A warrior. A Phoenix Rider.

Veronyka's heart swelled at the sight of her—of a woman—at last.

Then Veronyka noticed that Morra leaned heavily on a wooden crutch to support her left leg, which had been cut off from the knee down. And as the woman moved past, Veronyka saw that Morra's phoenix feathers were black on the ends—dipped in ink and ash, to honor a fallen bondmate.

Her stomach clenched. She'd had Xephyra too briefly to gather a feather, and with her braids gone, there was no evidence that she'd ever had a phoenix at all—no way to openly respect Xephyra's memory or commemorate their time together.

Even with her short height, Morra somehow managed to look down her nose at Veronyka, surveying her from head to toe. Despite the woman's humble appearance, when she edged around the table, Commander Cassian hastened to give up his seat to her and took a position standing in the corner next to the boy.

Morra indicated that Veronyka should take the chair opposite, and she did, perching on the edge and gripping her hands tightly together under the table.

They sat in silence for a moment. Who was this woman, and why did she do the commander's questioning?

A heartbeat later she had her answer.

A finger of magic prodded against the natural barriers of Veronyka's mind, testing the strength of her defenses. Fear sluiced through Veronyka's body.

Morra was a shadowmage.

*They called me the Feather-Crowned Queen, my brow
decorated with phoenix quills, my right to rule written across
the stars in fire. They called my sister the Council's Queen,
for she was nothing more than their puppet.*

- CHAPTER 14 -
VERONYKA

VERONYKA CLAMPED DOWN ON her panic and schooled her features into her best impression of Val's emotionless mask. Of all the things she didn't want to reveal about herself, her possession of shadow magic was high on the list. If they didn't trust her now, how would they react knowing she had the ability to see into and manipulate minds?

Morra wasn't *inside* Veronyka's head—not yet, anyway. She'd merely taken a cursory glance, and already she was receding, drawing her magic back in as she contemplated her next move. Her magical pressure was nothing like what Val was capable of, which probably meant her ability wasn't as strong—or not as well honed. It was such a rare skill that even in the Phoenix Rider glory days they hadn't tested people for it or educated them in its use. Val must have gotten so good because she used it constantly and because it was in her nature to want to control. Luckily, Val's expertise had trained Veronyka well in how to defend against it.

If she was very careful, she could show Morra enough to prove her answers truthful without opening her mind entirely. Everything she didn't want Morra to see, she'd lock up in her safe house. If it worked on herself and on Val, it would work on Morra.

With a soft exhalation of breath, Veronyka relaxed her mind. She often pictured her mental defenses as a wall of stones in the middle of a swirling river, the water surrounding her on all sides.

Veronyka stood inside that wall, and within it she was protected from outside influence. Whenever Val would tell her to guard her mind, Veronyka would imagine strengthening the wall, filling in the gaps with small rocks and pebbles, until nothing could get in or out.

When Veronyka's defenses were at their strongest, the wall was watertight, but she couldn't show Morra a mind as well protected as that, or she'd become suspicious. Veronyka had to loosen the stones, allowing cracks and crevices between them. This was her mind's natural state, and as Veronyka opened herself up to external influence, she felt water streaming in through the openings—the thoughts and emotions of the humans and animals nearby.

Veronyka had to ignore the influx of information—the commander's cold indifference and the boy's resentful impatience, not to mention the fiery haze in the distance that was surely the phoenixes.

Focusing on herself, Veronyka let her head fill with safe, harmless thoughts, the half-truths that would confirm her answers.

She allowed them to float to the surface of her consciousness, easy for the picking, before turning her attention to that dark corner where her safe house lived, solid and impenetrable. There, with her memories of Xephyra, she could hide the truth of her gender, her own shadow magic, and the source of the dagger. After burying every compromising memory, she reinforced the barriers, walling it off from the rest of her mind, hiding it in plain sight.

"I'm Morra, and I run the kitchens here," the woman said, drawing Veronyka back to the world around her. "What's your name?"

As she spoke, Morra's magic came back—harder and more insistent than before. Veronyka fought her instinct to draw herself inward and trusted that her safe house would hold.

Shadow magic only revealed *active* thoughts and feelings. . . . Morra couldn't find what Veronyka refused to think about. All a shadowmage could see was the surface of a person's mind—their current preoccupations. That was why Morra was questioning her rather than just taking what she wished from her mind.

"Nyk," Veronyka whispered, pushing the word through her tense lips.

As long as Morra found the truths she sought, she'd have no reason to suspect deception. She *was* Nyk. She let the truth of it fill her up—and the fact that Nyk was short for Veronyka was unimportant.

Seeming satisfied, Morra pulled back. "How old are you? Twelve, thirteen?" she asked.

"Sixteen," Veronyka corrected indignantly. She was used to people thinking she was younger than she was, and it was automatic to quickly—and somewhat defensively—set the record straight. In this instance, though, she wished she hadn't been so rash. Surely it would have been easier pretending to be a young boy than a young man.

The apprentice in the corner snorted in disbelief at her response, further proving Veronyka's theory.

"Where do you come from, Nyk?" Morra asked, speaking over the boy's reaction.

"From lower down the mountain, miss. Just outside Vayle." Again this was a truth, even if the *full* truth was that Veronyka was born in the valley, in Aura Nova. That, too, was hidden in her safe house. She knew, somehow, that any mention of the valley or the empire would compromise everything.

"Why, then, do you not speak with a Pyraean accent?"

Veronyka swallowed. "I . . ."

"Pyraeans on the lower rim speak with a certain lilt," Morra continued thoughtfully, "and have a tendency to draw out their vowels. It's very distinctive. Of course, there are more and more now living in Pyra who weren't born or raised here. Traders and travelers, refugees . . . spies . . ."

Veronyka clenched her fists. Her *maiora* had spoken in a rough Narrows accent, and her years of education with the Riders had never quite cured her of it. Val had insisted that Veronyka speak properly—like the noble classes of the empire, without accent or dialect—but it had never occurred to her how that would stand out in a place like this. A hundred excuses sat on the tip of her tongue, but she feared a trumped-up lie would raise more suspicion than the truth.

"My grandmother raised me, and she was educated in Aura Nova." She *had* been the one to teach Veronyka reading and writing, but Val was the one who'd drilled pronunciation and syntax into her, making up for what she saw as the old woman's shortcomings.

"Is she still with you, your grandmother?"

"No," Veronyka said, her voice wavering slightly.

"Have you any other family?" Morra asked.

Veronyka swallowed the surge of emotion. "Just my sister."

"Ah, yes, your sister. Beryk said there was an uncanny resemblance. . . . Are you twins?"

"No," Veronyka said carefully, keeping her thoughts and memories of Val as vague as possible, not wanting to reveal her face—or Veronyka's true feelings toward her at the moment—to Morra's prying magic. Being twins might better explain away her close resemblance to the girl who had approached Beryk in Vayle, but Veronyka didn't want to lie unnecessarily. At least now, if Morra did see Val's face pop up in Veronyka's mind, it wouldn't contradict her story. "We're a year apart."

"And this sister . . . She told you to come here? Why?"

"Yes. She overheard the steward, Master Beryk, speaking ancient Pyraean, and—"

"That's impossible," the boy burst out, cutting her off. He'd stepped forward and pointed an accusatory finger at her. "How could a country girl from Vayle know ancient Pyraean? It hasn't been spoken since the Reign of Wisdom and is only taught in empire classrooms or by tutors in noble households."

Clearly he desperately wanted her to be wrong, to be dangerous or devious so that he could justify his earlier actions. She felt sorry for him, but if only one of them was going to make it out of this interrogation unscathed, it would be *her*.

"My *maiora* taught me, and she was educated in Aura Nova," Veronyka repeated flatly, substituting the Pyraean word for grandmother to prove her point. It was true that most Pyraeans knew only a handful of words in the ancient tongue. It was considered a dead language, learned by the priests of Mori—god of knowledge and memory—to study ancient texts and by the empire upper classes as part of a well-rounded education. The Phoenix Riders used it as well, and many of their formations, training techniques, and communication cyphers were dependent upon understanding ancient Pyraean.

"Tristan," the commander said in a low, dangerous voice, and the boy stepped back from the table at once, as if scalded. "We will let Morra handle the questioning."

"What did your sister tell you?" Morra pressed, once the commander had nodded that she should continue.

"She said she'd heard mention of Phoenix Riders. When she spoke to the steward, he denied it, but he told her that when he did recruit, he was only looking for boys. So she thought I might have better luck."

"You traveled an awfully long way on such scant information."

"We don't have much, my sister and I," Veronyka said, speaking with complete honesty. "I want to be a Phoenix Rider. It's all I've ever wanted. I don't care about anything else."

Veronyka swallowed and looked down, avoiding Morra's eye so she could gather herself. Xephyra was fluttering against the walls of her safe house, trying to escape, but she couldn't let her break through. If she told them about Xephyra, then she'd have to tell them what had happened to her. Who in their right mind would give a phoenix to a girl who'd allowed her last bondmate to be murdered by her own sister?

"You don't have much, but you have a Ferronese steel dagger?" Tristan jumped in, apparently unable to help himself.

"I found it," Veronyka said, more firmly than she had to the commander when he'd first asked her. Tristan's aggression was making her own temper rise, but she was relieved to get to the heart of the interrogation. She might be lying about some things, but she was no spy. She focused: In her mind she pictured the knife lying in the dirt and clamped tight on her memories of the cabin that surrounded the dirt, closing out Val and Xephyra and the soldier and all that came before it.

"He's lying," Tristan said, looking between Morra and the commander. His tone was scathing, making it clear what he thought of liars. "That's an army-issue dagger. Look at the bottom of the hilt—that's a soldier identification number."

Veronyka frowned, glancing down at the knife where it lay on the table between them. Indeed, there was a series of numbers carved into the grip.

"There's no way he just *found it*. Best case, he stole it—it's probably worth more than his house." He looked away at his last words, as if recognizing that they were cold and uncaring—and probably true.

"It is," Veronyka admitted, her voice trembling slightly as she stared at the dagger. "I could have traded it, bartered it for gold or enough food to last my sister and me for a couple of months. But instead I saved it, hoping it was worth enough to buy a place here. I guess I was wrong."

Veronyka knew she was exaggerating and bending the truth, but she needed them to side with her.

When she looked up, there was pity in Morra's and Commander Cassian's eyes—and to her surprise, regret in Tristan's—and though she hated to appear weak and vulnerable, she knew it helped her cause.

So let them pity her. Let them believe her small lies and big truths. Let it be enough.

"You forget yourself, Tristan," Morra said in a low, disappointed voice. "You forget your roots."

"Leave us," the commander said to Tristan, his tone holding none of Morra's polite censure.

Tristan looked like he wanted to retort, a spasm crossing his face as he fought to control himself. "Yes, Commander," he said through clenched teeth. Then he strode out the door, slamming it behind him.

The atmosphere in the room changed with his departure, and Morra's presence in Veronyka's mind receded. She and Cassian shared a look, and Veronyka got the feeling that she had passed their inspection.

"Thank you, Morra," the commander said at last.

With a nod at Veronyka, Morra got to her feet, following Tristan out of the room. The commander retook his seat. They were alone.

"When I was a boy," he began, settling comfortably into his chair, "becoming a Phoenix Rider was a family legacy—something I inherited, much like my title and my lands." Veronyka was thrown by the turn the conversation had taken, but she tried to follow along. "For years I served, and our mission was clear: to guard the empire and protect its people. But," he said with a sigh, "the Blood War saw our duty muddled beyond recognition. I lived to see the Phoenix Riders change from a government-sanctioned military order to a rebellion, to something akin to a private army. Under Avalkyra Ashfire, we served *her* purpose—her ambitions and her goals—and no one else's. With her death, those of us who survived struggled to find our place in this new world order. I have since recognized that our mission, our purpose, cannot be to one person, one country, or even one province; it must be to all people, but especially to our fellow animages. We are united—not by political boundaries or cultural histories—but by magic. We are everywhere, and yet we *have* nowhere. We have no safe place, no home to call ours. I seek to rectify that. Azurec's Eyrie is a start."

Veronyka's heart swelled with his words. He was right. The Phoenix Riders that had served the empire for almost two hundred years were no more, and they had to come together for a new purpose.

"That being said," the commander continued, "we are a small operation at the moment, and I have to be prudent. We must build our strength slowly, cautiously. In the beginning it was just myself and Beryk—we'd flown together in the war, and I knew where he'd gone into hiding in the aftermath. It took us years to find Fallon, a young Rider who'd yet to see any action, and we stumbled upon him mostly by chance. Surely there are others, Phoenix Riders in hiding all over the empire and beyond, but we cannot go searching blindly for them and risk drawing attention to ourselves or to them. It wouldn't do for the empire to learn that Riders are mustering on Pyrmont. The empire may have little interest in reclaiming Pyra, but it would have great interest in destroying us."

"But I didn't—I would never . . . ," Veronyka began, confused. She'd thought they'd determined she wasn't a threat.

He waved her off. "What I mean to say is that recruiting has been difficult for us. While there are many with the gift of animal magic, there are few with the gold to fund their training. Raising, housing, and feeding phoenixes costs money, Nyk—*my* money—not to mention the price of a horse, fireproof saddle and tack, armor, and weapons. I have to feed guards and servants, pay wages, build and make repairs, and my coffers are not what they once were." He lifted the dagger from the middle of the table, turning it over in his hands before giving it back to her. "Phoenixes are too rare and precious for us to have poor peasant lads bonding with them, who are then unable to afford the cost of proper training. I'm sorry."

Helplessness seized Veronyka as she gripped the hilt of the dagger. Suddenly Phoenix Riding was only for the rich? The First Riders didn't have coffers filled with gold; they had *phoenixes*, the only wealth a person ever needed.

She swallowed a number of angry replies and fought to keep her voice steady. "There must be other ways, means of earning a place . . ."

"There are," the commander conceded. "When we recruit, the current Riders have the option of sponsoring one of the new applicants. Several of our current apprentices are being sponsored by Master Riders. They're called underwings."

"So, when you recruit again, I could apply as long as I found a sponsor?" Veronyka asked, a flicker of hope sparking to life inside her.

The commander looked uncomfortable. "Sponsorships are difficult to come by, Nyk. Those who can afford to take on an underwing are likely to pick friends and family—not a stranger."

"But I could still try," Veronyka pressed stubbornly.

"Indeed you could," he said, his voice resigned, "but I don't have plans for recruitment anytime in the near future, and we can't afford to board you here while you wait."

"There must be other ways I can earn my keep and help the Riders in the meantime," she said desperately, leaning forward. "I could cook, clean, be a servant—maybe work in the stables?"

The commander pursed his lips. Then his expression cleared, and he bowed his head. "I'm sure our stable mistress, Jana, would welcome the extra help."

Veronyka's heart leapt despite her disappointment. Sure, she'd come here to be a Phoenix Rider—not to muck out stalls and feed grain to pack animals—but it was still something. It was still a way to be involved. And it wasn't a no. She would work harder than anyone, show them she deserved to be here, that she had so much more to give.

And when the time came for the next recruitment, she'd have multiple sponsors lined up and would be the best damn applicant they had.

The *Sekveia*, or the "Second Road" in the Trader's Tongue, is a deserted path through the wilds of Pyrmont and a mysterious relic of the ancient world—both in origin and in purpose.

Some historians suggest it was built in an attempt to expand the Pyraean Queendom and connect some of its smaller settlements on Pyrmont, with the hopes of developing a thoroughfare for trade that could lead all the way to the valley, though this idea never came to fruition.

It has also been postured that the *Sekveia* was actually built centuries earlier by civilizations unknown to us, possibly the now-extinct Lowland peoples. This is supported by the fact that many of the ruined temples and structures that can be found along the Second Road bear no resemblance to Pyraean architecture built before or after the empire.

Perhaps most outlandish of all these claims is that the *Sekveia* leads to the famous lost treasure of the Pyraean explorer Wylan the Wanderer, who disappeared himself after declaring he would fly his phoenix around the world.

The details of his exploits have been chronicled in many songs and poems, perhaps none more famous than the play titled *The Wanderer's Fortune*. During a particularly successful run on Mummer's Lane, the lead actor had hundreds of false treasure maps distributed to promote the show. It created such a fervor that mobs broke out and several people were trampled to death, causing the play to be temporarily shut down.

—*Myths and Legends of the Golden Empire and Beyond*, a compilation of stories and accounts, the Morian Archives, 101 AE

I wonder what they would
call me now if they knew that I
was the one who killed her.

- CHAPTER 15 -
SEV

PACK ANIMAL DUTY WASN'T a popular assignment among the soldiers. Most had little love for the animals' smell and slow progress—not to mention the heaps of dung, with which Sev was well-acquainted—so nobody argued when he signed up for it day after day.

While he was frustrated about being given an assignment he didn't understand, Kade appeared downright furious. He seemed to take it as a personal offense, as if Sev were somehow undercutting his authority or encroaching on his territory.

Was his hatred as simple as their separate roles, bondservant and soldier? Sev had hated soldiers once. They were the thundering footsteps in Aura Nova alleyways, the looming shadows on the doorsteps of every orphanage and cookhouse. They were the waves on the beach of the Pyraean border, lapping ever closer, until they'd poured over the hills and overrun his family's farm.

Sev *still* hated soldiers, truth be known. And somehow he'd become one of them.

He couldn't blame Kade for how he felt, and while neither of them was happy with the arrangement, they didn't have a choice in the matter.

The one overwhelming positive was being near animals again. The llamas were sure-footed beasts, used primarily in the mountains, with long necks and sturdy padded feet. They reminded him a bit of the woolly, mild-mannered sheep his family had herded when he was a child.

Most of the time. He'd almost been bitten on more than one occasion and by more than one llama—though he'd begun to suspect one fellow in particular had a taste for him.

Sev knew it was risky, but he couldn't help interacting with the creatures . . . just a little. A pat here, a nudge there, and before he knew it, he was helping with saddles and filling water troughs. The other soldiers assigned to pack animal duty stared incredulously at the extra work he was doing, but as far as Sev could tell, they thought he was trying to gain attention and approval from superior officers and not relishing in his contact with the animals.

To Sev's surprise, he was enjoying his time with the bondservants as well.

At first the sight of them caused an ache in his chest, and it took a while for Sev to recognize it as envy. He knew it was strange for a free man to be envious of people forced into servitude, but as someone who had always hidden his abilities, he found being around animages who used their magic so openly was like watching someone guzzle gulps of cool water while he died of thirst.

Now Sev found their presence comforting. The thrum of magic, the hard but gratifying labor, and the way the humans and animals worked together—it all reminded him of his time on the farm. Tilla and Corem had herded sheep, the same as Sev's family, while the youngest bondservant of the bunch, nicknamed Junior, was from the small village near where Sev had grown up, and his family were fishermen. Or at least they had been.

"Don't know where they are now," Junior told him one day as they filled the water troughs. He had coloring and features similar to Kade, so much so that they could almost be brothers, except where Kade was tall and muscular, Junior was lanky and thin, all elbows and knees. "Empire got me before dawn, when I was checkin' the nets. I never saw my family again."

Sev realized he was *lucky* to know what had happened to his parents; even though they were gone, he knew they were at peace and not in bondage elsewhere. Though Junior was young, from what Sev understood, his parents had made a decent living selling their fish, and his term was seven years—half his life. While Sev often pitied the bondservants, Junior's story made him *angry*, and he had a sneaking suspicion that Trix might have intended for him to have these kinds of feelings. He guessed that she'd posted him with the bondservants to show Sev to whom his loyalties should belong. He was exactly like them. And yet, because of his choice to deny himself and his magic, *he* was free, and they were not.

Of course Sev wished life could be different. If the war hadn't happened, he would have been a sheepherder and a farmer, and every animage in the empire and beyond would be free. There would be no "mageslaves," the Phoenix Riders would have remained glorious—distant—heroes, and both his parents would still be alive.

But life *wasn't* different, and Sev's decision had saved him from bondage. How could he regret it?

While Kade was as gruff with Sev as ever, he completely transformed when he interacted with the llamas. His face—his entire being—lit up when he was with them, murmuring reassurances and praise and interacting so subtly and skillfully that Sev was more than a little bit impressed. He was clearly the strongest animage of the bunch, someone who had been using his magic since birth.

Sev *liked* this side of him. He was usually so grim—even hostile—but with the animals, the stiff line of his shoulders relaxed, and his severe features softened into delighted smiles and gentle laughter. It made Sev want to be near him, to watch and bask in the warm light of his magical glow. But whenever Kade saw Sev close by, he'd scowl and turn away, and Sev would reluctantly do the same. He wished he could understand why Kade disliked him so much and find a way to quell the animosity between them.

Early one morning Sev scrambled from his bedroll just before dawn. The soldiers had camped in the shadows of a steep cliff next to a series of ruined structures. While they'd left the Pilgrimage Road far behind, they did sometimes find themselves on twisting stonework paths that would appear as if out of nowhere only to be swallowed by the forest moments later. There were broken archways made from rectangular blocks of stone, strange pillars engraved with unfamiliar geometric patterns, and crumbled statues standing guard along the way, so old and weatherworn that it was impossible to tell what they were supposed to be or who had built them in the first place. Sev had heard Corem say the word *"Sekveia"*—the Second Road—which was supposed to be a mythical route through the wilds of Pyrmont. When he was small, Sev and the other farmers' children would go exploring in the Foothills, searching for the beginning of the legendary Second Road and the treasures it supposedly led to. Using it now as an empire soldier felt like some sick, twisted version of the childhood fantasy—especially if the "treasure" they sought at the end of this path was the Phoenix Riders' hidden lair.

Noise had awoken him, and when he squinted toward the pack animals, he saw Kade already starting his work for the day. He was hauling sacks of grain and barrels of water, his breath swirling around his face. He'd removed his tunic, and steam rose from his body in the cool morning air, his chain glinting in the pale dawn sun.

Sev hadn't slept well. Trix was nearby, muttering in her sleep as usual, and it had taken forever for him to drift off. He'd dreamed of the farm again, of rolling green hills and vast blue skies. Then he'd watched as it had all burned down.

Blinking to banish the images from his mind, Sev packed away his bedroll before making his way over to the paddock of llamas. His foot crunched on a small twig, and Kade whirled around, posture braced as if preparing for an attack.

He could be a soldier, Sev thought somewhat dazedly, scrubbing at his sleep-mussed hair, *except for the eyes.* They were intelligent and perceptive—but without cunning. They were kind eyes . . . until they recognized Sev.

"Oh," Kade said, straightening up. "It's you."

With a sigh, Sev hunched over a water barrel and splashed several icy handfuls onto his face before taking a long drink.

When he straightened, Kade was still standing before him. He was panting slightly, his chest rising and falling, muscles glistening with sweat. As Sev lifted the edge of his tunic to mop his sodden face, Kade's dark eyes followed his movements. His features were precisely carved, all angles and hard edges, and unlike Sev, whose chin was shaded with stubble, he'd kept up shaving his face, his jawline smooth. He was like a bronze statue of some ancient hero in a temple garden, gathering droplets of morning dew.

Sev inhaled sharply and cleared his throat, heat crawling up his neck. Since when did Sev care about temple statues? He realized with dismay that he'd been admiring more than Kade's magic recently. He glanced up at the bondservant's still-scowling face, and a bitter feeling settled in his stomach. Clearly the admiration was one-way.

Stepping around Kade, Sev spotted the stores of grain. He ripped one of the bags open and prepared to dump it into an empty trough, but Kade stopped him.

"What are you doing?" he demanded. His voice was its usual low rumble, but there was a raspy, gravelly edge to it—anger or annoyance, or maybe both.

Sev straightened, looking down at the grain in his hands. "Feeding them?" he said, his voice tilted as if it were a question. What had he done to earn Kade's ire this time?

"*Why?*" Kade asked, taking a step forward. He waved a hand at the animals. "*They* are not your charges," he said, then tapped a finger against his chest. "*I* am."

"You're not my charge," Sev said uneasily. He was meant to guard the pack animal train and make sure everything went smoothly. Yes, that involved keeping an eye on the bondservants, but that didn't make him Kade's master.

"Don't kid yourself, soldier," Kade snapped, wrenching the feed from Sev's grip. "You're one of *them*." He jerked his chin toward the rest of the campsite, where most of the soldiers were still sleeping.

"I know you don't like me," Sev began, clenching his hands into fists to stop from trying to snatch back the bag of feed. "But I think we're more alike than you realize."

Kade snorted, but Sev continued before he could make a snide comment.

"We both wanted to keep that girl safe," he pointed out.

"There's a difference between wanting to protect someone for their sake and wanting to protect someone for your own. You wanted to 'keep her safe' so that you didn't have to be the one to deal the blow. You wanted to ease your own conscience so you could sleep at night."

Sev bit the inside of his cheek, anger flaring in his breast. The words hurt, and the sting told Sev that Kade had struck close to home. Had Sev saved her neck only so he could save his own? Of course, Kade didn't see what had happened afterward, how close Sev had come to dying for his decision that day.

"You're a fair-weather ally—empty words and kind smiles—nothing more."

"I didn't ask for this, Kade," Sev said, his voice quaking slightly as he continued to suppress his outrage. "I'm doing my best."

"This is your best?" Kade asked skeptically, looking Sev up and down, taking in every imperfect inch of him. "I highly doubt that."

Sev frowned, trying to work out if Kade's words were some kind of backhanded compliment. Kade thought Sev was *better* than a soldier? The idea made him stand taller, even as he realized that Kade was mistaken.

"I . . . This is what I am, Kade. Sorry it's not good enough for you."

"I know *what you are*," Kade said slowly, almost threateningly. "And it's not this. This"—he gestured carelessly at Sev's raider uniform—"is what you *chose* to be."

It took Sev's body several moments to catch up with his mind. When it did, Kade had marched out of his reach, and Sev was forced to stomp after him.

"Hey," he said harshly, gripping Kade by the upper arm and turning him around. Sev was breathing hard—harder than he should when he'd walked only a few short feet. His heart was pounding in his chest, and there was a tinny ringing in his ears.

Kade stopped so abruptly that Sev's momentum carried him forward, and they almost bumped chests. Kade's body was tense, poised as if ready for a blow.

"What choice?" Sev asked, trying to be reasonable. "I didn't *enlist*—they forced me into the military. I could either live as a soldier or die as a laborer in the dank mines of Ferro or the sunbaked fields of Stel."

Kade's eyes sparked, and standing this close, Sev could pick out shades of amber and russet, warm against his black lashes and heavy brow. His angular face, twisted in rage, became even sharper.

"Not the choice I was talking about, soldier," Kade said, speaking through tight lips. He shrugged off Sev's hand, which had still been gripping his biceps, but then he stepped closer, his voice whisper-soft. "You think I don't see—that I don't know what you are, *animage?*"

Sev's stomach dropped, and the ground seemed to buck and dip beneath him. He staggered back. Kade knew Sev was an animage. Had Trix told him? Or had Sev been that obvious?

"You can pat the animals and get them their feed, you can talk and laugh with the other bondservants, but you're not one of us. You denied that part of yourself—*that's* the choice you made. So you don't get to play both sides. You don't get to be a soldier and a friend to animages—it's one or the other."

Sev had made a choice long ago to pretend he wasn't an animage, to hide his magic and suffer the consequences. He'd chosen to be a coward, to "not care" about the world, because it was easier than fighting. It was survival—or so he'd thought.

Animages like Kade had made a different choice. They'd rather risk bondage than hide who they were, and their bravery shamed him.

Worst of all, it shamed his parents, who had died for Sev. They had given themselves to the Phoenix Riders, to their fellow animages, and by denying that part of himself, he denied them as well.

Sudden heat pricked at the back of Sev's eyes, and before Kade could see more of his weakness, Sev pushed past him, bumping Kade's shoulder as he lurched away, past the line of animals and into the forest.

❧   ❧   ❧

Pacing back and forth between the trees, Sev gripped his head. The memory descended upon him like a heavy cloak, and in a blink, he was back home again.

Back where everything had gone wrong.

It had been two years since the end of the Blood War. Animages were fleeing the Golden Empire, making for the recently separated province of Pyra, and Sev's family lived right on the border. They kept the empire's forces back and helped families flee persecution.

It was less about politics, his father had said, and more about people. By making herself an enemy of the empire, Avalkyra Ashfire had made all animages enemies of the empire—whether they were Riders or not. The magical registry was being put violently into effect, and the empire was rounding up animages in droves, accusing them of rebel sympathies, of being traitors and conspirators.

It was only a matter of time before the soldiers came for Sev's parents and the rest of Hillsbridge, their small village. Before they came for Sev.

He'd been playing in the fields when he saw the soldiers approaching in the distance. His parents had always been very clear: If he saw empire soldiers, he was supposed to run back to the house. He was supposed to stay safe.

But back then Sev hadn't been the coward he was today. Back then Sev had wanted to be a hero.

He might have been young, but on the farm, as soon as you could walk, you could work. First it was scouring the bushes all day, so his father could make his famous blackberry pie, or helping his mother weed the garden. Then it was carrying buckets of water or feed for the animals and hitching their oxen to the plow.

During the spring thaw, when the river would flood and destroy their wooden bridge, Sev would turn the winch and raise the platform, keeping it safe until the waters receded. The river snaked around their farm, and when the bridge was drawn, Sev felt like they were on their own separate island, safe from harm.

As the enemy soldiers approached, Sev knew that if he could just reach the drawbridge in time, he could slow the soldiers long enough for everyone on the farm and in the nearby houses to get to safety. It was late spring, so the river waters were still high and couldn't be forded easily.

If Sev could just get there, he would be a hero. The thought of his parents' faces, shining with pride and admiration, filled his heart. He could imagine the villagers praising him for his quick thinking as they retreated to their safe houses. No one would get hurt. No one would die. All thanks to Sev.

The ground was muddy and slick as he ran down to the river's edge, and he skidded the last few feet as he approached the mechanism that controlled the bridge. The soldiers were much closer than he'd thought from his place on the hill, and fear made his hands clumsy as he struggled to turn the crank that would hoist the bridge, the sound of clinking metal and thumping boots reverberating around him. Sev pulled harder, panting, when the first raindrop splashed onto his face.

The single drop turned into a steady mist, making his hands slip across the metal lever and his feet sink into the ever-deepening mud.

The soldiers came to a halt on the other side of the river. Sev had managed to raise the bridge no more than a foot, and now it was too late to run.

There was a shout—a command, Sev thought—and a soldier stepped forward, a loaded crossbow in hand.

It was pointed at him, and Sev just stood there, muscles frozen, unable to move or think.

But then a fierce screech cut through the patter of the rain, and a fiery arrow pierced the heart of the archer before he could pull the trigger. Sev whirled and saw his mother rip past, fire blazing from her phoenix as she rained a dozen more arrows down on the empire soldiers in rapid succession. They ducked and raised shields, but before Sev could see more, strong hands gripped his arms and hoisted him up, up, into the air.

He was sitting in front of his father, mounted on his phoenix as they wheeled around, away from the fighting. It was Sev's first and only flight on phoenix-back, and he'd been crying the whole time, too teeming with fear to marvel at the dizzying height and powerful speed.

Before he knew it, his father was placing him on the path to their house.

"It's going to be all right, son," he said, leaping back onto his phoenix and turning around to face Sev. His voice was calm and soothing, like it always was, no matter that they were under attack and his wife was fending off soldiers on her own. "Now, I want you to run as fast as you can to the safe house. You remember where it is, don't you? Left at the fork. Run now, Sevro, and don't look back."

Sev did as he was told, his boots slipping and sliding on the muddy path. But when he reached the top of the hill, he disobeyed his father's last request and turned around.

Both of his parents were in full flame, swooping and diving, leaving bodies and swathes of fire in their wake. Despite his fear, Sev's heart swelled to see them make short work of the empire's soldiers, who had begun to scatter and retreat, back over the hills . . .

And into the swollen ranks of their reinforcements.

There was double, triple the original number, the soldiers cresting the hilltop in waves. The first regiment must have been the vanguard, and now a larger force was on the horizon.

Behind Sev, villagers and farmhands were scrambling to load themselves into wagons with whatever animals and supplies they could manage to gather. If his parents didn't stop the coming soldiers, they would cross the river and wreak havoc on all the people Sev had grown up with, friends and neighbors, cousins and relatives.

Turning his attention back to the fighting, Sev saw his mother and father flying high above, circling, signaling to each other. The bridge was on fire now, but the coming soldiers had wagons loaded with war machines, ladders, and catapults. The river wouldn't stop them. Nothing would.

Somehow, deep down inside, Sev knew what his parents intended to do. Maybe that was why he stayed there, watching. Maybe he knew it would be the last time he ever saw them.

Slowly his parents' phoenixes burned hotter, brighter . . . blistering, like the sun hanging low in the sky. Soon he couldn't even see his parents, or the phoenixes they rode through the air—all he could see was fire and light.

With a crackle and a cry that would sear itself into Sev's memory forever, his parents dropped, hurtling toward the enemy soldiers like blazing arrows. They landed in a fiery explosion, the heat waves rippling across the ground and knocking Sev, hundreds of yards away, off his feet. When he got up again, there was nothing but fire—soldiers running, screaming, while all around him, the crops began to burn.

Sev ran, just like his father had told him. He knew the fire would spread, would swallow their farmhouse, the stables, and the blackberry bushes. Everything Sev had ever known. He followed the road, trying to catch up with the villagers . . . but it wasn't until nightfall, when he still hadn't reached the safe house or seen the back of their wagons, that he realized he'd gone the wrong way at the fork.

He wound up at a small village farther down the river, one that was already in the empire's possession. He was deemed a war orphan, loaded into a wagon with a handful of others, and carted off to Aura Nova. He'd learned quickly that being an animage in the empire was a very bad thing, and so he'd hidden his true identity. He'd learned other things too . . . how to go unnoticed—whether it was from the larger boys at the orphanage, looking for sport, or from the soldiers on the street, looking to meet their quota—how to beg, borrow, and steal. He'd also learned how to look the other way when the old Sev would have stood up and fought.

He learned how to be a coward.

In some ways, he'd been running ever since that last day on the farm—following his parents' instructions at last. Run and hide. Stay safe.

Eventually it was hunger that got him captured, not his magic. He'd been caught stealing from a baker's cart, and as he ran from the proprietor's outstretched hand, he'd collided with a loaded merchant's wagon. The cart-horses startled, and the entire wagon tipped over—onto an empire soldier.

Looking back, Sev often wondered if he could've stopped it if he'd used his magic to calm the horses. But he hadn't, and someone had lost their life because of it.

Sev had been charged for the soldier's murder and hauled to the Aura Nova prison that night. The next morning he was given a choice: be forgiven his crimes and serve for life in the military or work himself to death as a laborer. Sev had heard horror stories about the criminal labor camps, but joining the ranks of the people who'd killed his parents? He had thought it was the hardest decision of his life, choosing to join his enemies in order to survive.

Now he wasn't so sure. Maybe Kade was right. Maybe he'd made a much worse choice long before in rejecting a part of himself.

Sev shook his head. It was too late to go back. All he could do now was move forward. He'd had enough of the guilt and the taunts and Trix's mad plans. Let her tell them what he was; he'd be long gone before any of it mattered. Trix expected him to run at night—it was the logical thing to do—but Sev didn't much feel like being logical.

The decision banked the fire burning inside him, and Sev's mind cleared.

In the cover of the trees, he watched as the campsite came to life, as the llamas were fed and watered and reloaded with their burdens. Tents were packed up, meals eaten, and soon their party began to move out.

More than once Kade glanced over his shoulder in the general direction of the trees where Sev had disappeared. He whispered questions to Tilla and Corem—asking after *him*, Sev guessed—but they only shrugged and shook their heads.

Sev smiled grimly. He might be a terrible soldier and a worse animage, but he knew how to hide.

When the pack animals drew into a line, Kade at the lead, Sev slipped back out of the trees. The animals always brought up the rear of their convoy, allowing the soldiers to clear a path ahead. There would be plenty of guards walking alongside the animals, keeping watch over their valuable burdens, but right now none were in place. Even the rear guards were not yet in position. The time before the procession moved out was always chaotic, with stragglers and confusion and shouting voices.

It was perfect.

Before Sev could overthink or hesitate, he snuck to the back of the line and took the lead reins of the nearest llama, carefully guiding the animal aside. He was loaded with several sacks of grain, plus a few personal packs.

As the rest of the line moved forward, soldiers catching up as they snaked through the trees, Sev remained still, pretending to fiddle with a harness, allowing them to move past. The grass was thick here, the bushes and brambles growing tightly together, with swaying fronds swishing back and forth as the convoy progressed. Along with heavy crates and barrels stacked high, obscuring the view, it was easy to get lost in the shuffle of bodies and the noise of their departure.

When no one was looking his way, Sev slipped back into the trees with the llama in tow, disappearing in a flap of ferns and bowing branches.

His heart hammered in his ears, the thump of adrenaline so loud, he didn't hear the footsteps of the person who followed him.

An arrow through the heart,
and my world went up in flames.

- CHAPTER 16 -
VERONYKA

THE FIRST FEW DAYS at Azurec's Eyrie were a blur, though most of what Veronyka did remember revolved around food. Never in her life had she been able to eat as much as she wanted—and even go back for seconds—for every meal of the day, and that wasn't including the extra sweet cakes and fresh rolls Morra slipped her every time she passed the kitchens. The cook didn't like to see people who looked underfed—particularly not young Pyraean children.

It was somewhat of a shock for Veronyka to realize that she'd never been properly full in her whole life. With it came a pang of sadness for the girl she used to be, hungry and scared and alone. Guilt threatened to surface when she remembered that Val was likely still living that way, but she refused to let it take hold. They could have had this life together if Val had ever listened to Veronyka or let her weigh in on their decisions. Veronyka had earned this comfort, and she was determined to enjoy it.

Her work as a stablehand kept her busy, running errands and tending animals from dawn until dusk, and she was so tired that she usually fell into bed at the end of each day—though she'd had to adjust to doing so in a room with over twenty other people. That also meant shoring up her mental defenses, lest she be plagued with dreams about families, hobbies, and romances that were not her own.

Her duties took her all over the stronghold and village, and she wasn't *just* in charge of mucking out the stables, as she had expected; she was responsible for the welfare of every animal they had. That meant the horses and hunting dogs, the llamas that provided wool and served as beasts of burden, and the pigeons that carried messages across the mountain. They took care of goats, rabbits, chickens, and even the cats that kept the stronghold free of mice and rats.

It had been strange, at first, to see so many people on a daily basis—stranger still that they were constantly smiling and nodding at her. Most of the servants, guards, and other occupants of the stronghold and village came from either Montascent or Petratec, the closest settlements on Pyrmont. There was the odd person from farther down the mountain—like Veronyka—but recruiting that close to the border was dangerous. By banding together, the people of Montascent and Petratec—who were usually rather isolated and closed off—had access to work and resources, and the Eyrie got the helpers, fighters, and craftspeople they needed without risking exposure.

The result was a familiar, friendly atmosphere—and Veronyka was surprised how at home she felt. She was used to keeping her head down to avoid notice and sticking close to Val's shadow, but here she could watch and wonder and ask questions all day long. Veronyka learned more in her first week than she'd learned in years, and very little of it was about animals or magic. She'd caught serious trouble for cutting through Old Ana's vegetable garden on her very first day, but by her fourth, Old Ana was enlisting her help in pulling up potatoes and mending the wooden trellis that held snaking vines of cucumber and sugar snap peas. It had taken Veronyka days of lurking outside his forge to work up the courage to ask the Ferronese metalsmith about his craft, but she now knew the exact color heated iron should be when it was ready to be worked, as well as the difference between forging, welding, and finishing.

Best of all, Veronyka spent most of her days outside, not skulking in a cabin. And every time a mounted phoenix soared through the sky on a training exercise or patrol shift, her heart leapt into the air—only to flop back down again. Xephyra should be here with her. They should be soaring through the sky together. Even the thought of joining the Riders someday sent a similar mix of joy and regret flickering through her, as if seeking a new bondmate were a betrayal of Xephyra's memory.

She often spotted Tristan among the apprentices, his squared shoulders and stiff jaw visible even at a distance, and Veronyka couldn't help the stab of resentment the sight of him produced. He'd been so willing to see the worst in her, done everything he could to prove her story false and bar her acceptance here. What if he was telling the other Riders that she was no good and turning them against her? She'd need one of them as a sponsor when the next recruitment came, and all she wanted was a fair chance to prove herself worthy.

The problem was, she wasn't the only one.

There were five stablehands aside from herself, and all of them were animages. She had no doubt that they were awaiting their chance for recruitment, the same as her, and it made for a somewhat tense, competitive environment.

"Can I help with that?" she asked Petyr one morning several weeks into her time at the Eyrie. They were saddling the new crop of horses the commander had recently purchased and readying them to meet their new riders—the apprentices.

Petyr, a local boy from Petratec, was struggling to bridle Wind—the most challenging of the horses and Veronyka's personal favorite—who was lifting his head high like the proud, stubborn creature he was, keeping his mouth firmly out of reach.

Petyr ignored Veronyka's offer and instead flipped the nearest barrel upside down and stood atop it to get a better reach. Veronyka bit her tongue, anticipating the trouble right before it happened. Wind obediently lowered his head—only to toss it directly into Petyr's chest, butting him from his perch. The boy went careening to the ground with a shout, and everyone in the stables looked in their direction.

Veronyka rushed to help him from the hay-strewn ground while giving Wind a stern, chastising glare over her shoulder.

Jana came hurrying up, and all it took was one look at the horse in question to give her a sense of what had happened. "Leave Wind to Nyk, Petyr, and help Loran with one of the easier mounts."

Neglecting Veronyka's outstretched hand, Petyr got to his feet and stormed off.

Veronyka sighed, bending down to scoop up the bridle.

It was always like this.

She had established her talent early on, and Jana, who came from a long line of Stellan horse breeders, was quick to use her whenever a challenging situation demanded it. Veronyka was only trying to help, but she could understand how her enthusiasm—and her skill—might be seen negatively by her peers, who were now constantly overlooked in favor of her. They were trying to prove themselves too, and so Veronyka did her best to ignore when the other stablehands whispered alone together or took their meals without her in the dining hall. She was sure she'd earn their respect—if not their affection—in time. Or at least, she hoped.

"I guess we're both everyone's least favorite, eh, Wind?" she murmured, rubbing her hand along his smooth flank. Digging in her pocket, she held out a carrot she'd begged from Old Ana before she'd arrived for duty that morning.

Wind perked up, but she held it out of reach. "Only if you're good," she chided, showing him the bridle. He huffed through his nostrils, then resentfully bowed his head.

Veronyka grinned.

She and the rest of the stablehands guided the horses in a single line—ten of them total—through the village and out to the pastures beyond the wall, near the steps down to the way station. The horses had been purchased from a breeder in the Foothills who specialized in crossing the elegant Stellan bloodlines of the valley with sturdier mountain horses.

A series of barrels, stones, and other objects had been set up in the open space before the village, and standing off to the side were Tristan and the rest of the apprentices. The moment his gaze landed on Veronyka, he scowled, but his expression shifted at the sight of the horses behind her. The muscles in his jaw clenched while he and the rest of the apprentices shifted and craned their necks, trying to get a better look. A mixed wave of emotions rose up from their group, their excitement, fear, and dread hitting Veronyka like waves lapping at a pier. She'd been keeping her mind guarded ever since her run-in with Morra, but still, spikes of heightened feeling managed to push through her defenses.

There was a makeshift paddock set up, where Veronyka and the other stablehands led the horses and left them to wait. A pack of hunting hounds was already inside, weaving through the horses' legs as they ambled through the tall grass, and a cage of messenger pigeons had been placed on a barrel. Glancing around, Veronyka saw Jana hide a crate of rabbits into the cover of the nearby bushes. What was going on?

A few moments later the commander appeared at the village gates, leading his dappled horse, Cotton, toward the apprentices. A hush fell over the group when he arrived, and in the ensuing silence, the commander explained the rather bizarre exercise that had been set up.

If Riders needed to fly out on an overnight journey—or travel a long distance—they would often have an accompanying land party with pack animals and extra supplies. The phoenixes needed to rest, and so did the Riders, so such provisions were necessary. They also occasionally scouted from horseback, allowing them to travel to more heavily populated areas, with their phoenixes reporting from the safety of the sky. As animages, they needed to be masters of more than just their bonded animals—they needed to be masters of every beast in their service, including messenger birds and even the dogs that served them in the hunt.

"Horse mastery," the commander continued, "has been an integral part of Rider training for centuries. As warriors of the highest sort, Riders were trained in warfare both on land and in the sky. While most of you are competent on horseback, none of you have practiced control of all your animals simultaneously."

Veronyka's ears perked up—finally she was going to see some real magic at work. Thus far, from what she'd glimpsed, the commander's training program seemed to focus on honing their skills as warriors over their abilities as animages. The sight had left her disheartened, as she had no weapons or combat experience. If ever she was to join their ranks, she'd be at a major disadvantage. Veronyka's single best skill was her use of magic, and she was eager to see how she would measure up.

"The horse of a Phoenix Rider must be comfortable in the presence of not only his rider, but whatever other beasts his master requires—including, of course, his phoenix. This is not an easy task and will take weeks of training and discipline, starting now."

A gust of warm wind rippled through Veronyka's hair, and a phoenix landed on the ground in front of them.

It was the commander's mount, Maximian. He must have been circling high above them all this time or perched on one of the jagged spears of rock just out of sight. Though Veronyka had already seen him close up, the first time had been in the crowded clearing on the mountainside. Now, in the wide open, she was free to appreciate his magnificence. This wasn't a juvenile like Xephyra had been, still small enough for Veronyka to hold in her arms. This was a full-grown phoenix, just as majestic on foot in the morning sunlight as soaring through the night sky on wings of fire. His plumage held more variations of red than Veronyka had ever seen in her life, each feather shimmering and jewel-bright, with fiery orange and brilliant yellow tipping his crest and long tail feathers. The phoenix's rib cage was about the size of those belonging to the horses behind them, who whinnied and neighed at the sight of the gargantuan firebird, while his wingspan was more than twice their length. His body shape was similar to an eagle's, with thick, wide-set legs and a short, strong neck. His eyes glimmered like black gems, and his hooked beak shone like gold.

One of the stablehands told her that after the war Cassian had gone willingly into custody, claiming his bondmate had died in the fighting, so Maximian could hide safely somewhere in the mountains. Some bonded pairs could remain in magical contact over thousands of miles, depending on the strength of their connection. When there was a permanent link, things like eye contact and physical distance, which were helpful when trying to use animal or shadow magic, were far less important. Still, it was a difficult thing to accomplish. Veronyka hadn't known it while they lived together—Val accidentally let the truth slip later—but her *maiora*'s phoenix had been alive their entire time in Aura Nova. In order to protect Val and Veronyka and to keep their identities as animages—and hers as a Rider and once-servant to Avalkyra Ashfire—a secret, her grandmother stayed in the capital city, while her phoenix remained in Pyra. Her *maiora*'s capture had lured her phoenix back to her side, and she was killed as she tried to defend her bondmate.

Veronyka had cried often for her *maiora* in the weeks that followed her death, but she'd cried for her phoenix, too. She wondered how many others might be living the same way . . . separate from their bondmates to avoid persecution or unable to reconnect because of bondage or the travel restrictions. Some people might have chosen to remain with their families over their phoenix, unable to get out of the empire or unwilling to leave livelihoods behind. It was a dark thought, at odds with the blue-sky day and the sight of the phoenix before her.

"You will watch Maximian and me complete the course, and then you will do the same. I do not expect perfection on your first attempt—but you should be expecting it of yourselves."

Encouraging, Veronyka thought as another wave of emotion splashed against her from the apprentices. Never had she been surrounded by so many animages all in one place, their emotions high and their magic strong, battering against her like a windstorm. She wished, not for the first time, that Val had taught her more about shadow magic.

The commander expertly navigated the obstacles, which seemed relatively simple—if he were just on horseback. That, however, was not the purpose of the exercise. Before he began, he ordered the paddock gate opened and the pigeon cage unlocked, calling a hound to his heels and a messenger pigeon to his shoulder. Doing the course with a phoenix soaring above, while keeping a skittish bird on his shoulder and an eager dog trotting alongside him, was another thing entirely.

As he worked, the commander spoke calmly but loudly, indicating various details of what he was doing and why it was important.

"You must guide the horse without the reins, so that your weapons will be within easy reach at all times," he announced, drawing his bow to hit a target halfway down the first leg of the course. Veronyka darted a glance at Petyr. . . . Apparently the bridle wasn't necessary after all.

Next the commander leapt several barrels, while keeping his bird calm and relaxed on his shoulder and his dog from running off in pursuit of the caged rabbits, their scent a tantalizing distraction on the wind. His phoenix continued to circle overhead, acting as a scout and guide and keeping him informed of any approaching Riders or threats.

"However," the commander said, on his way back toward the group after completing the roughly oval-shaped course, "there may come a time when horse and phoenix must work together, and as we all know, with phoenixes come fire."

A piercing stab of fear broke through Veronyka's mental barriers, so sudden and powerful that she turned, seeking the source. Tristan stood directly behind her, jaw set and sweat dotting his brow. Did the emotion come from him, or from one of the other apprentices clustered nearby?

Maximian dropped into a sudden dive, emitting an ear-splitting shriek as his entire body burst into flame. The sight was so awe-inspiring that Veronyka almost forgot her duty, and she sent delayed thoughts of calm and safety to the nervous horses shifting and stamping in the paddock behind her.

The commander's horse stood his ground, nostrils flaring, but otherwise showed no sign of fear or panic. The phoenix landed mere feet in front of them, burning feathers turning the air around him into rippling heat waves. Then, to Veronyka's surprise, the phoenix bowed his great head toward the horse and his rider. The commander dismounted and calmly greeted his phoenix with a pat to his flaming neck. Xephyra had been too young to ignite, so even though Veronyka knew that protection from your phoenix's fire was a part of the bond magic, she was still amazed that the heat had no effect on him.

With a final flap of his wings, Maximian put his flames out, and the commander faced the apprentices.

"For today we will forego the finale and focus on getting through the course without incident. Now choose your mounts."

Veronyka and the rest of the stablehands stood aside as the apprentices stepped through the gate of the paddock. While the messenger birds and hounds were shared by all, the horses would belong to one rider alone, so they had to be careful to choose an animal that suited them.

At once, the air around Veronyka filled with the presence of each apprentice's animal magic, their mental conversations with the horses like whispered words just out of earshot. Though Veronyka frequently crossed paths with the apprentices, usually inside the stables or at mealtimes, she didn't know any of them very well yet. Still, she had put some names to faces—there was Tristan, of course, and Elliot, the steward's assistant. She always saw him walking around the stronghold, either tight on Beryk's heels or running his errands at all hours of the day. There was Anders—tall and lanky, with prominent ears and a near-constant smile on his face—and Ronyn, one of the Pyraean apprentices. Staring at his bristly close-cropped black hair, Veronyka wondered if he'd cut off his braids to join them, as she had done, or if he'd never worn any at all.

While Jana moved around, offering her expertise and advice on a horse's skills or temperament, Veronyka and the rest of the stablehands waited off to the side in case any of the apprentices had questions or the horses misbehaved.

Every time an apprentice stepped toward Wind, he would stomp his hooves and toss his head, snorting irritably until the apprentice moved on. Veronyka worried that no one would choose him and that the horse might be sent back to the breeder.

While Wind's disposition seemed to push the other apprentices away, it actually drew Tristan toward him. He watched curiously as the horse deterred several of his fellows in a row, his brow furrowed in consideration, before stepping up himself.

While the apprentices varied in age and skill, Tristan was clearly top among them. Every morning Veronyka saw them running together on her way to breakfast, Tristan in the lead. They practiced their weapon and fighting skills in the training yard, and Tristan defeated every opponent, whether it was a fellow Apprentice Rider, a Master Rider, or even a stronghold guard. He was an expert at archery, spear and knife fighting, and hand-to-hand combat, and Veronyka was curious to see if his competency extended to his magic.

He waited patiently as Wind had his little tantrum, all the while emanating a calm—but firm—presence. The horse eventually relaxed, and Tristan moved close enough to let the animal sniff his hands and face. When it was clear Wind wouldn't bite, he patted the horse on his long, spotted nose. Then out of his pocket came a carrot, and Veronyka couldn't help but grin as Wind snuffled along Tristan's arm before snatching it up.

Clearly Wind had found his rider, and Tristan his mount.

Intrigued by their quick connection, Veronyka reached out to Wind, wanting to get his measure of the apprentice. Had his affection been bought with a carrot, or did stubborn, surly Wind perhaps recognize a kindred spirit in stubborn, surly Tristan?

In order to communicate with an animal, an animage had to open a doorway or channel in their mental walls, a passage for their magic to pass through. These were temporary and disappeared almost instantly after the animage released it—except with a bondmate, of course. That passageway was permanent, strong, and stable. Until it was severed entirely.

Taking a deep breath, Veronyka found Wind's consciousness, a familiar mix of sweet and stubborn. The more she interacted with an animal, the more easily the channel opened, and connecting with Wind was almost effortless.

The problem with reaching out is that it leaves the animage vulnerable. If they aren't completely focused, the chatter of other animals can slip in by mistake, weakening the connection to the first and making it difficult to maintain control.

And if the animage has shadow magic as well? Then it's not just animal minds the person has to worry about.

Before Veronyka knew what was happening, Tristan's thoughts began to infiltrate her mental barriers.

She was experiencing them *through* Wind—or at least that's how she perceived it. She was only hearing his interactions with the animal, not the full scope of his mind.

These weren't *projected* feelings, like the odd snatches of words and fragmented feelings that the other apprentices unconsciously released into the air. Veronyka had somehow become intertwined in the passageway that Tristan had established between him and Wind. She knew she should pull back—she hadn't meant to eavesdrop like this—and yet she didn't.

It was oddly thrilling to actively use the magic she'd spent her whole life fighting against—even though she didn't really know what she was doing. But after a moment of confusion, a haze of muddled feelings and extraneous thoughts, she found the thread of his interactions with Wind. He was sending out waves of compliments and praise, of encouragement and promises to be kind. She even discerned the words "*xe xie.*"

Tristan spoke to the horse the same way that she would to one of her own animal friends—not forcefully or imperiously, but with kindness and respect. She was surprised, given his explosive temper and haughty attitude toward her. Just as Veronyka's impression of him rose, the commander came up behind him, and the nature of his unspoken words changed. They turned hard, firm, and authoritative.

Wind bucked back abruptly, and Veronyka found herself ejected from his thoughts and disconnected from Tristan as well.

She frowned. One minute he was being kind, the next, dominating.

After the commander moved on, Tristan's stiff posture relaxed, and Veronyka assumed that firm control must be what they taught them here, even though she had never found it effective. Gaining an animal's permanent respect versus its immediate obedience had always seemed the smarter way to go. Val had never agreed, and neither, it seemed, did the commander.

Tristan notified Jana of his selection, then joined the rest of the apprentices who had chosen their horses and were now adjusting weapons and strapping on their gear.

The boy named Anders was to go first, and as he mounted up and called a hound and a pigeon, the rest of the apprentices gathered in a group to observe his run, their own horses waiting safely inside the paddock until their name was called.

Veronyka watched, breath caught in her throat, as Anders prepared to start the course. He silently called his phoenix, who appeared from the depths of the Eyrie, where the rest of the bondmates awaited their summons.

The boy's phoenix was half the size of the commander's, and so too was his performance. His horse kicked and reared, his hound bayed and leapt for the rabbits more than once, and his messenger pigeon took flight near the beginning and never returned. His phoenix behaved correctly, as far as Veronyka could tell, and when the commander demanded to know where the second patrol was, Anders's answer—relayed from the phoenix— seemed to please him.

At the end, his bondmate came to land gracefully in front of him, and while the horse started, it refrained from unseating its rider. The others clapped as he dismounted, shouting words of encouragement as Anders's narrow shoulders sagged in relief.

Eight more went through their paces, with similar levels of success. The multitasking was clearly very difficult, and while each shone in their own way—some at archery or jumping, others with the hound, the pigeon, or both—none were able to master it all. Veronyka itched to try it herself.

Tristan was last. The other apprentices, done tending their horses, stood to watch. It was clear by the focused attention of the other boys and the commander that great things were expected of him. Even the stable-hands watched eagerly.

Tristan easily outshone the others. Wind fought against his

control—Veronyka could sense it—but ultimately the horse obeyed, completing the circuit without rearing or kicking out. The hound and pigeon also behaved correctly, making Tristan's run almost flawless.

Almost.

Nearing his triumphant finish, Tristan called down his phoenix, the largest of the apprentice mounts, who flapped his wings and burst into dazzling flame. Everyone stiffened in surprise—except the commander, who watched without reaction or emotion.

Tristan's face was focused and intense, and Veronyka couldn't tell if he'd intended for the phoenix to ignite or if his bondmate had acted against his will. The phoenix landed in a wave of heat and sparks, the horses in the paddock whinnying and snorting while the rest of the phoenixes, who preened on the rocks at the edge of the grassy plain, squawked and ruffled their feathers.

Veronyka ignored all this, her eyes fixed on Wind. They had a special friendship, a connection, and even at a distance she could feel the horse's terror. His eyes rolled and his nostrils flared as he reared up in fear.

The phoenix puffed out his flaming feathers, standing his ground, while Tristan tried desperately to get his horse under control. Wind was having none of it, kicking and spinning around, causing the pigeon to take flight and the dog to dart away, tail between his legs.

Veronyka didn't think—she reacted.

She stepped out from the group, putting herself between the phoenix—who pulsed heat so suffocating that she staggered—and the horse, who continued to try to buck his rider. Tristan was halfway off his saddle now, in danger of a bad fall and possibly a trampling.

Despite the fear and panic assaulting her from all sides, Veronyka cleared her mind of everything and everyone except for Wind. She found the disappearing remnants of their earlier link and reopened it. Her eyes bored into his, strengthening their connection and drawing his focus away from the phoenix. She put all her magic into a series of calm, soothing emotions.

Look at me, she said gently in his mind. *Keep your eyes on me.*

He tossed his head and reared onto his hind legs, but she never wavered.

On me, she repeated, the words ringing in her mind. A second later the horse dropped to all fours as if Veronyka were a puppet master controlling his strings. He released one last snort of agitation, then remained still.

Tristan dropped from the saddle, panting as he gathered himself. He nodded at his phoenix, and the flames went out.

Everyone stared, including the commander, but it was Tristan who spoke first.

"What do you think you're doing?" he spat at Veronyka, his voice shaking. "How dare you interfere with an apprentice exercise?"

Veronyka was stunned. She hadn't thought beyond calming Wind and keeping him—and Tristan—safe. But if she had, she might've hoped for some recognition or praise. Not a scolding.

The commander stepped forward. "It's clear that all of you need more practice with this exercise. Some," he said, staring at Tristan, "more than others. This course will replace your morning map lessons and teach you the importance of focus and control. You, Tristan," he added as the apprentices moved to pack up, "will come in the evenings as well. Every night. Nyk here can help. It was lucky you found him. . . . Perhaps he can teach you a few things."

Tristan glowered at Veronyka. She didn't understand—she was to teach an apprentice?

"But, Commander," Tristan began incredulously. He spoke more quietly when he continued, not wanting to draw the continued attention of his fellow apprentices. "*Father,* he's—he's just a stableboy. What could he possibly teach me?"

Father? Immediately she saw it; he had the commander's light-brown eyes and widow's-peak hairline, as well as some of his natural confidence and physical presence. Veronyka reconsidered every interaction she had seen between them, filtered through the lens of family. Suddenly Tristan's bad mood made sense.

The commander's lips twisted as if in amusement. "What could he teach you? Humility, for a start," he said, mounting his horse and trotting back up to the village.

Tristan glared down at Veronyka, cold hatred in his expression, before storming off after the commander.

Veronyka helped the rest of the stablehands bring in the animals, avoiding their stares. She knew Tristan didn't like her much after his discovery of her had backfired and made a fool out of him—not to mention the way they had argued at her interrogation. But after today . . .

Angering a random apprentice was one thing, but making an enemy of the commander's son was something else entirely.

But fire forges weapons. Obsidian, steel . . .
even phoenixes. All are tempered, fortified, and made
stronger after passing through the flames.
The same can be true of people.

- CHAPTER 17 -
SEV

SEV SHOULD HAVE GOTTEN a knife.

He'd yet to get a replacement for the dagger the girl had stolen—and threatened him with—weeks ago, and the empty sheath on his hip made him feel more and more foolish with every step he took, struggling through dense undergrowth and heavy, hanging branches. It had been a Ferronese blade, pilfered from an officer's untended pack during a training exercise back in the capital. It had been plainly made—probably deliberately, in order to avoid theft—but Sev had recognized the stamp near the hilt that marked it for what it was: valuable. He'd hoped to sell it someday, but as he got caught in another snagging vine, Sev admitted that he'd happily take a butter knife at this point. He thought of the axes and short swords, the spears and scythes and numerous other weapons that were within his grasp mere moments ago and were now beyond his reach. Perspiration beaded his forehead, and he kept swiping at the phantom hair that had been hacked off when he'd been made a soldier. Without the thick strands to catch it, sweat trickled down his temples and dripped down the back of his neck.

The cursed llama was no help either. As luck would have it, Sev had grabbed a biter, and every time his back was turned, trying to clear a path for them, he sensed the beast's snuffling nose and open jaws, ready to snap at any exposed flesh.

Sev hadn't made it far when a distant crunching sound drew his attention. The biter's ears twitched, and Sev froze, scanning the forest until his pursuer stepped through the trees.

Kade.

Shock rooted Sev to the ground, and he quickly turned away to hide his reaction. He gripped the animal's lead reins in case the creature tried to bolt, but it was clear that Kade's calming presence was already at work on him. By the time Kade stepped into Sev's peripheral vision, the llama was butting its head against his outstretched hand. *Traitorous beast.*

"They do a head count," Kade said offhandedly, as if their meeting were happenstance and the information were of no real importance. As if he *hadn't* just caught Sev trying to run away.

"I know that," Sev said, heat rising up his already hot face. "But I'm on pack animal duty, so that means *I'm* the one who's supposed to do the count. Alec is too lazy, and Grier is too drunk," he said, mentioning the other soldiers assigned with him that day. "That's *pack animal* duty, by the way, not *pack animal bondservant* duty. I don't report on you."

Kade forced a slow breath out through his nose. "And when they don't get a count on the pack animals . . . you think they will just forget it?"

His voice was calm, reasonable—nothing like the angry, scowling boy from barely an hour before. For some reason, this soothing tone made Sev angrier. He was treating Sev like one of the llamas, like a simpleminded, temperamental pet.

He faced Kade at last, dropping the reins and clenching his hands into fists. "They'll march on long enough for me to get a head start. I don't care about the rest."

"They'll hunt you down." Again his voice was almost indifferent—but his eyes betrayed some hidden feeling, something that invested him in this conversation, despite what he was trying to project.

Sev frowned, trying to puzzle it out, before realizing the gravity of what was happening for the first time. Sev had run away, but by following him here . . . Kade had done the same.

"That's my problem, not yours. If you leave now, they'll think you were just lagging behind."

"I can't."

"What—why not?" Sev demanded. A flicker of hope stirred in his chest.

Kade placed a gentle hand on the llama's long neck. "Do you know what happens when a bondservant loses track of his charge?"

Sev swallowed, the warm glimmer inside quickly snuffed out. He . . . he hadn't thought this through.

And why should you? asked a harsher, more instinctual part of himself. Kade disliked Sev—he had made that very clear—so Sev should dislike him back. Kade was nothing to him.

Nothing.

It was selfish, Sev knew, but he'd *had* to be selfish in order to survive. Look what had happened to his parents. They'd been selfless, and it had gotten them killed. They'd left him all alone to fend for himself in a world that hated him for what he was. So he'd had to become something else. There were no more heroes soaring through the sky, protecting their people. There was the empire, and those that got caught under its boot. Sure, the Riders had supposedly regrouped, but they'd soon be killed as well. Trix and Kade were stupid for believing otherwise.

And yet somewhere in the back of his mind, Sev wanted to believe too. He wanted to believe in *something*, and whatever his mixed feelings about Kade and his cause, Sev couldn't let him take the fall for this.

Kade had been watching him, staring intently at his face. They were the same height, their faces on a level, but Sev was much narrower, thinner— like the sinewy string to Kade's carved bow, the supple branch to Kade's sturdy tree.

A dull pain shot up from Sev's hands, and he looked down, unclenching his fists. His joints ached with the release of tension, and his knuckles had gone white with the lack of blood flow.

Kade's hands still rested on the llama, and they were shaking. He was afraid. Did he fear being alone out here with Sev—or did he fear being *caught* alone with Sev?

Something dark and desperate unfurled in Sev's stomach. He was afraid too—but not for the same reasons.

"Come on," he said, turning around. "We're going back."

As the end of the convoy came into view, Sev realized it was no longer moving.

He looked at Kade, who had also noticed the halted progress.

"Just—let me," Sev said. He shoved the llama's reins into Kade's hands, then lengthened his strides.

As the three of them rejoined the party, Captain Belden—who had long since returned from his meeting with the informant—was standing at the back of the line. Sev's insides turned to liquid. This was not good.

Officer Yara, who was next to Captain Belden, noted Sev's approach and marched over.

"How dare you remove an animal from the convoy, mageslave?" she barked, speaking directly to Kade and ignoring Sev entirely.

A hot spasm of anger lanced through Sev's stomach, and a protective urge reared up inside him. He hated the way the soldiers treated the bondservants, and he hated the reminder that this was the very reason Kade disliked him in the first place. But they were in a dangerous position right now, and Sev had to be careful.

"It was me, Officer Yara," Sev said loudly, stepping forward. "I took both the llama and the *bondservant* with me," he explained, putting extra emphasis on the proper term for Kade's position. Though Sev didn't dare glance in his direction, he thought he sensed Kade's reaction to his words. Soldiers never stood up for bondservants.

Officer Yara, too, seemed surprised by them, raising her eyebrows and causing her burn scars to stretch and turn white against her brown skin. "And who gave you permission to abandon your post, soldier?" She jerked her chin at Kade and the llama. "They are the property of Rolan, governor of Ferro, and by proxy, Captain Belden. They are not yours to do with what you wish."

Property. Sev took a deep breath, composing himself. Lowering his voice to the slow, dim register the others were used to, he answered.

"The llama was limping, Officer Yara. The bondservant reckoned he had a muscle cramp and needed a quick rubdown, so we stepped aside to treat the animal. We didn't want to delay the convoy."

"Is this the lame beast?" Captain Belden asked, cutting in before Officer Yara could respond. He had been standing just behind them, consulting a map that his attendant held out for him. Waving the map impatiently aside, he stepped forward.

The captain was a weasel of a man with a pale, pointed face and thinning straw-like hair. He was battle-hardened, though, and had a reputation for cruelty, despite his taste for fine wine and embroidered silk.

"Yes, Captain. He's walking fine now, sir, and—"

"Stand aside," he commanded, and with a quiet *snick* and a flash of steel, he drew his dagger. The elegant weapon put Sev's stolen dagger to shame, with its embossed leather grip and swirling, knotted embellishments, not to mention the gleaming Ferronese steel blade. He snatched the llama's leads from Kade, who resisted for a breath before releasing them. Without a moment's thought or hesitation, Captain Belden drew the knife across the animal's throat.

Sev barely had time to register what was happening before the llama let out a strangled snort of pain, then collapsed, a shower of blood spattering across the ground as the warm flicker of his life was snuffed out.

Next to him, Kade staggered, and Sev fought to hide his own visceral reaction. Only an animage would truly *feel* the animal's death the way Kade did, and Sev couldn't give himself away—not while the captain stood there, bloody blade in hand.

There were plenty of misconceptions about animages in the empire. Many thought they were half-animal, wild and incapable of proper human emotion and intelligence. Others saw them as weak and overly sensitive, weeping at the death of every rat and cockroach and wanting to make even the lowliest creatures their pets and playmates.

Sev supposed that last part was true. On the farm, he'd had all manner of animal companions, but that didn't mean he was incapable of understanding that some animals had to be killed so that he could eat, that some beasts plowed fields and pulled carts, that they worked just the same as humans did.

Regardless, one truth universally acknowledged was that animages could feel the emotions of the animals around them. They felt their pain and their panic, sometimes connecting with them more deeply than they did with humans. It made them vulnerable, and Captain Belden had just exploited that fact.

As Kade and Sev stared down at the dead animal, Belden carefully cleaned his blade with a handkerchief his attendant gave him, the fine fabric stitched with his golden monogram. He did it slowly, almost reverently, and the care was in stark contrast to his rash, thoughtless treatment of the llama.

"You will now report to Officer Lyle and assist our hunting unit," he said to Kade, who visibly forced himself to straighten and face the man. "If you are caught anywhere near the pack animals, you will face strict discipline. Do you understand me, mageslave?"

Kade's nostrils flared, and his jaw clenched as he nodded. "Yes, sir," he grit out.

"We cannot afford to be delayed," Belden continued idly, examining the knife closely before removing one last speck of blood. "By anything."

He stared fixedly at Kade when he spoke the last two words. Sev understood the threat plainly. *This time it was the llama; next time it will be you.* Belden returned his weapon to its sheath and the blood-soaked rag to the attendant, then strode back to the front of the convoy.

"I'll deal with you later, soldier," Officer Yara said, following the captain up the line.

Sev looked at Kade, expecting to see anger or disappointment on his face. The hunting party was the worst duty available to an animage, who had to use their magic to lure in unsuspecting animals to be slaughtered. When Kade met his eye, however, he didn't look upset—he looked *panicked*, his gaze darting around the clearing, face leeched of color. That's when realization dawned on Sev for the first time.

Trix's mission.

He had no idea what Kade's task was—or for that matter, what his own was—but Kade had obviously been assigned to the pack animals for a reason.

And Sev had just screwed everything up.

Two soldiers dragged the llama carcass off to the side of the path, out of the way, while a handful of bondservants reclaimed the supplies that were strapped to its back. Objects, not life, were valuable here, and Sev was struck by the *senselessness* of it all. The creature had died in vain, for *his* selfish decisions, and worse, he'd somehow managed to drag Kade and Trix into it.

As the line started moving, Sev saw the old woman up ahead, staring at him.

He looked away.

Long have the Ashfires bled—
and burned—for our right to rule.

- CHAPTER 18 -
TRISTAN

TRISTAN SKIPPED LUNCH.

The rest of the apprentices were probably talking about what had just happened, and he didn't want to deprive them of the opportunity to gossip. The commander and his son, at odds again.

Rather than turning right toward the dining hall, he turned left, around the side of the temple and back to the apprentice barracks.

Inside, he paced.

Quiet as the mountain. Still as the mountain. Calm as the—

A surge of frustration reared up, and Tristan whirled, throwing a punch clean through the wall.

As quickly as his anger came, it leaked away. He sighed loudly, forcing the air from his lungs. He examined the hole in the wall, then his banged-up knuckles. Luckily, the wall was more of a screen, made from wooden slats woven together and not the heavy planks they used in the valley.

If the wall had been board or stone, like the exterior walls of the barracks, he'd have broken his hand. He laughed darkly, imagining how he'd explain that kind of injury to the commander. His knuckles bled, the skin scraped clean off, and the wall had obvious damage. He'd have to get the servants to fix it and hope his father never found out.

Tristan sank onto his hammock, swaying idly back and forth. The barracks was a long, narrow building, filled with fabric slings instead of wooden bed frames or pallets on the floor. The hammocks allowed them to fit as many sleepers as possible, sometimes stacked double with stools to help climb onto the higher beds, like in the servant barracks. Since they had only ten apprentices, though, many of the slings were empty, and Tristan had chosen one low to the ground and near the back door, where there was a fleeting sense of privacy.

Most thought the commander of the Riders would show favoritism to his only son and heir, but Tristan had found the exact opposite to be true.

He'd been itching to train with horse and phoenix for months, the last major hurdle to conquer as an apprentice before becoming a Master Rider. But his father had insisted on holding him back and waiting for the other apprentices, who were nowhere near as good as Tristan.

Then that nagging feeling had surfaced in Tristan's mind, the fear that his father knew his weakness. That his reasons for holding his son back were a lie. It wouldn't be the first—or the last—lie his father told him, and Tristan loathed having to second-guess every conversation and interaction between them.

Tristan guarded his secret closely; did his best to hide it, to recover when he made a mistake—like the exercise out on the bluffs—and come back twice as strong. But there was always that moment of paralyzing doubt, a flash of uncertainty or hesitation that he was certain his father would see, if he knew to look for it. And what if he did? What if he learned that his son was afraid of fire, the very thing that made the Phoenix Riders who and what they were?

But no matter how it jangled his nerves and set his teeth on edge, Tristan wanted this life. He refused to lose his dream over something that was, ultimately, within his own control.

After his father demonstrated the obstacle course today, Tristan had seen it as an opportunity, a chance to show that he was stronger than any flaws his father might think he had—that there was absolutely nothing that would hold him back. He'd thought he might even be able to convince his father to give him his own patrol—Tristan's ultimate goal.

Instead he'd made a fool of himself.

Actually, the stableboy Nyk had made a fool of him.

As if it wasn't bad enough to hesitate, to mess up *another* important exercise—but to have a stableboy swoop in and save him? The very same person who had already made him look an idiot once before? Word had traveled after Tristan's disastrous first patrol, and the apprentices had been quick to see the humor in Tristan "prematurely blowing his horn." Every time they saw Nyk, they'd cast Tristan sidelong glances and smirks, and now with this most recent blunder, his hopes of living it down were practically nonexistent.

Tristan had replayed the scene over and over in his head since he'd left the obstacle course, and he was convinced that if the boy hadn't stepped in, he could've gotten things under control. The fire made him panic—that was nothing new—but given another moment, Tristan would have told Rex to quench his flames, commanded the horse to stand down, and called back his dog and pigeon. He could've *fixed it*, but instead that runt of a boy ran into the middle of the scene, seconds away from being trampled and burned, and did the very thing Tristan hadn't yet managed to do—regained control. Almost effortlessly, it had seemed.

This boy was really starting to get on his nerves.

Tristan dropped his head into his hands, his hair curling around his fingers. As if being embarrassed in front of his fellow apprentices wasn't enough, he'd *seen* that familiar look in his father's eye. This mistake would be his excuse for holding Tristan back for weeks—months, probably. No matter how strongly Tristan performed from now on, his father would remind him of this failure.

Not only would he suffer, but the Riders would suffer too. The commander's opinions of him didn't change the fact that they needed more patrols—finding Nyk had only proven that. They needed to survey the areas of Pyra where empire spies and raiders might lurk, the lower rim and the Foothills and the wilds that weren't traveled by the locals.

Now, because of Tristan's mistake, the commander would hold back on what they desperately needed, just to prove a point. Just to *humble* him.

"You win, Father," Tristan muttered, getting to his feet. "I am humbled."

Several hours later, however, Tristan's weak grasp at humility slipped away with every step he took toward the obstacle course. How could his father do this to him? He was the best apprentice they had, and still he wasn't good enough. Sure, he'd made some mistakes, but only because his father pushed him to that brink.

By the time he reached Nyk, standing anxiously next to Wind, Tristan's mood burned hotter than Rex in a fire dive.

Calm as the mountain, he told himself, but the words held no meaning.

He didn't speak to the boy, who looked up at him with hair and eyes as dark as charcoal. He had a smudge of dirt on his short nose, and his servant uniform was filthy and ill fitting. Still, he had to be magically powerful, to pull off the stunt he did during the obstacle course. To calm a horse as wild as Wind and to approach Rex in full flame without fear or hesitation . . . He had the stuff of a Rider, Tristan had to grudgingly admit. But all the raw talent in the world didn't make Nyk an expert, and the commander assigning the boy to help Tristan—that cut more deeply than his fragile ego could bear.

Scowling, he snatched the reins, mounted up, and called his other animals. Without a word he began the course, leaving the boy behind.

Halfway through, however, Nyk caught up.

"I . . . I thought I was supposed to help you?" he asked, wide-eyed and uncertain.

Tristan paused before the target up ahead. "Do you ride?" he asked.

"What—horses?" Nyk said.

Tristan's nostrils flared. "Yes, horses," he said, forcing his voice into politeness. He knew the boy didn't ride horses, or phoenixes, or llamas for that matter.

"No," Nyk said, and Tristan nodded.

"And have you any skill with a bow?" Tristan indicated the weapon in his hands.

"No," the boy said again, looking down.

"No," Tristan repeated. "Have you used a messenger pigeon? Hunted with a hound? Have you done anything that I am doing in this obstacle course?"

Nyk shook his head, his gaze fixed on the ground.

"I didn't think so," Tristan said, focusing again on the target several yards away. He knew he was being harsh, but he couldn't seem to stop. *This is what you wanted, isn't it, Father? To make me more like you?*

"Why did he assign me to help you, then?" Nyk asked, looking up at last. Tristan felt an unwilling stab of compassion for him.

"That was just the commander toying with you. You'll get used to it— or not. I thought I had, and now look at me."

A rush of blood burned Tristan's cheeks—he hadn't meant to say so much, to reveal his true feelings. But to his surprise, when he glanced down at Nyk, there was deep understanding in his expression, as if Tristan's words hadn't been the nonsense ramblings of the commander's privileged, misunderstood son, but something he could completely relate to.

"What do you want me to do, then?" Nyk asked after several silent moments. As he stared up at Tristan, his eyes landed on the knuckles of his right hand—raw and bloody from his punch to the wall.

Tristan moved it out of sight and straightened in the saddle. "Just keep quiet and stay out of my way."

"Will you do the finish?" Nyk asked, gesturing toward their stack of supplies, which would certainly be in danger of catching fire if Rex ignited nearby.

"No," said Tristan, more sharply than he intended, "I—no, not tonight."

Nyk nodded, a slight frown on his face, and stepped aside.

Tristan squeezed his eyes shut. He couldn't face Rex in full flame again, not so soon after his screwup this afternoon, but he had to be more careful. Being on edge only made everything worse.

With a slow breath out his nose, Tristan straightened his shoulders and continued.

The course was exhausting, especially for the second time that day. Though he did his best not to show the strain—a habit he'd picked up after being constantly scrutinized by his father—sweat dotted Tristan's brow, and his concentration was waning. Keeping a firm grip on three animals, as well as a connection to Rex as he soared overhead, was draining. He soon began cutting corners, telling Rex to circle but not encouraging him to give reports on the landscape or goings-on in the stronghold's grounds.

Nyk became increasingly agitated, following along silently but clearly dying to say something. He opened and closed his mouth, gripped his hands tightly together, and kept moving closer only to jump back again.

Tristan couldn't take it. "What?" he demanded at last, coming to a stop. He didn't care much for what the boy had to say, but he needed a break, and he figured that if he let Nyk speak his mind, he'd stop fidgeting and Tristan could finish before the sun set. As it was, the glowing orange ball was cresting the mountains in the distance and would be out of sight in minutes.

Nyk hesitated. "It's just—you're, well, you . . ."

"Spit. It. Out."

His eyes narrowed. "Fine. You're doing it *wrong*," he snapped, before adding, "*sir*."

Sir. Given the fact that his father was the rightful governor of Ferro and Tristan was his heir, he should be addressed as "my lord." But as another man currently laid claim to that position, Tristan supposed that "sir" was the best he could hope to get. Still, it was wrong.

"I'm no *sir*. I'm an apprentice. Yes, Apprentice. No, Apprentice. Got it?"

"Yes, Apprentice," Nyk answered, his voice flat.

"Doing what wrong?" Tristan asked, looking down at himself. His technique, his form, everything was perfect.

"The way you use your magic," Nyk said, gesturing to the animals.

"You push too hard. Take Storm," he said, indicating the dog at Wind's feet. "Instead of telling him what you expect and guiding him through it, you force your will on him moment to moment. You keep constant pressure on him, draining yourself unnecessarily, and the second you let up, you'll lose him."

Tristan pulled a skeptical expression. He had never *enjoyed* lording over animals, but asking them nicely when they needed to obey was simply out of the question. Even his bond with Rex, which had developed into a trusting friendship, started out as Rider and mount. Master and servant.

If there was a mental equivalent to an eye roll, Rex did so just then, his exasperation seeping through the bond. To the phoenix, their connection made them a pair, equals. His magic strengthened Tristan's, and likewise, Tristan's human logic and understanding of the world increased Rex's intelligence. Phoenixes weren't like regular animals, and their centuries-long bond with humans was part of the reason why.

With a shake of his head, Tristan pushed Rex's thoughts from his mind. The suggestion that he could interact with a dog in the same way he interacted with a phoenix—to whom he was magically bonded—made no sense at all.

He looked up at the darkening sky; his time was running out. Nyk's words about control nagged at him, but they obviously came from youth and inexperience. Tristan was doing what he was taught to do, and surely his father—a veteran of the Blood War—knew more about animal magic than an unbonded sixteen-year-old kid.

"While your observations are fascinating, this is how animages have been taught for generations. We need these animals to be obedient; we don't need them to be our friends. And I will not lose him," he said, nodding down at the dog.

Tristan continued the course, leaving Nyk behind, pushing extra hard for fear that his tiredness would prove the boy right.

As he turned the corner and prepared for the final leg, Rex's boredom filtered through the bond, making it difficult for Tristan to concentrate. The pigeon on his shoulder itched to stretch her wings and dig for grubs, and Storm had caught wind of the rabbit cage again. The scent flooded the dog's nostrils, and anticipation coursed through his veins.

Then, out of nowhere, a loud *whack* echoed through the silence. It came from across the course, where Nyk stood just below the archery target, a tree branch in hand. He'd clearly just knocked it against the wooden frame, and the distraction stripped Tristan of his hold on the animals.

With a grim smile, Nyk cocked his arm back and flung the branch as far as he could. Before Tristan could scrabble to regain control, the dog was off after it, the pigeon took flight, and the horse beneath him tossed his head and reared, almost unseating him. The only animal who remained doing what he was supposed to was Rex, whose boredom had quite evaporated as he watched the scene below.

Without so much as a glance in Tristan's direction, Nyk strode to their supplies and readied for their departure.

Tristan didn't bother trying to finish the course or calling his lost animals back to the starting point. He rode over to where Nyk stood and leapt from his horse.

"What in the dark realms was that?"

Rex landed next to them, and his arrival was the first thing to make Nyk turn Tristan's way since he threw the stick. He gazed longingly at the phoenix, eyes bright with reverence.

"If you refuse to order your animals about, then tell me, how did you get the horse—"

"*Wind,*" Nyk interjected, whirling around to face him. "Your horse's name is Wind. You don't call this beautiful creature"—he gestured to Rex—"*the bird*, do you?"

Rex cocked his head, waiting for Tristan's response.

"What? No. His name is Rex."

Nyk nodded, staring at the phoenix. "Yes, that suits you, you regal-looking fellow."

"Stop that," Tristan snapped as Rex drew himself up straighter and puffed out his chest. Tristan's self-righteous anger was deflating in the face of this boy's obvious affection for his bondmate. "Scat," he told Rex, who ruffled his feathers and took off.

Tristan turned to Nyk. "If all you do is charm and flatter the animals, then how did you get Wind to obey you so easily this morning? You're telling me you asked nicely and didn't force your will, your magic, on him? Only Rex has ever obeyed me like that."

Nyk sighed, as if Tristan had asked him this question a thousand times and he was tired of answering it. He turned away before responding. "I just convinced him, is all."

"You just *convinced him*?" Tristan repeated skeptically. "Don't lie to me," he said, thinking of his father's constant games and deceptions. "There's nothing worse than a liar."

"I'm not *lying*," Nyk answered hotly. "And the reason he obeyed instantly, and without hesitation, is that he was familiar with me already. If you befriend the animals, if you treat them as equals, they'll trust you, and once they trust you, they'll obey you. Without a command and without question. That's what I meant with Storm today. If he trusted you, he'd have stayed by your side."

Tristan shook his head. It was absurd. "You're too soft-hearted for this line of work—like a little girl who wants to cuddle puppies."

Nyk's face contorted in outrage. "As opposed to you—too manly to admit when you're wrong? To admit that sometimes being kind is better than being cruel? Deny it all you want, but I know you're as soft-hearted as me, *xe xie*."

With that, Nyk stomped back up to the village, the rabbit cage tucked under his arm, while the pigeon, the dog, Wind—even Rex, soaring through the air—followed like a row of ducklings behind.

Tristan gaped after him, stunned that the boy had the nerve to speak to him that way. But as the shock wore off, his mind replayed the events of that morning, when he'd first met Wind. No matter what he said to Nyk, it *was* his instinct to be kind and gentle to animals. His father had done his best to change this, but whenever Tristan was scared or nervous, it was his default.

"Xe xie . . . ," he murmured, shaking his head. It was what his mother had called him as a young boy, the Pyraean words ingrained in his memory, while her face faded a little more each day. Sweet one . . . dear one . . . Tristan hadn't realized that he'd said those words out loud before. Maybe that was why his father had punished him so severely. The commander's ancient Pyraean was a little bit rusty, but surely even he would remember that phrase.

Tristan stood in the field for a long time, night descending around him, before finally walking back through the darkness alone.

POSTMORTEM EXAMINATION

Deceased: King Aryk Ashfire
Birth: Day 27, Twelfth Moon, 129 AE
Death: Day 6, Fifth Moon, 165 AE
Age: 35

Witness Account: Queen Lania of Stel
On the evening of Day 5, Fifth Moon, 165 AE, Queen Lania claims that King Aryk wished to retire early after dinner, citing stomach pains and exhibiting fever symptoms. When Lania joined him in his chambers several hours later, it was to find him in bed, unresponsive, with a burning fever and vomit-covered sheets.

The king was placed under High Priestess Deidra's care, and the court sat vigil at his bedside. The sickness took him before eighth bell on the afternoon of the following day.

Witness Account: Fenton, captain of the King's Guard
Captain Fenton claims King Aryk retired on the evening of Day 5, Fifth Moon, 165 AE, in good spirits, intending to have an early morning walk with his beloved hounds. He had no visible signs of illness or discomfort.

Physical Examination
Date: Day 7, Fifth Moon, 165 AE
Conducted by: Deidra, High Priestess of Hael, and Ilithya, Acolyte of Hael

No evidence of forced entry or struggle. An empty cup was found on King Aryk's bedside table, as he was well-known to enjoy a glass of spiced honey wine before bed, which he would fix for himself. The cask of wine, honey, and spices were all checked for poison or spoilage, but no toxic materials or signs of tampering were discovered. Body exhibited symptoms of intense fever, dehydration, and stomach illness.

Diagnosis: Death of natural causes, possibly phoenix flu, sweating sickness, or other airborne virus.

Update
Date: Day 10, Fifth Moon, 165 AE
Conducted by: Ilithya, Acolyte of Hael

Empty cup examined, and trace amounts of suspicious, dark residue discovered embedded into ridges of the embossed metal. The chalice was known to be the king's favorite, an Ashfire heirloom once belonging to Ferronese King Damian himself. Further testing required to identify the nature of the substance.

The only people with access to the king's bedchamber—and his private collection of favored treasures—were himself and his wife, Queen Lania.

Sometimes the title of queen is given; sometimes it must be taken.
And sometimes the honor becomes so drenched in blood and betrayal
that it is slippery to the touch, but we reach for it nonetheless,
poison on our fingers and vengeance in our hearts.

- CHAPTER 19 -
VERONYKA

VERONYKA HID IN THE kitchens during dinner.

She was still angry with Tristan, and he was definitely still angry with her, so she didn't want to see him any sooner than she had to. Morra put her to work the moment she sidled in, but Veronyka didn't mind. She picked at a plate of honey-drizzled sweet cakes that the cook set out for her, while using a mold to cut pastries from a flattened length of dough. She plopped the rounds onto a nearby tray, while Morra rolled the remaining bits into fresh sheets for her to cut.

As long as Veronyka kept her mind occupied, she didn't fear the woman's shadow magic. As far as she could tell, Morra didn't use it unless absolutely necessary.

Of course, Morra didn't need shadow magic to know that something was bothering her. When Tristan walked past the open archway that led into the kitchen on his way to the dining hall, Veronyka couldn't help the scowl that crossed her face.

"I think it's cut, lad," Morra said dryly. Veronyka looked at the woman, confused, until she nodded down at the piece of pastry Veronyka had been cutting—and which she had ripped in half with a savage jerk of the mold.

"Oh, sorry," Veronyka said, removing the cutter so Morra could gather the ruined dough and reroll it.

"What's your issue with the lordling?" she asked, nodding in the direction of the arch Tristan had just passed through. Her gaze was knowing as she sprinkled flour onto the stone table, pressing a roller over the ball of dough, her strong arms flattening it in several short strokes.

"He's the one with the issue," Veronyka said. She knew she was responsible for some of his animosity; she shouldn't have commented on his magic—or pried into it at all, even if it was mostly by accident—and she probably shouldn't have stepped in that morning at the training exercise. But it was clear he held other resentment toward her, thanks to her arrival on his patrol route and the questioning that came after it, and Veronyka refused to take the blame for that.

Morra laughed. "Oh, he's not all bad. He's got more of his mother in him than his father. Those of us who knew her see it—as soon as *he* sees it, things will go easier."

"What do you mean?" Veronyka asked. "Who is his mother?"

Morra absently rubbed the thigh of her amputated leg and reached for a mug of pungent herb tea she often drank to dull the pain.

"Tristan's mother, Olanna, came from a very old Pyraean family. Most think only Cassian can claim a noble lineage, being an ex-governor, but the history of the lesser kingdoms is young compared to the bloodlines of ancient Pyra. Olanna was a Flamesong, and their family tree goes all the way back to the First Riders."

Veronyka's heart leapt; she loved hearing about the First Riders. They were part of the Phoenix Rider creation story, legendary figures that were chosen by Axura in her fight against Nox.

Val had shown Veronyka a giant fresco in Aura Nova that had escaped the council's purge of phoenix-related artifacts, hidden between two old buildings in a narrow alley. The plaster was peeling and the colors were faded, but it was still the grandest thing Veronyka had ever seen. It showed the battle between light and dark—Axura's flaming phoenixes pitted against

Nox's darkness, depicted as ink-black birds trailing wisps of shadow. Strixes, Val had called them, and the word had caused a chill to crawl up Veronyka's spine. They were more than just death and darkness personified; they were harbingers of the end of the world.

The entire thing sounded more myth than history to Veronyka, but until this day Phoenix Riders claimed descent from those mighty warriors. Val said the First Rider Queen was an Ashfire, the start of an unbroken line that ruled for a thousand years—starting in the Queendom of Pyra and then in the Golden Empire, up until the Blood War tore everything apart.

"Cassian's family ruled Ferro—as kings in the beginning, and then as governors," Morra continued. "It was some great-great-great-uncle of his that married Elysia and ruled as king consort when the empire was founded and then elevated his brother to the role of governor in his homeland. Tristan's certainly got the look of his father, but right here"—Morra tapped a finger to her chest—"he's his mother. It's from her that he gets his compassion and his sense of right and wrong. His temper, on the other hand, is Cassian through and through." Morra leaned in, lowering her voice. "They say there's Stellan blood in the commander's line, and that's where he gets his love for plots and politics—though I'm sure he'd deny it until his dying breath."

Veronyka smirked. Stellans had a reputation as troublemakers and war-mongers. At least, that's what Val had told her. Stel was the largest and most powerful of the provinces, and before it was part of the empire, it was a commonwealth of more than a dozen kingdoms. The kingdoms spent centuries warring among themselves as much as with their neighbors—usually Ferro, with whom they shared a border—and had difficulty reaching satisfactory terms with Queen Elysia's growing empire. Stel was the last region to join and had apparently been heavily involved in the Blood War, backing Pheronia—who was Stellan on her mother's side—against Avalkyra and providing military and financial support.

"Did Olanna fight in the Blood War?" Veronyka asked.

"Oh yes. She served the Feather-Crowned Queen, same as her husband,

and even when the final battle was lost, she continued to fight. While Cassian met with the council, asking for clemency and offering up information in order to keep his governor position, Olanna was helping hide Riders and their families. It wasn't just Avalkyra's soldiers being captured and killed—anyone with animal magic was in danger. Olanna smuggled hundreds out of the valley and safely into Pyra. She smuggled me out, even though it looked like I might die from my wound. She was a good woman, Olanna."

Morra cleared her throat and got to work on the next lump of dough, her movements jerkier than before.

"Wait," Veronyka said, putting aside the cutter and facing Morra directly. "The commander tried to cut a deal while his wife was out risking her life? He ratted to the empire?" She couldn't contain the sneer that curled her lip or the contempt that tainted her voice.

"There's many who saw it that way, it's true," she said, putting aside the roller. "But it wasn't as simple as that. He and Olanna disagreed on methods, but their goals were the same. He thought if he could just retain his position on the Council of Governors, he could save us . . . he could save *her*. The magical registry was only an idea then, but it was easy to see how such a law could take hold amid the rampant fear and hatred after the war, and we needed *someone* on the inside, someone who could represent us and our interests on the council. So, he turned himself in. He offered information, but he didn't have anything of real value—mostly names of people already caught and condemned or bases long abandoned. But his efforts were for nothing."

Something about her tone made dread uncoil in Veronyka's stomach. "What happened to Olanna?"

"She was caught," Morra answered with a heavy sigh. "What she did was risky, and it was only a matter of time before she was brought in. Tristan had been sent away to live with some servants in the Ferronese countryside. But Cassian was still in the empire's custody when she was captured, and he attended her trial. All his connections, all his political maneuvering, and he couldn't save her. Olanna was deemed too dangerous to be kept alive and serve her term in bondage like so many others. She was executed for treason, and her phoenix beheaded. Her death sent shock waves through the empire and scared the last remnants of Avalkyra Ashfire's rebellion into submission. If, with all her status and wealth, Olanna could be butchered, then no one was safe. Cassian has not been the same since. They chose to spare his life but not his position on the council. I think they rather enjoyed seeing him broken and exiled . . . a once-mighty governor brought low. Perhaps they thought he could serve as an example or a cautionary tale. The council named some Stellan lord governor in Cassian's place and banished his entire family from the empire."

The disdain Veronyka had been feeling just moments ago slowly ebbed away. It was so incredibly cruel, and she couldn't help feeling a pang of pity for both Cassian and Tristan.

"Did you fight in the war?" she asked.

"Yes," Morra said, returning to the dough. "Though I didn't last long." She reached into her hair and pulled out an ash-covered feather. "I lost Aneaxi in a border skirmish. Those were dark days for me, but there's more than one way to fight a war—Olanna taught me that. We Riders who outlived our bondmates found other ways to serve our queen. They called us Mercies. We raked the burning buildings and smoking battlefields, seeking out survivors. And resurrections."

"Resurrections?" Veronyka whispered. "Phoenixes can be reborn in the middle of a battlefield?" Her heart stuttered inside her chest, and the image of Xephyra's cold ashes came back to her.

Morra nodded gravely. "All it takes is fire and bones, and there was plenty of both. I'd only just joined, but the older Mercies had strange stories to tell. I was determined to do my part, to find *someone*. . . ." She glanced at Veronyka, then shrugged, sliding the dough over for her to cut. "But my unit was ambushed before we'd even crossed the border. The others died. . . . I barely escaped with my life." She gestured down at her leg.

They stood in a small bubble of silence for several moments, while the noise and commotion of the kitchens clamored all around them.

"We're not as strong as we once were," Morra continued, "but nor are we as weak. The commander may seem brusque, and some of his methods are too rooted in the empire, but he is capable. Of those who survived the Blood War—with their bondmate, mind you—Cassian has the most military experience, the most wealth, and the most natural authority. Those who fought alongside him respect his ability as a leader, and there's no one among us to challenge him. Yet," she said with a wink. Quietly she added, "One day young Tristan will find his strength."

Veronyka had a hard time seeing Tristan as someone in need of strength. He was very like his father, as far as she could tell, but apparently Morra saw something else in him. As someone with shadow magic, she probably saw more than most.

Veronyka paced next to the obstacle course the following evening, waiting for Tristan's arrival. During the morning exercises, he didn't so much as look at her. He just went through the course, ignoring her advice and pushing his animals hard, overexerting himself. The rest of the day passed quickly, in the way that time does when you're dreading something.

Morra's words floated around Veronyka's mind all day. She was curious about what Tristan thought of his mother's heroic sacrifice. Did he think her brave, or did he blame her for their exile? And would he turn into the kind of leader she had been—a selfless supporter of her people—or would he be like his father, desperately clinging to his place in the valley?

It made her think about the kind of person she wanted to be too. Veronyka had been told hundreds of stories about the Phoenix Riders in her life, about Avalkyra Ashfire and her deeds, each more amazing than the next.

At eleven, Avalkyra was the youngest Rider in history to win both the flying *and* archery competitions at the summer solstice games, and she led her first patrol at twelve.

During court functions and official council meetings, Avalkyra insisted that she and her sister sit at the king's right hand—a place usually reserved for the queen—and forced her stepmother to sit on the king's far-less-dignified left.

When Avalkyra's father died and her stepmother tried to seize control, Avalkyra flooded the council with allies, dismissing many of the regent's confidants with threats and blackmail, allowing her to overrule the would-be queen's every move and order.

Even the Stellan Uprising, the largest military conflict before the Blood War, couldn't defeat Avalkyra. She won the battle with *half* the recommended soldiers, ensuring Aura Nova was not left vulnerable to her stepmother's machinations in her absence, and even brought Pheronia to the battlefield, ensuring the queen couldn't use her as leverage or turn her sister against her.

And when evidence came to light that the king had been poisoned by his own wife—the current queen regent—Avalkyra ensured that justice was served.

"What kind of justice, *Maiora*?" Veronyka had asked late one night as her grandmother told the story. They were in their usual positions in front of the fire—Veronyka curled up on the pile of mats and cushions that acted as her and Val's bed and her *maiora* seated on a rickety old stool next to her.

"The only kind that matters, *xe* Nyka," Val had said, slipping under the covers next to her. "Was Avalkyra to put her treacherous stepmother in a finely furnished cell, where she could continue to cause strife? Was she to rely on a trial run by cowardly politicians with agendas of their own? Death was the only punishment worth doling out: an eye for an eye."

"But what about Pheronia? I thought Avalkyra loved her sister. If she did, how could she kill her mother?" Veronyka had looked up, surprised to see Val and her *maiora* share a look over her head, an exchange that she wasn't meant to see.

"It's not as simple as all that," her grandmother had said. "Love and politics are like oil and water—they don't mix. What was best for the empire, and for Avalkyra's own claim to the throne, wasn't necessarily the best for her sister."

"So she chose politics over love?"

Val made an impatient noise in the back of her throat. "Avalkyra couldn't let the regicide of her own father go unpunished. People respond to strength, Veronyka. She was heir to the throne and had a duty to her king to see justice served."

But that decision had been the schism, the moment when the two sisters—always struggling *together* to combat the will of the council and the machinations of the governors—finally separated.

Later her *maiora* explained that Avalkyra thought the move would gain her support in her bid for the throne, but the opposite happened. People saw her as cruel and ruthless, and Pheronia gained public favor and sympathy. The sisters stopped speaking, and Avalkyra refused to attend the dead queen's funeral.

While Avalkyra never admitted to the murder of her stepmother, she was the prime suspect. She fled into Pyra, avoiding her own trial, and began the process of separating the province from the empire. Treaties were signed, boundaries redrawn, and Pyra became its own country again. Pheronia had not been crowned in her absence, as she was still underage, but the council ruled the empire in her stead, earning her the nickname the Council's Queen.

Hearing Morra recount hers and Olanna's stories made Veronyka reconsider what she thought she knew about the Blood War. She'd always imagined Avalkyra Ashfire as a hero, going down in a blaze of glory, the war ending with her last breath. But war wasn't one or two big moments; it was dozens of smaller ones, enacted by people like Morra and Olanna who continued to fight even after their cause had lost. Suddenly Avalkyra Ashfire's shining flashes of greatness looked rash and foolish. Avalkyra hadn't just fled persecution when she'd set up in Pyra. She'd turned her back on the people of the empire, leaving thousands of her supporters, as well as innocent animages, behind. Thanks to her actions, many were condemned to bondage, imprisonment, even death, and it was left to people like Morra and Olanna to make things right.

There's more than one way to fight a war. There were fiery battles and court intrigues, but there were also daring rescues and selfless sacrifices.

Veronyka thought of the bondservant she'd seen outside her cabin all those weeks ago, the way his face had lit when he'd seen Xephyra, when he'd seen *her*—a fellow animage, living in freedom. She remembered what Commander Cassian had said about a new purpose for the Phoenix Riders, about creating a safe place for their people.

Before, Veronyka's visions of being a Phoenix Rider involved soaring through the air and raining arrows down on some fiery battlefield. Now that picture changed, shifted. She saw herself protecting wagons of animages, children, old folks, and everyone in between—people like her, lost and afraid and in need of a home. The idea made her skin tingle. That was a battle worth fighting.

Lost in thought, it took her a moment to notice Tristan's approach. His bow and quiver were slung over his shoulder, and his soft brown hair rippled in the evening breeze. Veronyka went to Wind, making sure he was properly saddled—which she'd already done at least three times.

Tristan ignored her once more, mounting up. While he was still stiff and unsmiling, he seemed less angry than he had been the previous night—or even earlier that morning—as if his temper had finally cooled.

With a nudge of his knees and a wordless command, he turned Wind around, called the pigeon to his shoulder and the dog to the horse's heels. As he readied his weapon and moved to the beginning of the course, the distant sound of pumping wings told her that Rex was on his way.

She waited for Tristan to begin, determined to avoid any further arguments. After several moments, however, she stepped forward. Why wasn't he starting the course? Was something wrong with him, or with Wind?

"Are you—" Veronyka began, coming up alongside him, but Tristan interrupted her.

"I'm sorry," he blurted, staring straight ahead.

"What?" Veronyka asked incredulously.

He sighed and looked down at her. "I said I'm sorry. It's not—none of this is your fault. *I* was wrong to raise the alarm when I saw you on the mountainside, and *I* was the one who screwed up the obstacle course. If I were you, I'd have done what you did. Or at least I hope I would have. So can we just . . . forget it?"

Veronyka was stunned into silence. Growing up with Val meant Veronyka was extremely unused to apologies. All she could manage was a nod.

Tristan nodded back, cleared his throat, and began the course. He started stiffly, but soon loosened into his usual confident performance.

Veronyka stuck a hand into her pocket. She'd woven her shorn braids and their attached trinkets into something resembling a bracelet and had taken to carrying it around like a talisman. She often fidgeted with it, and she did so now, her fingers running along the familiar beads as she studied Tristan from a distance.

Ever since they'd met, he'd been nothing but angry, mean, and arrogant. It was hard to believe this calm, apologetic version of him was the same person. Of course, he'd been under a lot of strain, and his description of the commander's behavior had reminded her all too much of Val. Clearly his father had wanted to teach Tristan a lesson, and Veronyka had been drawn into the mess.

Now not only was he apparently sorry for his previous behavior, but his entire energy and demeanor were different.

"Nyk?" he said hesitantly, his voice carrying from the far end of the course.

Veronyka jogged over. "Yes, Apprentice?" she said.

The words seemed to irk him. He scowled for a moment before clearing his throat. "You can call me Tristan," he said.

"Oh" was Veronyka's response. What was *with* him?

He sighed. "Can you—I'll need you to do that distraction thing again. With the stick?" he added.

She hesitated. Was this some kind of test? "You *want* me to distract the animals again?"

"If I'm going to do all this"—he gestured around the field—"*extra practice*, I might as well push myself. We both know I can do this course, but that's not the point. The point is to keep calm in the face of distraction, to be able to command a large group of animals without losing focus or control. You might have inadvertently made a fool of me before, but you *deliberately* made a fool of me last night. I don't like to be bested—whatever the contest."

Veronyka frowned. "I thought you wanted to forget all that?" she asked warily.

"This isn't a trick. I . . ." His expression turned even grimmer. "I'm not like my father. I don't *want* to be like my father. I'm not trying to embarrass you in return or to prove a point. I mean what I say."

Veronyka nodded, understanding him at last. He wasn't being manipulative; he was simply expressing himself—without ulterior motive. The day he'd found her, he'd been angry and frustrated, and his scowling face and argumentative words had told the story. Yesterday he had been humiliated, and so that was how he'd behaved, lashing out at her. Now he wanted to start over, so he had apologized and was inviting her help. He might be one of the most honest people she'd ever met.

It made her uneasy. She wondered how he'd feel if he knew she was a liar.

"Okay," she said, peering around for a stick.

"There should be some in the bushes over there. Did you use your magic on the animals yesterday or just make the sound?"

"I didn't use my magic. All I did was distract them. . . ." Her voice trailed off, and she realized the thing she'd noticed about him, his change in energy. It wasn't just his attitude.

It was his magic.

Veronyka reached out to the animals, confirming her suspicion. His pressure, his hold on them . . . it was different from yesterday. The dog and the bird had a loose understanding of what was happening beyond what they remembered from doing the course before. Wind, too, was familiar with the exercise, but even so, the magic that told him to stand still and be calm wasn't a forceful push. . . . It was a request.

"Right," Tristan said, straightening in the saddle, oblivious to her revelation. "Do it whenever you want, and I'll try to keep them focused."

"Don't prepare them for it," Veronyka warned, tugging a branch from a tangle of weeds and walking backward to the target. "That's cheating."

She actually heard him chuckle. "Wouldn't dream of it."

There was a hurdle coming up where horse and rider had to weave through a series of staggered poles jutting from the ground, and Veronyka decided this was when she'd make her move. She waited until he was about to finish, then hit the target as hard as she could. The sound echoed loudly, and she turned to see what Tristan did next.

The horse's ears went flat, and the dog barked. Veronyka threw the stick into the air, and the dog leapt away from Wind—only to pause halfway across the clearing. Tristan was sweating, keeping Wind on course and the pigeon on his shoulder, and she could sense his pressure was increasing.

"Focus on the dog," Veronyka found herself calling, remaining as still as she could. "You already have the bird and the horse—trust them, and focus on the dog."

Tristan frowned, then gave her a small nod. His eyes closed. A heartbeat later the dog yipped and whirled around to rejoin him.

Tristan's eyes flew open, lips parted in surprise, and Veronyka cheered. Overhead, Rex let out a musical screech, and a trail of fire streaked out behind him. Tristan looked up, watching his phoenix's fiery arc across the sky, before looking back down at Veronyka.

He smiled at her, and the sight nearly knocked her off her feet. It transformed his usually haughty expression into something boyish and carefree. His cheeks dimpled on either side, and his brown eyes glittered with triumph. He looked like some mythical hero again, as he had the first time she'd seen him—except this time it was his smile that shattered the fanciful illusion, and not the fact that his drawn spear was leveled at her.

Veronyka swallowed, realizing that he had said something—and she hadn't heard a word.

"P-pardon me?" she said, still slightly dazed.

His smile twisted into a quizzical frown. "I said, I think I want to have another go—can you stay?"

Veronyka did a double take. He *wanted* her to stay with him? Was she no longer an annoying presence, a punishment laid down by his father? Did he actually value her help? Warmth spread from her chest all the way to her fingertips.

"Of course," she said.

He smiled gratefully, and the angry, mean boy from the days before was gone. Maybe that wasn't who he truly was. . . . Maybe she'd had him wrong all along.

As Veronyka expected, Tristan did even better the second time around. Though the dog still turned and darted toward the stick, he didn't move more than a few steps before Tristan got him back under control.

As they packed up, a cold wind whipped across the open field, and the lanterns atop the village gate swayed and guttered in the distance. Veronyka shivered, until a gust of warm wind enveloped her like a hug as Rex landed on the ground nearby.

Veronyka stared admiringly at the beautiful creature. His heat and his magic pulsed from him, leaving her both warm and covered in goose bumps. She couldn't believe she'd had a phoenix of her own, for however brief a time.

Veronyka closed her eyes. Xephyra's smoke-and-charcoal scent filled her nostrils, and her rustling feathers whispered in Veronyka's ear. It was as comforting as a caress, as painful as a freshly opened wound.

She clenched her jaw and reinforced her walls, burying both the good and the bad.

If Veronyka had come here with her bondmate, she could be an apprentice, like Tristan. Not a servant. Not a boy.

She could be herself.

"You can pet him, if you like," Tristan offered with a slight frown, as if he were trying to puzzle out her bizarre expression.

Veronyka hesitated, thinking about her future among the Riders. Could she really bond anew, with Xephyra still living in her heart? Could she still love the same way?

But as her gaze lit on Rex, some of the pain and anxiety disappeared from her mind—like the night's last shadows banished by the sun.

She rested a hand on the phoenix's neck. Rex stood tall and proud, his feathers almost hot to the touch, and softer than she'd have expected since he was full grown. While Veronyka could speak into the mind of any animal she chose, phoenixes were the only ones that had the ability to block that access—thanks to their own magic. But after a moment Rex opened himself to her, slowly and deliberately, like a flower beginning to bloom.

Veronyka's fears all but evaporated. Yes, she could move forward. Xephyra would always be with her, and bonding with one of her brothers or sisters wouldn't be a betrayal. Taking them into her heart would be like honoring Xephyra's memory, not abandoning it.

Focusing on Rex, she marveled at his calm, self-assured nature. He was clearly the stable counterbalance to Tristan's easy frustration, but the longer she remained connected to him, the more she understood that while he often calmed his bondmate, he was capable of peaks and valleys of his own. He had arrogance and a powerful temper, but humor as well.

Tristan watched them closely, and she wondered what he could sense of their interaction through his bondmate—if anything. The lines between shadow magic and regular animal magic were often difficult to discern, and mysterious at the best of times.

Coming to stand next to her, Tristan ran his hand along Rex's neck.

"You're going to make me say it, aren't you?" he said, eyes on the scarlet feathers underneath his fingers, and not on her face.

"Say what?" Veronyka asked.

"You were right," he said, dropping his hand and looking down at her. He sighed heavily, as if it pained him deeply to admit it. "I've been thinking about it all day, and when I tried it, just now . . . You were right about the animals, about the way we control them."

Veronyka smiled, patting Rex once more before repacking their water-skins into Wind's saddlebag.

Tristan crossed his arms over his chest. His face was almost impossible to see in the darkness.

"You're enjoying this, aren't you?" he asked.

Her smile grew wider before she forced it down and turned to face him. "Only a little."

He laughed, the sound as soft as a whisper across her skin. "Were your family Riders, then?" he asked, slinging his bow and arrows over his shoulder as they continued to pack up. "You seem to know a lot about animal magic."

"I learned it all from my grandmother, who was a Phoenix Rider. My parents were, too, but I don't remember them."

They were walking toward the village now, the soft thump of the horse's hooves and the steady pant of the dog at their feet almost lost in the swish of the grass in the evening breeze. Rex soared overhead, his warm glow like the last dregs of daylight on Veronyka's upturned face.

"You'd be a good Rider," Tristan said.

Veronyka's head jerked around. "What?"

Tristan glanced at her and shrugged. "You would."

Veronyka's chest was suddenly tight. "But your father—the commander—said you're not recruiting."

"Is that all he said?"

Veronyka frowned. What did that mean? "Well, he also said that train-ing costs money . . . that he couldn't have poor peasant lads bonding with phoenixes but then unable to afford proper training."

Tristan sighed. "It's one of the first things I'd change if it were up to me."

"What is?" Veronyka asked, her racing thoughts causing her to lose track of the conversation.

"You shouldn't have to be rich, or sponsored, to be a Rider. Plus, we should let girls join. It would double our numbers right out the gate."

Veronyka fought to keep her face neutral, though his words caused a tingle of heat to creep up her cheeks. "I don't understand the rule against girls to begin with," she said in what she hoped was an offhand voice.

Tristan shrugged. "It was practicality at first. When we began recruiting—well, it was expensive, starting up. So precedence was given to those who already had an egg, or who had the funds to purchase one of the few we had on hand. They also needed to be able to afford the food and supplies they'd need for training, and of course, any extra funding to help us rebuild the facilities was welcome. Latham—Loran's brother," he added, as Loran was one of the stablehands she worked with every day. Veronyka hadn't known he was related to an apprentice—surely when the time came to recruit and gain sponsorship, Loran would have no trouble getting in. "Their mother paid for the renovations to the practice yard, and Fallon's family supplied our first horses. The commander was also interested in those with existing combat training or weapons skills—that way we weren't starting at zero—and most who met those qualifications happened to be boys."

"Most, but not all?"

"Well, you know Elliot?" Tristan asked, and Veronyka nodded. "Both he and his sister wanted to join. They had the money, too. But we only had one egg available, so the commander decided to just admit him."

"Was he better?" Veronyka demanded, unable to keep the scathing note from her voice.

"He was the older of the two," Tristan said. "And seemed more eager, but he was pretty devastated when his sister was rejected. I guess it was easier to have no girls than one girl. . . ."

Veronyka seethed, but she didn't say anything. The commander's reasoning was flimsy. And yes, maybe the one girl Rider would have had to sleep with the female servants in their barracks, but was that really such an inconvenience? Even in the days of the empire, the Phoenix Riders had always mimicked the natural social structure of wild phoenixes, flying in smaller groups that were responsible for defending a given territory, and mated pairs were kept together. Older, solitary phoenixes often remained in the mating grounds and training complexes, helping to care for the hatchlings and tend the young. The gender divide wasn't something they practiced or acknowledged—patrols trained, slept, and ate together, whatever their sex.

Valley logic, Val would call it. The mountain-born Pyraeans had been the only matriarchal monarchy in the region, and their laws and customs were hard for some of the men of the valley kingdoms to swallow.

"But we'll have to change eventually," he continued. "We could make do without a horse for every Rider. We could modify old saddles and tack and start using obsidian arrowheads and spear points, which are cheaper than steel. Some time, sooner or later, the empire will learn that we've regrouped, and they'll come for us."

"And he just plans to sit here and wait for them? What's the point of being tucked away up here when our people are in bondage in the valley?"

"You're right," he said heavily, a note of frustration in his voice. "But two Rider patrols and ten apprentices don't make an army. We need to grow our numbers first, give the apprentices time to develop their skills. If we showed our faces in the empire now, we'd be slaughtered, and do more damage than good. Even still," he said, seeing Veronyka open her mouth to interject, "I've been pushing to become a Master Rider . . . ideally, the next patrol leader. That way we can graduate some of the older boys and make a third patrol. Hopefully after that we can open up recruitment and take on more apprentices."

Veronyka's blood was like lightning in her veins. "Will he listen to you? How many new recruits could you take on?"

Something in Tristan's gaze flickered, and Veronyka sensed hesitation when he replied. "It's—I don't know. We probably shouldn't be talking about this."

"You're the one who said—"

"I know what I said. But I'm just an apprentice. It's not my place to talk about or criticize the commander's protocols."

They walked on in silence for several moments. Veronyka chewed her lip.

Tristan wanted to change things here, to allow boys and girls, even the poor ones, to join. That sounded like the Phoenix Riders Veronyka had grown up on, the kind of Phoenix Riders she wanted to be a part of.

"Why haven't you become one yet?" Veronyka asked, breaking the silence. "A Master Rider or a patrol leader?"

Tristan laughed without humor. "The commander doesn't think I'm ready."

Veronyka thought about this. They'd have to *show* him that Tristan was ready. Maybe if they really pushed hard during these evening exercises, she could help him achieve his goal. And her goal too. She was still poor, but maybe as a patrol leader, Tristan could have more say in who they recruited and who was sponsored.

Veronyka knew it was a long shot, but if they were going to be doing all this extra training anyway . . . wasn't it worth trying?

"How long do you think the commander wants us to work together?" she asked, an idea forming in the back of her mind. They'd arrived at the stables, Veronyka opening the gate to guide Wind back inside, while Tristan undid the latch to the fenced area where the dogs slept.

Closing it behind the hound, he followed her into the stables, a frown on his face. "I don't know. Probably until his next inspection. He attends our lessons once a month, so maybe by his next visit he'll decide if I've been sufficiently *punished*," he said, smirking slightly at the last word, as if the idea was laughable now. It made her smile too. "Why?"

As Veronyka removed Wind's saddle and placed it on the rack, Tristan picked up a brush and started grooming the animal. He seemed to do it absently, as if helping her with her chores wasn't something he had to think about.

"No reason," she said, removing Wind's bridle. Tristan continued to frown at her, so she shrugged as she said, "It'll be a good opportunity, that's all."

Tristan stopped brushing to stare at her over the animal's back. "Opportunity for what?"

"To prove him wrong."

When Pyraean Queen Elysia (9 BE–37 AE) set her sights on expanding into the valley, she knew that alliances, not conquests, were the best way to protect her people and their future. With four royal sisters eligible for marriage, as well as herself, she intended to secure such treaties through wedlock.

The "Five Brides" have often been credited as crucial to the founding of the empire, for it was through these matches that they were able to unify many of the lesser kingdoms in a peaceful fashion. Hence Queen Elysia became known as the Peacemaker.

While her sisters married for duty and for position in this new world, it is said that Elysia herself married for love. When she and her sisters flew to Ferro to undergo peace negotiations with King Damian, they discovered that he was under attack by the neighboring Stellan kingdom of Rolland.

They traveled with haste to the battlefield, where King Damian and King Rol were locked in combat. When Queen Elysia landed among them, her four sisters beside her, the battle ground to a halt—none in the valley had ever seen such a sight as flaming firebirds with fierce, beautiful women astride them, descending like fallen stars.

As the soldiers on either side began to scatter, Queen Elysia faced the two kings. King Damian bowed at the sight of her, showing the respect that was her due. King Rol, on the other hand, took advantage of the moment of distraction and stabbed King Damian in the back. Before he could finish the job, Queen Elysia lunged forward, blocking his blade with her obsidian dagger. When Rol tried to run, the youngest of the sisters, Princess Darya, put an arrow in his chest. Though there would be decades of strife between the Stellan kings and Pyraean queens, many trace their enmity back to this solitary event in history.

As King Damian stood face-to-face with Queen Elysia, it was clear that he saw more than just a fiery warrior queen—he saw his future bride.

—"The Reign of Queen Elysia the Peacemaker," from *The Early Years of the Golden Empire* by Winry, High Priestess of Mori, published 79 AE

It is a fact of life that
one must kill or be killed.
Rule or be ruled. Win or lose.

- CHAPTER 20 -
SEV

FOR SEV'S PART IN the llama's death, he was given a week of latrine duty. The disparity in the punishments between him and Kade was enough to ensure that whatever anger Kade held toward him before his botched escape, it would now be tenfold. Word had also traveled along the convoy, blaming Sev for the delay and the extra-hard afternoon's march, and so curses and mutters followed him wherever he went, coming from servants and soldiers alike.

One benefit of marching until midnight was that Trix didn't confront him until the following evening.

Sev was hunched over and sweating as he dug the latrine, the activity a convenient outlet for his pent-up frustration. The steady *thump* and scrape of the shovel hitting the packed earth drowned out all his thoughts. It was almost peaceful.

"Drop that shovel this instant before I club you over the head with it."

Sev grimaced. He'd known this moment would come, but he'd been dreading it all the same. Slowly he turned to find Trix standing behind him, eyes sparking dangerously. Kade was there as well, looming like a wide, intimidating shadow.

"I . . . ," Sev began, but he didn't have any words lined up.

"The shovel," Trix barked. "Or maybe I'll drive it straight up your backside instead."

Sev released his grip on the spade, which fell into the dirt with a *thud*. The latrine was mostly finished anyway.

"Good. Now walk."

Sev had the uncomfortable feeling that he was being marched to the edges of the campsite so that he could be killed quickly and silently. He assured himself that was ridiculous, but with every step he took, Trix's rage seemed to grow, filling the air around them with the crackling intensity of a coming storm.

"Look, Trix, I—"

"No, you don't get to talk," she snapped, coming to a halt at last and turning to face him. Sev had never seen her upset before. She was always sarcastic and dark humored, but never truly angry or out of control. "For once you'll *listen*. Never have I encountered such a ridiculous, stubborn, *thick-skulled—*"

"Enough," Kade interrupted, and both Sev and Trix whipped their heads around in shock.

Sev couldn't help but gape: *Kade* was standing up for *him*—and against Trix? He was almost giddy with gratitude.

Kade looked between them, from the astounded expression on Sev's face to Trix's similar wide-eyed stare. He cleared his throat. "He came back, didn't he?"

Trix shook her head, as if trying to dispel a cloud of mosquitoes. She turned to Sev again; while her voice was quieter, her temper had not yet subsided. "Do you have any idea what you've done? You almost ruined everything."

"Of course I don't!" Sev said, his tone bordering on shrill. They stood in a dense copse of trees, the heavy branches muffling the sounds of their conversation. Still, he cleared his throat as he added quietly, "You don't tell me anything."

"I wonder why," Trix sneered. "You've had a foot out the door the whole time."

"The only reason my foot is *in* the door at all is because you black-mailed me, you sneaky, conniving witch."

Silence.

Sev worried he'd gone too far, that Trix might decide to do away with him after all.

Instead she burst into raucous, cackling laughter.

Sev allowed himself a small, cautious smile—and was shocked to see Kade returning it.

"I hoped you might have a backbone in there somewhere . . . ," Trix murmured, wiping at the tears of mirth that wet her eyes. Then she became severe once more. "But what you did was beyond foolish. Didn't I already catch you trying a ridiculous escape once before? Did you really think you could slip through *my* grasp so easily, never mind the empire's?"

Sev clenched his fists, but he didn't argue with her.

"Well . . ." She sighed, the rest of her anger seemingly spent. "You were right, of course."

Sev frowned—he was *right* about something?

She crooked him a regretful grin. "It was a mistake to get you involved, to try to coerce loyalty out of you. I thought you might want to fight for our people, like your parents did, but I accept that I was wrong."

"My parents . . . ," Sev repeated, all humor gone from him. "What do you know about my parents?"

She stepped forward, the dappled moonlight filtering through the trees playing across her wrinkled face. "I know more than you could possibly imagine, Sevro, son of Alys and Sevono."

Their names, unspoken for so long, echoed inside Sev's head.

"How?" he asked, his throat tight. "How do you know who my parents were?"

"It's been my business to know things for a very long time, boy. I had reason to keep tabs on loyal servants of Avalkyra Ashfire and the animage cause, even in the years after the war. Your parents were the final line of defense in the Foothills, and though they did not bear a noble name or boast a great Phoenix Rider lineage, they earned a title of their own, after their deaths. Among the Hillsbridge survivors, they were toasted as Alys and Sevono Lastlight. When their glorious flames were extinguished that day, many saw it as the true end of the Phoenix Riders. And yet even in their dying moments, they saved lives. Three hundred and sixty-seven by my count, including hundreds of animages and their families. A snuffed candle will cast light until its last breath—and so too did your parents."

"Stop," Sev choked out, unable to bear it anymore. "Just stop it."

"It troubles you, to hear tell of your family's heroic deeds? I thought you'd died that day, as did most people, but then you turned up on Captain Belden's roster. As I said, Sev is a unique name . . . and you look just like them, you know."

"Enough! I don't—"

"They are shining war heroes, and yet you skulk around as if they shame you."

"*I* shame *them*," Sev gasped, his heart hammering so painfully that he thought his chest might explode. "They died because of me."

Trix was silent at last, but Sev could feel her stare as he gathered himself, breath shuddering into his lungs. He couldn't bear to look at Kade, to endure his judgment, so he stared at the ground when he spoke.

"We had time to escape! They told me to run if anything ever happened, and . . . I saw the soldiers coming and thought I could reach the drawbridge in time. But I didn't get there fast enough, and they had to come and save me. They died because I wanted to be a hero like them."

"They died so you could live, Sevro," Trix said, not unkindly. "It was a most precious gift. Now it's up to you what you wish to do with it."

He shook his head. "I'm not like them."

"No," Trix agreed. "You are something else."

Sev looked up. He'd had the exact same thought about himself, but Trix didn't say the words with derision or disdain. She said them with admiration.

"I've been watching you for weeks, you know. Long before our little arrangement and long before you started watching me."

"Because of my parents?" Sev asked.

"Because information is power—but you know that, don't you, boy?"

"What do you mean?" Sev asked, unnerved by the cunning glint in her eye.

"What did I tell you? I've been watching you, Sevro, and I know you're a hoarder of information—just like me. You know every soldier's name and where he likes to sleep. Every night before bed, you wander the campsite with your bedroll as if looking for a perfect spot—but you never look at the ground; you look at the soldiers' faces. You've been studying the work roster, too, lingering just a few minutes longer than necessary every time you check your assignment, so you know where people will be and when. Smart stuff . . . *subtle* stuff. That's what I was interested in."

Both Trix and Kade were staring at him, and heat crept up Sev's face. It was true; he did collect information, often as a means of feeling comfortable in a new place. It had also helped keep Sev alive, from his time in the orphanage to his years on the streets, and now, as a soldier.

Though it seemed she meant the words as praise, something in her tone felt dismissive—regretful—and Sev didn't know what that meant.

"Was?" he repeated after picking through her words. "You're not interested anymore?"

Trix tilted her head at him. "I tire of trying to convince you, Sevro. Go on, back to your old life. Sign up for vanguard or rear guard or Captain Belden's personal footstool for all I care. Your debt to me is paid."

"I didn't do anything," Sev argued.

"Technically speaking, you *undid* months of careful planning. Thanks to yesterday's antics, we'll have to regroup. Still, I no longer require your services."

"Thya," Kade whispered under his breath, casting a glance at Sev. "The *packs*. There's no way anyone else will be able to memorize them in time."

"Memorize the packs?" Sev asked. Trix had started moving again, and Sev followed close behind. "You mean the soldiers' personal packs?"

While most soldiers didn't have much by way of possessions, each had their own pack that they stocked with food, water, liquor, and personal items—endless talismans for luck, love, or swift journeys, plus letters from family back home. The soldiers had to be ready at a moment's notice to go on patrols, take watch duty during the evening meal, or go on scouting missions, and whenever they did, their personal packs went with them. When they weren't in use, they were stored with the rest of the supplies and carried by the llamas.

"Yes," Trix said over her shoulder, still striding away from him. Sev tried to listen as she spoke in an undertone to Kade. "We could focus on the water supply, though there's still the question of *who* will. . . ."

As their voices dropped out of earshot, Sev slowed his pace. His limbs were tingling, his breath oddly shallow. After the events of the previous day, he'd been expecting a variety of grim outcomes, one of which ended with Trix choking the life from him while he slept. But this? To have her release him from their agreement just like that? He should be relieved. He'd no longer have to face Kade every day or try to unravel Trix's complicated motivations.

It would be like none of this had happened, and Sev could walk away unscathed . . . at least, for now. What was that she'd said about the water supply?

Then it hit him. "You're gonna poison them," he called to Trix's retreating back.

She turned, gaze flicking to Kade before settling on Sev. "Am I?" she asked mildly. "But I'm in charge of the messenger pigeons. How would I manage something like that?"

"*He* was gonna do it," Sev said, taking a step toward them and pointing at Kade. "Only now he can't, thanks to me. And the personal packs . . ." Sev paused, his mind picking through all that had been said and all he'd gleaned on his own. "You don't want to spoil all the supplies—you'll need some, when all this is over—so you wanted me to help identify them. Help keep track of which bags belong to which soldiers."

That still didn't explain everything. Whose packs would they choose to poison? Did Trix have other allies among the soldiers? And what of Captain Belden? All his possessions were kept separate from the rest of the regiment.

"This is no longer your concern, soldier," Trix said. "Remember? Don't worry. I don't forget my friends, and we *are* friends, aren't we, boy? I'll ensure you make your escape when the time comes, and you won't be one of my targets—but you'd best stay out of my way."

Trix made to walk away, but Sev grabbed her arm. "If the soldiers get sick all of a sudden, who d'you think will take the blame? Those who make their meals, those who handle the food supplies. You'll be putting all the bondservants' lives at risk."

"You're right. If the soldiers get *sick*, we don't stand a chance."

Sev stopped short, releasing her, and she continued to march on. After a stunned moment he caught up. "You mean to kill them all."

She turned back around to face him, her expression utterly remorseless when she said, "Dead men tell no tales—and point no fingers."

"But you work with the messenger pigeons, like you said. Why not send a message to the Riders right now and avoid—"

"Avoid what, boy? Death? What do you think would happen if the Riders knew there were empire soldiers making straight for them? Whether it's us dealing it or them, there will be bloodshed on this mountain, make no mistake. As for the messenger pigeons," she continued, her acid tone turning to one of worn frustration, "don't think it didn't cross my mind. But these are no proper messenger pigeons. They've been 'simpled'—trained in a very specific way for a very specific purpose. They can travel only to and from the same starting and end points within the same range, no deviations, no longer distances. They can't break loose and follow unique orders. Too much magical influence."

"And the wild animals have too little," Kade added, his voice subdued. "It requires a good amount of training for an effective message carrier. Wild animals would only obey an animage's orders for as long as their magic remained connected to them. . . . Eventually they'd become distracted or lose focus."

"I had a pair of real messenger birds during the war," Trix said, her tone wistful. "They could fly from Aura Nova into Pyra in two days. Nefyra and Callysta, I called them. What I wouldn't give for another pair such as them."

"This is what you wanted, isn't it?" Kade asked Sev, after several moments of silence. There was no aggression in Kade's tone, just curiosity.

"What is?" Sev asked, mind still on Trix's plans.

"A way out of this arrangement," he said. Though Sev could hardly see in the darkness, there was something like disappointment in Kade's crossed arms and downcast face. "Now you have it."

"You're free of us," added Trix. She smiled, patted him on the arm, and left, Kade following soon after.

Yes, this *was* what Sev wanted. He wanted to get away from the war and everything it stood for. But as he watched Kade's and Trix's retreating backs, he realized that he *didn't* want to get away from *them*.

You're free of us.

The words rang in Sev's mind, but it was one word in particular that he couldn't shake. *Us.*

It was powerful, loaded with meaning. "Us" was about community and commonality—animages, bondservants, allies, friends. Sev hadn't had an "us" in a very long time. When he was young, he'd belonged to his family. That was the last time he'd truly felt a part of anything. Now he was a soldier, but he'd never fit in. And before that he'd been one of dozens of orphans, always coming and going from the shelters. There was no friendship in that life, and it was the same on the streets, each of them out for themselves, scraping and clawing to survive.

Sev had thought being alone made him stronger, gave him fewer vulnerabilities.

But there was strength in "us," power in the unity of brother and sister. *This* was what his parents had fought for. Not for themselves, not to be heroes . . . They'd fought for animages.

They fought for us.

Was Sev going to sit back and be a soldier, complacent among his ene-mies, or was he going to stand and fight with his people?

"Wait."

Kade and Trix stopped, though they didn't turn around.

"I'll do it."

At that, Trix looked over her shoulder and grinned.

But victory does not come
without consequences.

- CHAPTER 21 -

VERONYKA

THEY TRAINED HARD OVER the following days. Tristan had his own motivation to want to succeed, and Veronyka knew she helped him *and* herself by pushing him as hard as she could. If he could prove to his father that he was ready to lead a patrol, it would get her one step closer to possibly being an apprentice. Of course, even if Tristan and the older apprentices were promoted, there was no guarantee Veronyka would be chosen as one of the recruits—or that she could convince someone to sponsor her.

One thing at a time.

As each day passed, Tristan's skills grew stronger. He'd begun to trust her advice, and the animals trusted him in turn. Veronyka's attempts at distraction were almost fruitless, so she moved on to quizzing him the way the commander had about what Rex saw from above.

"How many steps on the stairs that lead up from the way station?" Veronyka asked, struggling to find new questions after he'd answered several already.

"Two hundred and twenty-one," Tristan said instantly, clearly not conferring with his phoenix before answering. "I've counted them. Try asking me something I *don't* already know," he said with a theatrical yawn.

"How many lanterns line the—"

"Forty-five."

Veronyka scowled. Tristan's laugh echoed to her from across the course.

"Fine," she said, looking around, trying to find something to stump him. Seeing an extra quiver on the ground, she slid the arrows out and whirled around, hands behind her back. "How many arrows am I holding?"

Tristan rolled his eyes and looked over at her, spotting the empty quiver. "Fifteen. I know how many extra arrows I brought with me."

Overhead, Rex released a sharp caw. Tristan frowned, then looked more closely at her.

"Wrong," Veronyka said with a wide grin, but of course Tristan already knew that, thanks to Rex. "You're not doing the exercise properly. Tell me what Rex said."

"Sixteen," Tristan said, "But I only brought fifteen per quiver, and the rest are—ah, the target." He looked over her shoulder, where the target lay bare. Veronyka had removed the arrow he'd imbedded earlier, which had come from the quiver he wore on his back. "All right, you've made your point. I shouldn't assume."

"Or get cocky when you get a few right," she said, walking toward him and waving an arrow in his face. "Come on, let's go again."

During the next run-through, Tristan announced that he wanted to do the full exercise—including the fiery finish.

Veronyka didn't think anything of it, certain he'd have no trouble pulling it off after performing so well up until now, but as he progressed through the course, she sensed a definite tension in him growing with every step Wind took.

By the time he reached the last obstacle, sweat dripped down his temples, and his chest was rising and falling in erratic, rapid bursts. Wind's ears were twitching in agitation, Rex was flying faster, and the dog's tail was tucked between his legs.

Veronyka hesitated. Tristan was projecting his thoughts; she'd only have to open a crack in her defenses, and she'd know exactly what was bothering him.

"Are you okay?" she asked instead, clamping down on the urge to use her shadow magic, no matter how innocent her intentions. If he wanted to tell her his problem, he would.

He was frozen at the end of the course, as if waiting for Rex's descent—only the phoenix was still circling above, making no move to dive or ignite.

"Tristan," she said, coming to stand next to him. He was staring straight forward, his jaw clenched. Apparently he hadn't heard her the first time. "Hey—are you okay?"

He started, twisting in the saddle, and they locked gazes.

One way to strengthen a magical connection was to make eye contact, and Veronyka hadn't been prepared to defend against it. In one blinding flash of insight, she understood. She looked away, severing the momentary link.

Tristan was afraid of fire.

It was so surprising, she hardly believed it, and yet it explained why the course had gone so badly for him that first day—and only at the end, when Rex ignited. And now that she thought about it, she remembered sensing a surge of fear from his direction when Maximian burst into flame. Surely it wasn't impossible for a Phoenix Rider to be afraid of fire, especially when they weren't bonding as young children, like they had in the old days.

"Let's just call it quits for now," Veronyka offered, unnerved by his wide-eyed, tense silence. "It's been a long day."

Wordlessly she called Tristan's other animals—the hound and the pigeon—and packed up the supplies, trying to cover the silence.

"I . . . ," Tristan began, still seated on Wind in the same place he had been before. His head drooped shamefully. "I can't do it."

"You're tired," Veronyka said, forcing nonchalance into her voice. "Next time . . ."

"No—you don't understand," he said, and when he lifted his head, moisture glistened on his bottom eyelids. He stared at the sky, at Rex still soaring above, and choked out a strangled laugh. "I'm a Phoenix Rider who's afraid of fire."

When he'd collected himself enough to look back down at her, his expression was wary, as if he expected her to laugh or belittle him.

Instead she came to a stop next to him, patting Wind's neck, and shrugged.

"Bellonya the Brave lost her dominant arm as a child and had to relearn her fighting skills with her other hand. She became the fiercest spear thrower in history. King Worrid was deaf, so he designed a special saddle to allow him to fly without losing his balance. He also set up the Morian Archives, making sure the empire's histories were recorded by the priests and acolytes of Mori and not just passed on verbally."

Tristan frowned at her. "What's your point?"

"My point is that you have a condition, and now you have to deal with it," she said, realizing with chagrin that her gender was her own "condition" to overcome.

"I can't just *deal* with it. I'm a Phoenix Rider—fire comes with the territory. It's not like I can coat myself in *pyraflora* resin and carry on with my day."

He dismounted in a huff, and Veronyka actually smiled at the mental picture of him covered head to toe in sticky fireproof sap. She tried to fight it back, but luckily, when he caught sight of her over his shoulder, he smiled too.

A moment later, he sighed. "This is serious, Nyk."

"I know it is," she said. "But maybe you're thinking about it the wrong way."

"What do you mean?"

"Well, the problem isn't out here." She gestured to the world around them. She hesitated, then took a step toward him. "It's in here," she said softly, tapping his temple, his hair dark and curled with sweat. The touch sent a lightning bolt of awareness through her, and her entire body lit up as if her nerves were on fire. She'd never touched him before and was shocked at how *intimate* it felt—her fingers against his warm skin, their faces mere inches apart. . . .

She yanked her hand back, and he watched her sudden movement with wide eyes.

"I could try swallowing *pyraflora* sap instead?" he asked, his voice slightly breathless.

Veronyka forced a smile, avoiding his gaze and trying to shake the tingling feeling that was still crackling through her body. She was conscious of him now in a way she hadn't been before, how the breaths moved in and out of his chest and the way the sweat from his skin left her fingertip damp. She rubbed her hand against her leg and stepped back from him, trying to focus on their conversation.

"I have this thing I do when I don't want to think about something," she said as memories of Xephyra flickered before her eyes. "It's a way of keeping bad thoughts and feelings locked up inside my mind. Maybe you could do the same thing but put your fear there instead."

"Locked up?" he asked, frowning.

"Yeah. I call it my mental safe house," she said, explaining the method she'd used to bury her grief for Xephyra and to pass her interrogation with Morra. She steered clear of mentioning shadow magic and just focused on how she visualized her stone wall, how she put whatever she didn't want to think about inside and carefully stacked protective stones all around it. "I know it's sort of silly," she said as they moved to pack the rest of the supplies, "but it works for me. This way, whatever you don't want to think about isn't running rampant in your mind—it's trapped, cut off from everything, even yourself."

Tristan was nodding thoughtfully. She'd thought he'd scoff at the idea, but it seemed he was willing to try anything.

"It makes sense," he said. "I mean, we do it subconsciously all the time, don't we? Hiding from stuff we don't want to face or think about. But doing it on purpose . . ."

Veronyka nodded. "I hope it helps."

"Thanks," he said, expression earnest. "I . . . No one else knows," he blurted.

Veronyka gaped for a moment, taken aback—but pleased—that he'd trusted her. She tried not to let her surprise show and smiled reassuringly. "And they won't."

Some tension released in his shoulders, and he smiled back. "Where did you learn all that?" he asked, waving back to where they'd been standing when she'd described her mental safe house.

"I sort of came up with it on my own, I guess." She thought of Val, constantly berating her for projecting her emotions, and supposed her sister deserved some of the credit—or blame.

It had been strange without her, these past weeks. Veronyka was capable of taking care of herself—she'd known that all along—but it had meant something to prove it to herself. To prove it to Val . . . even though her sister wasn't here to see it.

"I had some trouble with magical control," she continued, "so, locking away certain feelings and emotions helped me find balance."

Val had been a hard teacher, but Veronyka had to admit that she'd learned from her and the cautionary stories she'd told.

"I heard that in the Last Battle, half the animals in Aura Nova went mad," Veronyka said softly as Tristan took a swig from the waterskin. The Last Battle was Avalkyra Ashfire's final stand, when she sent all of her troops to the capital city in an attempt to seize the Nest, the empire's royal palace and seat of power. "The Riders couldn't contain their magic, and their volatile emotions fell like rain from the sky. Horses broke through their stalls, cats clawed themselves bloody, and dogs ran down their masters."

Tristan finished his drink and trailed a hand absently along Wind's neck. "I wonder if it wasn't on purpose. . . ."

"What do you mean?" Veronyka asked, trying to clear the disturbing images from her mind. Ever since she'd heard the story, she'd dreamed of it from time to time, soaring over the carnage on phoenix-back. Her parents had died that night, and though Veronyka had no idea of the details or circumstances, she hated to think of the terror and bloodshed they'd had to endure in their last moments in this world.

"You have to admit, it's a potent siege tactic, turning half the occupants of the city against their human masters. It's like doubling your army."

Veronyka's stomach churned. "But . . . so many animals would die."

"Yes, they would. But humans died too, didn't they? And phoenixes?"

"But they *chose* to fight," Veronyka protested.

Tristan shrugged, his expression thoughtful when he said, "Maybe the animals did too." Veronyka frowned, and he gestured down at Wind. "Their devotion to the animages who feed and care for them is powerful. . . . If phoenixes have the desire to fight on behalf of the humans they love, why not other animals as well?"

Veronyka had never thought about it that way. What if the animals had joined in willingly? What if it wasn't a command or a pulse of anger that had drawn them into the fray, but love and loyalty of their own? Maybe the animals had fought to protect people like her parents. The idea warmed her heart and helped to banish the bloody images from her mind.

In the distance the hourly bell chimed, announcing the change in watch shift.

"Ten bells already. I'm sorry for keeping you so late," Tristan said, dismounting. "I should have sent you back in hours ago. Once the sun sets, the commander won't know I'm out here alone."

"It's okay," Veronyka said, and she meant it. Working with Tristan was the most fun she'd had since she'd arrived, especially now that they weren't fighting.

"What if I made it worth it for you?"

"What do you mean?" she asked.

Tristan paused as he put away his arrows, considering her. "Well, I can't promise I'll be made patrol leader—or that you'll become an apprentice when I do—but I can help you prepare. There's more to Riding than bonding with a phoenix. Combat, archery . . . You said yourself you didn't know any of it. I just thought . . . maybe I could help you, like you're helping me. What do you think?"

"I think . . . yes, of course," she said, stunned by his generosity.

Tristan beamed, all uncertainty gone. "Good," he said, sliding the last arrows into the quiver.

As they walked back to the village, Veronyka's good mood turned dark.

"How does sponsorship work?" she asked. That would be the final hurdle she'd have to face if they decided to recruit in the near future. She could practice all she wanted, but if she couldn't afford the supplies or convince a Rider to sponsor her . . .

Tristan's brow furrowed. "Well, usually a Rider recommends a friend or family member for recruitment and offers to cover the costs of training. If they show aptitude and pass some basic tests, then they're admitted."

"Oh," Veronyka said, her heart sinking. She had to have a sponsor in place before she would even be allowed to take the tests?

As they arrived at the stables, Tristan opened his mouth to say something when Elliot emerged, followed by a flutter of wings as a pigeon took to the sky out the rear window of the pigeon coop.

Elliot started at the sight of them. "Oh, Tristan," he said, looking between them with a strangely accusatory stare. "I was just sending an order for new leathers for Anders and Ronyn."

He paused, as if he were expecting Tristan's approval or permission.

"Oh, right." Tristan glanced at Veronyka. "We were just training."

Elliot made no move to smile or greet her. Veronyka glanced at Tristan, but whatever he'd been about to say when they arrived, it was clear he didn't intend to say it in front of Elliot.

Veronyka fought a pang of disappointment that their night was cut short so abruptly.

"I guess I'll see you later," she said to Tristan before grabbing Wind's reins and leading him inside.

Later, Veronyka tiptoed through the shadows of the courtyard.

The stronghold was deserted, save for the sentries posted atop the walls, and she avoided even their notice as she scurried toward the bathhouse.

She'd been too afraid to go up until this point and had taken to washing with a rag and a bucket of cold water from the well. But it had been more than a month since she'd first arrived, and she couldn't hide from it any longer.

The bathhouse was a low stone hut between the servant and apprentice barracks. There were two doors, one for men and one for women. Veronyka edged through the men's entrance and peeked inside.

The hut was filled with steam and burning incense—but no naked men, thank Axura. A fireplace burned in the wall that divided the bathhouse, heating both sides, while small oil lanterns hung from the ceiling. There were three round tubs sunk into the ground, each big enough to fit five or six people. Wisps of steam sat on the surface of the water, along with the pale, fragrant petals of the *sapona* plant.

Veronyka grabbed a towel from one of several woven baskets, then paused, listening for approaching footsteps. All was peaceful, save for the constant trill of crickets and frogs.

With a deep breath, Veronyka stripped naked, stumbling out of her dirty tunic and pants. She flung herself into the nearest tub, sloshing water onto the stone floor, washing as quickly as she could. She scrubbed furiously, watching the water fill with streaks of grime and foamy bubbles from the soaptree petals. The interior of the tub had a carved bench for soaking, and as she watched, the dirty water was sucked out a hole near the side, while fresh, clean water bubbled up from another hole in the ground. The water stayed warm as well, somehow heated or perhaps coming from a natural hot spring.

The water eased Veronyka's aching muscles and relaxed her breathing. She hadn't had a proper soak in a bathhouse since they'd lived in Aura Nova. And considering her secret, it could be some time before she'd be able to enjoy them with any frequency. Her true body was now a burden, and her secret to bear. She'd already had to steal scraps of linen for her monthly bleeding and to hide behind a dressing screen to bind her breasts every morning, causing the other servants to tease Nyk for his "shyness."

It would be a worthy sacrifice, though, if it gained her a place among the Riders. And with Tristan's offer to help her train . . . surely she'd be one of the best new candidates.

Veronyka blinked, realizing that she'd lost track of time.

Footsteps sounded from the courtyard beyond, growing steadily louder, and Veronyka's insides tensed. She leapt from the tub, splashing more water everywhere, and hastily dried herself off. She struggled frantically with the towel, only just managing to drape it around her shoulders like a cloak when the door swung open.

Tristan stood in the entryway, his face obscured by the mist and incense of the bathhouse.

"Nyk?" he said in surprise, letting the door swing shut behind him, the gust of air dispensing the cloud that surrounded him. "Why aren't you in bed?"

"I . . ." Veronyka's voice was so high, echoing in the domed hut, that it hurt her own ears. She cleared her throat and tugged the towel more tightly around herself. "Why aren't you?"

"Oh—I couldn't sleep," he said, walking over to the linen baskets. When he turned around again, he held out Veronyka's dirty, sweat-soaked tunic. She must have flung it there in her haste to undress.

Face burning, she took it from him with a nod of thanks.

"Are . . . are you cold?" Tristan asked, eyeing her curiously as she clutched her towel tightly to herself. The room was stiflingly hot, and people usually walked around naked inside bathhouses, not wrapped up like a caterpillar in a cocoon.

"I . . . yes," Veronyka stammered, as a single drop of sweat trailed down her temple.

Tristan nodded dubiously, then took a towel for himself, staring at the rolled-up cotton in his hands.

"What if I sponsored you?" he asked abruptly.

"What?" Veronyka said, hardly daring to believe her ears.

"I've been thinking. . . . I have some savings, and when the time comes, I could put your name forward, if you wan—"

"*Of course I want!*" Veronyka blurted, taking an unconscious step forward. "But . . . why would you give up your savings for me?"

He shrugged, as if determined to keep things light. "Sponsorship isn't all fun, you know. You'd have to run my errands, help me care for my weapons and armor, clean my rooms . . . all on top of your own training."

When he finally looked up again, he seemed surprised at the way Veronyka was gaping at him. But how could she not? He was offering up her dream on a silver platter and then apologizing that it wasn't gold.

She'd take her dream if it were served in a bucket.

"Tristan," she said with a breath, hands trembling as she adjusted her towel. "I don't know what to say."

"Say yes," he said, smiling hesitantly.

"Yes," she whispered.

He beamed, his dimples reappearing, and Veronyka bit her lip to fight her own stupid grin. A swell of happiness was rising in her chest. She was bewildered by his kindness and kept trying to figure out why he would put himself on the line for her. Then she remembered Sparrow. . . . Not everyone wanted repayment or needed a reason in order to help someone.

Still smiling, Tristan dropped his rolled-up towel next to the nearest pool. Then, to Veronyka's dismay, he began to peel off his tunic.

She gaped, her heart pumping as she realized what was about to happen. Not only was Tristan not leaving her alone to dress, but he was undressing himself. He obviously hadn't come to the bathhouse to talk; otherwise he wouldn't have been surprised to see her. Which meant he planned to stay awhile. To bathe. Naked.

This is normal, she kept telling herself, her cheeks hot. *Men and boys bathe together, just as girls do. No problem.*

But no matter how she tried to calm herself, Veronyka's eyes went wild, darting from Tristan's bare chest to the door, back to Tristan, and around the entire bathhouse. Where was she supposed to look? How was she supposed to get dressed with him here? There was no escape. There was nowhere to hide. When his fingers reached the strings on his pants, Veronyka felt lightheaded and stared resolutely at her feet, though she barely saw them. Her gaze wandered up again, as if dragged there by some uncontrollable force.

He wasn't standing naked before her, but had already immersed himself waist-deep in the pool. He'd walked in calmly, making barely a sound, rather than splashing in as she had. It was a relief to have some kind of barrier between them, even though the steaming water didn't entirely obscure the dark trace of hair that trailed down his muscled stomach and into the water below.

He submerged his head, and when he came back up, water streamed down his body. He smoothed his hair back and blinked at her. "You should get some sleep, Nyk."

Then he turned away, sinking onto the bench with his back facing her. He reclined and closed his eyes.

Veronyka sagged against the wall, her muscles trembling. She dressed at top speed, stumbling into her pants and fumbling far too long with the laces. She slipped out the door and ran to the barracks, determined never to have another bath again.

Day 5, Third Moon, 169, AE

Xe Onia,

I know you are angry with me, but we can't fall apart now. This is what they want. Don't you see that?

I have sent this with Nefyra, my best messenger pigeon. Your response will get to me in two days.

Please respond.

—Avalkyra

I was banished, chased from the very empire
my foremothers had built. Was I to give up then
and fade away into obscurity? Was I to fall
onto my knees and beg?

- CHAPTER 22 -
VERONYKA

TRISTAN'S PROMISED HELP WITH training began early the next
morning and continued doggedly over the following days.

Rather than taking her to the target range or teaching her combat moves with knife or spear, Tristan took her running. Veronyka was
severely disappointed, but he insisted that fitness and stamina were more
important.

And so every morning before dawn, they met in the courtyard. He
would lead her over the village walls and up tightly winding stairs to the
higher fortifications that enclosed the stronghold. He took her along narrow
tracks that ran all over the mountaintop, through bushes and long grasses,
and down the steep inclines of the cliffs that surrounded the plateau. Veronyka knew he slowed his pace for her, but it was still the most exhausting
thing she'd ever done.

Tristan was eternally patient, nudging her if her eyes began to droop
while they stretched and taking frequent breaks to "catch his breath" that
were obviously just for her.

Nearly a week into their new routine, Veronyka's sluggish start had
them returning a bit late for their regular duties. As they jogged through the
gate into the stronghold, the sun had already risen, limning the mountain

in gold, and the other apprentices were gathering in the training yard, preparing for their own early morning lesson.

They saw Tristan and waved him over, and Veronyka followed. Her lungs felt like they were on fire, and her legs were unsteady beneath her. Tristan, on the other hand, had a fine sheen of sweat on his face but appeared otherwise relaxed and at his leisure. Veronyka, gasping with her hands on her knees, hated him for it.

"Who's your shadow, Tristan?" asked Anders, separating from the rest of the apprentices. He had the cool, light-brown skin of Arboria North, and his dark hair curled around his rather large ears. His parents were part of an acting troupe, and Anders had certainly inherited their love of theater and entertainment, if not their talent; his less-than-stellar singing voice could often be heard from the apprentice barracks, the dining hall, or from high above as he and his phoenix soared by. Arborians were famous for their arts, and beyond music and theater, they made the best furniture and woodcarvings in the empire, as well as fine leatherwork. Anders had a pair of thick leather cuffs etched with songs, poetry, and family motifs, though he wore them only at dinner. The commander forbade any embellishments that didn't follow his strict apprentice uniform, which included matching practice tunics and armor on patrols, and hair that was kept neat and short and faces that were clean-shaven. Even in their prime, the Phoenix Riders employed a similar dress code for their apprentices, and only the Master Riders had earned the right to wear braids and whatever cultural or personal ornamentation they pleased.

"Oh, this is Nyk—he works in the stables," Tristan said.

"Since when do stablehands train with apprentices?" asked Latham. He looked a good deal like his brother, Loran, with the same fair skin, spun-gold hair, and dark-blue eyes common in the south where they were from.

"Since the commander said so," said Elliot helpfully, reminding everyone of Tristan's punishment, to which they'd all been witness.

"Ah, yes!" Anders said with his usual broad smile, shooting Tristan a mischievous look. "The commander's most recent disciplinary decree. Tell me, Nyk, have you gotten this poor apprentice up to scratch yet?"

Tristan just shook his head, a faint smile on his face as he stared at the ground. Veronyka wondered why he would take their joking without retaliating—he certainly had no problem arguing with her—when she realized his awkward place here. It was his father they were talking about, and his position of power over them put Tristan in a tough spot. He couldn't be a regular apprentice, because they would always see him as the commander's son, and yet he wasn't technically in a position of authority. No wonder he was so eager to be promoted, to have the lines more clearly drawn.

"He was already up to scratch without my help," Veronyka said stoutly, and Tristan flashed her a surprised, grateful look.

"Well, if they want to send servants over to help the apprentices, I'd be more than happy to let one of the washer girls whip me into shape," Latham said, grinning and waggling his eyebrows. "Or maybe one of Morra's kitchen maids . . ."

"Poor Latham, always pining for company. Almost as bad as Elliot here, going on and on about the girls back home," said Anders, slinging an arm around him.

"I'm not *pining*," Elliot protested, blushing as he shrugged Anders's arm off his shoulders. "And I don't go *on and on*—it's my *sister* I talk about, not—"

"Leave him alone," said Ronyn, sounding bored. He was one of the older apprentices and had clearly had his fill of Anders's and Latham's antics.

"Nyk here agrees, don't you?" Anders asked, tossing his arm around Veronyka instead. "You'd like to see more girls about, wouldn't you?"

"Of course," Veronyka said. The others laughed in delight, but she didn't mean it the way they meant it—she just wanted to see female Riders. She cast an exasperated glance at Tristan, but to her surprise, he avoided her gaze. His face seemed oddly flushed; was he embarrassed by her being there? Veronyka didn't mind the teasing—it was far less malicious than Val's constant jibes and sarcastic remarks—but it seemed that Tristan did. She felt the need to change the subject.

"What I meant," Veronyka said, copying Elliot and throwing Anders's arm off her, "is that there should be girl apprentices. For training."

"Well, there's something you and Elliot can agree on," Anders said, still smirking. "So, is that why you're here?"

Veronyka's heart skipped a beat. "What do you mean?"

Anders raised an eyebrow. "To train?"

"Oh—yes. Well, sort of. I . . ."

"I'm helping him get in shape for the next recruitment," Tristan said.

"What's the point?" said Ronyn.

"What do you mean?" Veronyka asked. She couldn't tell if his tone was negative or just disinterested like before.

His gaze flicked to Tristan and the others. "There, well—"

"We don't have any eggs," Anders cut in, the jovial attitude missing from his voice for the first time. "Haven't found any in months. You'd have a better shot laying one yourself than finding one here."

The tone of the group changed, the laughing and joking replaced by a somewhat strained silence. Veronyka was staring at Tristan, but he wouldn't look at her. He'd known this all along. Why hadn't he told her? Why had he pretended she had a chance—offering extra training and even promising to sponsor her—when he'd known there was no way it would actually happen? Maybe that *was* why he'd done it. . . . It was a debt he'd never have to repay.

When Beryk walked into the fenced area and called them to attention, Veronyka took the opportunity to slip away, past Tristan and out of the training yard.

It was still an hour until Veronyka would be expected to begin her duties for the day, but she went to the stables anyway. It was dark and quiet inside, and the presence of the animals soothed her. Veronyka's magic had grown strong in her time here, the way it had when she'd been with Xephyra. While being around phoenixes strengthened her powers, bonding with one had helped even more.

Before Xephyra, and before Veronyka's arrival at the Eyrie, she would have to see an animal in order to connect with them and communicate.

Now she was able to walk through the dusty room with her eyes closed and sense what horse was behind each door, which cats were slinking in the shadows, and if there were any doves or starlings perched up in the rafters. Birds and mammals were always easiest for her magic to find, reptiles and water creatures the most difficult. Apparently it had to do with the similarity in mind and behavior. The larger the differences between them—like habitat and diet—the more difficult to connect to.

Familiarity helped, too, so Veronyka was able to reach out to the animals inside the stable with the barest thought.

Finding Wind's stall in her mind, she opened her eyes and slipped inside. Taking a seat on the ground next to him, she patted him gently on the nose as he drifted back to sleep, swaying slightly to the steady rhythm of his breathing.

Helplessness was weighing her down, the sensation familiar after years of Val controlling her life. Now that Veronyka was free from that, she *hated* the idea of sliding backward into that same futility. After her time training with Tristan, she'd started to feel like she was on the right track, building toward her future, but now? It felt like she was right back where she'd started.

"Nyk?" came a hesitant voice from beyond the door.

Veronyka froze. She wasn't sure she wanted to be found, but her hiding place wasn't exactly foolproof. A minute later the door swung open, and Tristan stood there.

"How did you find me?" she asked ruefully.

"I saw you run toward the stables, and then I asked Wind," he said, glancing at Veronyka's stall mate, the corner of his mouth quirking. He patted Wind's hindquarters and sidled into the room, sinking down onto the ground next to her. He leaned against the wall and drew up his knees, resting his elbows on them.

Veronyka scowled at the horse, who blew a dignified puff of air out through his nostrils.

"Don't you have training right now?" she pressed.

Tristan shrugged. They sat in silence for a moment, then . . .

"Why didn't you tell me?" she blurted. "Why pretend like you could help me—all that stuff about extra training and sponsorship—when you knew it was never going to happen? Why lie? Did you feel sorry for me or something?"

Tristan dropped his knee and turned to face her. "No, it's not—it wasn't like that. And I didn't *lie*. I just didn't bother mentioning it because it's not *never*. It's just not right now."

"If you don't have any eggs—"

"We'll get some," Tristan said firmly.

Veronyka put her head in her hands. "I don't know what I'm doing here."

"You're helping me," Tristan said, forcing a smile. "You saw the mess I made during that first obstacle course. If you weren't there, things might have gone really bad for me . . . and Wind," he added, reaching up to pat the horse's wide, barrel chest.

Veronyka tried to smile too, but she just couldn't muster it.

"We need smart, talented people like you here," he continued. He was staring resolutely at the ground between them when he added, "*I* need you here."

Veronyka swallowed with difficulty, her throat tightening. The surge of happiness she felt at his words was quickly replaced by heavy guilt. He'd trusted her with his darkest secret, and yet she hadn't reciprocated. But how could she? Tristan hated liars—he'd said there was nothing worse. Sure, he might have skirted the truth about the eggs, but being Nyk every day, Veronyka was *living* a lie—it colored everything she did, every interaction she had. Veronyka didn't feel like a boy on the inside—she wasn't like some of the other children she'd known growing up who might be born as boys or girls but didn't feel like they fit that category, and so they dressed in a way that felt right to them. That was their truth, no matter what the world saw. But Veronyka wasn't *Nyk*; she was Veronyka. Nyk was a lie.

In some ways it would have been easier to tell Tristan the truth before he'd revealed something so personal about himself. Now that they were closer, her lies felt like a bigger betrayal—and the stakes for revealing them felt that much higher. She didn't want to lose what they had.

There was a look he gave her sometimes, a secret smile that made his eyes shine and his face flush with color. . . . Veronyka feared he would never look at her like that again, that even if he could accept her lies and forgive her for them, whatever it was that lay between them, as fragile as spun sugar, would shatter.

"I . . . I just don't know if it's enough. I *need* to be a Rider. Without that . . . ," she began, then faltered. How could she explain all that she'd lost? That her heart felt broken, empty, *wrong*, and that she feared the only thing that would make her whole again was another phoenix to fill the void?

"Something's missing?" Tristan offered. Veronyka stared at him, surprised at his apparent understanding. "I think that's how I feel about being a patrol leader. Like, if I can just *get there*, if I can *make* it happen, everything will fall into place. But it's a dangerous game to play . . . putting the key to your happiness in someone else's hands. Even when I was a kid, all I wanted was to have a phoenix—I thought that once I did, I'd be invincible." He grinned, straightening his legs and leaning his head back against the wall, his arms crossed over his chest. "But nothing is guaranteed in life. Rex could die, or my father could decide I'll never make a proper patrol leader—and then what? I can't be broken forever. I have to make my own happiness."

His words struck a chord deep inside Veronyka. She'd been looking outside herself for answers, for a way to bandage the wound she had inside. But maybe she had to heal herself before she could hope to find a phoenix that would want to bond with her. She didn't know if she'd ever fully recover from the loss of Xephyra, but she could start by trying to feel whole again, by trying to find happiness instead of constantly striving for things beyond her control.

And what had made her happiest since she'd lost Xephyra? Training with Tristan, being a part of things here—even as a lowly stablehand.

Veronyka stared at Tristan's profile, at his sharp jaw and strong shoulders. She had the sudden urge to touch him, to ground herself in this place, with him. She wanted to let everything else fall away and just be here, in this moment.

He glanced down at her, his eyelashes casting shadows on his cheek-bones. She felt inadequate next to him, short and scrawny, her eyes too big and her nose too small, while he was all muscle and long limbs, with his artfully tousled hair and dimpled smile.

"You make me happy," Veronyka said—and then was so shocked she'd said the words that she almost clapped a hand to her mouth. Instead more words burbled up from inside, trying to drown out the memory of the first ones. "I mean, training with you . . . helping you, and you helping me, has made me happy. And being near Rex—and the others—but mostly you and Rex, and . . ."

She squeezed her eyes shut, praying for one of Nox's deathmaidens to come carry her to the dark realms so she never had to face Tristan again.

"Me too."

Veronyka's eyes flew open. Tristan wasn't looking at her, but his throat bobbed with a dry swallow. "So . . . what do you think?"

"About what?" she asked in a daze. Wind's stall felt impossibly small all of a sudden, and the quiet of the stables pressed in on every side. All she had to do was extend her arm and she'd be touching Tristan, alone in this cool, dark place.

"Will you stay? Give it a chance?"

Before Veronyka could answer, the front gate creaked open, followed by the crunch of boot on straw.

The footsteps drew nearer, and then Wind's stall door burst open, revealing the commander standing in the doorway.

"Sir," Tristan said, leaping to his feet. Veronyka did as well, though she knew the damage was done. They were hiding away inside a shadowy stall, covered in bits of dirt and hay, and scrambling up from the ground as if they'd been caught doing something illicit.

Then she remembered that Tristan was supposed to be in lessons, and her anxiety spiked even higher.

The commander surveyed them closely, his gaze cool and precise, as if picking up on every minute detail. "You have lessons this morning, Apprentice."

"Yes, Commander Cassian. I was just—"

"Socializing?" He made it sound like a dirty word.

Veronyka kept her head bowed, her hands clasped tightly behind her back, unsure if she should jump in or let Tristan handle things.

"It's lucky I needed a quick word with Beryk, else I might never have known that you ducked out of your lesson and shirked your responsibility."

Tristan's lips twisted, as if "lucky" was the last word he'd use for this situation.

The commander leaned forward. "There is a time and place to fraternize with servants and stableboys, and the middle of your lessons is not it."

"I'm sorry, sir," Tristan said in appropriate chagrin. "Please, do let me know when and where that is."

Veronyka groaned internally and had to press her lips together to stop the grimace—or was that a smile?—that was trying to force its way through.

The commander stared at his son, nostrils flaring. "Clearly you are not taking your training seriously. Perhaps it's time for my inspection. I know it's a week early, but I'm quite eager to see how far you've come and if your extra lessons have taught you anything of value. I do hope you're prepared, Tristan. I'd hate for you to make a fool of yourself . . . again. I'll see you in one hour's time, Apprentice."

Veronyka's anxiety was like a wild animal burrowing inside her stomach as she stood next to the obstacle course with the rest of the stablehands.

It wasn't Tristan's abilities that had Veronyka's insides tied in knots—it was the commander's reaction she most feared. Even if Tristan executed the course flawlessly, it might not be enough. The commander was always hard on his son, but after he saw Tristan skip a lesson this morning—and assumed that Tristan wasn't taking his training seriously—Veronyka worried he'd be impossible to please.

Commander Cassian was just like her sister, and people like Val didn't do what was right for the sake of it. The commander was a shrewd man, but more than that, he was controlling. And for whatever reason, he didn't want

Tristan to be a patrol leader. Instead he used the possibility of that prize as a means to keep his son in line. No matter how well Tristan performed, the commander wouldn't give that up unless he absolutely had to, unless Tristan gave him no other choice. But could they push the commander to that decision?

When he called the apprentices to attention, Veronyka noticed commotion at the village gate in the distance. Beryk and the rest of the Master Riders, dressed in their full armor and riding leathers, were walking toward the obstacle course. The commander smiled as the apprentices whispered and pointed—clearly he'd asked the patrol members to come and watch, and the students had known nothing about it.

Perfect, Veronyka thought with grim satisfaction. She wanted to force the commander's hand, and what better way to do that than in front of an audience that could hold him accountable? There's no way the commander could maintain that Tristan wasn't skilled enough if the entire Rider force— apprentices and masters alike—saw him excel. Veronyka just needed to give them incontrovertible proof. Tristan couldn't simply do what the rest were doing. . . . He had to go above and beyond.

The commander spoke a few words and indicated that he'd invited the Master Riders so that they could "see what you lads have been up to," but Veronyka recognized manipulation when she saw it. The commander had invited the small crowd for added pressure, not to satisfy the Riders' idle curiosity.

Still, they did appear interested, leaning against the paddock fence as the apprentices lined up and prepared to demonstrate their skills on the course. Unlike with their first run-through several weeks ago, they were expected to attempt the final flourish and have their phoenixes ignite at the end.

Veronyka knew this would be Tristan's true challenge.

He had done it multiple times in their extra practice sessions, but now the pressure was higher than ever before.

As Anders began the exercise, one of the stablehands rushed to latch the gate shut before a hound slipped out. It was Petyr, and though he managed to close it in time, it gave Veronyka an idea.

A plan began to form in her mind, a plan that was risky and downright foolish. Not to mention the fact that it had the potential to blow up in her face—and Tristan's. She needed to talk to him, but he remained too close to the commander.

Most of the apprentices had improved, but no matter how well they did with the course, every time a phoenix ignited, horses bucked and dogs howled. Two pigeons took flight and circled back to the village, and somehow a quiver of arrows caught fire.

When Tristan guided Wind over to the beginning of the course, Veronyka rushed forward to fuss with a strap. Her hands shook with adrenaline, but she did her best to angle her body to hide her face from the audience's view. Tristan glanced down, a perfect mask of haughty impatience on his face, though he could see quite plainly that there was nothing wrong with the saddle.

"What is it?" he whispered, pretending to help adjust a buckle.

"I'm thinking about doing something . . . reckless," she said. She looked up at him, half hoping he'd tell her no, and she'd be free to hide behind the horses and wait until it was all over.

Instead he straightened in his seat and batted her hand away from the strap. "Okay," he said, before wordlessly calling his hound and his pigeon. Just like that, he'd accepted her words and given her permission to do whatever mad thing she could think of.

Okay.

While everyone watched Tristan make his way through the course, Veronyka quietly moved behind them. She didn't have a lot of time, and she'd get only one shot at this.

Though she didn't give Tristan her full attention, she was proud at how well he was doing. She looked up whenever the others murmured in reaction to a perfect shot at the target or an expert jump over a barrel or crate. The commander shouted questions to him, as he did with the others, making sure the apprentices were connected to the phoenixes as well as the other animals.

As Tristan guided Wind through the poles near the end of the course, Veronyka knew the moment had come. Tension hung over the group as everyone remembered how badly this had gone for Tristan the last time his father was in attendance.

Rex cawed, beating his wings as he soared in a wide arc, then dipped his head and dove.

Surely my dear, sweet Onia knew
I'd never bow my head.

- CHAPTER 23 -

TRISTAN

TRISTAN BRACED HIMSELF AS Rex hurtled toward the ground.

Any second his bondmate would ignite, and Tristan knew that everything depended on what happened next.

He had barely a breath to prepare himself, to reinforce the safe house in his mind, as Nyk had taught him. He'd been practicing for days, and the walls were already there, his fear ensconced within.

But that wasn't enough. Tristan had to fill every gap and crack, ensuring his terror had no way of surfacing.

In some ways his fear *was* a luxury, just as his father's favorite quote had always maintained—an indulgence he turned to in moments of weakness. But putting it in the safe house made it unreachable, protecting him from himself.

It was sort of like separating thought from emotion. . . . His rational mind knew that Rex's fire was no danger to him, but his emotions allowed the fear to take root, to overpower his logical thoughts and turn him into a mess of nerves and anxiety and hesitation.

Tristan knew he did not like fire, and that was okay—by locking his fear up, he took control over it. In time maybe he could eliminate it completely.

But for now he would do whatever it took to get through the exercise. He clamped tight on the wall in his mind and waited.

With a searing flap of his wings, Rex burst into flame.

Tristan marveled at the way Rex exalted in his fire, able to appreciate the feelings that rippled through the bond for the first time. Fire was sacred to a phoenix, a part of their very existence. . . . Fire was life and death and power and magic, and all of it barreled through Rex, crackling in his veins as he landed before Tristan, singeing the grass at his feet.

Tristan remained perfectly upright in his saddle, his mind calm. His fear was nowhere in sight.

Exhilarated, he checked in with the other animals, noting their fear and hesitation but keeping them steady and under control—until a surge of energy drew his attention to the paddock.

The horses inside jumped and tossed their heads—as they had each time a phoenix ignited—but somehow the latch had come undone, and horses were streaming from the gate.

Several of the stableboys tried to stop them, but Tristan could swear that Nyk was only pretending to join in, reaching a hand half-heartedly as the animals barreled past.

Ah. So, *this* was his reckless plan. Why had Tristan blindly agreed to this? With a calm he didn't know he possessed, Tristan pushed a slow, even breath out through his lips.

One . . . two . . . three horses were freed before Jana closed the gate, and even as Tristan told himself not to panic, that he could handle a few extra horses, he noticed the half a dozen hounds that had snuck out with them.

He was going to kill Nyk.

Everyone was looking around at one another, trying to decide what to do. Even the commander stepped forward, clearly intending to intervene, but with a curious glance at Tristan, Beryk restrained him.

So, they were going to let him try.

Closing his eyes, Tristan blocked out the commotion around him and focused on the animals. Again listening to Nyk's advice, Tristan trusted that

Wind, the first hound, and the pigeon would remain in position, and sought the other animals instead. He'd never tried to manage so many at once, but then again, when he looked at it the way Nyk did—not constantly putting pressure on each one, but rather reaching out to them individually, making his request and then receding—it wasn't nearly so strenuous. Both the dogs and the horses had been through this multiple times before, so once Tristan reminded them of their duty to behave and remain still, they were much easier to get under control.

It was a bit like gardening. Tristan's mother had loved flowers, and their house had always smelled of roses and violets and bloodred Fire Blossoms. He'd helped Old Ana tend his mother's garden after she died—though being so young, he had no doubt he'd been more hindrance than help—and when they'd left home for good, he and Old Ana planted new flowers outside the village. According to her, it was more about being a guiding hand, not a constant overseer—and animal magic was the same. Just as the plants would naturally reach for the sun, so animals instinctually sought out animages.

While some resisted his touch more than others, eventually the freed horses slowed their pace and looped back around, while the hounds yipped once or twice before doing the same. Sweat trailed down Tristan's forehead, but he ignored the mental and physical strain as he reined in the disorder around him.

A hush fell over the group as, one by one, horses and hounds lined up alongside Tristan, creating a half circle of perfectly obedient animals.

Tristan gave Rex a final command; the phoenix lowered his head, and with one last flap of his wings, his fire went out.

It was as if a bubble of silence had popped, and the world burst to life around him once more. The apprentices and Riders cheered, rushing forward to congratulate him, while the stableboys moved to recapture the escaped animals.

The commander stayed put, and as Tristan dismounted, he heard Beryk say, "That's mighty impressive, Commander—I couldn't do that."

Tristan was pleased, if exhausted, but he tried to smile and nod as he waded through the crush of bodies, distracted.

Finally the crowd parted, and his eyes fell on Nyk.

He gave Tristan that familiar, shy smile—clearly unsure if Tristan was going to thank him or strangle him for his so-called reckless plan.

Despite wanting to murder him in the moment, Tristan felt nothing but overwhelming gratitude. Yes, mastering the escaped animals had been challenging, but it was the silent, unknown battle that Tristan was proudest of. The battle only Nyk knew about.

For the first time in his memory, Tristan had faced a phoenix in full flame, and he hadn't hesitated. He wanted to shout from the mountaintop, to roar his triumph and exhilaration for all to hear.

Instead Tristan pushed the others aside, determination propelling him forward.

He barreled into Nyk, throwing his arms around him as the noise receded and there was nothing but the two of them, pressed together.

"You did it," Nyk gasped, apparently surprised by Tristan's sudden, fierce embrace.

Remembering the crowd around them, Tristan drew back, avoiding Nyk's curious expression, and forced an easy smile. "Thanks to you."

When gentle King Hellund married ferocious Queen Genya, there was much celebration and fanfare in the empire—though the newly minted queen was not there to see it.

The instant the ink dried on their marriage contract, the young bride leapt onto the back of her phoenix, Exiline, leaving her groom behind. With fine silk and Fire Blossoms trailing in her wake, she hunted down the infamous group of bandits that had been terrorizing her beloved's reign. It was on this campaign that she earned the nickname "the General," and it wasn't long until she returned home triumphant.

In a bold romantic gesture, she presented the severed head of the gang leader to her husband as a belated wedding gift, and he promptly fainted into his barley soup.

—A popular cookhouse tale

We were Shadow Twins, half sisters,
but we couldn't have been more different.

- CHAPTER 24 -

VERONYKA

VERONYKA DIDN'T KNOW WHAT to do with herself that night. She was dying to know what—if anything—had happened with Tristan and the commander, but she hadn't seen either of them since the obstacle course.

She still couldn't believe how well everything had played out—the planned *and* unplanned parts, like the accidental release of the hounds. She'd been so focused on the horses, ensuring only a handful escaped, that she'd completely forgotten about the dogs. One moment they were on the far side of the paddock, quite absorbed in chasing and snapping at one another, and the next they were barreling through the gate along with the horses and causing an additional distraction Veronyka wasn't sure Tristan would be able to handle.

But he had. He'd taken it all in stride, pushing outward with his magic while trusting the animals he already had under his power. Even in the face of Rex's crackling flames, Tristan had been the picture of confidence and control.

He'd been magnificent.

Veronyka kept thinking about the way he'd hugged her afterward, the gleam of triumph—and something else she couldn't quite place—sparkling in his eye. Her heart had stopped at first, the thought of her bound breasts pressing against him making her dizzy. But he didn't seem to notice, and then before she knew it, they were apart again. The other apprentices had pushed in, and Veronyka had stepped aside to attend to her duties.

Now she awaited the commander's verdict. Whether he decided Tristan was ready to lead a patrol or not, Veronyka was quite certain he would deem their extra lessons no longer necessary.

The thought caused an unexpected pang of sadness. Their nightly time together had transformed from something to dread into something she spent her entire day looking forward to. From their first meeting, Tristan's success and progress had been tangled up in her own, and though they had embraced their fate and willingly helped each other, they would no longer be *required* to train together. If he became a patrol leader, his daily schedule would change, and he probably wouldn't have time to practice with her at all.

Needing some fresh air after the dinner that Tristan and the commander did not attend, Veronyka decided to take Wind for a walk out to the obstacle course. It was the one place Tristan might go looking for her, and besides, Wind had grown accustomed to the nighttime exercise and had been emanating impatient thoughts from the stables all evening. Veronyka reasoned that even if Tristan never turned up, she could try riding Wind on her own.

The horse snorted in irritation as Veronyka tried to mount up. She'd been watching closely as the other apprentices rode their horses and thought she could mimic the basics. However, after three attempts she dragged one of the crates over from the nearest obstacle and used it to climb into the saddle.

She tried to steer Wind to the right, but pulled too hard on the reins, causing the horse to toss his head. Veronyka loosened her grip, focusing on her right leg instead. It worked, but when she looked up, it was to see that he'd turned them around in a complete circle. Using her animal magic, she told him to stop, then remembered she wasn't supposed to do that and told him to ignore her. And so he kept turning to the right, taking them around for a second loop.

"Are you lost?" said a voice from nearby, and Veronyka stiffened. Wind stopped his movement as Tristan appeared, putting a gentle hand on the horse's head. He smirked up at her. "The course is over there."

"Tell the horse that," Veronyka muttered, face hot with embarrassment.

"Wind." Tristan's smile widened. "His name is Wind."

Veronyka scowled, remembering when she'd told him off for the same thing.

Bite him, Veronyka thought to Wind, who angled his head, sizing up Tristan's bare forearm. She hastily called him off and dismounted. Luckily, she didn't fall.

"So, where have you been all night?" she asked. "I didn't see you at the dining hall."

"Eating with the commander," he said, petting Wind absently.

"And?" Veronyka pressed. His reluctance to speak was making her even more impatient to get the information out of him.

"He wanted to—very grudgingly—congratulate me on my progress. I told him I had the extra lessons to thank for that," he said, and Veronyka fought the grin that tugged at her mouth. "And he thought I was being insolent. So, really, a typical conversation for us."

Veronyka laughed.

"After that, he promised I could be a patrol leader."

"Tristan, that's great!" Veronyka said, wanting to touch him but hesitating when she caught sight of Tristan's peculiar expression. He was still smiling, but it looked somewhat forced—as though he were pleased, but something was holding him back from true happiness.

"What's wrong?" Veronyka asked.

He tossed his shoulders in a dismissive shrug. "He said I can't graduate to my new position yet."

"Because of the eggs?"

Tristan nodded. "So, basically, we're right back where we started."

Veronyka shook her head firmly. "No, we're not. You did something amazing today, Tristan, and your father promised you the position you worked hard for. This is a good day."

He smiled more earnestly now and nodded his agreement.

The movement showed Veronyka the bow and quiver he was wearing over his shoulder.

"Do you want to get in more practice?" she asked hopefully, indicating the weapon.

"Nah," he said, swinging it off his shoulder. Veronyka's heart sank, until . . . "I think it's time we gave you a try."

"At the obstacle course?" she squeaked, then cleared her throat.

He chuckled. "No. That's a bit advanced for you. Let's try your hand at the bow and arrow first."

The bow he held out was smaller than what a standing soldier would use, made from dark, polished wood and curled at both ends.

"It's recurved," he explained, tracing the reverse bends at top and bottom, "which gives maximum draw with minimal effort. Riders usually shoot while mounted, so they need smaller, more agile weapons. This works in your favor, compensating for your, uh, limited strength."

Veronyka had to give him credit for *trying* to be tactful, though he'd failed.

Tristan showed her how to string and unstring the bow, but she couldn't seem to get the hang of it. The strength and coordination it required to bend the wood and hold the string taut was more than she would have assumed, and soon her muscles began to tremble.

After watching her struggle, Tristan finally took pity on her and helped. "It'll get easier," he said, reaching around her to add his strength to hers, pushing the bow down so Veronyka could fasten the loop.

His sudden proximity filled her senses, the scent of cool green grass and woodsmoke mingling with the cotton of his tunic and the smell of his skin, salty with sweat and still warm from the day's sun. When he released the bow and stepped back from her, Veronyka took a deep breath of the Tristan-free air and collected herself. Her nerves were on high alert because of the new challenge archery presented, she was sure, and *not* because of the way the commander's son smelled.

Taking the bow from her, he demonstrated proper technique, drawing the string effortlessly. He pointed out the position of his feet, spread and evenly balanced, along with the angle of his elbow, and how far he drew the string, anchored to his chin. The position displayed his lean, muscular body to its best effect, and Veronyka took as long as was acceptable to stare at him.

To help my technique, she told herself, looking away at last. *Yes,* he was attractive—strong and smart and talented. And *yes,* she loved being with him. But he was also her training partner, the commander's son, and with any luck, her sponsor someday. She couldn't afford to get distracted.

He handed her the bow, and she tried to mimic him, drawing the arrowless string back and doing her best to remember his square, balanced posture.

He walked around her, nudging her elbow up, kicking her feet farther apart, and squinting at her grip.

Then he rested a hand, idly, against her chest.

His palm splayed against the fabric, his smallest finger mere millimeters away from the gentle swell of her flattened breasts. Immediately her chest constricted and her breath hitched.

"No, no," Tristan said softly, the other hand resting on the elbow that drew back the string. "Deep breaths—that's where your strength and posture come from. In and out, come on," he encouraged, tapping her chest lightly.

Veronyka thought she might faint right then and there. Bad enough that she was a girl pretending to be a boy, her secret a fingertip away from being discovered, but Tristan's very proximity was enough to make her lungs tighten and her body shake.

Veronyka, you fool.

Focusing on the bow in her hands, she relaxed and did as he ordered. Deep breath in, slow breath out. On the next breath in, she tightened her grip and drew back the string, feeling her muscles bunch and expand and her posture straighten.

"There it is," he said softly, his breath tickling the back of her neck.

She glanced over her shoulder at him. He was so close, Veronyka could see the barest shadow of stubble along his jawline and the way his throat bobbed when he swallowed. Once. Twice.

His hand lingered for a moment longer. Then it dropped, and she released the string, her body's tension collapsing in on itself in a grateful moment of release.

Tristan cleared his throat and reached for the quiver. He was brusque when he took the bow again, avoiding her eye as he showed her how to hold the arrow, curling his fingers to pull it taut against the string and angling the shaft against the bow, with a finger below to guide it.

He was an excellent teacher, patient and thorough, and when it was Veronyka's turn, she did her best to follow his instructions. Her form seemed accurate enough, but when it came time to actually shoot the weapon, the arrow flopped to the ground scant feet in front of her.

Tristan covered his mouth in a gesture that she knew was hiding laughter, and he collected the stray arrow before waving for her to try again. She got the hang of it eventually, firing weak shots in the general direction of the target. Before long the muscles in her shoulders, arms, and back began to ache, and her fingertips were rubbed raw.

"There are gloves and armguards to make you more comfortable," Tristan offered, seeing her shake out her aching fingers after another unimpressive shot, "but it's better to toughen the skin and develop calluses."

"It's fine," Veronyka said in frustration. She'd managed to embed only a single arrow, on the outermost edge of the target, but nothing more.

"You have other strengths, you know," Tristan said quietly.

Veronyka *knew* she sucked at this, but his words confirmed it. How was she going to be a mounted warrior when she could barely draw a bow? If Avalkyra Ashfire could be the best markswoman in the summer solstice games at age *eleven*, beating out hundreds of older, more experienced archers, Veronyka could learn too. She *had* to.

"If you want to be a Rider, you have to be an archer," she gritted out.

She'd just have to practice more, find ways to shoot late at night or early in the morning. . . .

"Yes, archery is important," Tristan conceded, coming to stand in front of her, arms crossed. "But every Rider has their talents. Anders is an amazing flyer, fast and unpredictable. Fallon has incredible balance—he can ride standing, sitting, or even on his phoenix's tail. Ronyn is by far the strongest of any of us; he can throw a spear almost as far as I can shoot an arrow."

As Tristan continued to list off each Rider's remarkable skills, Veronyka felt smaller and smaller. How could she think she belonged among them, when she had no such astounding abilities?

It seemed Tristan could read her mind. "But *your* strength, Nyk, is your magic."

Veronyka gave him a disbelieving look. "We all have magic," she said, unable to keep the embarrassing sulkiness out of her voice. Of course, Veronyka *did* have a magical skill that most of them did not—her shadow magic—but it had no bearing on how she'd fare as a Rider. In most cases it was a terrible inconvenience and a liability.

"Not like yours," Tristan said forcefully.

A pleased smile spread across Veronyka's face, despite her having a hard time actually believing his words. Val's praise had always been scant, and usually bracketed on both sides with snide jabs and insults. Her *maiora* was kind and patient, but their time together had been so limited. Val had been the one to teach her the most about magic.

Veronyka's first recollection of *having* magic involved Val. She and her grandmother had been inside their home when a girl kicked in the front door. It was strange, and Veronyka must have been very young, because in her memory, the girl had been a wild and terrifying stranger. It had been Val, of course, her dark eyes peeking through the strands of her matted, so-dirty-it-looked-brown hair. In one hand she'd held a bit of scrap metal, sharp and wicked-looking. In the other, a slithering, writhing snake.

Her *maiora* had lurched to her feet when Val burst in, but then she stood frozen, face white as plaster as she stared at the girl. Next thing

Veronyka remembered, Val was bending down and releasing the snake. Veronyka wasn't *afraid*, exactly—but she had definitely been uneasy. When the snake drew close, though, something shifted, and Veronyka felt calm, as if the serpent were an old friend. She bent down, running her fingers along its strange, slippery hide, and after the two became acquainted with each other, it was a simple thing to wrap her small hands around its undulating body and hold it up for closer inspection. It lunged once for her face—she could remember her *maiora* making a fearful sound—but Veronyka chastised the snake for its bad manners, and that was the end of it. The entire thing had seemed like some sort of test. . . . Maybe Val didn't know if Veronyka had any magic at all and wanted to be sure. She didn't like to think what would have happened if she *hadn't*. Val always acted as if Veronyka were a burden, even though she had the same magical powers as Val. If she'd been nonmagical, Veronyka knew Val would have made her feel completely and utterly worthless.

She stared off into the distance, wondering where Val was at that moment. Had she left the hunter's cabin? Or had she remained stubbornly behind? The thought that Val might have moved on, that Veronyka would have no idea where to look for her, left a hollow ache in her stomach, even as her brain told her that she shouldn't care.

"You're the strongest animage I've ever seen," Tristan continued, drawing Veronyka to the present again. He rubbed the back of his neck, oddly shamefaced. "What you did with Wind that day . . . I was already connected to him, and you just took over. I would have been impressed if I weren't so embarrassed."

Veronyka grinned. "Yeah, but look at what you did during the commander's inspection today. That was far more difficult."

"But you're the one who set that up and taught me how to properly control the animals in the first place. If you hadn't explained about trust and guiding rather than controlling, I couldn't have done it."

Veronyka beamed. His respect meant so much to her. It meant everything.

"And that other thing you taught me," he continued, furrowing his brow and pointing up at his head, "about the mental walls? It, well . . . I've never been able to face Rex's fire without seizing up in panic. But when I do the mental safe house . . . it's like the fear is happening to a different part of my brain, like it's nothing but a memory. It's amazing."

Maybe she was staring at him with too much feeling, too much intensity, because Tristan ran a hand through his hair and looked away. "So, what I'm trying to say is: Trust your magic, all right?"

"Okay," Veronyka said, accepting his advice. "I'll still need to learn this though," she added.

"And you will. This is your first try, and you're tired," Tristan said bracingly. "It's also hard in the failing light. I wish you could have a go in the training yard. This target's a bit high—it's meant for archers on horseback—and the markings are worn out. . . ." He trailed off, staring at the target with a frown.

"What?" she asked after a silent moment.

"Got any plans tomorrow?"

"Tomorrow?" Veronyka asked blankly. "I'll be in the stables."

"No you won't. Tomorrow is Azurec's Day," he said.

Veronyka blinked. She'd lost track of time since she'd been at the Eyrie. Azurec's Day—also known as the summer solstice, the day with the most sunlight of the year—was always a big festival day in the empire. It was the one time a year when Val would let them walk the streets together, watching the street performers and maybe even buying sweet cakes from a vendor. The largest celebrations were always in Aura Nova. Before the Blood War, the king and queen would attend, tossing handfuls of coins onto the streets, and at night their phoenixes would put on a fiery display in the sky.

"Oh, right," she said, remembering that there was traditionally no work on festival days. "What are you suggesting?"

"The training yard will be empty. We can spend the whole day there."

Veronyka's heart leapt at the prospect, but it felt suspiciously like charity. "You don't want to spend the day with your friends . . . the other apprentices?" she asked.

He gave her a half shrug. "We see enough of each other, and we still have the feast."

Veronyka nodded, and they packed up their things.

"And *you're* a friend, Nyk," he added, leading the way back up to the village.

"I am?" she asked, a strange bubble expanding in her throat. Friendship had always been a loaded term for Veronyka, a thing just out of reach. She'd tried once or twice in her life, running the cobblestones with the other bare-footed kids on their winding Narrows' street, or sharing whatever meager food she had with some of the beggar kids in the Forgotten District, the neighborhood that housed the city's orphanages. No matter who it was, Val would shut it down at once, chasing the other children away or swatting the food from the cowering street rats' outstretched fingers.

"They're nothing but filthy mongrels," she'd say. Or, "Feed them once, and they'll be following you forever."

Veronyka would look down at her own tattered rags and wonder how they were any different. She'd wonder what was so wrong with feeding them more than once.

Veronyka had known she and Tristan were more than just training part-ners, but they had gone from fighting to laughing to awkward moments so quickly that she could hardly keep up. Was that friendship? All she'd ever had was her sister, but now that Xephyra—and Tristan—had come into her life, Veronyka realized that Val had never really been enough. There was a difference between friendship and family, between the people you chose to surround yourself with and the people you were stuck with, good or bad.

And just as Xephyra had done, Tristan had chosen her.

"Of course," he said, nudging her with his shoulder. "More than a friend, really—I mean," he said, laughing nervously as he realized what he'd insinuated, "you're a *close* friend. Closer than the apprentices."

Veronyka smiled at him, heart light as a feather as they walked through the village, Rex flying above. Veronyka stared at the phoenix, watching golden flame rippling across his body in gentle waves.

"I don't know how you can stand to be parted from him each night," she mused. While the phoenixes roosted in the Eyrie, the apprentices lived in barracks similar to hers. Her connection to Xephyra had been so primal, so fierce, that the thought of putting piles of rock and buildings between them each night would have been painful. Of course, what had actually happened was much, much worse.

Tristan looked up. "It was hard at first, when our bond was new and more fragile. But now we're connected no matter how far apart we are."

Rex cawed his agreement, soaring lazily above them.

Though Xephyra was gone, Veronyka still felt the lingering remnants of their severed bond, like a broken bone begging to be set. The more she ignored it, the more it seemed to ache.

"Still, it'd be nice to move into the Eyrie with the Master Riders—that's where they sleep. It was carved centuries ago. All this"—he gestured to the village and the wall that surrounded it—"is fairly new. The village was here to serve the pilgrimage route, but it was mostly small shops selling phoenix idols, feather talismans, and other tourist junk. It had been abandoned since the Blood War, so we basically had to rebuild it all when we arrived two years ago. We added the wall, and the stables and everything inside the stronghold is recent. The caverns inside the Eyrie extend underneath the stronghold and deep into the mountain. Some of the passages were caved in, but we were able to excavate most of them."

"It must be beautiful," Veronyka said, wishing with all her heart that she might one day be a part of this world, of the history that defined her people.

Tristan looked at her a moment, and Veronyka worried that she'd given herself away somehow. But she needn't have worried.

"It is," Tristan agreed quietly. Then he added, "I'll show you."

We were night and day, moon and sun—
darkness and light.
We were nothing without each other.

- CHAPTER 25 -
TRISTAN

AS THEY APPROACHED THE carved archway that led into the Eyrie, Rex soared overhead in a wide circle before diving dramatically into the darkness beyond.

Nyk's eyes widened, his face glowing with unreserved wonder.

Show-off, Tristan thought to Rex, whose smug self-satisfaction blazed through the bond.

Nyk's reaction reminded Tristan of a younger version of himself. He thought of the first time he'd seen his father's phoenix, how small he'd felt before the great Maximian, awed—and of course, terrified—by the crackle and hiss of the fire that burned beneath his brilliant feathers. Admiration had filled his heart at the thought that his own father rode into the sky on such a breathtaking beast. From that day forward, all Tristan had wanted was to be a Rider.

He'd asked constantly, but the commander had never indulged Tristan with personal stories or sentimentality. For his father, being a Rider was just another duty, like running the Eyrie and reclaiming what their family had lost since the war.

Their exile often made Tristan ashamed—but not for their loss of position and wealth. He was ashamed because of his father. Cassian had denied their cause and offered up information, forsaking those who had fought and died in the war, just for a chance to keep his beloved governor position. He'd been willing to side with the very people who'd tried to wipe out the Riders.

The people who had killed Tristan's mother.

Tristan could barely remember her and had only his father's words—and the odd fragmented memory of braided hair and fierce laughter—to keep her alive. When he was young, people told him he had her spirit. Now Tristan feared he was becoming increasingly like his father, cold and calculating and more focused on personal pride than on doing what was good and right for their people.

But at times like this, when he forgot about his ambitions and his constant need for his father's approval, Tristan felt closer to his mother, and that was a good feeling.

They climbed the wide steps that led to the archway, which was cut through a jagged spur of mountain rock and chiseled into the shape of the animals sacred to the gods. Beasts slithered and crawled and snarled overtop one another, including Teyke's cat and Mori's owl, while Azurec's spread-winged phoenix crowned the entrance at its apex.

They passed through, and the Eyrie lay before them.

It was carved into the heart of the mountain like a great, stony bowl. It reminded Tristan of an amphitheater, with a flat space far below and tiers rising wider and wider from the bottom up. The levels acted as walkways and roosts for the phoenixes, while at the very bottom of the pit, a stone courtyard was ringed by an arched gallery. Rough, uncut peaks of stone surrounded the bowl like cupped hands, hiding it from view of the mountain below.

Directly in front of them was a jutting spear of stone, like a plinth or a platform, which thrust into the open air of the Eyrie. Though the top was smooth and flat for walking, the rock supports underneath were carved in the shape of another massive phoenix. The path stretched across its back, while its head capped the end of the plinth and its wings spread wide to reconnect with the walls on either side.

Tristan gave Nyk some time to take it all in before pointing out the basic function of the space. "See those doorways along each ledge? Those are where the Master Riders live. When we moved in, they spent months scouring the tunnels, searching for lost eggs."

"Did they find any?" Nyk asked.

Tristan nodded. "A few. It's where most of the apprentices got their mounts. One or two had an egg from their families, and three Riders still had their mounts from before the war. The commander, Beryk, and one of the instructors and leader of the second patrol, Fallon. He was only a child during the fighting."

"Was that where you found Rex?" Nyk asked.

Tristan shook his head. "I inherited my egg from my mother's side. He'd been passed down for years, waiting for me."

Tristan had never been more anxious for anything in his life than when he'd incubated his generations-old phoenix egg. What would happen if things went wrong and he wasted this most precious of family heirlooms?

But all the worry had been for nothing. Rex had deemed him a worthy bondmate, and Tristan was proud to ride such a beautiful creature—fire and all.

As they looked on, Rex made himself comfortable on a nearby ledge, his feathers sending up sparks as he shifted into position. All around, other phoenixes settled in for the night, roosting in small clusters.

Only the top two levels of the Eyrie were in use, but Tristan liked to imagine what it might have been like a few hundred years ago, when every cavern was occupied and flaming birds perched on every ledge.

Nyk's eyes were fixated somewhere below. "There're more phoenixes down there," he said, his voice oddly strangled. "There's an enclosure, or a fence. . . ."

Tristan withdrew his gaze. "It's the females," he said heavily. "That's where the breeding cages are."

He risked a glance at Nyk and instantly regretted it. Nyk looked shocked, disgusted, and his reaction made Tristan feel dirty—as if it had been his idea.

"They aren't bonded," Tristan explained, lowering himself onto the ground next to the archway. He leaned his weary back against the cool stone wall, and Nyk copied him. "So they have to be restrained, or they'll leave. The Riders are trying to get them to mate."

Tristan could see that his words upset Nyk, and if he was honest with himself, they upset him, too. After knowing the mind of a creature as intelligent, powerful, and ancient as a phoenix, it was hard to believe putting them in enclosures—cages, essentially—and using them for breeding was at all right.

Nyk crossed his arms. "And has it worked?"

Tristan sighed heavily. "We got one last year—"

"*One* egg?"

"Yes, *one*," Tristan admitted reluctantly. He ran a hand through his hair, the curls stiff with the day's dirt and sweat. "But whether the bird was already carrying or not, we don't know. She was wild; they managed to trap her, and she laid the egg soon after. Every other attempt has gone badly."

"Badly?" Nyk repeated.

"They've maimed every single male who got close to them. You know, when they hurt, *we* hurt," he added, and Nyk nodded—confirming he knew this already. "I remember a couple months back, Fallon was limping for days because his phoenix was in the breeding cages and had been slashed by one of the females. They're stronger than the males and usually grow to be larger."

Nyk seemed pleased by this information.

"The same is true of, well, pleasure," Tristan said, staring resolutely at his knees. Heat crept up the side of his neck, and he forced a laugh as he continued. "We feel *all* their emotions, good or bad, and apparently if the phoenixes actually did mate, the bondmates sense it in some way. So that's weird."

That startled a horrified laugh out of Nyk, and Tristan grinned, gratified that he'd been able to make him smile and break the awkward tension.

"In the old days Riders worked in pairs," Tristan said, arching his back to stretch his stiff muscles. Nyk watched him idly, and his attention was unlike anyone else's—not the intense scrutiny of his father or the vague affection of someone like Beryk or Morra. It made Tristan's senses sharpen and his shoulders straighten. "For hunting and tracking and fighting. The phoenixes would become a mated pair for life, and so would their Riders. I guess their bonds, they bled into each other, so it was almost like the Riders were bonded in the same way the phoenixes were."

"Like Nefyra and Callysta," Nyk murmured, his tone thoughtful.

Tristan smiled, pleased that Nyk knew about the First Riders. There had been hundreds of famous pairs throughout Phoenix Rider history, but Nefyra, the First Rider Queen, and Callysta, her second-in-command, were Tristan's favorites. Even though they married others for alliances and for children, they remained committed to each other above all else. They refused to leave each other's sides—in battle, in life, and in death. When Callysta succumbed to an arrow wound, Nefyra followed her soon after, dying of a broken heart.

"So, if the breeding cages don't work and you don't have any eggs, why isn't your father searching Pyra, the abandoned watch towers and outposts?"

"We have," Tristan said. They hadn't searched *thoroughly*. He knew that, but there was never enough time. Any day now the empire would learn about them, and they had to be ready. Nyk opened his mouth, probably to argue his very valid points, but Tristan was tired of defending his father's methods—especially when he hardly agreed with them himself. "Listen, Nyk, I dislike it as much as you do. But if you ever want to be a Rider, we need more phoenixes. This is the only way we know how."

Nyk fell silent; clearly talk of the breeding cages was dimming his initial pleasure at seeing the Eyrie for the first time. This disappointed Tristan.

He reached out with his magic. With some prodding, he was able to convince Rex to leave his roost and visit him at the end of the phoenix walkway. When Tristan got up, Nyk followed a second later, a frown on his face.

Standing near the edge of the plinth, Tristan felt the warm rush of air that signaled Rex's approach. Nyk stopped next to him just as the phoenix burst from the depths of the Eyrie; a gust of wind rippled through Tristan's hair, and streaks of light momentarily marred his vision.

Arcing above, Rex burst into full flame at the peak of his ascent, then dove downward into the darkness below. Nyk crouched in alarm as Rex hurtled toward them, then he leaned over the edge to watch the bird's descent. It was part of the solstice dance, the display Rex and the other phoenixes would put on the following evening.

Again Rex flew high into the air, only to turn around and soar in a fiery coil toward the earth. As Tristan had hoped, soon other phoenixes joined in, ruffling their feathers in puffs of sparks before igniting. Sometimes Tristan thought phoenixes were natural performers, always game for a bit of theater, a bit of the dramatic—especially if it involved showing off their elegant flight and brilliant flame.

Seeing them like this was surprisingly easy—their fire was a faraway spectacle, not a dangerous threat. He could appreciate the beauty of it in a detached way, as distant and otherworldly as the sun and stars.

While watching one phoenix fly into the sky and then come careening back down was beautiful, watching half a dozen was spectacular. Nyk gripped Tristan's arm, his mouth hanging open as the firebirds twisted and spiraled, leaving flaming tracks in the air. The moon hung in the sky behind them, fat and bone white, and dull in comparison.

Now that they had begun, Tristan knew the phoenixes would be at it for a while. He nudged Nyk, whose large round eyes reflected the fiery performance, and returned to sitting against the wall near the entrance. Nyk followed, walking backward so he didn't miss a single second of the show.

Tristan didn't know if it was guilt over how he'd first treated Nyk or gratitude for the help he had given Tristan since, but for some reason—he didn't want to think too hard on it—making Nyk smile made Tristan's own heart lighter. Nyk had a way of bringing out a happier, more positive side of him. Barely an hour ago he'd been ready to deem his long-desired promotion to patrol leader a failure just because it wasn't happening as quickly as he'd hoped. But Nyk had made him truly appreciate the success for what it was: a step in the right direction. And before that, when Tristan had blurted out his fear of fire, Nyk hadn't laughed or ridiculed him. He hadn't even batted an eye, instead listing off famous Riders with issues of their own so he wouldn't feel alone and then providing Tristan with a life-changing solution.

It wasn't that their friendship was all fun and laughter—in fact, Nyk was one of the few people, besides his father, who called him on his arrogance and bad temper. But unlike his father, who held Tristan's every bad decision against him, Nyk never seemed to hold a grudge. After their rocky start, Nyk had been steadfast and loyal, a constant friend in a place where Tristan didn't really have any. He'd never fit in much with the other apprentices, and he wasn't yet a Master Rider. He was stuck somewhere between, which was often a hard place to be.

But then he'd look at Nyk, and his endless hope would make Tristan want to hope too, just like Nyk's faith in Tristan made Tristan want to have faith in himself. He wanted to be the person Nyk seemed to think he could be, and he needed Nyk by his side to remind him of that.

He needed Nyk by his side because he never felt more himself than when they were together.

They continued to watch in silence as the phoenixes painted the night sky. At one point Nyk's head drooped onto Tristan's shoulder, and Tristan let his own head fall back against the rough-hewn wall.

Eventually the birds gave up the dance and returned to their roost. The night around them grew darker, until only Rex remained. With a last flash of light, he took his final descent into the shadows.

Tristan bade him good night and thanked him before moving to get to his feet. Nyk slumped against the wall, fast asleep. Tristan prodded him with a foot, then gave him a gentle shake with his hand, but Nyk was dead to the world. Everything about him was bright and vivid, as if Nyk didn't do anything by half—couldn't, even if he wanted to. When he ran, no matter how tired, he pushed until his legs buckled beneath him. When he talked about phoenixes and Riders and animal magic, his whole face lit up.

And even when he slept, he did so with reckless abandon—his shock of messy black hair standing on end and his mouth slightly open.

With a smirk, Tristan bent down and lifted him, carrying Nyk in his arms back into the stronghold. It was strange, holding him close like that—having Nyk's face pressed against his chest. It was a relief to unburden himself when he reached Nyk's bed in the servants' barracks, but when Tristan stepped away, he felt strangely bereft as the cold air rushed into the places where Nyk's warmth had been.

Tristan knew that he should have told Nyk about the eggs. But he'd feared the information would cause Nyk to leave, and the idea made Tristan miserable. There had to be a way. He would go searching himself if he had to. The last time he'd disobeyed his father's orders, he'd been assigned extra lessons with Nyk—and the time before that, he'd found Nyk wandering the wilderness. Both instances had worked out far better than he could have imagined.

Maybe if he did it again, something even better would befall him.

Maybe Nyk would be made an apprentice and Tristan a patrol leader. And when it came time to choose his second-in-command, Nyk would be top of the list.

Together we could have
been unstoppable.

- CHAPTER 26 -
VERONYKA

VERONYKA AWOKE SUDDENLY, DISORIENTED as she stared up at the wooden ceiling. She blinked into the darkness and saw the familiar rows of hammocks that filled the servants' barracks. Slowly the night before came back to her: the stone-carved Eyrie, the fire-drenched phoenixes . . . and Tristan.

She must've fallen asleep, and—Axura above, did Tristan *carry* her to her bed?

Heat prickled her cheeks, and she couldn't tell if she was mortified or pleased. It was kind of Tristan to let her sleep, but she'd begun to fear that kindness. She didn't want to *need* it. As unrealistic as it felt, she wanted them to be equals. While he'd called them friends, she felt the imbalance between them: He was older, stronger, more experienced, while she was younger, weaker, and new to this place. He was the commander's son and would rule one day. She was . . . nobody. Not even an apprentice. It was similar to her equally disproportionate relationship with Val, and Veronyka never wanted to feel like she owed someone her life again.

She reached into her pocket for her braided bracelet, fingering the familiar beads.

The Eyrie was at once better—and worse—than she'd been expecting.

All the history and beauty was there, and the feeling of magic was powerful, as if embedded in the stones. But then there'd been that sense of wrongness, that fluttering, agitated tremor in the air.

Breeding cages.

Veronyka had never even considered such a thing. When she'd thought about the Riders trying to get more phoenix eggs, she'd always assumed that meant *searching*, not trying to produce them. Guilt gnawed at her belly, as if she were somehow complicit in their imprisonment. All this time she'd been here, there were females locked away in cages somewhere out of sight. How did people like Morra stand for it?

Val had told her that phoenix mating rituals were highly mysterious, that even the ancient Riders didn't know much about them. They often bred and laid their eggs in secrecy, which was why caches of eggs could still be found all over the mountain, untouched for centuries, waiting to be hatched. It was only during the last fifty years of the empire that phoenix eggs were deliberately hidden to keep them safe. There was trouble brewing long before the Blood War, the divide between animages and nonmagical people growing more pronounced with each passing year.

The Phoenix Riders had always been a symbol of the empire's power, the force used to unify the lesser kingdoms and to keep the peace and protect the people ever since. But where their loyalties lay was always somewhat elusive. In the beginning a Phoenix Rider always sat on the throne. First it was Elysia Ashfire, the Peacemaker, and then her daughter, Ellody. Many more followed, both sons and daughters, because when the Pyraeans took control of the valley, they vowed to respect and adopt the customs of all its people. Now the heir to the throne was always the eldest child, whatever their gender, and not the eldest daughter as it was in Pyraean culture, or the eldest son as it was done in most of the lesser kingdoms. The crown thrived, and for decades, man or woman, a Phoenix Rider sat in the empire's golden seat.

If, as in the case of King Hellund, the heir was not an animage, they were swiftly married to one in order to keep magic in the royal line and to appease the animage supporters. During King Hellund's reign—before his marriage to Queen Genya the General, a brutal fighter and Phoenix Rider—there were several recorded instances of the Phoenix Riders refusing to take orders from their king. Their allegiance was with their commander, which was often the position held by the local governor where they served. So, when King Hellund ordered the troops positioned in Ferro to fly across the empire to deal with a band of brigands terrorizing Arboria South, their Phoenix Rider commander simply refused. King Hellund's marriage to Genya set things to rights, but not all the governors and politicians of the empire could forget that the Phoenix Riders' loyalty wasn't so much to the crown as it was to their own kind.

By the time Avalkyra and Pheronia were born, the foundation for the war between them was already firmly in place. Those without magical blood saw themselves in Pheronia, who had the support of the nonmagical councilors, merchants, and governors. Of course the Phoenix Riders sided with Avalkyra, who was one of them—and whose mother had been a renowned warrior in her own right—but that didn't buy her political support. And the Phoenix Riders' numbers were small compared to the empire's growing army of conscripted foot soldiers. Eggs became highly valuable, things to hoard and hide, not parade out in the open, and it had been that way ever since.

A shudder ran down Veronyka's spine as she thought of those majestic birds, trapped against their will and forced to breed. It was like caging and breeding *people*. Phoenixes were no ordinary animals; they were highly intelligent even without a bond and had powerful magic all their own. But what were her chances of ever getting a phoenix again without the cages? And furthermore, what were the *Riders'* chances of expanding without more eggs?

If Val hadn't been so controlling and cruel, Veronyka could have come to the Eyrie with her own phoenix. She could've met Tristan as herself, as Veronyka, and trained with him and the other apprentices. He would have been better than her at first, but she'd have caught up to him. She'd have taught him what she knew about animal magic, and he would have helped her learn horseback riding and archery. Before long they would have soared through the sky as equals: Riders, warriors, and friends.

Tristan was already there when she arrived in the training yard later that morning, leaning against a barrel of practice weapons and dressed in his fitted training gear.

He opened his mouth to greet her, but Veronyka interrupted him, unable to bear it a second longer. "Thanks for, uh, getting me back to my bed last night."

Tristan appeared startled at first. Then he grinned shyly, the barest hint of his dimples showing. "No problem," he said, handing her the recurved bow that Veronyka had practiced with before.

After several shaky attempts, she managed to string it, and they made their way over to the targets. The training area was tucked against a corner of the stronghold's walls, with a wooden fence on two sides. Targets lined the base of the stone wall, while soft sand combat areas and padded dummies filled the rest of the space. Next to the targets was a small wooden shed, which Tristan disappeared into, emerging several moments later with two quivers and a longbow.

"Might as well get in some practice," he said, in response to her unasked question. "Don't worry. You'll still have my undivided attention should you need it."

She felt moderately better that he was at least getting in some exercise for himself instead of devoting his entire day to her. Again the sense of the imbalance between them nagged at her.

A group of servants cut through the far corner of the yard, accompanied by Anders, Latham, and some other apprentices. They laughed and chatted excitedly, and Tristan glanced in their direction. They waved and called him over, but he shook his head and indicated his bow.

"Are you sure you don't want to go with the others?" Veronyka asked, keeping her eyes on the bow in her hands—and not his face. They couldn't have a proper solstice celebration up here, since the last thing they wanted was to draw attention to themselves, but the commander did allow a small group of villagers from Petratec and Montascent to come and participate. Apparently most of the servants and craftspeople who lived at the Eyrie were from those two villages, along with several of the Riders.

The visiting villagers brought arts and crafts to sell, fine clothes and jewelry, and participated in the games that were being held in the open field where the obstacle course usually took place. Later there would be music in the dining hall, while everyone enjoyed a large feast. At the very end of the night the phoenixes would take to the skies.

Tristan's feet moved into her line of sight, and she looked up to meet his eyes. He was frowning. "I already told you I don't want to do that. This is about getting you some time with proper targets and equipment."

Veronyka nodded, but she didn't answer.

"What's troubling you, Nyk?" he asked, sticking the pointed end of his bow into the ground and leaning against it for support. "Do you not want to train?"

Veronyka struggled with the words. "No, of course I do! I just—I'll never be able to repay you for all this help."

He considered her for a moment, the morning sun casting his features into a haze of warm brown and gold. "I never said you had to. Besides, it's thanks to you the commander is even giving me a patrol in the first place."

"You'd have gotten that on your own eventually," Veronyka said. "But what you're giving me . . . the chance at being a Rider . . . I can't give it back. I can't match it."

"Nyk—we're friends now, all right? And that's not how friendship works. Besides, we've both got a long way to go. I'm not patrol leader yet, and you're not an apprentice. So, enough talk, and show me what you've got."

He jerked his chin toward the targets. With a reluctant smile, Veronyka did as she was told.

They shot arrows all morning, moving from the large beginner targets to smaller, more difficult shots. Veronyka thought she was getting the hang of it, even though her muscles were stiff and screaming with pain. Tristan shot from much farther back, his longbow's range outstripping the small bow she used.

At lunchtime Tristan disappeared into the dining hall and returned with a flagon of water and a basket of fruit, bread, and cheese.

They were just talking about calling it quits, the late-afternoon sun stretching their shadows across the ground, when they heard a commotion from outside the training yard. The open gate revealed a swarm of people around the entrance to the stronghold.

Tristan grinned. "The minstrels are here."

Along with artisans and fellow revelers, Petratec and Montascent always sent a troupe of performers, including minstrels and puppeteers. They carried their instruments and dolls in oiled bags or carefully sealed boxes and wore colorful tunics and headscarves. They were welcomed warmly and directed into the dining hall to unload their supplies. One little girl shrieked with glee at the sight of a Princess Pearl puppet dangling from a box, while others begged for their favorite songs and stories.

As the crowd shifted, one of the headscarf wearers turned, and a wisp of red hair, twisted with braids and beads, slipped out from underneath its cover. Veronyka spotted a shimmering seashell, sparkling in the hazy sunlight.

Her heart stopped.

Slowly, as if she could sense Veronyka there, the scarf wearer lifted her head. Dark eyes locked onto Veronyka's, and the blood drained from her face.

Val.

Day 29, Third Moon, 169 AE

Pheronia,

You are forcing my hand. The longer you
remain silent, the more dangerous our situation
becomes. Do you think you are infallible, locked
away in your fortress? Do you think you have
won already?

I am coming, xe Onia. Prepare yourself.

-A

But apart we were lesser, weaker
versions of ourselves. How they rejoiced
to see us torn asunder.

- CHAPTER 27 -

SEV

I'LL DO IT.

The words rang in Sev's ears from the moment they left his mouth, as if the entire world had shifted in the speaking of them. He heard them over and over during the following days, as he went about his chores, eating and sleeping, a constant refrain in his mind.

Trix had smiled like a fool when he'd volunteered, and Sev saw in her face that she'd known he'd come around, that the whole thing had been a bluff. For some reason, it didn't bother him the way it once might have. After constantly suffering at the hands of others, he was at last an active participant in the events around him, finally giving his parents something to be proud of. It made Sev's every footstep lighter, his thoughts almost carefree.

But as the details of Trix's plan unfurled, he knew that his decision would come at a cost. He would be expected to kill, to become a traitor to his fellow soldiers. Sev didn't relish the thought, but his loyalty didn't belong to them. For most of his life it had belonged only to himself, but no longer. Being a soldier at all was a betrayal of his parents and all they'd fought for, and if anyone deserved his loyalty, it was them. He would serve the Phoenix Rider cause, whatever the cost.

When Trix decided it was time, the cooks and bondservants would poison the evening meal. They were using a toxic mountain flower called Fire Blossom, which could be dissolved into food or drink. Captain Belden and the others didn't know about the flowers, which Trix's cohorts had to pick as they traveled. Clusters of the Fire Blossom tree dotted the mountainside, their fat red petals dangling like drops of blood from their knotted, twisted boughs.

"But what are you waiting for?" Sev asked one night, spotting a *pyraflora* tree and tugging a bright red flower from a hanging branch. "Fire Blossoms are everywhere. Why not poison them now, before we risk getting caught?"

"This," Trix said, plucking the flower from his hand, "is about as poisonous as black stew. Which is to say, quite poisonous—but not poisonous *enough*."

Then she popped the blossom into her mouth. Sev gaped at her, and she gave him a wide, wicked grin.

"Iron stomach," she promised, before moving on.

"So you need time to turn the flowers into poison—into something lethal."

Trix nodded. "Boiled. Dried. Crushed into a fine powder. All this has to be done after our regular duties and out of sight of the captain. Besides, we must choose our moment carefully. You soldier types aren't often all in one place . . . what with scouting up ahead, hunting for game, or breaking off to meet informants or purchase llamas. We can't risk poisoning too few and wind up on the edge of a returning soldier's blade."

Sev hadn't considered that. Suddenly her task seemed impossible. "So when?"

"We will have *one* opportunity when no hunting parties or forward scouts leave camp: the night before the attack. They'll need to ensure everyone returns to the campsite to nail down assault plans, assign positions, and prepare to strike with force. *That's* when we'll deliver an attack of our own. One blow to the main camp and . . ."

"Another to the perimeter guards," Sev said, seeing his role at last. Despite Trix's confidence that they could poison the majority of their party in a single stroke—including Captain Belden, whom she intended to deal with personally—at any given time at least five guards were on watch duty at the edges of their campsite. Sometimes more, depending on their location.

With his gift for memorization, easy access to the duty roster, and his position with the llamas, Sev was ideally placed to poison the personal packs of the soldiers assigned to perimeter guard before they left for duty. They didn't have a lot of the Fire Blossom to spare, and of course, they didn't want to spoil all the supplies. If they were successful, the other bondservants, cooks, and anyone else loyal to Trix would need them to make their way back down the mountain—or wherever they intended to go. Most would probably seek out refuge somewhere in Pyra, where they could be free from bondage—and the empire—and start their lives anew. Sev would seek out what was left of his family farm in Hillsbridge, but he didn't know where Trix would go. Or Kade.

No matter how hard Sev tried, he couldn't figure the bondservant out. Kade had argued against Trix's hasty dismissal of Sev the night he volunteered, insisting they needed him, but now Kade seemed unhappy that Sev had to decided to remain. It didn't make any sense.

Without their interactions during pack animal duty, the only time Sev saw Kade was at night with Trix. He remained frowning and distant as they discussed plans and strategies, and sometimes he didn't turn up at all.

"Were you one of her generals?" Sev asked Trix a few nights after she'd revealed her plans, the pair of them sitting together around a rare fire. It was very late, with everyone but the perimeter guard asleep, and Kade was nowhere to be found.

They were camped in a deep gorge, with steep stone spears rising above them, completely blocking the sky. Giant boulders were scattered in random heaps and piles, as if tossed there by a god's careless hand. To the west, the ground fell away steeply, giving Sev the impression that their entire campsite was perched on some precarious ledge and one good gust of wind could blow them clear off.

Luckily, their fire was tucked up against one of the large stones, far away from the cliff and protected from view of the campsite.

"No . . . I was never much of warrior. I served my queen in other, less obvious ways."

Sev stared at her thoughtfully. "You said it's been your business to know things for a very long time," he began, thinking out loud, "and that you advised Avalkyra Ashfire. Before you claimed that being famous 'would have quite defeated the point' of whatever you were doing in the war. Now all this stuff with poison . . . You were a spy, weren't you?"

It seemed obvious, all of a sudden, with her penchant for scheming and blackmailing and all her talk of information as power. Trix managed Captain Belden's messenger pigeons, and Sev suspected she spent as much time reading the captain's messages as she did sending them. She'd already mentioned that Belden was in constant contact with scouts higher up the mountain, and Sev had no doubt that was how she had so much information about his plans.

"I traded in secrets," she said, not addressing Sev's assumption directly but confirming it all the same. "My life began in the Aura Nova slums, and I will have the touch of it on me for the rest of my life, the same as you. Back then, joining the empire's military was a great honor, not a forced conscription. It was a guarantee of food, shelter, and work—and of course, joining the Phoenix Riders meant being a part of its most prestigious ranks. I almost flunked out of training," she said, chuckling as she poked at the fire with a stick. "But my aptitude for codes, patterns, and puzzles set me apart from my fellows. I'd learned to write thanks to my time serving Hael, god of health and healing, and was able to put my knowledge of herbs and medicines to use as well. My queen saw something in me and elevated me to serve at her side. War has a way of making regular people into heroes."

"Or fools," Sev said before he could stop himself.

Trix laughed loudly at that. "One and the same, are they often not? But this is why I need you, Sevro, animage soldier and common thief. Heroes have their uses, but we have ours, too. We're not popular, people like us," she said, her shrewd expression soft at the edges. "Too many deceptions, too many whispered secrets and mysterious missions. But we're *useful*. That's what it comes down to at the end of the day. Be useful, boy, and you'll never want for a position in this world. Find what you're best at and use it. If you're sneaky, then sneak. If you're a liar, then lie. If you're wicked as the south wind and devious as a deathmaiden, then, well . . ." She shrugged helplessly, arms wide, and Sev snorted.

Her words had made an impression on him, though. Maybe he wasn't a lost cause after all.

"What do you know about the informant?" Sev asked. It had been on his mind ever since Trix first told him about Belden's meeting. He couldn't help but wonder who would sell out their own people that way—what they had to lose and what they had to gain.

"Not much," Trix conceded, her mood turning dark. "I've not been able to intercept a letter since we were in the capital. I have no idea what happened at their meeting outside Vayle or if this traitor is still in play. That is why this battle cannot happen—why we must stop Belden's plan before it can be carried out. I don't have the network and resources I once did, and my blind spots nag at me."

Her expression was brooding. Sev tried to change the subject.

"What was she like, Avalkyra Ashfire?"

Trix seemed startled by the question at first, then considered it for a while. "She was . . . terrifying. Avalkyra Ashfire didn't need a crown of metal and jewels—she was a *born* queen, and no piece of gold could change that. People in the empire used to call her the Crownless Queen, trying to dismiss her claim to the throne, but Avalkyra would not be dissuaded. She was a ruthless fighter and a fearless leader—a more natural Rider I never saw. Like poetry on wings, soaring through ash and flame."

She held out her hand, dipping and curving it, as if her palm were a phoenix gliding on the wind. She dropped it.

"Soon our glory will be restored and our people made safe. If I can see them once more before I die, I will consider it a life well lived."

"Phoenix Riders?"

"Yes. There are . . . Well, I'm certain I have friends and loved ones among them. That is what sustains me—that and devotion to my queen's cause."

"How did she lose?" Sev asked, leaning back and stretching out his legs before the warmth of the flames. "She had the Phoenix Riders, the best part of the empire's military, and the support of Pyra and Ferro." Stel was rumored to be involved in the plot against Avalkyra, putting all their funds and forces behind Pheronia, whose mother was of Stellan descent. The governor of Ferro was a Rider and so supported Avalkyra Ashfire's claim, while the governors of Arboria North and South remained reluctant to join the fray.

"She was single-minded to the point of obsession, and vengeance was all she cared about. She made rash decisions and put her warriors in vulnerable positions. She flew her entire force to Aura Nova for the Last Battle, leaving their families and their non-Rider allies vulnerable. It was all or nothing with Avalkyra. There was no middle ground."

Taking her stick, Trix drew in the dirt in front of her. With a few hasty lines, she had a rough map of the Golden Empire, with divisions marking the provinces of Ferro, Stel, Pyra, and Arboria North and South. In the middle was an *A* for "Aura Nova," the capital city and its own, separate district. Aura Nova was built on neutral territory, so that no one province would have political power over another, and was ruled directly by the council and not a separate governor.

"They were cornered," Trix explained, using *X*s to mark the Phoenix Rider forces, and *O*s for the empire's foot soldiers and horse-mounted cavalry. "When Avalkyra led her troops to the Nest, the empire's forces circled around, blocking their escape. They could obviously fly out of range, but the empire's catapults were placed strategically around the city. And besides . . . Avalkyra would never approve a retreat. By taking the battle to the empire, we were forced to fight on their terms—on their turf, so to speak. Avalkyra had been forced to flee the capital and set up residence in Pyra, but everyone knew she wanted the Nest. Pheronia's generals took advantage of that and waited.

"Phoenix Riders are best in open fields or high terrain, not in cramped cities. Our attack patterns are usually sweeps—a small unit rips by, loosing arrows and trailing fire, before circling back around. But in such tight quarters, those kinds of assaults were difficult. There were too many hiding spots for the archers below—they just camped out in upper-story windows and picked us off. Most of Aura Nova is stone, but even still, the entire city was on fire. Everything that could burn did . . . buildings, trees, and flesh. Ash fell from the sky and blanketed the streets like a rare winter snowfall. Luckily for the poor folk squatting in wooden tenements and cheap, run-down cookhouses, the majority of the battle took place on the Rock."

The Rock was a thrust of stone that held the Nest, the name of the palace that had housed the royal line since Queen Elysia the Peacemaker built it when she founded the empire. They said Queen Elysia chose the rocky outcrop because it reminded her of their abandoned home atop Pyrmont. There, the palace was built, and on the flatter ground surrounding it, the public service buildings, courthouses, and temple district. Marble Row, the street of lavish houses where the provincial governors lived while they were in the city, along with wealthy merchants and other people of importance, was situated on the eastern side of the Rock, where they had a view of the harbor and the Fingers where they sliced through the capital.

Marble Row had been decimated during the battle and had been in a constant state of rebuild for the fourteen years Sev had lived in the capital.

"And on the Rock is where the war ended. Just as they were born, they died—together," Trix continued.

"Who did?" Sev asked.

"The princesses—the Ashfire heirs. They were False Sisters, you know. Shadow Twins. Siblings born mere moments apart by the same father and two different mothers. It creates a kind of bond, a connection that goes beyond blood. Avalkyra's mother was queen, a Rider from an old Pyraean line who died in childbirth, and her sister's mother had been a wealthy Stellan consort—until the death of the queen, when the king decided to marry her next. Even though Avalkyra was the first *legitimate* child of the king, his second marriage made Pheronia legitimate as well. And of course, no one was sure which princess was born first. The king never officially named an heir, the old fool, so the girls were pitted against each other from day one. She loved her, though, Avalkyra—she loved her sister, but it's the strongest love that turns into the strongest hate. And hatred wins wars." She paused. "*Usually*. In truth, neither sister won the Blood War. Avalkyra's phoenix, Nyx, was gravely wounded—I watched from a tower window as both Rider and mount fell from the sky. They landed amid the rubble and destruction near the outer walls of the Nest. Before long, the flames engulfed them both."

Her voice had gone hoarse, and she cleared it before continuing.

"Riders are immune to their mount's fire, of course, but only while their phoenix is alive to protect them. As for Pheronia, the foolish girl left the safety of her tower room—looking for her sister, some say, hoping to make peace or surrender—and was taken by an arrow as she roamed the palace walls. They brought her to me, you know," she said, and Sev straightened. He had no idea she'd been so closely involved. He'd assumed that as a spy, she'd simply watched from the shadows.

"Oh yes. I was an assistant healer working inside the Nest, and of course all the properly trained practitioners were busy elsewhere. They brought that dying princess to me and wanted a miracle." Trix sighed. "The arrow went clean through her chest. There's no saving someone from that sort of wound. Still, I did what I could for her. . . . People like to talk about the princesses as if they were seasoned politicians, analyzing every fault and misstep. But seeing her there, dying on my table . . . she was just a girl, barely eighteen, alone and afraid."

Sev was eighteen, old enough to be considered an adult and allowed to join the military instead of the labor camps for his criminal sentence. It was hard to imagine having the weight of an empire on his shoulders when he could barely keep his own life together.

Trix's gaze was distant, as if she were reliving the past inside her head.

Finally she seemed to come back to herself and poked at the fire once more.

"Now we have no princesses, no queen or king. The governors bicker and squabble, back to their old ways, fighting against one another for every scrap of power and control. It's been sixteen years, and they've yet to get a majority vote for someone to succeed the throne. The prudent ones fear a civil war; the power-hungry ones are simply biding their time. Their provincial armies are only just now coming back to full strength, but soon someone will make a move and seize the power that is there and waiting."

"Do you think the Phoenix Riders could do it? That they could put someone on the throne again?" Sev asked.

Trix looked at him sharply, as if surprised by the question. Her eyes were dark, shadowy pools when she replied. "In truth, I don't know what their purpose is, hidden as they are up in the mountains. But yes, I believe that one day, they *could* put a Phoenix Rider queen on the throne again."

Sev wanted to ask if she thought they *should*, but he held back. Surely it would mean more fighting, more wars, and he couldn't help but feel that the struggle might not be worth it . . . that the Phoenix Riders would return only to be wiped out once more.

"And what about . . . what happened to your phoenix?" Sev asked hesitantly. Whatever had happened to Trix's bondmate, it couldn't be good, but curiosity got the better of him.

She stared at the flames. They'd burned quite low, only just gilding the bottom of her face. "Her name was Bellatrix."

I'd like to be called Trix. She was silent for a long time, and Sev thought the conversation was over.

"We survived the fighting in Aura Nova," Trix began, her voice heavy, "because we weren't in it. I was already positioned inside the Nest and had to maintain my cover. Bellatrix was with the youngsters at Avalkyra's home base on Pyrmont. It was terrible to be apart, but as I watched the phoenixes drop from the sky, I was grateful. Sick with cowardice and grateful all the same. In the days and weeks that followed, we tried to keep the rebellion alive. I fled my post, but I couldn't risk leaving the capital—everyone traveling in or out had to provide travel papers and identification. Laws were passed; friends were executed as traitors. To exist was an act of rebellion. Even in Pyra, we were not safe. Avalkyra left nothing in place, no precautions in case she did not return. We were leaderless, all our best warriors dead or imprisoned. Raiders wreaked havoc on our borders, and animages were chased deep into the mountains. But hope lived. *She* lived."

"Who lived? Your phoenix?"

Trix stilled for half a heartbeat, pain flickering across her face before tossing her stick aside. "Yes. She lived, for a time. She begged me to run away with her. There were still safe places for people like us, deep in the wilds. But I couldn't."

Trix was speaking steadily faster, the words pouring out of her in a rush.

"I have a duty to my queen, and my work is not yet done. I told Bella that, again and again—she had to remain in hiding, lest she give us both away. When she railed against my orders, I commanded it, with all my might and all my magic. She didn't listen. Bella was a stubborn old thing," Trix said, aching tenderness in her voice. Then, in the blink of an eye, her tone went hard. "When they found me at last, they dragged me to the city square. I must admit that I was afraid. I was a spy, so I was always prepared for my own death—but *facing* it is an entirely new beast. And facing Bella's? That, I was not ready for. She came for me, wings blazing, shrieking her fury. A dozen soldiers were dead before they managed to hook her with a net and drag her down to earth. I could hardly see, for the tears in my eyes. Bella called to me, and her fear was like fire in my belly. Before I could do more than cry her name, they raised the ax and cut off her head with one fell swoop. A phoenix that's been beheaded cannot be reborn. That death is final. There was blood everywhere. . . . It sizzled as it spread across the cobblestones."

Sev stared at her, unable to banish the horrible image from his mind. "I don't know what to say."

"Say nothing," she said briskly, clearing her throat. "It was years ago now. Water under the bridge. Ashes in the wind."

"I'm sorry, Trix," Sev said eventually.

"Ilithya," she corrected. "That's my true name. Or at least, it used to be. Ilithya Shadowheart. It's about time you knew it."

Sev felt the weight and significance of that name and the fact that she'd given it to him. Thya was short for Ilithya, and Trix was short for Bellatrix.

There's so much in a name.

"I'm sorry, Ilithya," he corrected.

"You know what? I prefer Trix," she said, and gave him one of her wide, mad-looking smiles. Sev found it oddly comforting.

"Time for sleep, I think," she said, getting creakily to her feet. "Nothing like tales of the bloody past for a bedtime story. Sweet dreams, Sevro."

She squeezed his shoulder, then puttered off to bed, leaving Sev alone by the fireside.

He wasn't at all ready to sleep. He wouldn't be surprised if Trix really *did* think the history of the Blood War made a good bedtime story, but Sev did not. His mind was racing, filled with images of battles and blood and death.

He put another log onto the fire and stared into the growing flames.

Sev knew there was a chance he wouldn't survive what was to come—that Trix and Kade might not either. But if Trix's plan succeeded? He and the others would be free. Sev could go anywhere, do anything, with no soldiers left to drag him back to the empire. As much as that was exciting, he ached to have a place to *belong* when all this was over. To have "friends and loved ones" like Trix. Now that he'd had a small taste of it, he wasn't ready to let it go.

"Can't sleep, soldier?"

Sev squinted into the darkness, and a second later Kade appeared from the shadows. Sev hadn't heard his approach, which made him wonder how long the bondservant had been lurking there, just out of sight.

"Have you been eavesdropping?" he demanded as Kade lowered himself onto a log opposite him.

"There's nothing Ilithya could tell you that I don't already know. Besides, I didn't want the old woman interfering."

Sev settled back into his seat, wary. Kade's presence always put him on the defensive. "She prefers to be called Trix."

Kade snorted. "She's just being difficult. When we first met, she asked me to call her *Princess Pearl.*"

Sev found himself smirking, and Kade grinned too.

"Are you sure you're up to this, soldier?" Kade asked eventually, his smile gone. His hands were knitted together in front of him, and he spoke to the flames, not to Sev.

"You don't want me involved," Sev said, not at all surprised by the fact, though still put out by it. He had thought, when Kade argued against his dismissal after the llama incident, that Kade was looking at him differently. That maybe he'd wanted Sev around after all—or at least saw value in his skills. But Kade made no move to deny his words. He took up Trix's abandoned stick and jabbed angrily at the fire. Obviously Sev was wrong.

"Well, you don't have any other choice," he said bitterly. "So you're stuck with me."

"We can figure something else out," Kade said, shifting onto the log next to Sev's, leaning forward as he spoke. "We can find another way."

Sev continued to prod at the fire, but he wasn't really seeing it. "I know I've made some mistakes," he began, trying to keep his voice steady, "but I can do this."

"We can't afford mistakes, soldier. People's lives are at risk."

"You think I don't know that?" Sev asked.

"You're not thinking this through. You realize you'll be poisoning your *fellow soldiers,* looking them in the eye right before you turn around and stab them in the back."

Guilt gnawed at Sev's stomach, but he refused to let Kade's words dissuade him. Of course what they were doing was terrible, but they didn't have any other options. Besides, if Sev didn't do it, someone else would.

"Why can't you see past it?" Sev demanded.

"Past what?" Kade asked, his brow furrowed.

"The fact that I'm a soldier. It's not who I really am."

"Did you see past it before you were one of them? Did you see past it when hundreds of them marched on your family's farm?"

"Shut your mouth," Sev snarled. "I am what the empire—what those soldiers—*made* me. A motherless, fatherless animage with nowhere to go and no one to trust." He tossed the branch into the fire and lurched to his feet, stepping over the log and making to stride away.

Kade stood in front of him, blocking his path. "Do not make the mistake of thinking you are the only person here who's had a hard life. That you're the only 'motherless, fatherless animage' to be found in this camp."

Sev stared at him, at Kade's rising and falling chest. Was Kade a war orphan too?

Before he could ask, Kade huffed an exasperated breath and continued. "I understand that life has been hard for you, but people can only judge you by what they see. By your *actions*."

"And what have my actions told you?" Sev demanded.

Kade shrugged and looked away. He was attempting to stay calm, Sev knew, but the strain was evident in the tense cords of muscle in his neck and the way his jaw clenched. He ran a hand over his short hair, then cast Sev a sidelong glance. "You're a liar. You're selfish and reckless. And you care nothing for our cause."

Sev couldn't deny the first three things. He'd lied about being an animage since he was four, and for years he'd only ever looked out for himself. If his two escape attempts weren't reckless, Sev didn't know what was. He used to loathe those parts of himself, the same as Kade, but Trix had changed that. When *she* looked at Sev, she saw all his negative qualities as his greatest potential. She saw someone capable—someone with hidden talents and a dark past.

Someone just like her.

"I didn't care, at the start," Sev admitted, addressing Kade's last comment. Or rather, he hadn't *wanted* to care. Life was easier when you didn't care—or so he'd thought. He'd spent so much time afraid of hurting, of losing everything again, that he'd forgotten life wasn't worth living—worth saving—if you had nothing to live for. "But that's not true anymore."

"What changed?" Kade asked, hand dropping to his side. "You all but begged to be done with this mission."

"I don't know. I . . ." Sev swallowed. Sure, he felt guilt over messing things up, for disrupting Trix's plans and getting Kade punished—but that wasn't what had changed for him. The circumstances hadn't changed, but Sev had. "I'm not sure how things changed, but they did. And I'm not quitting," he said, shaking his head resolutely.

Kade stared at him, an odd expression on his features, almost indiscernible in the flickering light of the fire. Was he surprised that Sev was fighting back . . . or maybe pleased?

"What about you?" Sev asked, carefully avoiding Kade's eyes. "You hated me at the beginning. Has that changed?"

"I never hated you," Kade said quickly—too quickly.

Sev forced out a rueful laugh. "Now who's the liar?"

Ignix was the world's first phoenix, a female, and Cirix was the first male. Just as they were a mated pair, so too were their Riders.

Cirix was bound to Queen Nefyra's lover, Callysta. When she died, Cirix promised to join her, if only for a moment, before coming back to bond with her daughter. And so he did, again and again, remaining in Callysta's family line for many generations.

Ignix, on the other hand, has no death or resurrection on record. It is believed she lived through all the ages of the queendom until the founding of the empire, when she was finally lost to history. Most believed she remained in Aura, forever haunting those golden ruins.

Despite her long life, Ignix never bonded again.

—*Famous Phoenixes throughout History*, Princess Darya, published 12 AE

There is strength in unity, it is true.
The bond of blood, the bond of magic.
And love, the most powerful bond of all.

- CHAPTER 28 -
VERONYKA

VERONYKA WATCHED, NUMB, AS Val made her way toward them. The crowd parted for her, as Veronyka had known it would—she wouldn't have been surprised if the very mountains moved to make way for her sister. The bow in Veronyka's hand fell from her slack fingers, and the sound of it hitting the packed dirt echoed in her ears as if from very far away.

She wanted to run. She wanted to scream. She wanted to scrape that cold, impassive look from her sister's face.

"I have to go," Veronyka heard herself saying, the words slightly muffled as she forced them through unmoving lips.

"Nyk?" Tristan said, but Veronyka was already pushing past him, through the open gate of the training yard, and intercepting Val before she could enter.

"What are you doing here?" Veronyka whispered angrily, grabbing Val's arm and steering her aside. The familiar sight of her sister was unwelcome, *wrong* here in this safe place Veronyka had found for herself. All she could think about was what Val had done to her. All she could see in her mind were Xephyra's eyes bulging as she'd fought for life. The memory of the poison was fresh as spring blossoms, and the dizzying, heartbreaking betrayal was like rot in her belly.

"I go where I please, Ver—"

"Don't call me that," Veronyka snapped. She was leading Val back out the stronghold gates and through the village—she'd have marched Val all the way to the switchback stair, but Val finally planted her feet just outside the metalworker's quiet shop and refused to move.

"What shall I call you instead? *Nyk?*"

Veronyka reared back slightly. "How did you—"

Val rolled her eyes. "Look at you. If I hadn't heard that boy say it, I'd have figured it out when I saw you."

Veronyka forgot that Tristan had called her name before she'd abandoned him inside the training yard. A pang of guilt surfaced at the way she'd left him, but she didn't have the mental space to dwell on it.

Veronyka stared at her sister. Val looked the same as she always did: tall and beautiful, head held high—no matter the tattered clothes she wore—and always that distant, unfeeling facade on her face.

"How did you find me?" Veronyka demanded. "What do you want?"

"Who's the boy?" Val asked, nodding back toward the stronghold.

"Nobody," Veronyka said sharply.

Val laughed, the light, tinkling sound raising the hair on Veronyka's arms. "Oh, come now, little sister. You can lock your feelings up all you want, but you cannot hide them from me."

Or have you forgotten?

Veronyka lurched back, hastily reinforcing her mental walls, seeking out the gaps in the stones. She'd gotten lazy in her time away from her sister, not constantly on her guard as she'd had to be all her life. Now the barrier felt flimsy, as if cracks and crevices had appeared in the time she'd stopped tending the wall so diligently.

"You still haven't told me what you want or why you're here."

Val shrugged dismissively. "I came back for you," she said at last.

Came *back*? That didn't even make sense. Was Val delusional enough to think that she was here for *Veronyka's* sake? That Veronyka needed her help?

"We're family," Val added, her voice stripped of her usual scorn. "I would go anywhere, do *anything*, for you. Surely you know that."

Yes, Veronyka did know that. Val *would* do anything—she was a person without limits, it seemed, and so full of self-righteous conviction that she could justify any dangerous action or bizarre behavior—and that was an exhausting burden to bear.

"And now you're here," Veronyka said. "What it is that you want?"

Val crossed her arms stiffly, looking uncomfortable. A surprising thought occurred to Veronyka. Had Val come to apologize? Could it be that she regretted what she'd done and she wanted to make things right?

"I know we didn't part on the best of terms," Val began, resting a hand on Veronyka's shoulder. "But that's in the past."

Nope, no apology. Veronyka jerked out of reach. "The *best of terms*?" she repeated, her voice shaky. The shock of seeing her sister, the resurfaced memories of hurt and betrayal . . . they were catching up with Veronyka, making her dizzy and light-headed.

"You're still angry with me, for culling your—"

"Culling?" Veronyka choked, the word torn from her constricted throat. "She was my bondmate!"

Val pressed her lips together, her nostrils flaring. Then she took a slow, measured breath, as if Veronyka were an irrational child throwing a tantrum and Val were searching for patience. Veronyka glanced around, knowing she shouldn't have shouted, but no one was nearby. Voices and laughter could be heard from the field beyond the gate, where everyone gathered, but the village itself was quiet. She had to keep her temper under control. . . . She had to keep *Val* under control.

"We don't have time for this, Veronyka. I need you by my side. We're stronger, *better*, together."

The words grated. How could Val even think that? Over the past few weeks Veronyka had seen what real friendship was—how two people could work together and help each other, and that wasn't what her relationship with Val had ever been, or would ever be.

"With me you can be yourself," Val continued, gaze roving Veronyka's face. "You've cut your braids and forgotten yourself, posing as—what? Some peasant boy-child?"

"I *am* myself; I haven't forgotten anything. And there's nothing wrong with dressing like a boy," Veronyka said, fighting for composure. "Queen Malka did it. She bound her breasts and kept her braids short."

Val rolled her eyes, but before she could reply, Veronyka added, "And I'm not just a peasant; I'm a stablehand."

"A stablehand? You abandoned me, your only family in the world, so you could live a lie as a no-name *servant*?"

"So what?" Veronyka asked, her voice rising again. "There are worse things than serving those you respect, than paying your dues until . . ."

"Until what, *xe* Nyka? You think I don't know, that I didn't ask around, didn't pry into heads and hearts and figure it out the moment I stepped foot in this sorry excuse for a Rider outpost? No female Riders and only a dozen masters—half barely out of childhood and the rest wrinkled, old men? They have no eggs, and no eggs means no phoenixes and no future."

Veronyka shook, unnerved that Val had gleaned so much so quickly. "I wouldn't need to be here, waiting for a phoenix egg, if you hadn't *killed my bondmate*."

Val's hands clenched and unclenched, her face twisting with anger. She turned abruptly away, as if she wanted to punch something, but after a deep breath, the rigid line of her back loosened. She looked over her shoulder. "If that were different—if *things* were different . . ."

"If things were different, I'd be a Phoenix Rider." Veronyka's rage was shifting, twisting and swirling, spreading like wings inside her chest. Xephyra's face flashed in her mind, and Veronyka pushed the dark feelings away before they engulfed her. "But I'm not."

"Hey, Nyk—is everything okay?"

Veronyka spun around to see Tristan standing a few feet away, approaching them hesitantly. How much had he heard? His expression seemed mild enough, if a bit concerned—their tense body language made it obvious that Veronyka and her sister were arguing.

"Everything is fine," Veronyka said, hating that he was here, within her sister's eyeline. "This is my sister, Val. And, Val, this is Tristan, one of the apprentices."

Tristan nodded, frowning slightly as he considered them. Veronyka knew they looked nothing alike, and she could only hope Val never crossed paths with Beryk or Elliot.

Val was looking at Tristan, too, no doubt measuring his worth and deciding what way he could best be used to her advantage.

"Why do you not allow females to train as Riders?" Val demanded without preamble.

Veronyka squeezed her eyes shut, stifling a groan.

"Well," Tristan began, gaze flicking to Veronyka as if wondering how much she'd told her sister. "We didn't have a lot of eggs, in the beginning. So we had to be, uh, selective."

Val tilted her head, and Veronyka could sense the magic spill from her, almost see the way she poked and prodded into Tristan's mind. Veronyka felt sick being witness to the violation and even worse that she didn't know how to stop it. "But you do have female phoenixes, don't you . . . ?" Val whispered, almost to herself, distracted as she searched his thoughts.

"In the breeding enclosure," Tristan said.

"Breeding enclosure?" Val repeated, her voice dangerously flat.

"Can we have some time alone?" Veronyka blurted as Val's eyes sparked with anger.

Tristan nodded, looking slightly hurt at the quick dismissal. She wished she could tell him it was for his own good, that she was protecting him, but all she could do was smile encouragingly.

"Nice to meet you," he said to Val, and turned around, hands in pockets as he strode back up the street and toward the stronghold. Veronyka felt even worse knowing that she'd kept him from the rest of his friends only to abandon him now in the middle of the festivities.

Val's breath was heavy when she spoke, her face twisted with indignation. "Females imprisoned. You'd better watch yourself here, *xe* Nyka. If they find out you're a girl, you might wind up in a cage next. How they *dare*, when Ignix herself might be among them."

Though most famous phoenixes had their deaths noted in the history books, no such record existed for Ignix. It was part of why phoenixes were always treated as sacred beings—there was no way of knowing for sure just who they had been, or how long they had lived.

"I doubt they've captured and caged the first phoenix in existence, Val," Veronyka said, her voice weary. She hated the breeding enclosure too, but Val's dark paranoia knew no bounds. "Surely Ignix would come forward and make herself known."

Val's voice was oddly hushed as she replied. "Maybe she is afraid. Maybe the world has changed too much." Seeing Veronyka's confused expression, she cleared her throat and shrugged. "Or perhaps she's not here at all. It's the principle. One does not cage or breed a phoenix, any more than one would cage or breed a queen."

Distantly the bell rang for the feast, evening slowly descending around them like an ink stain on paper.

Crowds of people headed in their direction from outside the village, laughing and singing as they made their way through the growing twilight toward the dining hall.

"Why do you stay here, *xe* Nyka?" Val asked, when the last villagers disappeared around the corner. She was fighting to keep the disgust and disappointment from her voice—and failing. "You've seen for yourself how they treat females. You *will* get breasts eventually," she said unkindly, eyeing Veronyka's bound chest, which was relatively flat with or without the extra fabric. "You can't be Nyk forever, and then what? You think they will accept you and release the phoenixes from their cages? You think they will give *you*—a girl and a liar—one of their precious eggs? Even you can't be so foolish as that."

Veronyka didn't answer, but her eyes flicked back to the stronghold, where Tristan was no doubt seated with everyone else, enjoying food, drink, and entertainment.

Val understood at once. "You think he will save you? He's just an apprentice."

"He's the commander's son and practically a patrol leader already. He'll be the one running this place one day, and he said he'll do whatever he can to help me be a Rider."

"But he's promised to help *Nyk*, the poor, helpless stableboy, not *Veronyka*—the girl who has lied to him from the start."

Veronyka's chest felt tight. "I'm not lying about who I am," she said, even as she knew it wasn't technically true. She wasn't faking her personality, but then again, she also wasn't showing Tristan her whole self—gender aside. He didn't know she was a shadowmage, after all, or that she'd already had—and lost—a bondmate. "Besides, he's not like the commander. He hates the breeding cages and the fact that they don't let girls and poor kids become Riders. He's different."

"Are you so blinded by your feelings for him that you can't see how ridiculous this is? He'll inherit from the commander in ten or fifteen *years*—if you're lucky. Are you willing to wait that long? And just because he dislikes a thing doesn't mean he can change it. He'll still have to answer to the other Riders—who will have loyalties and agendas of their own. These aren't *our people*."

"Nobody is, according to you," Veronyka snapped. "You hate the empire, and now you hate Riders, too. . . . Who *are* our people, Val?"

"You're my people, Veronyka, and I am yours."

The words echoed between them. Veronyka didn't know what to say. Val *was* all she had, her only family. And before she'd come here, Val was the only person in the world who would have cared—or noticed—if she'd lived or died.

Veronyka hoped that now there might be at least one more.

"I have a gift for you," Val said.

Veronyka quailed at the thought. The last gift Val had given her had been a phoenix egg.

"I don't want it," Veronyka said, taking a step back from her. Whatever it was, Veronyka would not, *could* not take it. Even if Val had found another pair of eggs, did she really want a repeat of what had happened last time? She didn't think she could survive it.

"Just come with me, Veronyka," Val said confidently, cajolingly, as if it were the easiest thing in the world. All she had to do was follow—but Veronyka was done being led around by her sister.

"I'm not going anywhere with you. I'm happy here. I want to stay."

"I'm asking you—*please*," Val said, lips pursed, as if the word were bitter on her tongue. Then her tone changed, becoming breathless, almost panicky. "It must be now, Veronyka—we don't have time to waste."

"*No,*" Veronyka said, frowning at the urgency in her sister's voice.

The sound of music burst suddenly from the stronghold, rising above the din and floating into the air to mix with the muffled conversations and laughter that filled the night.

"You would stay here, putting your faith in these men who would see you humbled and subjugated, rather than leave with me? *Why?*"

"You know why," Veronyka said, her voice shaking with barely controlled fury. How dare Val act sad and hurt when Veronyka was the victim here? "I *did* have faith in you—and you betrayed it."

"But we could become Riders on our own terms—not theirs," Val said, her eyes bright and glittering. "No rules, no waiting. Just you and me."

"There would be rules, Val—*your* rules. And even if we succeeded, then what? Live on the outskirts forever? Shun other Riders because they aren't *us*? We've been doing that all our lives, and I hate it. I want to be a part of something, Val. . . . I want to be a part of the Riders, not a Rider all on my own."

"You wouldn't be alone," Val said quietly. "You'd have me." Her hard features had gone soft, her fiery voice hesitant. Vulnerable.

Her pretense at frailty, at weakness, only made Veronyka angrier. "We tried that, remember?" Veronyka asked in a strangled voice. "We tried to go it alone, and look what happened! You gave me what I wanted only to tear it away from me again just to prove that you could. Just to be in control. So tell me again, why did you come here? Are you going to kill Tristan or the commander? Are you here to take it all away again?"

"I came here to give you—"

"I don't want it—I don't want *anything* from you!"

Veronyka turned away and ran for the stronghold. She couldn't stand being around her sister any longer. Her mind was racing, and her heart was a skittering, lurching thing inside her chest. She needed to get away from Val, away from everything.

When she stepped through the stronghold gates, Veronyka was shocked to see Tristan standing there, just outside the double doors to the entrance hall, as if he was waiting for her.

"Nyk," he began, unhitching himself from the wall and stepping toward her. Then, seeing the look on her face, he paused. "What's wrong?"

Before Veronyka could answer, scraping footsteps sounded behind her, and she knew that Val had followed. Tristan's eyes narrowed at her sister, and there was something hard and protective in his expression. Veronyka longed to give in to it, to trust in someone else's care and not fear it, as she had to with Val.

"Are you coming to the feast?" Tristan asked, looking between them as he came to stand next to Veronyka.

Val started talking, but Veronyka didn't hear it. The world around her went silent as she was hit with a powerful wave of emotion—emotion that was not her own. She staggered, trying to sort through her own feelings and those assaulting her.

Fear, rage, and confusion—she thought they belonged to Val at first, or maybe Tristan, but when she turned to face them both, she knew the sensations didn't come from either of them. Veronyka whirled, staring into the dark corners of the courtyard. The feelings were familiar somehow, and when she reached out with her magic, a wild, savage screech filled the night.

Shouts echoed from the guards along the walls, who were pointing up at the sky. A flaming phoenix soared above, circling the stronghold in wide, erratic arcs, flying ever lower. Someone tugged Veronyka's arm, trying to pull her back, but she resisted it.

The phoenix's flight was dizzying—or maybe that was the swirl of emotions still spinning inside her. There was a pulse of intense heat, and then the phoenix landed on the cobblestones, mere feet in front of Veronyka. A powerful wave of its wings, and sparks danced across the ground.

The phoenix was juvenile, near the size of most of the apprenctice mounts, except its scarlet plumage was edged in deep purple that shimmered in the torchlight. Tracks of flame shone like lava between its feathers, and its eyes, black holes limned with fire, latched on to Veronyka's and held her gaze.

A gasp escaped her lips, and she dropped to her knees.

Xephyra.

Day 11, Fifth Moon, 170 AE

Princess Pheronia and the Council of Governors,

I, Avalkyra Ashfire, the Feather-Crowned Queen and rightful ruler of the Golden Empire, hereby officially claim my throne.

It grieves me that I have been deemed a criminal and a traitor, when I have always acted for the good of my family, and of course, for the good of the empire.

I will be in Aura Nova one week hence, in order to discuss the terms of my ascension. You are welcome to negotiate your position in my new regime—but be warned, I have the might of Pyra, Ferro, and the Phoenix Riders behind me.

—Queen Avalkyra Ashfire

P.S. Happy eighteenth birthday, Princess.

*But one must be cautious who they
bond themselves to. Once fastened, those ties
do not easily come undone.*

- CHAPTER 29 -
VERONYKA

VERONYKA KNEW IT, FELT it, even as her eyes refused to believe it. Her mental safe house burst open, flooding her mind with memories, and in them, Xephyra was still small enough to carry. The creature before her now was almost the size of a pony, her claws sharp and her wingspan as wide as the cabin she'd be born in.

*Re*born in. Xephyra had come back. Somehow Veronyka had managed it. Somehow that cold pile of ash had turned into her phoenix once more. No matter how much she'd grown in their time apart, there was no mistaking the bond between them. The instant their eyes met, it had sparked back to life, like fresh tinder on the smoldering embers of a banked fire. The connection crackled between them, shock and recognition setting Veronyka's very soul ablaze.

Xephyra was on fire too—there were great billowing waves of it, rippling over her scarlet feathers, so hot they burned bright, blisteringly blue. But these weren't the flames of happiness, of a phoenix and Rider rejoined. . . . They were the flames of danger.

Veronyka looked over her shoulder, noticing the crowd of people there for the first time.

Apprentices, servants, and villagers were huddled near the entrance to the dining hall, where they had undoubtedly spilled out in reaction to Xephyra's fierce shrieks.

Stronghold guards were there too, with bows and spears pointed directly at the newly appeared firebird.

A spasm of fear—hers or Xephyra's, she wasn't sure—pulled Veronyka off her knees and onto her feet. Her mind was galloping in a hundred directions at once, and the reappearance of her bondmate did nothing to quell the confusion inside.

Veronyka clenched her teeth and focused.

Xephyra was in danger here—the phoenix sensed it, and it made her behave wildly, which only put her in greater danger. Unless bonded, phoenixes were erratic, unpredictable creatures, and the stronghold guards were on high alert because of that fact. One wrong move, and this could turn very, very bad.

Veronyka had to get Xephyra to calm down. Once her bondmate was under control, the guards would stand down, and the immediate threat would be neutralized.

Taking a shaky step forward, she reached out with her hands as well as her magic.

"Nyk, no!" Tristan shouted, though it sounded as if it came from a lifetime away. She supposed it did. Tristan existed in a world where Veronyka was Nyk, and Nyk had no phoenix. But that's not where Veronyka truly was. No, Veronyka was here and now, reunited with her dead bondmate and afraid for her life.

When she made contact with Xephyra's mind, Veronyka staggered—it was bizarrely unfamiliar, and yet nothing had really changed. It had the feeling of a childhood home that was now inhabited by new people—it was at once exactly the same and astoundingly different. It was a miraculous thing to realize that the bond survived death, but their connection wasn't unchanged by it.

It was clear that Xephyra was wary too, and confused by their reunion. Veronyka kept seeing herself in her phoenix's mind—long black braids, the cottage, their pallet on the floor—and she seized the images.

Yes, it's me, she said, pressing a hand to her chest. Tears welled in her eyes as Xephyra cocked her head, hesitating. *It's me.*

Veronyka sensed the commotion around her, felt the shifting bodies and shuffling feet, but she blocked it all out. All that mattered was her and Xephyra. With every second they spent staring at each other, their flickering, fragile bond strengthened. But no matter the soothing thoughts and comforting emotions Veronyka funneled through their link, Xephyra refused to settle. Her hackles were up, her instincts on high alert, and the upheaval in the courtyard did nothing to stifle her fears.

"Step aside, boy!" came the commander's voice, like a general on a battlefield, breaking Veronyka's concentration.

A metallic scraping noise sounded, sending a sliver of foreboding down Veronyka's spine. She craned her neck, searching for the source, and spotted two guards holding a length of greasy-looking iron links.

A net.

"No—please," Veronyka cried, but before she could say or do anything more, Xephyra panicked and reared up, sending a sweltering wave of heat and sparks over the crowd.

Veronyka raised an arm to protect her face, shocked at the intensity of the heat. At the edges of the courtyard, bits of straw and fabric caught fire, while the onlookers gasped, rippling and recoiling from the hot air like grass in the wind. Tristan was at the forefront and had been reaching for her before Xephyra's flames had forced him to stagger back. Val was there too; her face shone with intensity, her gaze manic, *hungry*, as she stared at the scene before her.

Hatred roiled in Veronyka's gut. *Val.* Did she have something to do with this? Did she know all this time that Xephyra had come back?

The commander was shouting again, and the sound caused Val's unblinking stare to falter. With one final glance at Veronyka, she allowed herself to be bumped and jostled, disappearing into the crush of bodies. Did she fear what would happen now that the commander was involved? Or did she sense Veronyka's rage and know that it was directed at her?

"Nyk, move—you'll be hurt," Tristan shouted, forcing his way forward once more. "Get out of—"

Before he could finish, his head jerked up to the sky. A second later Rex ripped through the air above with a resounding screech. The phoenixes weren't supposed to leave the Eyrie unless summoned, but it was clear that Tristan had not called his bondmate to his side. Before he could do anything, Rex was joined by another phoenix, and another, and soon the sky was alight with their flaming tracks.

Veronyka tensed. They might be there in support of Xephyra—phoenixes did not like to see one of their kind attacked—but they were only making the situation worse. Their presence was fanning the flames of her bondmate's already wild emotions, and as they dipped and soared, weaving a mesh of fire above, Xephyra expelled a great rush of heat and flame in response.

No, Xephyra! Veronyka shouted through the bond as the guards closed in and panic seized her heart. *Calm down, and everything will be fine. Just calm—*

But Xephyra was too far gone. She reared up again, backing away from the surging guards and bumping into the side of a storage shed. Barrels went flying and beams of wood caught fire. If Veronyka didn't get Xephyra under control, the stronghold would burn.

An arrow whizzed by Xephyra's head, meant to scare her back and away from the other wooden buildings, but the sight of it drove icy fear deep into Veronyka's bones. She held her breath as another arrow flew in the same direction, and then a third, which veered slightly off course *just* as Xephyra staggered forward. It grazed the muscle of her wing and zipped past; there was a scream—and it came from Veronyka's own throat. She fell to the ground again, and a strong arm slipped around her stomach, heaving her backward.

"No!" Veronyka shouted, shoving the arm—which belonged to Tristan—aside as she got laboriously to her feet. Her wild eyes flitted from Xephyra to the guards with their raised weapons, to the phoenixes above, and back down to the flames licking across the ground. "No, no—*stop!*"

And everyone did.

The entire yard stilled for a strange infinitesimal moment, just long enough for Veronyka to realize that she'd accidentally used shadow magic. To command. To control.

The knowledge sent shock waves through her, and as if released from a trance, the crowd expelled its collective breath. No one seemed to have noticed what had happened . . . no one except for Val. She was staring at Veronyka as if she'd never seen her before.

Veronyka didn't have time to spare for her sister. She whirled around, seeking out Xephyra, who was still motionless from Veronyka's magic— though her flesh continued to hiss and crackle with heat.

The sight of her like that made Veronyka's throat ache. Not only had she apparently commanded a crowd of people, but she'd commanded her bondmate, a thing she'd sworn she'd never do.

There was a gust of air, bringing with it the tang of steel. The net whooshed over Veronyka's head and settled onto Xephyra with a heavy, metallic rattle that echoed in the courtyard. She flapped her wings and snapped at the links, but it did no good.

Veronyka lunged for her, but the sudden movement caused black spots to speckle her vision. She'd used too much magic, depleting herself, and she staggered into Tristan.

"Where are they taking her?" she demanded, using Tristan for balance as she struggled to see over the crowd of guards closing in on her bondmate. He avoided her eye, his expression grim. "Where are they—Commander!" she shouted, spotting the man as he crossed the courtyard and releasing her grasp on Tristan to follow him.

The commander turned, and then nodded, as if he'd been expecting her. "Good," he said, his gaze flicking over her shoulder to where Tristan stood. "Both of you, come with me."

Veronyka didn't want to leave Xephyra. But she needed answers, and the commander was the only person who would have them. Still, her heart thudded painfully as she left her bondmate behind. They had only trapped Xephyra because they thought her a danger. Once she calmed down, they'd release her.

She told herself that over and over again, though her chest remained tight.

The instant the door shut behind them in the commander's meeting room, Veronyka spoke. "What are they doing with her?" she asked as Cassian moved to stare out the window into the courtyard below. The smell of burnt wood wafted in, along with the sounds of sweeping brooms and scraping shovels. "You have to tell me where they're taking her."

The commander raised his brows in a puzzled look. That's when it hit her. . . . He didn't know. Nobody had figured it out yet. Veronyka's pulse quickened. To everyone here, Xephyra was an unbonded, wild female phoenix, and Nyk was just a stableboy that had been caught in the crossfire.

"The phoenix is a her, then?" asked Tristan, looking between them. Yes, the phoenix was a her, and Veronyka knew exactly what they did with female phoenixes at the Eyrie. "So she'll be put . . ."

"In the breeding enclosure," the commander finished with a curt nod, taking a seat in his chair.

Veronyka's stomach roiled. This . . . She couldn't let it happen. She had to tell them, explain to them that the female phoenix was bonded—to her.

But that would mean revealing herself as a liar and risking her position here. All she'd worked for . . . gone. Whether she had a phoenix or not, she needed Tristan's support in order to become a new recruit, and she knew he'd feel betrayed by her deception. He had shared his most shameful fears, and Veronyka had been too cowardly to reciprocate.

It wasn't just her lies, either; there was the *how* of it. She'd used shadow magic to deceive Morra, and it was a notoriously distrusted ability. She wasn't *just* a liar, but a shadowmage as well. Trust was paramount in a Rider patrol. Trust was everything. And if no one trusted her, no one would want to sponsor her.

She'd have a phoenix to ride, but she'd be no Phoenix Rider.

Veronyka's thoughts were spiraling out of control. Surely they wouldn't turn away a bonded pair. . . . Surely there was a way to make this work.

" . . . time we discuss Nyk's position here."

With a jolt Veronyka realized that the commander had been speaking, and now both he and Tristan were looking at her. She replayed the last few words she'd heard. *Nyk's position here.*

Veronyka looked at the commander. If her position was in question, then he must have figured out her secret after all. The knot in her chest loosened somewhat. Maybe it was for the best. Better to get it over with, to squash her dreams once and for all. She might never be a part of the Phoenix Riders, but at least she could do right by her bondmate and get her out of that cage.

"He deserves to be a new recruit," Tristan said, and Veronyka stared at him. Here he was, standing by her, when their entire relationship was about to be torn to shreds. "I know we don't have eggs," Tristan added hastily, before his father could point out the obvious, "but Nyk more than displayed his capability as an animage tonight. To have talent like that working in the stables is a waste."

"I quite agree," the commander said. Tristan's mouth snapped shut, and even Veronyka found herself shocked into stillness. "The boy should not be tending the horses and the hounds, not when his connection to the phoenixes is so strong."

So the commander *hadn't* figured her out. Veronyka's head was spinning.

"Maybe we can start a secondary apprentice unit," Tristan said eagerly, pulling out the nearest chair and taking a seat, heartened by his father's attitude. "One where Rider hopefuls can get a jump on training. They could participate in weapons and combat exercises, our fitness regimen, and observe the rest of us when we ride our mounts. In the meantime, I could put together a third patrol to go hunting for more eggs. If we had permission to skip lessons for a week or two, I bet we could—"

"You're missing the point here, Tristan," the commander said, loosening the buttons at the collar of his embroidered tunic and relaxing into his chair. "We've just captured a third female. With any luck, we'll have a clutch of eggs before the winter solstice. There's no need to go gallivanting across Pyrmont."

He was talking about Xephyra as if she were a broodmare, as if her only purpose was to be a container for phoenix eggs, a kiln for baking precious warriors, and not a phoenix in her own right. It made Veronyka's blood boil.

"But the cages don't work. How many years are we going to keep those females locked up before you accept that?"

"And when will *you* accept that I will not grant you a patrol just so you can traipse across the countryside and get yourself killed?" the commander said, slamming his hands on the table.

A tense silence fell.

Tristan's chest was rising and falling rapidly, his lips parted as if he meant to loose a defiant retort. After staring intensely at his father for several weighted breaths, he closed his mouth and dropped his gaze.

Veronyka studied the pair of them. She had never before considered the possibility that it was love that made Commander Cassian hold Tristan back. She was surprised she hadn't recognized it before, for it resembled Val's behavior in some ways. How easily a person could convince themselves they were doing the right thing, no matter the damage they did to the person they supposedly cared about, if it was out of love.

But while Veronyka wasn't sure if Val could truly love anything or anyone, she believed that the commander did. He'd lost his wife under terrible circumstances. It wasn't hard to understand why he wouldn't want his son to risk his life for the same cause that had claimed her.

"What, then, Commander Cassian?" Tristan asked, looking up again. "We sit here and wait?"

Now that Tristan's voice was steady and his anger in check, the commander removed his hands from the table and sat back in his chair. He seemed pleased to have regained control of the situation and forced a determinedly light smile. "For tonight? We celebrate. We won't go hunting like a pack of wild dogs or train dozens of new recruits, stretching ourselves beyond our means. Instead we will use the resources we have available to us. Given the display I saw this evening, the best course of action is to move Nyk from the stables to the enclosure. I believe his gifts will make the greatest impact there, and with a third female, our luck will surely begin to change."

Veronyka's body went cold, like she'd been plunged into an icy lake.

"The enclosure . . . ," Tristan repeated, his eyes flicking to Veronyka. "You want Nyk to serve in the breeding cages with the females? But—"

"Furthermore," the commander continued, his voice rising and betraying his simmering anger, telling Veronyka that he hadn't forgotten his earlier argument with his son, "as you seem so determined to assume a patrol, I think it's time you showed me what kind of leadership you are capable of. As you know, the best leaders do so by example. You have put a premium on new eggs, and so you shall volunteer your phoenix for the next round of mating attempts. Your bondmate, Rex, has long since reached full maturity. He would make an ideal candidate for breeding, don't you think? Perhaps together with your friend Nyk, you can encourage a union that results in new eggs and new Riders. You are dismissed."

Like an anchor, love will hold fast
in a storm, but it can also pull you under.

- CHAPTER 30 -

VERONYKA

VERONYKA BARELY HEARD ANYTHING as Tristan tried to argue. There was a roaring in her ears, a rush that drowned out all thought and feeling. Too much had happened that day, too many shocks and surprises and gut-wrenching realizations.

Xephyra was *alive*. Axura above, Veronyka's bondmate was alive. This should be a night of joy—of pure, perfect euphoria.

But it wasn't. As much as she reveled at being reunited with her bondmate, everything was weighed down by dread.

She'd made a terrible mistake.

She should have told Xephyra to leave, should have sent her away the moment she recognized her. But when the guards surrounded them, she'd thought only of calming Xephyra, certain that the danger was in her phoenix's volatile reactions, not in her obedience.

Rather than telling Xephyra to flee, Veronyka, in a panic, had *commanded* her to stay. All this time she'd abhorred and refused that kind of power, and then she'd gone and used it in the worst possible way. It was their bond that had drawn Xephyra to the stronghold in the first place, and Veronyka's command that ensured her capture.

She'd been told to report to the Eyrie the following morning. It was almost like a dream come true. Almost.

Veronyka gripped her head to stop herself from screaming—or crying. She was worse than Val, worse than the commander. She had betrayed her own bondmate—surely there was no more severe a crime than that.

And somehow her secret was still safe . . . but what did it matter? She couldn't stay here—not with Xephyra in a cage—and as soon as she told them *why* Xephyra couldn't remain inside the enclosure, it would all be over anyway.

Sour regret gripped her. She should have told them the truth, should have gotten it over with straightaway rather than allow Xephyra to remain locked up for one more minute.

But she hadn't. She was a weak, pathetic coward. Even the thought of it was enough to make her heart stutter and her breaths grow thin. She was utterly overwrought, and she didn't have the strength to deal with it right now.

Outside, the stronghold had gone quiet. The dining hall was empty, and the guards were back at their posts. The celebrations had been cut short; there would be no fiery phoenix dance tonight.

Val was waiting for her, seated on a barrel with a shawl wrapped around her shoulders. It had grown cold, and a bitter wind whipped across the abandoned courtyard.

Veronyka ignored her sister and headed toward the barracks.

Val caught up, walking beside her in silence. After several steps, Veronyka decided she wanted to talk to her after all.

"Did you do it?" she asked, turning abruptly to face Val.

"Do what?" Val asked, staring down the length of her nose at Veronyka.

Veronyka shoved her, relishing the idea of getting into a fight, of releasing all the anger and heartbreak that was building up inside. "Those ashes were cold and dead when I left that cabin. How is she here?" Veronyka demanded, fighting to keep her voice from rising to a shout. "What did you do?"

She thought back to that day, sitting in front of the empty hearth. She was certain she'd failed, had felt nothing from her bondmate, nothing in the weeks since . . .

Actually, that wasn't true. She'd put Xephyra in her mental safe house, blocked her presence and shut her out. Veronyka had thought she'd been stifling painful memories, but she'd actually been shutting out her bondmate's newly reborn attempts to connect with her.

Val stared at the place where Veronyka had dared to touch her, but she made no move to retaliate. "Don't blame me for the threads Anyanke has woven for you. I had nothing to do with your bondmate's resurrection."

Veronyka scowled. It was all too convenient, too awful, to have happened by accident. But the logistics of it weren't easy to dismantle, not when Veronyka was already so mentally drained. It was impossible to control a phoenix you weren't bonded to, let alone travel with one for weeks. Val couldn't have done this. "Since when do you believe in the gods?"

"Since always. Believing is one thing—worshipping on bended knee is something else."

Veronyka rubbed her arms, trying to banish the chill night air.

"Have they kicked you out, then?" Val asked, a determinedly light note to her voice—as if it was of no importance to her at all.

"No, they didn't. I'm . . ." The hollowness in Veronyka's chest was spreading, clawing its way up her throat and making it difficult to speak, to *breathe*. "They're putting her in the breeding enclosure. And I'm to work there as well."

Saying the words out loud was like a slap across the face, and the gravity of what was happening finally caught up with her.

A breath escaped Val's lips, as if she'd been hit in the stomach. "Do they know that you're bonded?"

Veronyka shook her head. She was oddly grateful for Val's shock, relieved to have someone on her side—but she dismissed the idea at once. Val was only ever on her own side.

"They think I have a gift with calming animals. I did the same thing

with a horse once, and . . . they want to keep Xephyra in a cage, force her
to mate, and . . ."

Her throat hitched, tightening painfully until she couldn't speak at all.
Against the cold numbness of her body, hot tears spilled down her cheeks.

"You cannot stand for this," Val said, taking a step toward her. "You
must free her."

"You think I don't know that?" Veronyka demanded.

"*Xe* Nyka," Val said softly, reaching for her, but Veronyka dodged her
touch.

"This is all your fault," she snarled, before running to the servant barracks, leaving her sister standing there, her arm outstretched.

That night Veronyka dreamed for the first time in weeks.

She sat in a crowded, smoky room, at the foot of a large wooden bed.

*She held a hand in hers and was unsurprised to find that it belonged to the
same dark-haired girl as in her last dream. She seemed older now, in the early
years of her womanhood, and their hands fit perfectly. Together they bent their
heads in somber silence.*

*There was a man in the bed, apparently unconscious, buried in fine blankets
and propped on embroidered pillows. His skin had a sallow tinge, and his brow
was dotted with sweat.*

He was dying.

*In her dream Veronyka knew this, even without recognizing the black-robed
priests of Nox or noticing the veiled mourners in the background. Incense burners
filled the room, choking the air with their bittersweet smoke.*

*Dream-Veronyka had fond feelings for the dying man, but she loathed the
woman who stood next to him with a hatred that made her stomach churn.*

*Dozens of others stood vigil in the room. Men and women, all dressed in
the finery of the wealthy Golden Empire elite. One of the courtiers caught
Veronyka's attention, and the recognition she felt was almost enough to jolt
her from the dream.*

Tristan.

No, that couldn't be right. This man was older than Tristan, but he had the same eyes, the same strong nose and stiff posture. Something in her mind clunked into place, and she knew this was Cassian she looked at. A much younger Cassian, but the distinctive widow's-peak hairline was evident, along with the indents that would become dimples on either side of his mouth when he smiled.

What she was seeing . . . it must be the past, then—but whose past? She looked at the girl next to her again. There was something familiar about her, but of course, Veronyka had been visiting this girl in her dreams for years.

A low rush of murmurs drew her attention. A stillness had come over the dying man, and a healer moved forward, checking his hands and neck before shaking her head and drawing the blanket up over his face.

The hated woman let out a wail, but it was nothing to the fierce chasm that had opened inside Veronyka. She clutched at the hand she still held as all around the room, the richest and wealthiest people in the empire turned in her direction and bowed. . . .

Veronyka awoke in the dark. She was more tired than when she'd fallen asleep, and her eyes were dry and puffy. The dream had been strange, but what had come before it had been stranger; Azurec's Day had delivered Veronyka the pieces of her old life again, except they didn't fit back together as they once had.

Xephyra's arrival had helped clarify things, putting Veronyka's position into perspective. Her bondmate did *not* belong in a cage, and if that meant Xephyra didn't belong here, with the others, then neither did Veronyka.

It made her ache to think of leaving Tristan behind, of what they might have become together if things were different.

But as she'd said to Val: If things were different, she'd be a Phoenix Rider.

Veronyka slipped out of the barracks before sunrise. She doubted Tristan would come by for their predawn run, but she wanted to avoid it in case he did. There was no point in pretending or getting her hopes up, and she wasn't ready to see him just yet.

The stars were still out, her only companions as she made her solitary way through the stronghold. She had several hours until she had to report at the Eyrie, and she sensed Xephyra sleeping comfortably through the bond. Her time was her own.

She started in the grassy field in front of the village, where the remnants of the previous day's celebrations still remained. The obstacle course was gone, but after so many nights spent going through the exercise, Veronyka could still see it in her mind's eye. This was where everything had changed for her, and it was where she felt most at home at the Eyrie.

Though the sky was growing paler to the east, Veronyka could pretend this was any other night, that Tristan was by her side, and everything was as it had been. But in that scenario, Xephyra was dead. So instead Veronyka imagined a new reality, one where she and Tristan did the obstacle course *together*, Rex and Xephyra by their sides.

Her heart lifted, and she let the vision dissipate.

Next Veronyka wended her way through the village. She spotted Old Ana hunched over her summer squash, tugging up weeds, and Lars, the metalsmith, waved as he started the fires for his day's work.

The stables were dark and quiet, the calming rustle of sleeping animals the only sound to punctuate the silence. Veronyka soaked it in, running her hands along horse flanks and murmuring soothing words as she passed. She poked her head into the fenced area where the dogs slept and received several sleepy tail wags in response.

The dining hall was mostly empty, so Veronyka took her time over a warm meal of oats and honey. Morra was busy getting started on the baking for the day, though she paused long enough to give Veronyka a wink and to slip an apple into her hand as she passed.

Veronyka forced her muscles to smile and kept her mind guarded as tightly as she could as she said her silent goodbyes.

෪ ෪ ෪

At first light Veronyka reported to the Eyrie for duty, just as the commander had instructed.

She was eager to see her bondmate. Maybe once she did, she'd have the strength to do what needed to be done.

The man who tended the female phoenixes was a local animage named Ersken. He and Beryk had grown up together in Petratec, and he was an expert at breeding hunting falcons, which was why the commander had enlisted him—with Beryk's help.

It was clear, however, that Ersken was out of his league in trying to breed phoenixes. He was grave but honest, telling her that most of his chores involved feeding the birds and cleaning the enclosure. They also needed to be exercised daily, preferably when the other phoenixes were out flying. The so-called breeding happened only once a month, for a week, and with virtually no success—unless you counted the single egg that was probably fertilized outside the enclosure anyway.

Though the Eyrie was open to the clear blue sky several hundred feet above, the bottommost levels were shady and cool, untouched by the early morning sun.

Ersken led her around, pointing into workrooms and storage areas, but Veronyka was too distracted to pay much attention. All she cared about was seeing Xephyra.

At last they climbed down the stairs of the gallery, which ran the length of the circular space, and into the courtyard below.

The enclosure stood before them.

While the area was large and clean, it was still a cage, excavated directly from the stone of the mountain, with bars that enclosed it on both sides: where it opened into the Eyrie, and at the back, which gave a view of the gorge and steep mountain cliffs beyond. There appeared to be a matching enclosure next to the first one, but it was dark and unused—awaiting more females, Veronyka thought darkly. The pair of them reminded her of prison cells.

A rustling sound from the first enclosure drew her attention—phoenixes stirring in the shadows—then suddenly Xephyra lurched forward to greet her.

The space inside was high enough that they could perch out of sight in cracks and crevices and wide enough that they could stretch their wings and fly from side to side. Ersken seemed surprised by Xephyra's warm welcome of Veronyka and took the chance to fill the phoenixes' water trough from a nearby barrel.

At the sound of the sloshing water, the two other females came forward, but with far more wariness than Xephyra. The nearer of the two was just a bit smaller than Veronyka's bondmate, eyes bright with curiosity. The one behind was larger, her purple crest and tail almost black at the tips, and emanated nothing but cold, fierce hate. She puffed out her feathers, making herself look even bigger, and returned to the shadows of the enclosure after inspecting Veronyka with a detached stare. Veronyka had the sense that she was very old, though she couldn't be certain—the phoenix's mind was locked tight.

Xephyra's beak pushed eagerly between the wide bars, and with a glance to make sure Ersken was occupied, Veronyka stroked it gently. Even after everything, Xephyra still wanted to be near her, still loved her. Veronyka tried to think of words, of apologies and reassurances and regrets, but she found that she didn't need them. Xephyra knew. They were bonded, after all, and while they might need time to mend the strong bridge they'd once had between them, it was still there, and Xephyra knew her heart.

There were endless questions to ask as well—about where her bondmate had been and what had happened in their time apart—but Veronyka let them rest for now. They had forever to catch up.

The feathers along Xephyra's neck were smooth and silky, and with a bit of searching, Veronyka located the barest hint of a scar in her shoulder joint, where the arrow had grazed her wing the previous night. Phoenixes healed quickly, and the wound had been superficial.

The relief Veronyka felt at being here with Xephyra, seeing her safe and unharmed, was powerful. She actually had to grip the bars for balance, pushing slow, steady breaths through her nostrils. It was okay. Xephyra was okay. She had known it, would have felt it through the bond if Xephyra had been harmed, but it still meant something to see it with her own eyes.

Suddenly everything else seemed more manageable. Veronyka and Xephyra were together again. Truly that was all that mattered.

Still, Xephyra was confused by her confinement, and her mind was somewhat frantic and scattered. Val's face kept popping up, but Veronyka supposed that her sister's actions had left their mark on her bondmate. She had *died*, after all. Veronyka wondered if Xephyra even understood what had happened to her. It had been about two months since she'd been poisoned, and their weeks apart had put a bit of a communication barrier between them, as if Xephyra's development had been stunted without constant contact with her bondmate.

Finished with the water, Ersken straightened up, and Veronyka stepped back from the bars. He explained that they always exercised after eating in the morning, and that he used the food to lure the phoenixes close and distract them so they could be fitted with cuffs linked to coils of chain. This allowed them to fly but not escape. They were fed well, at least. The bowls of dried fruit and nut porridge looked very much like the breakfast they'd served in the dining hall that morning, flavored with a heavy dose of honey. Phoenixes could survive on almost anything, but they tended to prefer sweeter fare.

Veronyka watched uneasily as Ersken placed the leashes on their legs. Like the metallic net that had ensnared Xephyra, these cuffs were treated with flame-resistant resin made from the sap of the *pyraflora*—the Fire Blossom tree—which protected against the intense heat of phoenix fire. The petals of the Fire Blossoms, sometimes called Phoenix Flowers for their fiery red color, could also be made into a vicious poison. Veronyka wondered if that was the same poison Val had used on Xephyra. Surely it was the most readily available in the wilds of Pyrmont.

There was an old Pyraean song her *maiora* used to sing about the *pyraflora* tree, and though Veronyka couldn't remember every word, fragments of it ran through her head as Ersken uncoiled the chains.

> . . . *feathers red and petals dead, ash and bone make up its bed,*
> *fire bright as blood soon bled, ever will you rest your head* . . .

When the metal cuff slid onto Xephyra's leg and clanged shut, she reared back in confusion and alarm, the chain rattling loudly against the bars. Veronyka tried to soothe her, while fighting to keep her own emotions in check. Tears stung at the back of her eyes, and rage simmered in her stomach.

"It always takes a bit of gettin' used to," Ersken said, seeing the pain in Veronyka's face as she swiped at her cheeks. "For them an' you."

Veronyka nodded, though she couldn't keep her eyes off Xephyra. She might be well cared for, safe and unharmed, but this was no life for a phoenix. The sight caused a crackle of clarity to shoot through her mind.

Veronyka had two choices: tell them the truth and suffer the consequences, or flee with Xephyra in secret. She couldn't decide which option was scarier. It seemed that running away would be easier *now*—and certainly less daunting than facing Tristan, Morra, and the commander and admitting that she'd lied to their faces repeatedly—but what would happen to them in the long run? Where would they go?

But if she told them now, they might decide that, after proving herself to be an untrustworthy liar, they would be better off without her. They might force her away—or worse, lock her up as some kind of criminal, the way they'd tried to do when she first arrived. And what would happen to Xephyra then? Why not avoid the hurt and disappointment on Tristan's face—and the danger to herself and Xephyra—and just sneak out of here in the middle of the night?

Of course, while telling everyone the truth presented the *possibility* of leaving the Eyrie, ashamed and alone, running away now guaranteed it. Veronyka didn't think she could handle the smug look on Val's face if they rejected her after she revealed the truth of who she was, but slinking away like a coward felt wrong. It might save her the judgment of the people she'd come to care about, but would it save her judgment from herself? The fact that it was most certainly what Val would do made Veronyka want to do it even less. If she ran away, wouldn't she and Xephyra just wind up with Val again, settling back into their old pattern?

There was also the matter of the other female phoenixes to think about. If Veronyka found a way to release Xephyra, surely she'd have to release the others as well. She owed it to them, and yet . . . would she be dooming the Phoenix Riders forever? Dooming Tristan?

Once Ersken finished with Xephyra, he fitted the other two phoenixes with cuffs, introducing them as he worked. "This sweet lady is called Xolanthe, though I call her Xoe, more often than not. She's right curious—and a bit impulsive, truth be told," he said fondly, patting her neck after the leash had been secured. Xoe twitched and ruffled her feathers as the cuff was fastened but otherwise allowed him to do his work.

"*Her Majesty* Xatara, on the other hand," Ersken said with a sigh, "likes to make trouble." He frowned as he tried to reach the leg of the older, larger phoenix, who was spreading her wings, forcing her smaller competition away from the food. "She's fierce as fire and twice as hungry. Her Highness demands respect, and so I give it to her. Best to cuff her last. That way—" He cursed, drawing his arm back as a cut opened near his elbow, courtesy of Xatara's sharp claws. He reached back in with clenched teeth, closing the clasp with a snap before stepping back and reaching for a rag. "That way if you're wounded, you can tend to it straightaway."

He mopped at the blood and examined several bright red burn marks. He wore a leather jerkin and armguards to protect himself, but they didn't cover the entirety of his skin. The exposed flesh near his elbows and hands was covered in pale scars and partially healed scabs.

"Xolanthe and Xatara?" Veronyka asked. They matched the names of two warrior phoenixes from *The Pyraean Epics*, an anthology of songs and poems written during the Reign of Queens. Val had memorized the collection and used to recite it when they were trapped inside for days during the cold, rainy winters. "Are they sisters?"

Ersken chuckled. "No. They were named by the commander, who has a taste for poetry, it would seem. Suppose he'll need to name this new one now," he added absently. Veronyka's lips tightened at the thought of her beloved bondmate being renamed without her consent.

Ersken nodded to a lever on the far side of the enclosure, next to the opening for the food. "You can do the honors, if you'd like. That lifts the back hatch."

Veronyka's eyes widened. Could it be that simple? All she had to do was turn one lever, and Xephyra and the rest of the females could fly away?

Hands shaking slightly, she wrenched on the heavy switch, and a loud groaning sound reverberated through the enclosure. As she pulled down, a length of chain rattled somewhere out of sight, and the barred gate at the opposite side of the cage slowly creaked open.

With a wave of anticipation, the phoenixes took flight, though they were reminded of their chains soon enough. They tested their range once or twice, snapping and tugging at the metal leashes, before settling into the rhythm of flight. The chains were at least a hundred feet long and set on a rotating tether, which stopped them from getting tied into knots as they circled and banked around one another.

Veronyka and Ersken watched from a balcony next to the enclosure. The sky was pale blue, and the view of the gorge below was breathtaking. Jagged peaks faded into the distance in every direction, while rich greenery, growing brighter daily with the coming summer, coated the landscape.

Veronyka would miss this place. It felt more like a home than any of the houses, apartments, and cabins she and Val had lived in since they'd left their *maiora* behind. Even when she'd lived with her grandmother, Veronyka had been friendless and powerless on the unsafe Narrows streets. She wanted to belong here, but maybe she didn't. Couldn't. Maybe she'd just have to let it go.

Xephyra only flew two or three circles before she looped back around, drawn to Veronyka's presence. Ersken staggered back as the phoenix approached, but she landed on the rock just below them. Veronyka crouched and reached out a hand, wary of the long drop.

"That one's taken a likin' to you, eh?" he said, frowning slightly. Unless bonded, phoenixes never took a liking to anybody. Veronyka grimaced, knowing they were in danger of revealing themselves and yet unable to turn

Xephyra away. She allowed herself to pat her bondmate once before mentally encouraging her to enjoy the exercise while she could.

"She's bonded before, I'd wager," Ersken said as Xephyra flew off in a gust of warm air. Veronyka glanced at him warily, yet she didn't sense any suspicion there, only a mild observation from a man who'd spent too much time with captive phoenixes. Ersken had a kindly face, and he wasn't the nasty jailer she'd imagined. He was past middle age, barrel-chested and brown-skinned, with his graying braids pulled into a horse's tail behind his head. His wide, owlish eyes lightened with pleasure as he watched the beautiful birds soar in the air above them, and he'd shown them a gentle hand when fastening their chains.

Veronyka hadn't met a lot of animages—or Riders—in their thirties and forties, and it just occurred to her why that might be: Most of them had probably been killed in the war or put into bondage for their involvement with it afterward. It seemed that Pyrmont was littered with parentless children and grizzled old folks, and hardly anybody in between.

"It's the bonded ones who're more trusting of humans," Ersken continued, rubbing a hand against the stubble of his chin. "Poor thing. Probably lookin' for her bondmate and then she wound up here. Most of them will go to ash if they don't find their Riders, though there's a rare few that'll search forever."

"Go to ash?" Veronyka asked.

"Y'know . . . die. It's a hard life for a phoenix, if they survive their bondmate. It's a hard life for an animage, as well," he added, and Veronyka silently agreed. He didn't have any feathers or obsidian is his hair, so Veronyka didn't think he'd ever been a Rider—still, he was an animage, and it wasn't hard to imagine how the death of a bondmate could devastate a person.

"There were plenty of Rider-less phoenixes after the war, but most chose death or rebirth. Maybe some flew home, to Aura."

Val had always spoken of the Golden City with awe and reverence, as if it were as ancient and mysterious as the stars above. While the rest of

Pyrmont remained inhabited, none had lived in Aura since the Riders abandoned it almost two hundred years ago. Most, like their *maiora*, thought the city was cursed and haunted by ghosts, and even local Pyraeans were afraid to climb to the mountain's highest peak.

Not Veronyka, though. Her heart thrilled at the idea of flying there herself some day, soaring among the ruins and relics of another age.

"Has the commander ever sent anyone to Aura to check?" she asked. Tristan had mentioned they'd gone looking, but she wondered just how far those searches went. "For phoenixes, or for more eggs?"

Some people believed there were hundreds—maybe even thousands—of eggs in the old capital, laid over centuries and never retrieved. Maybe the Rider-less phoenixes were there right now, hatching their young and living in peaceful seclusion. Veronyka felt guilty for wanting to disrupt them, but if there were truly caches of phoenix eggs there, ready for the taking . . . it could change everything.

Ersken made a disdainful noise in the back of his throat. "Oh, he did— or so he says—but his patrol sure came back in a hurry. Too cloudy, nowhere safe to land, strange sounds, and 'the phoenixes didn't like it'—more like *they* didn't like it, and the phoenixes acted oddly because it called to them in strange, long-forgotten ways. But he's valley-born," he added conspiratorially, as if this explained all the commander's shortcomings. Maybe it did. Veronyka didn't want to admit that she was valley-born too, despite her Pyraean looks.

"More often than not, I find myself thinkin' of the phoenixes *below*, not above," Ersken said gravely. When Veronyka frowned at him, he continued. "Down in the valley. After the war, they usually beheaded the Riders' mounts so they couldn't be reborn. But other times they'd put the Rider in bondage and keep their phoenix locked up to guarantee good behavior. Some say there's dozens of phoenixes being held prisoner by the empire, deep underground. Even if they wanted to ignite and go supernova, they'd be reborn inside their cells."

A wave of cold crept over Veronyka, despite the warm breeze. Separating bondmates sounded like the worst kind of punishment imaginable. Worse than losing your bondmate to death, as Veronyka had already done. At least in death, one of you was at peace, even if the other had to go on living without them.

The thought made her feel desperately lonely, and she was surprised to realize it was a familiar sensation. The truth was, she'd gotten *used* to that feeling. Even now that Xephyra was back in her life, Veronyka was still trying to solve her problems on her own.

But Veronyka wasn't alone. Not anymore.

The future she was fretting over would be *their* future, and Xephyra had a right to weigh in on it too. For better or worse, they'd make this decision together.

Since Queen Nefyra, it has been tradition for the rulers of Pyra—and eventually the Golden Empire—to fashion a new crown for their coronation.

In Aura Nova such items are on display in the Hall of Legacy, though not often available for public viewing. Some crowns are delicate as fine crystal, while others will rust and tarnish without careful preservation. It is lucky they are under the jurisdiction of the Morian Archives; otherwise they might have gone the way of many other phoenix-related relics in the wake of the Blood War and the fall of the Ashfire line.

The oldest crown on display in the Hall of Legacy dates back to Queen Elysia the Peacemaker, who has the distinction of being the only ruler to date to fashion more than one crown. The gold and obsidian circlet she wore for her coronation in Aura and throughout her conquest was abandoned the day she founded the Golden Empire. She replaced that crown with one made of materials from each newly established province, including iron from Ferro, ornately carved wood from the forests of Arboria, horsehide leather from Stel, and obsidian from her homeland of Pyra. The iron, wood, and leather twisted together into a ropelike crown, dotted with shining spears of obsidian, symbolic of unity and inclusiveness, both characteristics that would define Elysia's reign.

All the crowns that came before Elysia's remain in the ruins of Aura, lost to the modern world. In the queendom such relics were placed upon the memorial stones for their dead queens, forever commemorating their glory.

According to Pyraean superstition, it is the restless spirits of these queens that haunt the long-abandoned Golden City, their earthly relics binding them to the cold ashes of their ancient queendom.

Notable of these lost coronets is the Fire Blossom crown of Queen Liyana, mother of Lyra the Defender, which was made of fresh *pyraflora* blooms that, according to legend, never withered or wilted. There was also the brutal crown of bones crafted by Queen Otiya, fashioned from her fallen enemies after a rival Rider family tried to usurp the throne. Some stories claim Queen Nefyra wore a "crown of fire," but it is of course more likely that she wore a crown of fire *glass*, commonly known as obsidian.

The last crown on record is that of Avalkyra Ashfire, whose phoenix-feather circlet was lost in the Last Battle of the Blood War, just like the would-be queen herself.

—*A History of the Crown*, the Morian Archives, 147 AE, updated 171 AE

*I had known from the outset that
we were doomed, that loving her would
be the greatest mistake of my life.
And I loved her still.*

- CHAPTER 31 -

SEV

THOUGH SEV HADN'T RECEIVED any official word, either from Trix or Captain Belden, it became clear as the days wore on that their journey was reaching its final destination. With every step he took, the paths they traveled grew narrower, the climb steeper, and the landscape wilder.

When they came to rest in a system of wide, low caves, Sev was certain it would be their basecamp. The caverns were deep and echoing, with a series of waterfalls spilling over the craggy sides to join the rest of the River Aurys somewhere down the mountainside.

Here they could leave all their extraneous packs and supplies behind, taking only what they needed to wage war. Captain Belden had obviously chosen this spot very deliberately. With the forest hemming them in, they were as secluded as they'd been so far on this journey.

It made Sev uneasy. Any manner of ill deeds could be carried out here, and the bodies would never be found.

Sev's suspicions were soon confirmed. Two days after settling into the caves, Captain Belden called his officers together to consult maps and work out battle plans. All the soldiers away from the camp slowly trickled in, including a hunting party with Kade in tow, as well as scouts and additional lookouts.

As they took their breakfast in the watery morning sunlight, Captain Belden officially announced the purpose of their mission: They were here to defeat the empire's enemies and eradicate the rebel force known as the Phoenix Riders.

A low hush fell over the group while Captain Belden spoke, but as soon as he returned to his tent, whispers filled the air, like wind through brittle grass.

The soldiers would begin their march the following morning, which meant that the true fight—the one Trix had carefully orchestrated—would happen tonight, during the evening meal.

A cloud of nervous energy hung over the camp for the rest of the day, as both soldiers and bondservants prepared to go to war.

For his part as a soldier, Sev was assigned to a small regiment that included Ott and Jotham. While the others napped or huddled together to sharpen blades and share battle stories, Sev remained outside by the animals.

He moved among the llamas, his mind quietly spinning. Two hundred names, two hundred packs, each with something unique inside or out to help Sev identify them. It hadn't been easy, but he had found a way to break it down. First of all, only certain soldiers were ever chosen for perimeter guard—usually those with more experience—so Sev focused most of his energy on them. The officers' packs were different from the regular soldiers', and the regular soldiers had their own subdivisions—archers, spearmen, and foot soldiers like Sev. They also had hunters and trackers in their midst, with larger packs stocked with different kinds of supplies. Eventually Sev had figured it out. It was like a puzzle, a game to keep him occupied on the long marches and sleepless nights.

Jotham's pack had a fraying strap, like the Scarecrow's hay-stuffed tunic.

Ott's reeked of smoking leaf and had a mysterious, dark stain across its front.

Yara's was perfectly maintained and spotlessly clean—so much so that it stood out from the rest for its lack of identifying marks or damage.

Despite Sev's hard work, there were still a handful he didn't know for certain. All he could do now was hope that they weren't the names drawn for duty tonight.

The animals were picketed together at the edge of one of the smaller caves, where they'd stored their supplies. The waterfalls were nearby, their steady rush drowning out the noise and bustle of the campsite.

"May I speak with you, soldier?"

Sev jumped, surprised to find Kade standing there, hands clasped behind his back. They hadn't talked since the night by the fire, and Sev didn't want to see him as he prepared to carry out the very deed Kade didn't think he could do. Would he try to stop Sev *now*, when they were almost out of time?

"I . . . okay," Sev said warily.

Kade walked toward the waterfall, glancing over his shoulder to ensure no one saw him so close to the pack animals. The ground sloped down toward the river, and he came to a stop next to a stand of trees and shrubbery that mostly blocked them from view.

He stared at Sev a moment, the steady patter of the waterfall singing around them and leaving droplets of condensation clinging to his dark hair. A shard of afternoon sunlight poked through the trees, slicing his face, showing that what Sev had taken for a stiff jaw was actually wavering, as if suppressing pent-up emotion or frustration.

"I want to explain. The other night . . ."

"You don't want me involved, but it's too late. There's nothing more to say."

"There is," Kade ground out. "I . . . I did hate you. At first."

Sev forced a smile, though he didn't find the information at all amusing.

"I knew . . . about your parents," he said haltingly. He paused, as if expecting Sev to lash out in anger like he had the last time they were mentioned. When Sev remained quiet, he continued, "I'd grown up knowing their names. I lived in that safe house they protected; I watched the fires burn from the back of a wagon as we escaped. I owe my life to your parents, and when Ilithya told me their son had survived, I . . . Well, I was eager to meet you."

Sev felt strange, weightless—disconnected from his body. Kade had known who his parents were all along? Had lived in the safe house? Sev had been there several times, when raids happened to nearby villages, or when soldiers were spotted along the border. Sometimes he and his parents would drop off whatever extra food or supplies they had—anything to help. He and Kade might have seen each other, even played together, and if Sev had listened to his parents, he'd have been on a wagon alongside him, on his way to safety.

"I knew that you'd be something special, that you could help us win this war. Only . . ."

"Only I wasn't," Sev said dully. "I wanted nothing to do with your war."

"It made me angry. That day, outside the cabin . . . I expected you to charge in like a hero, to stand up to Jotham and Ott and to rescue that girl. It's taken me all this time to realize that you did."

Sev frowned. "Did what? I didn't—"

"Don't you see? My methods would have only made Jotham and Ott more determined to do whatever they wanted. They'd have sent you away, put someone else as lookout, and then *they* would have been there when that animage girl turned up, not you. Who knows what might've happened."

"Luck," Sev said with a half-hearted shrug, unwilling to allow himself to enjoy—or truly trust—Kade's praise. "Teyke having fun at our expense."

Kade shook his head. "Fate. Anyanke weaving our threads together."

A thrill shot through Sev at Kade's words. He had felt it too. Some indiscernible current always putting them in each other's paths. Even now, there was a tug deep in Sev's abdomen, drawing him to Kade.

"I accused you of saving your own neck that day. Maybe you were, in some way, but you saved hers, too—when you didn't have to. If she'd been found, if they knew you'd tipped her off . . . things would have gone bad for you. Very bad. And the day you tried to run, you didn't come back for yourself. . . . You came back for me. Just because you do things differently than I'd do them doesn't mean they're wrong."

"So . . . is this a roundabout way of you saying you're sorry?" Sev asked, mouth quirking up in the corner.

Kade chuckled, the tension lightening between them somewhat. "It's my way of saying yes."

"Yes?" Sev asked, confused.

"To your question before, by the fire. Maybe I hated you in the beginning, but that has changed." Warmth spread from Sev's chest all the way to his fingertips. "I couldn't see—didn't *want* to see—what Ilithya saw in you. I was jealous, I suppose, of the way you two connected with each other. I've spent years of my life trying to be a worthy successor to Ilithya Shadowheart, but that's not my role to fill anymore. It's yours."

Sev swallowed. He'd only just come around to the idea that he belonged with Trix and Kade and the rest of the animages, but being her successor?

"That's—I'm not—"

"Not yet," Kade conceded, a ghost of a smile flickering across his face. "But you'll get there. And I'll help."

Sev thought back to the moment Trix first assigned him to pack animal duty. He and Kade hadn't been getting along, and Sev had thought she was being spiteful, putting them together—or that she wanted him to see all he had in common with the other bondservants. Now he couldn't help but wonder if *this* hadn't been her plan all along. She needed them both—not just now, but later, for the future. If they were going to save the Phoenix Riders, it would require more than just stopping this one attack. It would mean stopping every attack and rebuilding Avalkyra Ashfire's rebellion from the ground up.

"We're mirror images of each other—have you noticed?" Kade asked, tilting his head as he studied Sev. "Same age, same size—more or less," he added, his lips quirking into a half grin. They might be the same height, but Kade definitely outweighed *and* outmuscled him. "And here we are, in the exact same place, but opposite sides of the looking glass. Soldier and bondservant."

"We're not on opposite sides," Sev protested. "Not anymore." He needed Kade to see that. He'd thought all the same things about them, their differences and their strange similarities, but Sev wanted to bridge the gap.

Kade nodded, though his face had turned grim again. "I just . . . Well, I don't want to see you throw your life away trying to prove something to me—to anyone. You . . ." His mouth twisted, as if he was searching for words. "You already proved yourself to me."

"I did?" Sev asked, fighting down the wild hope that was building up inside him. "How?"

Kade shrugged, a determinedly offhand gesture. "First you came back. Then you stayed."

Sev's throat was thick, and he needed a moment to collect himself. "Even if I die, I'm not throwing my life away," Sev said, rubbing a hand against the back of his neck. "I just want . . ."

His arm dropped, and it felt oddly heavy by his side. Sev went to raise it, to reach for something . . . but he found he lost his courage partway, and it hovered in the air between them.

"I just want to rest easy when I die—whether that's today, tomorrow, or in a hundred years—knowing that I did the right thing for once in my gods-damned life. That I finally made the right choice. I want to stand with people I'm not ashamed to stand next to. . . . I want to stand with you."

He couldn't meet Kade's eyes, so instead Sev's focus had landed on the hollow between his collarbones, where his pendant hung. Sev wanted to read it, to know Kade's sentence and his crime, but the edge of his tunic covered the words. The day was still hot, and sweat glistened on his skin as his throat bobbed up and down in a swallow.

"What I can't figure out," Kade began, his voice soft and rich, "is why hating you was easy, but liking you has been . . ."

"Been what?" Sev asked, somewhat breathless at the idea that Kade *liked* him.

"*Difficult,*" Kade said, his expression intent. He took a step forward, pushing into Sev's outstretched hand, causing Sev's fingers to splay against his chest. They stared at each other, and Sev stepped backward—not a retreat, but a question. An invitation.

After a breath of hesitation, Kade followed him. Sev's next step brought him to the exterior wall of the cave, the stone cold and slightly damp against his back.

Kade filled the space between them, filled it with his rich brown skin and gemstone eyes and those wide, impossibly broad shoulders. Sev was trembling, the pressure against his palm making him want to both push Kade away and pull him nearer, nearer, until all was obliterated except for them.

The sunlight was gone from Kade's face, but the warmth remained. His eyes became hooded, his lips parted ever so slightly, and Sev's fingers clenched against the muscle of his chest. Slowly, as if not to spook him, Kade raised his arms, one on either side of Sev, and placed his hands against the stone, caging them in.

They stayed frozen in that shining golden moment for what felt like ages—or maybe it was several heavy, weighted heartbeats. Just when Sev had mustered the courage to close his eyes and lean in, the roll call sounded.

As if pulling his head out of water, Sev returned to their surroundings. He had to check in with Ott, his squad leader. After that Trix's plans would begin.

Sev's hand went to the back of his neck again, and Kade's arms dropped.

"You know the names?" Kade asked, his voice as slow and smooth as honey. Sev became lost in it, and it took time for his brain to understand what Kade was asking. The perimeter guard roster for that night—the packs he was meant to poison.

Sev cleared his throat. "I'll get them now." The duty roster was usually drawn up in the morning, but with the impending attack, all their schedules had been shifted.

Kade dipped his head in response. "I'll leave you to it."

As the sun disappeared over Pyrmont's distant peaks, the cooks began preparing the evening meal. Pots were hung over cook fires, kettles began to boil, and poison was sprinkled in.

Sev pressed a hand against his pocket, where a lump indicated the small supply he'd already been given. Two pinches of the poison per waterskin and three for any barley cakes or dried meat. The powdered petals of the Fire Blossom would dissolve best in the liquid, but even a dusting of it atop other supplies, once rewrapped in cloth or pouch, would begin to emit noxious fumes that would penetrate the food. The watch shift changed at sundown, and Sev knew he had no more than ten minutes to attend to the packs.

The names from the duty roster were like midges, buzzing around his head. He'd seen death before, but he had dealt it only by accident. He'd yet to engage in any real battle as a soldier, and Sev found he was having difficulty with the idea of killing in such a cold, calculated way. He didn't know any of the targets particularly well—did that make it right? It made it easier, but Sev couldn't decide if that was a good thing or not. These soldiers might have children, parents, brothers, and sisters—entire lives tethered to them. In comparison, he felt like some kind of wraith—tied to nothing and no one.

Not anymore, Sev insisted, forcing his mind to remain on the task and not on the soldiers. Sev wasn't killing for pleasure or personal gain; he was doing this for the Phoenix Riders, the only protectors his people had. He was part of Trix's re-formed rebellion, part of an "us" at long last.

As the noise of the campsite faded into the background, Sev made his way over to the pack animals. They had ten lookouts tonight—not because they were camped in a particularly vulnerable position, but rather, because they were so close to the Phoenix Rider lair.

Sev looked up into the sky, scraps of it visible between the trees and rocky caves, and gathered his courage. He thought of his parents, sacrificing themselves for him and for other animages. He thought of Kade and Trix, of Junior and Tilla and Corem—of all the bondservants—who deserved freedom.

He could do this.

Sev identified eight out of the ten packs with ease. Their personal effects were an extension of their very lives, and Sev imagined himself cutting the threads that connected the object to the person as he carefully poisoned their stores. The crumpled petals stuck to his fingers and left a dark, reddish smear the color of blood. It was one of the reasons Trix had wanted to poison the evening meal and not breakfast. In the darkness, the traces of the poison would be far more difficult to see.

Once the eighth pack was tended to, Sev considered the ninth name, the one he couldn't match. He was one of several soldiers who traveled without any personal items and only the most meager of supplies. There were around a dozen packs like that, and Sev didn't have enough to poison them all.

Time was ticking on. The soldiers would come for their packs at any moment to relieve the current perimeter guards. He had to make a decision.

The steady rumble of the distant campsite was interrupted by a sudden piercing whistle.

Sev froze; this wasn't a part of the plan.

Another whistle answered the first. Sev craned his neck to see the cooks and attendants pause in their work while the soldiers stood, heads turned toward the east.

Then a stream of armed soldiers poured through the trees, descending upon their camp.

We're under attack, Sev thought wildly, the fear so sudden and true that his insides turned to water and cold sweat scraped across his forehead.

But the newcomers weren't challenged or rebuffed—they were welcomed as friends with smiles and clasped hands. Captain Belden stood outside his tent, ready to greet the arriving party's leader.

The truth crashed down on Sev like a thousand tons of rock: They weren't the only empire soldiers heading up the mountain.

His mind reeled. They didn't have enough poison for all these soldiers, and even if they did, the new arrivals likely brought provisions and servants of their own.

Trix had been reading some of the captain's letters, but not all of them. Clearly this was information she had missed. All this time, they'd assumed they were a small strike force meant to deal the Phoenix Riders a stealthy—but still fatal—blow. But now, with twice their original numbers, maybe even more, they were a significantly larger threat. They couldn't march directly to the top of the mountain together—two hundred was a difficult enough number to conceal—so they'd had to travel separately to the same meeting point, ensuring they were both ready to attack at the same time.

Sev looked around, terror ratcheting his heartbeat to a painful rhythm. It was too late to call everything off; the dinner pots and waterskins had already been poisoned, and it was only a matter of time before their contents were eaten and their ill effects shown.

At the mouth of the nearest cave, one of the cooks tried to dump her pot, while a bondservant poured extra flour into a bowl of batter. If diluted, they might make only a few guards sick and spare their lives. All around Sev there was feverish panic, while the glint of steel and the tread of heavy boots muffled the rush of whispers and the sight of Trix's cohorts trying to abort their plan. A secondary line of pack animals and the bondservants who managed them came into view, making their way toward Sev. He looked for Kade or Trix or anybody he recognized, but they were lost in the crowd.

As the arriving soldiers settled into their camp, stew was served up, bread was fried, and waterskins were passed around. The Fire Blossoms were meant to work within thirty minutes, ensuring that everyone in the camp would be eating by the time the effects started to show.

The leader of the second party joined Captain Belden in his tent, and Sev wondered how his presence might complicate Trix's plans—if she still intended to go through with them. If they managed to kill both captains, would that be enough to put a halt to the attack? Even if it was, it wouldn't guarantee the survival of the bondservants. There were too many soldiers now, too many packs and stewpots and mouths to feed. It was a disaster, and all Sev could do was wait for it to unfold.

It started with retching.

Followed by gagging, spitting, and cursed complaints of stomach pains.

Then several soldiers ran into the forest or the darkness of the caverns, staggering off to empty their stomachs or their bowels.

Sev didn't know what was worse: the sound or the smell.

Others followed those that didn't come back, and soon waterskins and liquor jugs were sniffed and poured out. Rust-colored smears dyed the fingers of the soldiers who examined the contents, and bowls of food were dumped into the grass.

Shouts, cries, and accusations. The food was disgusting; the food was spoiled.

The food was *poisoned.*

Once those words were uttered, the camp dissolved into chaos. Attendants and cooks were rounded up, dragged through the dirt and grass and thrown onto their knees. Sev saw crying servants, begging for mercy, executed with blades across their throats, while those who tried to run were taken down with arrows or spears. Sev squeezed his eyes shut, praying Junior and the others had the sense to keep quiet and stay out of the way. The bondservants didn't officially have anything to do with meal preparation, but they did manage the transportation of the food supplies, and it seemed that everyone except for the soldiers was under scrutiny.

The packs! Sev remembered, whirling around. With the new soldiers arriving, no one had come to relieve the perimeter guard yet. If he managed to hide the evidence of what he'd done, he could hopefully save the bondservants on pack animal duty from suspicion. He pushed through the crush of llamas—who tossed their heads and stomped their feet in the face of all the commotion from the camp—struggling to find the supplies he'd tampered with.

Sev was fumbling with a strap when footsteps sounded behind him. They were uneven, stumbling, and with a slight drag.

He turned and saw Ott standing there, wavering slightly on the spot, sweat dotting his brow and what looked like a smear of vomit across his chin. Sev wasn't surprised to see him sick—he never missed a chance to be first in line to get food, drink, or his choice of assignment. He held his trusty crossbow loosely in one hand, as if he could attack the poison that was slowly killing him from the inside.

Ott blinked at Sev, gaze drifting from his hands—halfway inside the nearest pack—to the food on the ground, which Sev had hastily dropped and stomped on. He lurched forward, faster than Sev would have thought possible given the state he was in, and gripped Sev's arm. Ott yanked Sev's hand from the pack, twisting it to reveal the dark-red smears across his fingers.

Shoving the arm back with a sneer, Ott raised the crossbow, leveling it directly at Sev's forehead.

"Traitor," he slurred.

"Ott," Sev said, glancing to either side of him. He was blocked in on all sides, the llamas a mass of woolly bodies who skittered and shuffled nervously. His other hand was still inside the satchel, and he tried to surreptitiously check for a weapon or something heavy, anything he might use to help him escape. "I don't know what you're talking about. I—"

"Shut your mouth!" Ott shouted, his voice hoarse. Around him, the llamas' panic was a palpable taste on Sev's tongue, and his own fear was ripe.

Ott bent double and coughed, lowering the crossbow as he hacked and spit. Sev tried to make a run for it, but Ott had the weapon back up the moment he saw Sev shift his feet.

"Don't—you—dare," he forced out. More footsteps sounded nearby, and Ott perked up. "Hey, hey, over here!" he called frantically, but his voice was too weak to carry. He took a deep breath and filled his lungs before calling out again, *"Over here. I caught—"*

Ott's words were cut off by a loud crunch. Out of nowhere, a heavy branch cracked into his head, knocking him to the dirt in an unconscious heap.

Standing over his prone body was Kade.

He tossed aside the stick and picked up Ott's dropped crossbow.

Then he aimed it directly at Sev's heart.

*I cared not for the romantic love of men and
women. All I wanted was the throne that was
my birthright and to have Pheronia by my side.
She would be my heir, and her children after her.*

- CHAPTER 32 -
SEV

NO, KADE'S CROSSBOW WASN'T aimed at Sev's heart, but at his shoulder.

Before Sev had a chance to inhale, a bolt whizzed by his head and landed with a *thump*, right into the chest of another soldier sneaking up behind him. He whirled, gasping, his brain catching up with the thunderous pump of his heart. It was Jotham; he lay on the ground, blood spreading from the quarrel embedded in his ribs. The llamas skittered away from the noise and the body—though Sev suspected Kade was calming them; otherwise they'd probably have trampled the pair of them in panic.

True night had fallen, and by the time Sev looked up from the corpse, he could barely see Kade as he took Sev's arm and dragged him away. They left the pack animals and ducked behind the same copse of trees where they'd spoken privately together mere hours before.

Sev stared numbly at the chaos of the camp, just barely glimpsed between the branches, until he realized Kade was no longer next to him. There was a steep slope down to the waterfall and the gurgling pool, and there Kade crouched, silhouetted in the mist that rose from the water.

He was digging.

His shock receding, Sev scrambled after him, skidding down as quickly and quietly as he could. Did Kade mean to bury Jotham's and Ott's bodies? What would be the point, when the entire camp was about to be a graveyard?

Once he came to a stop next to Kade, Sev saw half-empty sacks of grain sprawled in the darkness beside Ott's abandoned crossbow, their golden contents spread across the ground like scattered stars.

And there, piled on the ground next to them, were a dozen smooth gray rocks. But the way Kade handled them, delicately and with both hands, told Sev that they were more than just stones. This must have been what Kade was doing when he heard Ott accost Sev. But what *was* he doing?

Their eyes met, Kade's features barely distinguishable in the twilight. "Those aren't rocks, are they?" Sev whispered.

Kade slowly shook his head and held one up for Sev to see more closely. Its surface was rounded, like a stone found in a riverbed, its shape carefully smoothed after years under the steady flow of water. In fact, the shape reminded Sev of—

"Eggs," Kade said, his tone was almost reverent. "Phoenix eggs."

Sev's mind flashed back to the conversation he'd had with Trix, when she'd said Sev had almost ruined everything after his failed escape attempt. He'd figured she was talking about getting Kade in trouble, but maybe it was more than that. These sacks of grain, were they concealing these priceless treasures all along? Had Sev unwittingly almost stolen a llama loaded with phoenix eggs?

Shouts echoed from the campsite, and Kade hastily put the egg into the small ditch he'd dug.

"I was supposed to take them to the Riders," he said, reaching to add the others. "I've been watching these eggs from the moment we left Aura Nova, never letting them out of my sight—well, until your escape attempt. But now . . . I don't think any of us are getting out of here alive." He swallowed, eyes frantic. "I can't risk them being discovered. All of this," he said, his voice heavy with defeat, "for nothing."

"Not for nothing," Sev said fiercely. "We're both here—both still alive. We'll take them together."

"There are soldiers everywhere. If they—"

"Exactly," Sev interrupted, "and I'm one of them."

Kade reached for an egg, then hesitated. "Sev, I . . ."

"Load up a bag," Sev insisted, "and we'll carry them together. If we're stopped, I'll tell them I'm under orders. Come on, quickly."

Kade nodded, looking around for something to pack the eggs into.

Sev jogged up the slope, retrieving a satchel from one of the llamas. He emptied what he could and held it open for Kade to load.

The eggs were about the size of one of Sev's hands, and as heavy as true stones. With twelve of them packed together, the straps cut deep grooves into Kade's skin as he slung it over his shoulder.

Arms and legs tingling with adrenaline, Sev straightened and took in their surroundings. The river was the outermost boundary of their camp, enclosing them on its eastern side. If they followed it south, away from the falls, they could find a place where it was narrow enough to cross. Then, once over the water, they could proceed more quickly, deep into the wilderness, praying to Teyke that no other soldier parties were descending on the camp tonight.

Judging by what Sev had gathered from their attack plans, in order to find the Rider lair, they needed to travel northeast. Hopefully they'd find it—or be spotted by Rider scouts—and be able to warn them before the soldiers regrouped.

"You, mageslave!" a voice called out, stopping them in their tracks.

Kade was walking just to the side of Sev, but his size—and the chain on his neck—made him stand out. Sev bristled, his patience with that word all but evaporated. Then a warm hand gripped his arm, as if Kade could sense that Sev meant to do something stupid. He flashed a warning look, and with a shaky breath, Sev nodded and turned to face the coming soldiers.

"Is there a problem?" he asked, his voice taut with suppressed anger. He angled his body in front of Kade's, hoping to take the brunt of their attention. Luckily, these soldiers were strangers from the newly arrived group and not people who knew him as a meek idiot.

"Yeah, there's a problem. You not seen the campsite?"

There were two of them, the glow from the cook fires behind casting their faces into shadow.

"'Course," Sev said, shrugging dismissively. "That's why I'm taking this one upstream for fresh water. Captain's orders."

"What's wrong with the water here?" asked the smaller of the two, jerking a thumb at the stream directly behind Sev and Kade.

"Yeah, and where's your bucket?" added the other.

"Have you seen what those soldiers back there are doing near the water?" Sev asked, going for affability, though his throat was dry. "The captain didn't want to risk it, so we're going farther upstream. And what d'you think's in the bag?" he asked, giving Kade a dismissive nod, and hating himself for it. "Rocks?"

The soldiers chuckled, loosening their stances.

"We best be off," Sev said, knowing that the longer they remained speaking to these soldiers, the worse their chances would be of getting away. "Don't want to keep the captain waiting."

He turned, not allowing them a chance to argue, and with a nudge to Kade, began to walk back the way they'd come. Once the soldiers had moved on, they'd have to figure out another way to cross the river.

"Wait," the taller one called, and Sev turned, his hand clenching against Kade's tunic. "Which captain?"

Sev swallowed. "Captain Belden," he said—what else could he say? He didn't know who was in charge of the arriving party.

"Captain Belden?" the man repeated, his voice sharp. The short one's hand dropped to his belt. "Captain Belden is indisposed. When did he give you this order?"

Sev's heart skipped a beat, and he sensed Kade's muscles tense under his hand.

As Sev searched for what to say, a breath of air slipped across his neck, carrying Kade's voice with it. He felt the words before he heard them, the world slowing around him, all his senses hyperaware.

He felt the heavy *thump* of Kade's satchel hitting the earth, heard the intake of breath and crunch of gravel underfoot as he tore off, and smelled the last dregs of him disappear in the gust of wind he left in his wake.

Though Sev seemed to experience it all in some frozen, crystalline moment, the soldiers bolted after Kade at top speed. They forgot Sev entirely, seeing the running bondservant as the only threat, and leaving Sev standing alone in the middle of the forest.

Kade ran like a Stellan horse, an agile blur as he leapt obstacles and slipped between trees. His pursuers shouted, their voices swallowed in the swish and snap of the undergrowth.

Sev became aware of his body, poised to run after Kade, to help him as he ran for his life. But then Kade's words came back to him, rattling around his head like precious, forgotten gems inside an empty jar.

"You know what you have to do," he'd said, before dropping the bag and running off.

Sev looked down at the satchel at his feet.

You know what you have to do.

Kade had sacrificed himself, leading them away from Sev and away from the precious phoenix eggs. Sev had to warn the Riders that the soldiers were coming; he had to get the eggs there safely.

He squeezed his eyes shut, barely daring to breathe as he listened for a grunt of pain or a shout of triumph that would tell him Kade had been taken down. But the campsite was too loud, and his blood rushed in his ears, louder even than the waterfalls, drowning out all other sounds.

Bending down on shaky legs, Sev hoisted the satchel over his shoulder. It was even heavier than he'd expected, and he knew it would be a challenge to carry it across camp, never mind across the mountainside.

Then he thought of Trix. *She* would know what to do, if she was still alive. She would fix everything. He would give *her* the phoenix eggs, and once the eggs were safe, he could go looking for Kade. Kade was smart, capable. . . . He could outrun the soldiers, fight them like he had Ott and

Jotham, or hide until the coast was clear. Sev just had to find Trix, and everything would be all right again.

He cut back up the sloping hill, skirting groups of soldiers hunched over and retching, and slipping past the cave of supplies, where more soldiers were cutting open sacks and upending barrels. The noise muffled his footsteps, allowing him to pass unnoticed.

Up ahead, the captain's tent loomed.

If Belden was "indisposed," as the other soldier had put it, that meant that Trix's plan had succeeded—that he had eaten some of the poison. With any luck, she would be somewhere nearby, planning her next move.

There was plenty of action around the captain's tent, soldiers coming and going, bearing platters of food and casks of wine to check for poison. Sev hastily crouched out of sight in the trees, peering inside through the half-open flap.

The attendant who served Belden his meals was on the ground, blood pooling on the woven mats. Food was splattered along the tent walls and across the tabletop, while Belden held a massive ax in both hands. The weapon dwarfed his wiry frame, and the weight of it caused his muscles to strain as he leveled it toward a bondservant, forced onto her knees before him while a soldier held her arms behind her back.

Sev's stomach lurched. The bondservant was Trix, and the razor edge of the ax rested just below her throat.

A trickle of blood oozed from the corner of her mouth, and an already purpling bruise spread across her cheek. Her eyes reflected the light of the brazier, and even on her knees, her face was proud and her chin held high. She would die a warrior's death by ax point, just as her beloved Bellatrix had done.

Belden was screaming at her, the words difficult to hear over the commotion all around them. Spit was flying from his mouth, and he kept pausing to clutch his stomach and gag.

Sev shifted slightly, trying to get a better view, and Trix's eyes latched on to him. They flitted over him, around him—looking for Kade, Sev guessed—until she saw the bulky satchel over his shoulder, the round, smooth objects straining against the leather. Relief flooded her features. Then she narrowed her eyes before flicking her gaze to the side, an almost imperceptible expression, but Sev understood well enough: *Go.*

Sev wavered. There must be a way to help her. He couldn't leave Trix to die. He couldn't walk away from her the way he'd been forced to walk away too many times before: from his parents, from Kade.

He cast about the tent for ideas or options, but Trix would have none of it. Her nostrils flared, and she looked to the side once more, her eyes bulging with urgency.

Sev clenched his teeth and shook his head. *No.* This was all wrong. *He* was supposed to be the one to die, the one who was risking his life. Why did everyone else have to go and leave him all alone?

Belden drew nearer, and Trix looked up at him, her lips twisting into a sneer—no, a smile. A terrible, deadly smile, her teeth red with blood.

"She lives," Trix announced, and though she faced Belden, her gaze fell upon Sev. She pinned him with her stare, as sharp as a knife. "Avalkyra Ashfire lives. And she will burn your beloved empire to the ground."

A shiver slipped down Sev's back at Trix's bloody proclamation. The captain lurched forward with a snarl, and in a great, sweeping arc, he lifted his ax and brought it down over the back of Trix's neck. It clanked against her chain before lodging deep in her spine, going down with her as she crumpled to the ground. Blood splattered everywhere, and after jerking the weapon violently from her body, he brought it down again. And again. Her corpse twitched with every strike, until Belden tossed the ax aside and bent over to vomit onto the ground.

Sev tried to do the same. His stomach clenched and his insides heaved, but nothing came up. His throat was so tight that he could barely breathe, and his limbs were numb with shock.

Turning away from the harrowing sight of Trix's mangled, lifeless body, Sev staggered backward, tripping over branches and stumbling through the darkness. *She lives.* Did Trix really mean that, or was she trying to get a rise out of Captain Belden? She'd told Sev how both sisters died in the Blood War. It didn't make any sense.

The bag on his shoulder weighed Sev down, physically and mentally, as he forced himself away from it all—away from the blood and the death and the knowledge that Trix would never see another phoenix again.

You know what you have to do.

Sev had to warn the Riders; he had to get the eggs to safety.

Shouts rang out, loud and nearer than the rest—had they seen him? Sev didn't look back, didn't hesitate, just ran as fast as he could through the forest. Footsteps—were those his, or a pursuer's?—echoed in his ears, along with crackling leaves and snapping twigs.

He came upon a small clearing with thick grass and gnarled roots underfoot. At the far end was a cliff that hung over an expanse of black. It was so dark, Sev couldn't be certain of the drop or what was at the bottom—more soft grass? The river? Or was it a trench of jagged, life-ending rocks?

You know what you have to do.

More shouting, more footsteps. Sev wasn't moving, and the sounds were getting closer. The clang of drawn weapons and the thrum of a released bowstring. Something thudded into Sev's shoulder, and the momentum made the decision for him. Searing pain ripped through his body, pushing the breath from his lungs, and his heart flew into his throat as he tumbled blindly over the edge.

In ancient Pyra there was a position of great prestige in service to the queen. Unlike her flaming warriors, who stood blazing and bright by her side, this person worked in the darkness, in the shadows cast by such shining lights.

A poison brewer, a whisper catcher—a spymaster. This person moved unseen, unnoticed among the Pyraean ranks of fighting queens and flying heroes. As such, their deeds are often lost to history, and even their names exist in no surviving record books—except one. Shadowheart.

Pyraean surnames are either inherited through ancient lineage and powerful magical bloodlines, or they are earned. A Shadowheart could rise up from the lowliest of births and stand proud among the queen's most loyal servants.

It is said that when the empire was founded, the position of Shadowheart was no longer utilized. The council demanded transparency, so such clandestine affairs were no longer tolerated.

Then again, it is the nature of the Shadowheart to be unknown and unremembered. Perhaps they have been here all along.

—"Queen and Council," from *Government, Then and Now* by Olbek, High Priest of Mori, published 137 AE

I would have given her everything.
Everything.

- CHAPTER 33 -

VERONYKA

ERSKEN WAS BY VERONYKA'S side for the remainder of the day, giving her no opportunity to sit with Xephyra and explain their circumstances. Maybe Xephyra was happy here, or maybe she was desperate to leave. Veronyka wanted to know. There was so much she'd missed out on, weeks of their lives together lost.

Though she was eager to have some alone time with Xephyra, Veronyka wasn't thrilled at the idea of burdening her bondmate with the harsh realities of what being in the breeding cages would mean. She'd just have to take it slow and get a sense of how Xephyra was feeling before she caused more pain and fear. Her phoenix needed some time to recover. They both did.

Veronyka figured her best chance to spend time alone with Xephyra would be after nightfall, when the majority of the stronghold's occupants retired. She wiled away her evening in the kitchens, begging food from Morra and helping where she could. When Tristan entered the dining hall, she watched him as he craned his neck and scanned the tables, only to drop dejectedly into a seat next to the other apprentices. Was he looking for her? The thought made her ache.

Later, when the stronghold was quiet, Veronyka made her way back to the Eyrie. She was halfway down the steps to the enclosure when a sudden tremor rippled through the bond.

Xephyra.

Veronyka pressed a hand to the wall, steadying herself, and turned inward. She found the place in her mind where Xephyra's connection lived, but the thoughts and sensations funneling through were muddled and incoherent. Veronyka had forgotten what it was like to have a bond, to keep a part of yourself open at all times, and perhaps Xephyra had lost that instinct as well. All Veronyka could discern was that Xephyra was being fitted with a leash again. What was happening?

At the bottom of the stairs, Veronyka slowed her pace, willing herself to relax. Maybe Ersken allowed them an evening fly as well as an afternoon one. Maybe this was normal.

Still, her heart was a wild thing inside her chest—and not just because of the dozens of stairs she'd just run. Xephyra's confusion was her own, and the sensation reminded Veronyka all too much of the moments before Val had poisoned her.

Pausing just inside the shadows of the gallery, Veronyka peered down into the courtyard below.

Ersken was standing next to Commander Cassian, facing the enclosure as if watching a show. They murmured together, but Veronyka couldn't hear them or see what they were looking at from her vantage point. Xephyra was calm for now, but it didn't change the feelings of unease she was emitting.

Instead of continuing down the stairs and entering the courtyard, Veronyka edged along the gallery. At last she saw Xephyra, but she wasn't in the enclosure with the other two females.

She was in the matching enclosure next to them.

A hand dropped onto her shoulder, and Veronyka whirled, her heart jumping into her throat.

Tristan stood in the shadows just behind her, a frown on his face. "Hey, are you okay?" he asked softly. His eyes raked her face, taking in the details of her strained expression and the way she kept looking down at the enclosure below. "What are you doing?"

He followed her line of sight and spotted Xephyra, separated from the other females. His face hardened.

"*That's* why he asked me to come down here . . . ," he muttered.

The questions bubbled up in her throat, but she didn't speak them—she already knew the answer. Veronyka hadn't given the second enclosure much thought earlier today, but it was clearly used for mating. A tremor rippled through Veronyka's body. She thought she'd have *weeks* to figure this out, but it had been less than a day.

"No," Veronyka whispered, her voice faint. She craned her neck, seeking Xephyra, reaching through the bond. "She's too young. She's never . . . She's not—" Veronyka was blathering, but Tristan cut her off.

"I know," he said grimly. He stared at her and seemed to come to a decision. He turned away and strode down the steps.

"Tristan, you're late," the commander said by way of greeting. "Call Rex down, and let's get on with this."

"Don't you think this is a bit quick?" Tristan asked, coming to stand in front of his father but making no move to follow his orders and call his bondmate. "The phoenix was captured yesterday. She's clearly young and frightened," he said, pointing at Xephyra, though at that moment, she looked nothing so much as politely curious.

Biting her lip, Veronyka reached out to Xephyra. She didn't want to actually scare her, but instead she simply asked: *Xephyra, do you trust me?*

The answer was swift as breath. Not a word, exactly, but a feeling.

Yes.

Warmth spread inside Veronyka's chest. Soon she wouldn't even need to ask; soon they would be completely in sync again.

Smiling, she asked her bondmate to have a bit of a tantrum. She was happy to oblige, squawking indignantly and flapping her wings so her chain rattled.

Tristan seemed puzzled by her abrupt change in attitude, but also pleased, gesturing to the phoenix as she proved his point. "Her wound has barely even healed. Do you really think this is a conducive environment for breeding?"

"Ersken has measured her tail feathers. Their length indicates an age between three to six months. She is fully mature."

Veronyka swallowed, her throat thick. Xephyra was large for her age—she always had been, even in her first life. She might have lived for over three months cumulatively, but *this* life, *this* body was closer to two months.

"Female phoenixes are extremely defensive creatures, Tristan," the commander continued. "The sooner we engage in breeding exercises, the better the chances she will not yet claim this place as her own. Xolanthe and Xatara have both exhibited territorial behaviors in their mating attempts. This is our chance to counteract that."

Tristan's expression was hard. He set his feet and crossed his arms, bracing himself. "I won't do it. I—this—it's not right. It's not the best way. I can't stop you from doing it, but I can stop Rex and myself from being a part of it."

"Excuse me?" the commander said, taking a step closer to his son. Ersken looked between them, eyes wide. "Are you refusing a direct order?"

Veronyka could see Tristan's throat work, even from a distance, but he didn't lower his head or avert his glance. "Yes, I am."

"This could cost you your patrol, Tristan," the commander said, lowering his voice to a deathly whisper. "I want you to think carefully right now."

"I am—and I have," Tristan said, speaking at full volume. "You told me the best leaders do so by example. I don't believe in this, so I can't in good conscience participate in it. If it loses me the patrol leader position, so be it."

The two stood nose to nose, staring at each other. Veronyka noticed for the first time that Tristan was actually a hair taller than his father. Maybe he had always been, but something about challenging the man was making Tristan stand straighter.

Pride in him radiated from her lungs, filling her up with each breath she took.

Commander Cassian's lips were pursed, but rather than explode in anger, he merely shrugged. "So be it. If you don't want to do what needs to be done, then I'll find someone who will. Run and notify Elliot that he and his bondmate will be required at the breeding enclosure immediately."

Renewed terror spiked inside Veronyka's veins, and Xephyra screeched in response.

Tristan looked her way, face frustrated and apologetic, but the instant their gazes locked, something happened. Veronyka's mental walls felt weakened by her sudden, visceral fear, and now her magic spilled blindly outward.

And it found Tristan.

Veronyka tried to pull back, but their connection was fast and strong.

It wasn't like when she'd glimpsed his mind before, accessing him through the animals he was connected to, or in small, momentary flashes. She was linked *directly* to Tristan.

It had happened almost effortlessly, as if there was a place in her wall that led directly to him. Before, when she'd heard him at the obstacle course as he communicated with the animals, it had been like listening through a keyhole. Now she stood before an open window.

Of course, just like a real window, the opening she'd made wasn't simply a way to see out, but a way to see in, too—a vulnerability that she had unknowingly cultivated, a weakness built from familiarity. Just as it did when she opened herself to the same animal over and over, it seemed all the times she'd skirted around Tristan's mind made connecting with him now much easier than it should be. This was something she needed to examine more closely, but as Tristan's thoughts came through the window in a deluge, it was all Veronyka could do to keep herself standing.

The high-stress situation was causing a rush of worries and fears to flood the surface of his mind. There was a shadow where the commander stood— watching, judging. Everything was a test in his father's eyes, and this was no exception. But she sensed that part of his anxiety had to do with her. . . . He didn't know Xephyra was her bondmate, but he'd known how much she hated the breeding cages. If it was challenging to understand a phoenix's mind, trying to untangle a person's felt near impossible. Tristan's thoughts were like guttering candles, bursting to life only to flicker out a second later, one after another, impossible to string together or follow along.

Veronyka tried to disengage herself, to separate his feelings from hers, to regain her balance. It was like being underwater, drowning in him. . . .

Then there was a spark, a ripple of sunshine in the corner of his mind—not a guttering candle but a blazing torch.

It was her.

Veronyka focused on that light, extending herself toward it—only she reached too far. She lost the tether to her own mind—the solid ground upon which she always stood. She felt weightless, disembodied, and another wave of dizziness washed over her.

She was wrenched from her place of safety. Veronyka's vision doubled, then split, and she was looking at the scene before her through *Tristan's* eyes. There she was, a small figure in the darkness of the gallery, crouched near a pillar.

The sight of herself sent a jarring spasm of alarm through her.

Somehow, rather than just sensing Tristan's mind, she'd slipped *into* it—mirroring, it was called. It was something Riders did with their phoenixes, and it allowed them to make use of their mount's incredible vision and to essentially be two places at once if they happened to be apart. It was the skill Tristan and the other apprentices were practicing during the obstacle course, and apparently a gift that took many years for fully qualified Riders to master perfectly.

And Veronyka was mirroring with a *person*. With Tristan. Could he feel her there? Could he hear her thoughts at this very moment?

She reeled, blackness closing in. Tristan's mind swirled around her in a whirlpool, swift and rushing and fathoms deep.

Distantly she heard a shrill squawk—it came from Xephyra—but before Veronyka could reach for her bondmate, the current pulled her under.

But I never had the chance.
I made my decision; I chose my path,
and there was no going back.

CHAPTER 34

VERONYKA

VERONYKA AWOKE WITH A start. She'd been dreaming of fire and ash, and she couldn't figure out what had jolted her awake.

Then it came again: a horn blast, shortly followed by another.

She scrunched up her face, trying to understand what it meant, when the events in the Eyrie came rushing back to her, and she lurched into a sitting position.

Veronyka wasn't in the servant barracks, but rather, was laid out on a pallet in a darkened chamber. She looked around the scant, empty room, seeing a basin of water, a satchel against the far wall—and her sister watching her from the shadows.

Veronyka's heartbeat hitched, picking up a painful, jagged rhythm. How long had Val been standing there?

"You're awake," she said, coming to kneel next to the pallet. Seeing Veronyka's suspicious look, Val rolled her eyes. "Oh, relax, Nyka, I haven't stolen you away. You collapsed."

Veronyka flashed back to the last thing she could remember—the sensation of losing herself in shadow magic as she fell deeper and deeper into her connection with Tristan. She shuddered.

Val's gaze roved her face, and inside, her magic nudged against Veronyka's mental barriers. Veronyka had the feeling Val knew—or at least suspected—how she'd managed to lose consciousness, but she made no comment.

"What happened? How did I get here?"

"They wanted the healer to have a look at you," Val began, and Veronyka's stomach clenched at the thought of them poking and prodding her unconscious body and discovering her secret. *"But,"* Val continued, smirking at Veronyka's look of horror, "I told them there was no need. I said you sometimes collapse when you're overtired. I offered my room so you could have some peace and quiet. Don't fret. They haven't figured you out yet, and they suspect nothing of your magic or your bond. You're welcome."

Veronyka scowled. She'd rather swallow soaptree leaves than give Val such an undeserved thank-you. "You were following me," she said instead, her tone accusatory. How else could Val have gotten in the middle of things if she hadn't been lurking somewhere nearby?

Val's expression flickered slightly, the tiniest chink her in self-assured armor. "I went *looking* for you," she corrected. "And figured you'd be with your bondmate. I arrived just in time to see you hit the ground."

Veronyka felt like there was more to the story than that. Had Val been in the Eyrie for other reasons?

"Your phoenix was so worked up, they decided to abandon the exercise after you were carried away. Your mistake has earned you a victory, if only a temporary one."

Veronyka's mouth twisted. Her *mistake*. Without another word, she reached across the floor for her boots.

Val watched her every movement. "Do you have any idea what you did down there?" she blurted, and Veronyka was shocked to hear her voice shake slightly.

"No, I don't. How could I, Val?" Veronyka demanded, getting to her feet. "You never taught me anything about shadow magic, did you? Nothing worth knowing, anyway. You wanted me to be unskilled and untrained so you could use it against me however you liked."

"I was saving you from yourself!" Val snarled, standing as well. "Your control has always been wild and erratic. You think I didn't see you in the courtyard the night your bondmate returned, commanding dozens of people *by accident?*"

Veronyka's stomach dropped. Though she'd noticed Val's attention at the time, she'd secretly hoped her sister didn't fully understand what she'd done. But of course she had. Veronyka had completely lost control of herself and her magic, and somehow she'd managed to force her will on a whole crowd of unsuspecting people.

"So yes, Veronyka, I've withheld information from you. To protect you. I was trying to stop you from doing something even more reckless, something like what you did last night," she said, gesturing vaguely in the direction Veronyka assumed was the Eyrie.

"And what exactly was that, Val?" Veronyka asked. Her feelings of guilt ebbed away in the face of Val's arrogance and superiority. Veronyka failed to see how what had happened with Tristan—one person—was any worse than what had happened in the courtyard. "What is it you think I've done?"

Val hesitated, and before she even opened her mouth, Veronyka knew she wasn't getting the whole truth. "You almost gave yourself away. You were neck-deep inside that apprentice's mind, and if your own body hadn't dragged you out, you might have drowned in him."

The thought sent a shiver down Veronyka's back. Could a shadowmage actually delve so deep into another's mind that they lost track of their own?

She considered her sister's words. Whenever Val disliked someone, she refused to use their proper name. Xephyra became "your phoenix" or "your bondmate," and Tristan became "that apprentice." Even their grandmother was often treated with scorn and called "old woman." Veronyka had always assumed Val's hostility toward the people in Veronyka's life came from a false sense of superiority, but what if it was something else? What if it was fear? Not of danger or darkness or any of the usual things that scared people, but fear of being replaced?

Their *maiora* might be gone, but Xephyra and Tristan were both occupying important places in Veronyka's life, places that, for sixteen years, had belonged to Val. But now Val had to *share* that space, and sharing had never been one of her strengths.

Exhaustion seeped into Veronyka's bones. She didn't know how to go on from here. There was so much she still needed from her sister, things that only family could give. But Val refused to fill that role.

Voices and the clank and jangle of weapons filtered in from the court-yard, and Veronyka remembered the horn calls that had awoken her. "I have to go," she said. She hesitated—why, she wasn't sure—but Val made no move to stop her.

Outside, mist clung to the ground in the early dawn light, distorting shapes and muffling sound as she made her way through the stronghold.

The commander's booming voice soon distinguished itself, and Veronyka followed it to find him atop the ramparts. He was conversing with one of the guards, and Beryk and his phoenix were perched on the wall next to them.

As Veronyka approached the commotion, Tristan fell into step beside her.

"You're up," he said, his face lit with relief. Veronyka wondered if he'd had a hand in getting her to bed again and quickly banished the embarrassing thought.

"Yeah," Veronyka said, avoiding the still-concerned furrow of his brow. "I'm fine. Sorry about all that. It's been a crazy couple of days, and . . . I guess I was just tired."

"I know what you mean," he said. "I was so nervous standing up to the commander, I was feeling a bit light-headed myself."

Veronyka's stomach twisted. So he *had* felt her in his mind, even if he didn't understand what he'd experienced. It was some measure of relief to know he hadn't glimpsed her thoughts the way she'd seen his, but she still felt immensely guilty. Based on Val's reaction, Veronyka suspected at least some of her concern over what Veronyka had done was genuine—that what had happened wasn't common or particularly safe. She had to be more careful.

The commander descended the nearby stairs, joining the handful of

Riders who were congregating in the courtyard, hastily strapping on armor and weapons. Apprentices were there too, helping with buckles or carrying quivers of arrows. Elliot kept fumbling with Fallon's wrist guard, his face pale and drawn, while Latham handed out waterskins with trembling hands.

"What's happening?" Veronyka asked.

"Apparently there was smoke coming from one of the riverside villages," Tristan answered, following his father as he made his way through the crowd. "Beryk was on patrol and saw it, so he raised the alarm—three blasts of the horn."

"What does it mean? Did some buildings catch fire?"

"No. This isn't regular wood smoke. They lit a pyre of long grasses and leaves used to create black smoke. A signal. It means they're calling for help."

"From the Riders?" Veronyka asked, perplexed. She thought their existence was supposed to be a carefully guarded secret.

"No. The signals are meant to notify nearby villages of raiders. When attacks happen on the lower rim, we usually can't respond. Not only would we probably not get there in time, but they're too close to the empire— we can't risk being seen. But this signal is coming from one of the closer villages. . . ."

"Are the Riders going to respond this time?" Veronyka asked.

Tristan didn't answer. Instead they both leaned in to hear what the commander was saying.

". . . should be able to assess the situation without exposing your patrol. Keep a safe distance and do not engage unless absolutely necessary."

"It's probably just a regular raiding party," Fallon replied, while his fellow Riders nodded. "No doubt it'll be over by the time we arrive. We'll approach on foot and help with the cleanup if we can."

"There's never been a raid this far up the mountain," Tristan said, speaking from the back of the group. The Riders turned to face him. "Didn't you say it looked like it was coming from Rushlea? There hasn't been a raid higher than Runnet since we've been here."

The commander's eyes flashed in his son's direction, before returning to their usual calm. Veronyka wondered if he was still angry about Tristan's defiance the previous night.

"There's a first time for everything," he said dismissively. "Ride out at once, and send a pigeon as soon as you can."

The patrol hurried to the Eyrie to mount their phoenixes and depart. The commander's attention shifted to Tristan, and Veronyka backed away slightly. He definitely still *looked* angry.

"I don't want to cause a panic," the commander said under his breath, so quietly that Veronyka had to strain to hear it—but strain she did. "So keep your observations to yourself, Apprentice."

The throne was mine,
and I would seize it with
both hands.

- CHAPTER 35 -

TRISTAN

SO KEEP YOUR OBSERVATIONS *to yourself, Apprentice.*

Tristan should have known his father wouldn't invite his opinions, *especially* after their conversation in front of the breeding enclosure. Commander Cassian did not like to be questioned or debated—least of all in front of others. It had been only Ersken and Nyk last night, but that had been enough. Tristan was ashamed to admit that Nyk's collapse had been very well timed—dealing with his friend had provided the perfect escape from his father's wrath.

Until now. Tristan feared his small act of defiance would keep him on the sidelines forever, but he couldn't bring himself to regret what he'd done. It had been exhilarating to stand up to him, and letting the idea of the promotion go was surprisingly freeing. Without that dangling over him, Tristan could do and say what he wanted, and his father could do nothing to stop him.

Except exclude him, of course. Tristan sighed.

Luckily, all the commotion meant that any talk of the breeding cages was forgotten for the time being.

The fog remained for most of the morning, clinging to the Eyrie and the stronghold like an ominous cloud. Rather than the five or so guards who usually manned the walls, there were close to twenty prowling the ramparts, and even more stationed in the village and at the way station down the mountain. All lessons for the apprentices were canceled, as half of the Riders—some of them instructors—were gone, and it was too dangerous to have the phoenixes flying when there was an unknown threat nearby.

The entire Azurec's Eyrie complex was on lockdown—which meant that any local villagers who still remained after the solstice festival weren't allowed to leave for safety reasons. Rushlea was more than halfway up the mountain, uncomfortably close for a raider party to attack.

Tristan fumed at the idea that they could have prevented this, that if they'd had more patrols, they could have stopped such an assault from happening. He understood his father's concerns, that they'd stretch themselves too thin, but the longer they left Pyra unguarded, the greater the chances that the empire would gain a foothold here.

Since Tristan had none of his own lessons or duties to attend to, he joined Nyk down in the enclosure with the female phoenixes. The birds were riled up and restless, snapping when Nyk slid the food through the slot and even more agitated as the day wore on and they weren't allowed out for their exercise.

Nyk seemed less upset to be down there than he had the previous night, Tristan watching with a smile as the new phoenix interacted with one of the other females—Tristan was pretty sure his father had named her Xolanthe—and actually laughing when the two playfully nipped and trilled at each other. Tristan's heart lightened at the sound. He had done the right thing standing up to his father against the breeding cages, no matter what it cost him personally.

Tristan did his best to assist Nyk with his duties, since Ersken was busy tending the apprentice mounts, but he sensed he was more of a hindrance than a help. Every sound from the stronghold above—the bells tolling the hour or the shout and clang of servants going about their usual work—caused Tristan to jerk upright or strain his hearing, often knocking over barrels of feed or stumbling into Nyk in the process.

Lunch came and went, and still there was no message or word from Fallon's Riders. Patrols rarely took this long—and if they did, a pigeon was usually sent with an update. The commander remained poised atop the battlements, and the atmosphere in the stronghold was tense.

By midafternoon Tristan couldn't sit still and had taken to pacing in front of the enclosure. His father had told him off for doing the same thing out on the walls, where everyone could see, so he'd returned to the bottom of the Eyrie.

Nyk seemed stressed too, or maybe Tristan's mutterings and shuffling feet were putting him in an agitated mood. He *had* accidentally stepped on Nyk's toes more than once, and he expected he was one stomping away from being told off, when a horn blast echoed off the stone walls rising all around them.

Tristan froze, and didn't move again until the second and third blasts sounded.

He stared up at the sky, brows knit together.

"Does that mean . . . did they light another signal?" Nyk asked, looking between Tristan and the upper levels of the Eyrie. "Is there another attack?"

Tristan shook his head slowly, uncertainly. *Yes*, he was about to say, though he didn't want it to be true. What other reason would they blow the horn three times? "I have to go," he said, and ran up the stairs. Nyk's footsteps sounded in the stairwell just behind him, and together they emerged into the courtyard.

Tristan's heart sank. He could actually see the thick column of smoke that was rising in the distance, visible over the soaring cliffs to the east. This wasn't the original signal, and it was clearly from a different village altogether.

Two raiding parties?

Tristan found his father and waited impatiently as he spoke to some guards. The instant they were dismissed, Tristan spoke.

"That looks like it's coming from Petratec," he said. "Someone has to go."

The commander must have recognized the look on his son's face, because he answered the unasked question with a forceful jerk of the head.

"Absolutely not—you're not ready," he said, and Tristan deflated. "I will go."

Tristan forgot his disappointment at once. His father was about to go to battle. Tristan had been barely a year old the last time his father had been in combat, and the reality of the situation hit him in a way it hadn't yet. For the commander to get personally involved . . . things must be truly dire.

His father hailed Beryk and gave him instructions. With a nod, his second-in-command hurried back to the Eyrie with the other Riders from their patrol in tow. The swell of energy within the complex changed, anticipation crackling in the air. The commander was about to fly out to meet raiders, preparing for the first aerial battle since the Blood War.

The Phoenix Riders were truly back.

His father turned to him. "Tristan, you will be in charge in my stead," he said.

The breath caught in Tristan's throat. "Me?" he asked faintly. The world seemed to shrink around them, until it was just Tristan and his father. A tingling, weightless sensation swept through his body. "But—you just said I wasn't ready, and after last night . . ."

The corner of the commander's lips quirked ever so slightly. "I asked you to show me your leadership skills, and you did. I respect your conviction and your willingness to sacrifice your own ambition for what you believe is right. Just because I don't want you flying blind into a dangerous situation for your very first patrol does not mean I don't think you a worthy leader and a valuable asset to the Phoenix Riders."

Tristan swallowed thickly, and to his intense embarrassment, the back of his eyes pricked with coming tears.

His father's amusement shifted and his expression turned soft. "You'll do well, Son," he said at last.

"Thank you, Father," Tristan said, his voice as steady as he could make it. He raised his chin and straightened his spine.

His father nodded in approval. "You will work closely with Captain

Flynn, and send a pigeon immediately if anything should change here. If all else fails, light the beacon."

He clapped a hand on his son's shoulder, gripping it tightly for a moment, before following his patrol to the Eyrie.

Tristan watched in stunned silence as, several long minutes later, the Riders flew from beyond the archway, leaving a blazing trail across the cloudy sky.

"Tristan," said a voice near his elbow, and Tristan turned to find Nyk standing there. "Are you okay?"

"Yes," he said at once, arranging his face in his best approximation of calm self-assuredness. "Of course."

Nyk lifted a brow at him, and Tristan knew his efforts at bravado were wasted. He glanced around, looking for something matter-of-fact to do or say, but he was distinctly overwhelmed. Guards were rushing back and forth across the courtyard, their weapons clinking together and their boots thudding on stone as they called out reports and took up new positions. Servants continued about their work, though they watched the commotion with wary stares.

Tristan faltered; what did someone do when they were in charge?

The question was soon answered for him when a guard summoned Tristan to the top of the wall.

Happy to have something to do, he mounted the steps near the front gate, and Nyk followed. The guard pointed to the edge of the field, at the top of the steps to the way station.

A ragged figure was visible, helped by a guard across the grassy plain toward the village gates. As they watched, three more guards poured from the village to meet them. They surrounded the newcomer just as he fell to his knees, a bulky satchel weighing him down.

Tristan frowned. He looked like a raider.

As the raider and his guard escort made their way through the village, Tristan barreled down the staircase, where more guards and servants milled around the entrance to the stronghold. He forced his way through, Nyk close to his back.

The boy was being helped through the double doors. His clothes were ripped and sweat-soaked, his skin bruised and smeared with dirt. His eyes were hooded—not exactly closed, but unaware of his surroundings. His skin was ashen around the shadows of his eyes, and his breath rattled unevenly—probably thanks to the arrow protruding from his shoulder. He was unarmed, and yet his leather-padded tunic, tall boots, and weapons belt marked him for what he was: a fighter. Given that he wore no uniform or crest indicating an employer, Tristan could only assume he was a raider.

A small crowd gathered to have a look, and Nyk stood among them, staring down at the raider with surprising intensity.

Tristan turned to the nearest guard, the one who had helped the boy from the top of the way station stairs. "Why did we just take the enemy into our protection?" he asked.

The guard wiped his sweaty brow and straightened. "Says he has information about the attacks." He waved at the arrow wound. "I don't think he parted with his comrades on good terms."

Tristan had to agree—the raider was in rough shape. His tunic was so bloodied it appeared dark brown in color, when the hemline told Tristan it had once been closer to white. A satchel hung loosely off his good arm, and red lacerations from the strap crisscrossed the exposed skin of his neck. Whatever burden he bore, it was heavy.

Still, Tristan didn't want to take any chances, and he waved for several guards to keep their spears trained on the raider as Tristan knelt before him. A healer approached, and Tristan nodded, allowing her to press a skin of water to the boy's lips. Drinking seemed to bring him somewhat back to life, even though it was clear that every swallow caused him pain. As he drank, the healer examined his wound.

"What's your name?" Tristan asked, drawing the boy's attention. His eyes fluttered for a moment, blinking as he tried to focus.

Tristan scanned the crowd, then spotted Ian, a wizened old guard.

At a word from Tristan, the man produced a small flask. As soon as Tristan unscrewed the lid, the pungent stink of liquor singed his nostrils. It was *petravin* or "rockwine," a distilled Pyraean liquor aged with a blend of local herbs and flowers, and made only in Petratec, the small village's claim to fame.

"Try this," he said to the boy, despite the healer's objection.

The smell alone made him sit straighter, and he choked a mouthful down. He muttered darkly, but when he handed the flask back, his eyes were clearer. He nodded his thanks to Tristan.

"Your name?" Tristan prodded.

"Sev," the boy said, his voice rough and thin. "I've . . . come . . . to warn you," he said, gasping as he fought to say the words. "There are soldiers . . . coming up the mountain, and—"

He stopped abruptly, clutching at his shoulder while the healer peeled aside the stiff, blood-soaked fabric that stuck to his skin.

"We know about the raiders," Tristan said, drawing Sev's attention back to their conversation. "They've struck two villages, and our best Riders have flown out to meet them."

"No," Sev said, eyes widened in alarm. "They're not raiders—they're soldiers, sent by the empire."

Silence met his words. Tristan was oddly frozen, unable to react. *Soldiers sent by the empire . . .*

"They're coming *here*," Sev continued through a grimace. "Those others—they must be traps. Tricks or decoys."

Before Tristan could think of what to do or say, Elliot burst to the front of the group.

"Was there a girl with them?" he demanded, speaking directly to Sev. He flung himself to the ground and gripped the front of Sev's shirt, eyes frantic.

When Sev gaped at him, clearly stunned, Elliot's face contorted with rage, and it looked like he might start shaking him. Tristan had never seen Elliot lose his temper. He was always cool, distant—detached, even. There was usually a stoic rigidity to him, but not anymore.

His shock subsiding, Tristan lurched to his feet and grabbed Elliot's arm, drawing him back. "What are you doing?" he demanded, but Elliot fought against his grip.

"Did they have a girl? A hostage?" Elliot continued, still speaking to Sev. "Her name is Riella. She's only thirteen—"

"A hostage?" Tristan repeated sharply, jerking Elliot around to face him. "Your sister was taken hostage? When?"

Elliot blinked, focusing on Tristan for the first time. His eyes bulged, as if he'd only just realized what he'd done. He took a long, shuddering breath.

"It happened right after your father recruited me." Elliot seemed to deflate, his shoulders slumped and his head drooped. "The man was a captain in the military and said he was working on behalf of one of the empire's governors—but he never said which one. They were watching my family because of my father's work with the Office for Border Control. Suspected him of 'animage sympathies' and of helping people cross into Pyra undocumented. When they saw Beryk, a known Rider, make contact with my father, they told me I had to go with him. I was actually *happy*, at first," he said, his voice hollow. "I didn't understand what they really wanted until the commander denied my sister. They were going to take our father, but then they took her instead. They said if I didn't do what they wanted, or if my father or I told anyone, they'd kill her."

"Why did they take her, Elliot?" Tristan asked, forcing his voice to be smooth and steady despite the jagged edge beneath it. Hostages were taken as a guarantee. . . . What was it that Elliot had promised to deliver?

Elliot looked up, tears rimming his eyes. "They wanted me to tell them about the operation here. Where it was . . . how many Riders . . . procedures and protocols . . ."

"So you were their spy," Tristan said, his voice cold now, but he could help it no longer. Elliot's interest in being steward, all the errands and letters supposedly on Beryk's behalf—all of it had been a lie, a cover, so he could move about the stronghold unquestioned.

"They said they would kill her," Elliot repeated, tone pleading.

"You should have told us. My father has connections in the empire. We could have gotten—"

"If your father reached out to anyone, they'd know I told. Tristan, *please*—I tried to back out. The last time Beryk and I went to Vayle . . . I met with him, the captain who had my sister. I told him I needed proof that she was okay before I gave them any more information. But they didn't bring her," he said desperately. "Just gave me some letter, could have been written by anyone . . ."

Tristan released Elliot roughly, his voice shaking with frustration. "You never should have done that alone. We could have *helped* you. We could have given them false leads, invited your sister here, come up with some excuse to extricate her—anything would have been better than this. What did you think would happen here, Elliot? What did you think they were going to do with the intelligence you fed them?"

The tears fell down Elliot's cheeks now, and they made Tristan's throat tight. He couldn't afford to get so emotional, but it was hard to look at the face of the person who had doomed them.

"I didn't see her," Sev piped in hoarsely from his place on the ground. "There was no girl with us, no hostage. Maybe they were lying."

Elliot squeezed his eyes shut, his face crumpling.

Tristan raked a hand through his hair. With a nod, he ordered two guards to escort Elliot away for further questioning.

Low murmurs broke out as he left, and the other apprentices exchanged stricken looks. Nyk stared at Elliot's retreating back, his expression bleak. Tristan ignored everyone's reactions and drew a deep breath, squaring his shoulders. He tried to channel his father, his sense of unflappable confidence and infinite capability.

Instead he felt like a child marching around in his father's oversize Riding boots.

He turned back to Sev. "How many?" he asked. They needed to devise a defense strategy, but to do that, Tristan needed more information.

Sev swallowed, blinking slowly. The brief burst of energy the rockwine had given him was already fading away. "Near four hundred, I think. We had two hundred in my regiment, and we met with a second group last night. But those village attacks . . . they must have come from another group of soldiers, traveling somewhere else on the mountain. There's no way our party could have gotten there in time. So there could be more . . ."

Tristan closed his eyes, nodding, as if merely confirming the number of guests at a dinner party. *At least* four hundred armed soldiers, coming here? When all their best fighters were gone?

He opened his eyes again. "How do we know you aren't a part of the diversion?" he asked, considering the boy before him. Elliot's betrayal had shaken him, and he did not want any more nasty surprises. "You're a soldier, aren't you? And you betrayed them. Why should we trust you?"

Sev stared dully at him, but made no answer. Tristan tried to think of what his father would do.

"Get Morra," he said, twisting to address a guard behind him.

"Already here," came Morra's gruff voice as she moved her way to the front of the crowd. The guards made room for her, and she paused before Sev, propping both hands on her crutch as she considered him.

Tristan's father trusted Morra implicitly. He said she had an uncanny ability to tell truth from lies, a knack for sniffing out information. Tristan had heard Beryk and the others whisper the term "shadowmage," but of course his father didn't hold with superstitions. There was no proof or written record that shadowmages were real, but Tristan knew the stories. If even half of them were true, he had no doubt that Morra was one of them.

It made a chill run down his spine. Tristan was honest by nature—possibly to a fault, given the trouble it had gotten him in with his father—but Morra still made him a bit uneasy. It was the secretiveness of her magic that bothered him, not the magic itself. Shadow magic could be used to sniff out lies, but it did so in a deceitful way—snooping and sneaking around. If people were just truthful, there would be no need for such magic—or for people to keep the fact that they had that magic a secret.

Or maybe Tristan was fooling himself. His fear of fire was something he hid from others, and maybe the threat of exposure was what made him dislike the idea of shadow magic.

Still, he couldn't deny that it came in handy.

"Who have we here . . . ?" Morra murmured, expression thoughtful. "Friend or foe?"

"Friend," Sev said. His face was clammy with sweat, but he sat up straighter as he continued. "And I was sent by another friend, Ilithya Shadowheart."

*Pheronia was not fit to rule, and the
council manipulated her every move.
I had to step in.*

- CHAPTER 36 -

VERONYKA

VERONYKA TOOK AN UNCONSCIOUS step forward.

She'd been in a daze since she recognized the soldier they'd dragged in, filthy and bloody but unmistakable. The boy who had saved her life outside her cottage, and in turn, whose life she had saved from Val's wrath. By convincing her sister to stay her hand, Veronyka had allowed this boy to deliver his message and warn them of the impending attack. Her head spun.

His arrival had been shocking enough—not to mention his dire message and Elliot's betrayal—but nothing thus far had surprised her more than his last two words.

Veronyka thought her heart might have actually stopped.

Ilithya Shadowheart.

It was her *maiora*'s name. Well, the first half, anyway. When Veronyka was a child, Ilithya was too difficult to say, so she had simply used "grandmother" or "*maiora*." Veronyka had never heard her called Shadowheart before, but something about it made a prickling awareness shoot through her.

And she wasn't the only one to react so strongly.

"How do you know that name?" Morra demanded.

Veronyka stared between the two of them, breathless in anticipation.

"She was a bondservant with the soldiers' party—working against them

from the start. She tried to poison them all . . . to stop the attack, but . . ."
He halted, panting, and Veronyka saw more than physical pain on his face.
Nothing he had said confirmed this was the same Ilithya she'd been raised by,
but nothing had contradicted it either. "I came instead to warn you and to
deliver these." He twitched his good arm, and the bag slid from his shoulder.
He opened the flap, revealing that it was packed full of smooth gray stones.

Veronyka inhaled sharply at the familiar sight. It couldn't be . . .

"Miseriya's mercy," Morra muttered under her breath, leaning closer. She
turned to Tristan. "Are those . . . ?"

Tristan reached for the bag, hastily examining the contents before closing it again. He didn't say a word, but his entire body crackled with suppressed energy. The crowd pushed in, but most hadn't seen what was in Sev's
satchel—and it was plain that Tristan meant to keep it that way. Now was
not the time to lose focus. If what the boy said was true, they had a small
army coming for them.

Still, a bag full of phoenix eggs—a dozen by Veronyka's count—was
hard to ignore in a place like this.

Her arms tingled with something as bright and glittering as the sun on
the River Aurys.

It felt like possibility. It felt like hope for the future . . . if they could
survive the night.

Morra turned back to Sev. "Why would Ilithya choose you and not a
fellow animage?"

"I *am* an animage."

"An animage soldier?" she repeated skeptically, and Veronyka knew she
was probing in his mind, using her shadow magic to discern if his words
were true or false. She soon nodded, expression apologetic.

"Where is she now?" Morra pressed. "Ilithya?"

Sev opened his mouth to speak before swallowing thickly and shaking
his head.

Morra swayed slightly, eyes glazed over—as if she was seeing something
the others could not. Something from the soldier's mind.

"Is she dead?" Veronyka whispered, looking between them. She itched to use her own shadow magic but knew she couldn't risk it.

Sev nodded, and all the air left Veronyka's lungs. If it was truly her *maiora* Ilithya, and she'd been alive all this time . . .

Veronyka thought back to the day Val had told her their grandmother was dead. Veronyka had figured Val had seen it, heard it—*knew it*—in the way she knew all manner of things Veronyka did not, and like a fool, she had taken her sister's word as truth. Veronyka should have known better, even then, and was frustrated with herself as much as with Val. She scanned the surrounding faces for her sister, wanting to speak with her that instant, but she was nowhere to be found.

Morra straightened, blinking as she came back to herself. "Everything he says is the truth."

A ripple of reaction spread through the crowd, as those at the front whispered what she'd said to those behind, while still more questions and concerns bounced back again.

"But how could a number so great move this far up Pyrmont unseen?" one of the guards asked, looking around the group. "A smoke signal should've been lit weeks ago, when they first started their climb."

"They'd know better than to travel the main routes," said a villager, while others nodded or murmured their agreement.

"Elliot's information likely helped them avoid our scouts," added Ronyn, his voice somber.

"They also traveled separately," Morra said, echoing what Sev had said earlier. "That helped them draw less notice and placed them in strategic positions across the mountain. The closest regiment made camp in the Vesperaean Caves. They're no more than half a day's walk from the Field of Feathers, which means they could be here before nightfall."

"Apprentice Tristan," interrupted one of the guards, pushing through to the front of the group, Captain Flynn next to her.

"Yes?" Tristan said, clearly sensing her urgency.

"There's a party of armed soldiers making its way up the Pilgrimage

Road," she said, slightly breathless. She spoke only to Tristan, but the onlookers leaned in to hear. "They will reach the way station within the hour."

A bucket of icy water cascaded into Veronyka's stomach. *One hour?*

"And it's barely seven bells," muttered Morra.

"What are their numbers?" Tristan asked.

"Near three hundred," the lookout answered, face grim. "But there could be more under cover of the trees."

Sev had told them to expect four hundred, so the soldiers must have divided their forces again, possibly planning separate or staggered attacks. The courtyard had gone quiet, the guards, servants, and villagers who stood nearby awaiting Tristan's command.

He lifted his chin and drew himself up to his full height. He looked just like his father in that moment, and seemed to expand to fill the space around him.

"I want all villagers inside the stronghold immediately," he told the lookout, who nodded and ran off. "Captain," he continued, turning to the man the commander had put in charge alongside him, "I suggest you send your men to aid in the evacuation, as many as can be spared. As for the village gate . . ."

"I'll see to it personally," the Captain said. "We'll barricade the doors, and I'll choose a contingent of my best fighters to stay behind and defend it. The rest I'll send up to the stronghold."

Tristan nodded. "Use a runner to keep me informed, and ask Jana to ready the pigeons. We've got messages to send. In the meantime," he continued, raising his voice over the noise of his orders being carried out, "I want every willing, able-bodied servant and villager lined up in this courtyard in fifteen minutes. We'll hold the fort until the commander and the Riders return."

The group around them began to disperse; Captain Flynn sent guards running this way and that, while servants hurried to prepare provisions. Morra left to question Elliot, hoping to glean more details about the coming attack.

Amid the tumult, Tristan crouched down in front of Sev. "Thank you," he said, gesturing for the healer to relocate him to a safe place. "We are forever in your debt. These . . . ," he said, gesturing to the eggs, "keep them with you, for now."

As Veronyka moved to get out of the way, Sev's gaze latched on to her. His eyes flickered with some distant recognition, but they were hazy with pain. Before Veronyka could react, he was lifted from the ground and carried out of sight.

She rubbed her aching temples. If Sev recognized her, if he asked after that girl he'd once met . . . It was a complication she did not need right now.

When she looked up, Tristan was already walking away, making straight for the temple. She frowned. "Where are you going?" she called.

"To light the beacon."

As the courtyard buzzed around her, a surge of adrenaline coursed through Veronyka's veins. So much was happening, so much was at stake. Soldiers and traitors and phoenix eggs. But with an army on their doorstep, one thing was for certain: Tristan had called for volunteers to protect the stronghold, and Veronyka intended to fight.

The courtyard was chaos as the battle preparations began—villagers being ushered into the empty barracks, clutching their children and whatever worldly possessions they could carry to their chests, while guards rolled barrels of grain across the cobblestones and servants hoisted sloshing buckets of water to the kitchens.

A small girl bumped into Veronyka—a girl with wild hair, a bird on her shoulder, and a homemade spear clutched in both hands.

"Sparrow?" Veronyka said incredulously, but already the girl was lost in the crowd. When had she come to the Eyrie? Had she arrived with Val and the minstrels, or had she been here even longer, skulking around the village and gathering all the gossip she could get her hands on?

Before Veronyka could locate her again, a loud crackling sound, followed by a searing hiss, filled the air.

She thought one of the phoenixes had ignited at first, but when she searched the sky, a flare of light drew her eye to the golden statue atop the temple. Apparently it doubled as a beacon, but rather than black smoke, like the village signal fires, whatever special leaves or grasses the Riders burned changed the smoke into vivid scarlet, tendrils of it crawling over the statue's surface like a phoenix in a fire dive.

As Tristan made his way down the ladder, people moved swiftly in and out of the building below, carrying bedding and crates of supplies. The sacred space was being transformed into a kind of infirmary, and Veronyka wondered if Sev was in there now, and how many more would join him before the night was out.

Meanwhile, the courtyard was filling with volunteers—cooks, villagers, servants, and stablehands—and Veronyka lined up next to them.

She wiped her sweaty palms against her thighs, her heart hammering, and tried her best not to think about the reality of what was happening—of what volunteering to fight would mean. It felt like crossing some imaginary line, as if by participating, she was deciding to stay here once and for all. Whether or not that was true, she couldn't just stand aside while Tristan and the others risked their lives, and she didn't want to see the empire strike another blow to the Phoenix Riders.

As Tristan crossed the cobblestones, Veronyka caught sight of Val, standing in the shadow of the temple. She watched the volunteers with idle curiosity, but she made no move to join them. Veronyka fought against a pang of disappointment. Since when did Val shrink back from a fight? But then again, her sister didn't think this fight was theirs to begin with.

Tristan's face was grim as he surveyed the group. A few stragglers joined the ranks, and he began his progression along the line of volunteers. Next to him, a guard pushed a wheelbarrow of weapons, helping the new fighters choose a sling or crossbow or whatever best suited their abilities and size.

Veronyka couldn't hear more than a low murmur, but one by one volunteers were given weapons and assigned positions. There were some children from the village that Tristan gave safer duties, like running messages or carrying waterskins, and Veronyka thought she spotted Sparrow among them.

At last Tristan turned to Veronyka.

"I'm ready to fight," she said, not waiting for him to speak.

He took a long time to respond, so long that the silence between them grew from a breathless moment to a yawning chasm. Was he going to deny her? The thought hadn't even occurred to her until now, and for once his emotions were locked up tight and out of her reach.

He forced a smile and laid a bracing hand on her shoulder. Veronyka knew immediately that this was not going to go as planned. Her breath came more shallowly, and she was suddenly aware of the dozens of eyes on her.

"You've only just begun your training," he said quietly. "I can't expose you to danger atop the walls, knowing that it was my decision that put you there. We could use more runners, or—"

"A runner?" she repeated, her voice flat. "Like the children?" Her neck and ears tingled with heat as whispers broke out around them.

"Nyk," he said, but she didn't let him continue.

"We're *all* in danger here," she said, hands gripping the rough fabric of her trousers to stop them from shaking.

"*Nyk,*" he said again, leaning in close, "there are plenty of other important tasks, not just running messages. Ersken will need help tending to the phoenixes in the Eyrie—not just the females." He said this last bit as if he thought it would cheer her up. Maybe, a couple of days ago, it would have. She remained stony before him.

"Please don't make this harder than it is," he begged, eyes glittering with some suppressed emotion. Guilt? Pity?

She couldn't believe he would deny her this in front of everyone, *shame* her in front of the other apprentices who watched nearby. He'd promised to help her and had told her that she belonged among them. That she'd make a good Rider. Now he was treating her like someone weak and useless and in need of protection.

He was treating her like Val always did.

Veronyka's throat tightened with unshed tears, but she forced out her next words.

"Harder for who?" she asked, not bothering to keep her voice low. With that, she pushed past him and ran from the courtyard.

Veronyka went to the Eyrie. Not to carry out Tristan's wishes, but because she didn't know where else to go. She kicked a water bucket and screamed every curse she'd ever picked up at the Narrows docks or border village cookhouses.

Xephyra cocked her head at Veronyka, curiosity filtering through the bond as she tried to decipher the swear words that Veronyka barely understood herself.

Footsteps approached, and Veronyka knew who it would be.

She got to her feet and stared into the shadows. It was already dark in the depths of the Eyrie, the day's muted, overcast light quickly fading away.

"What do you want, Val?" she demanded as soon as her sister emerged from the stairwell. She halted at Veronyka's words.

"Don't be angry with me because your precious Tristan didn't want you fighting by his side. I told you this would happen, Veronyka. I told you these aren't our people."

Val meant to wound her on purpose, Veronyka knew that, and still her words cut deep—because there was truth in them. Tristan *didn't* want her by his side.

"Tell me what happened to *maiora* Ilithya that day," she said, crossing her arms over her chest.

"What?" Val asked, frowning, though Veronyka knew it was a performance. She hadn't seen her, but she felt strangely certain that Val had been there hiding somewhere out of sight when Sev arrived. Val was like the rain—sometimes, when Veronyka paid attention, she could feel her presence like an ache in her bones.

"That soldier said he was working with a woman called Ilithya,"

Veronyka said, pointing up to the courtyard. "He said she was a bond-servant and—"

"Don't be ridiculous, Veronyka. There must be hundreds of women with that name."

"Ilithya Shadowheart." There, a flicker—something shifting in Val's eyes. Veronyka wished she knew how to properly use shadow magic, so she could reach out and snatch the truth from her sister's head. "Our *grandmother*. You told me she was dead."

Val actually rolled her eyes. "She was not our grandmother, *xe* Nyka. You know that." She paused, chewing her lip. "She was dead to us either way. Her bondage was a life sentence."

Veronyka squeezed her eyes shut, her blood pounding in her ears. All those years, lost. They could have looked her up, found where she was working and tried to visit her. They could have written her letters. They could have done *anything*—anything and everything was better than the nothing they had actually done.

"I know you're upset, Veronyka," Val said, her tone soothing. "Everything has come undone. But this is for the best. Fate led these soldiers here; they were guided by Anyanke's own hand. I've tried to be patient, to give you as much time as possible, but this is what I've been waiting for—this is our chance to escape. To get both you and your bondmate out of this cage the Riders have built for you. Now, while they're distracted with the defense preparations, we'll free your phoenix and escape. We'll free the other females too, if we can manage it, and then we'll sneak out through the underground service entrance."

Veronyka stared at her sister. As a child, Veronyka always said that Avalkyra Ashfire was her hero, the person she most wanted to be like. But in truth, Val had been the one she'd looked up to. Whenever they were in trouble, she knew Val would get them out of it—and she did, though Veronyka often disagreed with her methods. Val had always seemed fearless, and maybe that was what Veronyka most admired.

Now she couldn't help but look at her sister and see a coward. It wasn't fearlessness that guided her sister; it was selfishness.

Veronyka thought of her *maiora*, who had sacrificed herself so the girls could run to safety. Even at her lowest point—her family lost, her phoenix gone, her life in bondage, and her queen dead—she *still* fought.

That was what a warrior did, a true Phoenix Rider. Val and the others were wrong. It wasn't some rank to be earned, some standard to be met or a legacy to be lived up to. Phoenix Riders were the protectors of their people, warriors of light, and right now the empire soldiers represented the darkness come to swallow them whole.

Maybe Veronyka had been wrong to look up to Val and the Feather-Crowned Queen. Maybe she'd had a much better hero, her *maiora*, all along.

"Nyk?"

A voice echoed down from the stairwell. Both sisters jumped, but Val recovered first. She stepped backward, gaze darting around, as if looking for a place to hide—or a position to attack from.

Ersken had left a stack of storage crates lined up next to the enclosure. Val trailed a hand along the makeshift wall, then, discovering a narrow opening between the boxes, slipped into it and vanished.

"Val, where are you—" Veronyka began, but she froze when Tristan emerged from the mouth of the stairs. He strode purposefully toward her, but faltered halfway, his expression wary.

Veronyka tried, but she couldn't conceal the pain the sight of him produced. Everything else faded away, and it was like she was back in the courtyard again.

"Why?" she demanded, swallowing around the lump in her throat.

The sky was a dark, dusky gray, and the flickering lanterns on the gallery above—along with the reddish glow from the lit phoenix beacon—limned Tristan in a halo of red and gold. His face was shadowed, but when he took another wary step forward, his grim features came into clearer view.

"Look," he began hesitantly. "This wasn't . . . I didn't—I made a mistake." Veronyka blinked in surprise. He looked around, as if trying to find words, and then gripped his hair with both hands. "I don't know what I'm doing. Can't you see that?" he practically shouted, his composure crumpling. "I don't how to run this place, and what if the commander—my *father*—never comes back?"

The words were strangled, and seeing his anguished expression, Veronyka extended herself to him. It was instinctual, like reaching for a knife that was falling, even though she knew it was dangerous. But for some reason, reopening the channel between them didn't feel wrong or forbidden in this instance. It felt right, like it did when she connected with Xephyra. It wasn't about spying or controlling; it was about empathy—about sharing in his pain.

That was the difference between her and Val, she realized. Val used her knowledge as a weapon, to hurt, always seeking out weaknesses and ways to exploit them. Veronyka used her shadow magic to understand those around her, and it provided her with compassion and insight.

Maybe shadow magic wasn't a dark temptation; maybe it could it be both good and bad, just like people.

Still, Veronyka knew she had to be careful. She had already used her magic against Tristan once before, teasing him about calling Wind *"xe xie,"* just to prove a point. That had been small and relatively harmless, but that didn't make it right. Shadow magic could be a slippery slope. First Veronyka only wanted to understand Tristan, and then she went looking for things, and after that? How far a stretch could it really be to go from stealing thoughts and emotions to implanting some of your own? Every time they argued, would she plumb ever deeper, seeking newer and better ways to hurt him?

Like Val?

No, Veronyka thought firmly. *I am not like her.*

As the link between them opened, Veronyka saw just how tumultuous his emotions truly were. His mind—like any she'd ever connected with, human or animal—had a distinctive texture or feeling to it. Val was smoke and iron. Xephyra was bright, pure sunlight. Tristan was earthy and fresh—like dewy grass and the patter of warm summer rain. Usually. Right now his mind felt more like a thundercloud, swirling and crackling and rolling overhead.

"I'm not ready for all this," he continued, breathing heavily. "None of the apprentices have real combat experience, and Elliot . . . I don't know what to do with him. I can't bear the thought that all these people are counting on me, looking at me to lead. If I can protect at least one friend, if I can protect *you*, I should do that. I should *want* to do that, because it would be the right thing. But I don't want to—don't think I *can*—do this alone. I want you there next to me. I trust you more than anyone, but I promised, and—"

"Promised?" Veronyka repeated sharply, that one word piercing the bubble of joy that had been swelling inside her chest. "Promised who?"

Val stepped out of the shadows.

Though she was nearer to Veronyka than Tristan, all her attention was focused on him. Veronyka was almost bowled over by the wave of shadow magic her sister was emanating, funneling it like a gale that practically blasted Tristan off his feet. He slammed into the wall behind him, his face slack as Val bore down on him, her smoldering shadow magic scent heavy in Veronyka's nostrils.

Veronyka, who remained connected to Tristan after opening herself to him moments ago, heard what Val forced into his mind.

Stop. Don't speak. Don't think. You remember nothing. You—

"Val, enough!" Veronyka shouted, flinging her roughly aside. Val seemed to lose her focus and break the connection, and the air between them lost the crackling energy that had filled it. The terrible sound of her sister's voice was ripped from her mind, and from Tristan's as well.

Veronyka reinforced her barriers, though she could do nothing to protect Tristan.

He shook his head, blinking several times as he tried to understand what had just happened. While Veronyka understood the voice inside his mind to be Val's, she wasn't sure how someone without shadow magic experienced its use. To him, it might have been an incoherent rumble, a sudden, unconscious desire, or maybe the sensation that his own thoughts were spiraling out of control.

"Tristan, what promise?" Veronyka pressed, afraid of what Val might have done to his mind and his memory.

"You can't trust a word he says," Val began, but Veronyka cut her off.

"No. I can't trust *you*," she spat. "Tristan, please."

He cast a wary look at Val before facing Veronyka. He seemed to have come back to himself, though he plainly struggled to understand everything that was going on. "Don't be angry, Nyk. Your sister, she was worried about you, that's all. Didn't want you involved in the fighting unless you absolutely had to be. So I promised I'd keep you off the wall and out of danger."

His voice was pleading, but Veronyka didn't have an ounce of feeling to spare for him. She whirled on her sister.

Val didn't want her safe—she wanted her excluded, and most of all, she wanted her to feel completely, utterly alone.

Suddenly, everything came together in Veronyka's mind. *This is what I've been waiting for. . . .*

Val had known the soldiers were coming.

It was a horrifying thought, but Veronyka felt its truth immediately. Hadn't Val arrived at the Eyrie mere days before them? There's no way a shadowmage as accomplished as Val could fail to notice hundreds of soldiers climbing the mountain nearby. Veronyka always kept her magic close, guarded, and internal, but Val stretched her magic wide like a net. This was why she'd wanted Veronyka to leave right away, why she'd been so insistent. She didn't warn the Riders so they could prepare; she kept the information to herself, gambling countless lives so she could have Veronyka back under her control.

Since she'd arrived, Val had worked hard to sow fear and doubt into Veronyka's heart. She'd insulted the Riders, questioning their motives and their loyalties, and criticized Veronyka for serving them. When Xephyra appeared and was put into the breeding cages, Val was even closer to her goal. Going after Tristan, asking him not to let Veronyka fight, was the final move to strip her sister of everything that made her happy. All this heartache, all this agony, so that when this moment came, Veronyka would have nothing to hold on to.

"Did you know she had come back?" Veronyka asked her sister. It was the one thing she hadn't yet figured out, the last question that needed answering. She'd tried to ask before, but had let Val get by with deflections and vague answers. Not this time.

Val seemed surprised by the change in subject, but she lifted her chin, eyes blazing. "Yes."

"And you led her here . . . to me?" Veronyka's tone was flat, emotionless. "Yes."

"How?" Veronyka asked, a slow, steady heat climbing up her throat.

Val shrugged, the gesture so careless, so dismissive, that Veronyka had to clench her jaw to stop from breathing fire.

"You're impatient, Nyka, always have been. Resurrections are not for the faint of heart. It was a full week before she made her return. The phoenix sought you out, but I was the one who was there. It was no small thing, to keep her under my control, but I managed it. She followed you, and I followed her. Now here we are."

Veronyka's entire body was burning now, the scorching flames devouring her insides, begging for release. Val had called her "Nyka" right in front of Tristan, but it seemed almost trivial in the face of everything else.

"Why didn't you tell me?" Veronyka demanded.

"I tried," Val bit out. "I told you I'd brought you a gift. But you wanted nothing to do with me, remember? So I called her here instead."

Veronyka finished the sentence in her head: *to try to get you kicked out, only they stuck Xephyra in a cage instead.*

She shook her head slowly, sifting through Val's words for the heart of her confusion. "How could you control her—how could you call her here? It shouldn't be possible. You're not bonded to her."

Tristan latched on to the word "bonded," his gaze flicking toward the females' enclosure, but Veronyka was too preoccupied to care.

Val tilted her head, considering Veronyka for a moment. Then, deep in the back of Veronyka's mind, a door burst open.

Instantly she knew what it was—a permanent connection to Val. It was a kind of bond, she thought, but while her connection with Xephyra went both ways, wide-open and easily accessed, this channel was narrow and unstable—open, but still guarded.

Veronyka understood in a blazing moment of clarity that Val had somehow used this connection to make Xephyra trust her. Veronyka's presence was a part of Val, a constant fixture in her mind, and Xephyra had sensed it. It reminded Veronyka uncomfortably of the strong connection between her and Tristan—and the way Val had reacted to it. If Veronyka was a part of Val's mind, then Val was a part of Veronyka's, and she must have felt Veronyka accidentally opened a similar channel between her and Tristan.

While Tristan was unaware of their connection, Val had known about her link with Veronyka and exploited it, using Veronyka's bond to Xephyra to get what she wanted. It filled Veronyka with blinding fury. The things Val had done in her name made her feel contaminated and dirty. And it wasn't just recently. Veronyka's life was filled with instances of Val doing shocking, terrible deeds—and always, supposedly, for Veronyka's sake. Val had kept so much from her, kept her in the dark her whole life. Not just about Val and their grandmother, but about Veronyka and her magic.

And Veronyka had had enough.

She bore down on her mental barriers, and the connection between them flickered. The doorway slammed shut, but it wasn't gone entirely, and its presence changed everything between them. There were no imaginary boundaries and no false sense of security. Val was inside her mind, and nowhere was safe.

Veronyka couldn't speak. She couldn't breathe, either, except for a shallow inhalation that wheezed into her lungs.

"I hate you," she said at last. The words were quiet, and Val leaned in, unable to hear them. *"I hate you!"* Veronyka screamed, and cocked her arm back and slapped her sister across the face.

Val stiffened, her face alarmingly still, save for the red mark slowly blooming across her cheek. At her sides, her hands curled into fists.

Veronyka was panting slightly, shocked at what she had done, though she felt no remorse for it.

A spasm flickered across Val's features before her gaze dropped. Veronyka thought she looked oddly chastened—until she slowly drew a dagger from her belt. The blade was obsidian set in a bone handle. It looked ancient, but age didn't make it any less sharp.

Time shuddered to a stop, and Veronyka was brought back to that fateful moment in their cabin when Val had pulled a knife on Xephyra. Her bondmate let out a soft croon from inside the enclosure beside them, but otherwise, everything was quiet.

Tristan tensed, as if he meant to take a step forward. While he clearly didn't fully comprehend their argument, the flash of the blade kicked him into action.

Val thrust the knife between them, causing him to halt in his tracks, the point inches from his throat. Seeing the weapon leveled at Tristan unfroze Veronyka's numbness, though she didn't dare move.

Val took a careful, measured step toward Veronyka and then moved the knife to rest against her cheek. Val's closeness filled Veronyka with a strange mix of feelings: the comfort and familiarity of her sister's scent, combined with the instinctual fear of the cold, sharp edge against her flesh. Veronyka barely breathed, afraid the movement would sink the blade into her skin. Her mind buzzed. Would Val do this? Would this be her last and worst crime?

Val, please, she whispered internally. But the door was shut, and there was no response.

"Val, please," Tristan echoed, his voice soft and desperate. "I don't understand."

"You will." Val spoke the words slowly, as if relishing this moment. Then, in a lightning-fast move, she angled the blade and plunged it downward.

Veronyka gasped as the knife slid across her skin—but it was the flat, dull edge that pressed against her body. The razor-sharp blade faced outward, tearing through her tunic and the fabric she used to bind her breasts beneath it. Veronyka's reactionary inhale of breath forced her chest to expand as her sister dragged the knife to the side, tearing her tunic in half and fully exposing Veronyka for the liar that she was.

"Let me introduce you to my *sister*," Val spat, her voice savage and ugly in her triumph. "Veronyka."

Day 18, Fifth Moon, 170 AC

Dear Avalkyra,

I am sorry that meeting did not go the way you wanted it to, but you know I could not sign that document. To annul our father's marriage to my mother would indeed lessen your sentence, and you would be charged not with the murder of a queen regent, but with the murder of a lowly consort. You would walk away after paying the funeral fee.

And yes, annulling my mother's marriage would also make me illegitimate, and therefore solidify your claim to the throne.

But things have changed, and I must think of the future.

These past months of silence have been hard for me, dear sister; I was not ready to give you forgiveness. I was not ready to understand. But we are out of time.

I must speak to you again, in private. I am sorry that I did not reply to your other letters. . . . I hope I am not too late in replying now.

Yours, Pheronia

*Sometimes
to protect those you love,
you have to hurt them.*

- CHAPTER 37 -
VERONYKA

VERONYKA FELL TO HER knees, clutching at the shreds of her tunic. The world around her closed in, and everything went black-and-white. There was no sound, no burning beacon or battle preparations. It was just her and Tristan and the girl who used to be her sister.

It took an eternity to meet his eyes. She wanted to cower, to hide away from him, but something had changed within her. Newfound bravery, coupled with a recent magical awakening, had her seeking out the door that belonged to *him*—the one she'd somehow created by accident, the one that was there and waiting, making it easy to connect with him.

Veronyka swung it wide, opening herself to him, inviting his wrath like a sunflower chasing the blazing heat of the sun. She wanted to *hurt*, wanted the pain that he, surely, must be feeling as well. She wanted to drink it in, to ache with it, to tear the wound wide open.

Only, it wasn't there.

There was *nothing* there. No anger, no betrayal—just stunned, empty silence.

While his emotions were oddly numb, his mind buzzed with activity, rehashing every conversation, every strange moment or word out of place.

Apparently there had been a lot of them. The bathhouse and the breeding cage. The way she'd calmed Xephyra and when Val called her "Nyka." Tristan was no fool, and while he hadn't put all the pieces together, he'd been collecting them one by one, stashing them away for later examination. The hardest thing for Veronyka to deal with was the way he looked at her in those memories . . . like she was someone special and interesting and deserving of his attention. Would he feel the same now, with lies tainting every word and special moment?

Several breaths passed, and the air between them grew thick with anticipation.

He turned, as if meaning to walk away, but stopped himself. He wavered, then looked back at Veronyka once more. She couldn't read his expression, and before she could begin to unravel his thoughts, he closed his eyes, bowed his head, and turned resolutely back to the stairs.

With the sound of his retreating footsteps, the world came alive once more: the commotion of the courtyard above, the shifting of feathers in the enclosure behind her, the smell of burning fires and oil lamps. Even the colors had returned, drenching the ground beneath her in fire-red and ash-gray.

It was as if nothing had changed. And everything.

"Come on," said Val, resting a hand on Veronyka's shoulder. Her voice was gentle but firm. "Let's get out of here, back to my room. You can get changed, and I'll take care of everything. I'll free Xephyra, and you'll never have to worry about the breeding cages again. You'll never have to hide who and what you are. We'll get out of here before the fighting starts and make our way to safety. Together."

The words washed over Veronyka. They were soothing, the kind of words a mother spoke to a daughter, a leader to their troops: confident assurances that everything would be okay.

Empty words, really.

Val *would* take care of everything. Veronyka knew that, and there was a tiny part of her that was tempted to give in to her sister's promises. But the relief that decision would bring would be temporary. Val was a warrior, and peace suited her for only so long. She didn't want to build a shelter from the storm; she wanted to break the very winds that would dare to shake her.

And Veronyka was tired of fighting a battle she knew she'd never win.

"No, Val," she said. She was still on her knees, staring at the ground beneath her, dark hair hanging in her eyes.

"What?" Val said, dropping her hand from Veronyka's shoulder.

Taking a deep breath, Veronyka got to her feet. The scraps of her tunic blew in the evening breeze, but she didn't cover herself. While exposing her might have revealed to Tristan that she had lied, it didn't reveal her true self. Veronyka knew that person, and Tristan did too, and nothing about her body changed that.

"I said no," Veronyka repeated, fighting to keep her voice steady. "Never again. It will never be you and me, together, *ever again*."

"*Xe* Nyka—" Val said, but Veronyka cut her off.

"Don't call me that—don't you dare call me that. I've had enough, Val," she said, her throat tight with a lifetime of pent-up emotions. "I've tried to give you the benefit of the doubt. I've tried over and over to see you as a good person, to believe that *you* believed you were doing the right thing. That you wanted to protect me, that you cared about me."

"But I do," Val said. Veronyka looked into her eyes and knew that Val believed her own words—or maybe she'd gotten so good at lying, she didn't know when she lied to herself.

"If you cared about me, you wouldn't have killed my bondmate. You couldn't possibly understand the pain it caused me, but if you had even considered it, you'd never have done it."

"You're wrong," Val said, but Veronyka spoke over her.

"You came here with one goal in mind: to ruin my happiness. This is the only place I've ever felt like I belonged, like I was safe."

"You were safe with *me*," Val said, eyes blazing.

"But who would keep me safe *from* you?"

"You think *he* will?" she spat, pointing to the stairwell where Tristan had disappeared. "You think he can protect you and care for you the way

I have? This so-called safety and belonging you felt? It was based on a lie. He doesn't even know you. He doesn't know *who* you are *or* what you're capable of."

"He knows me better than you," Veronyka said, and Val laughed disdainfully. Veronyka shrugged, refusing to let her sister get under her skin. "And what he doesn't know, he'll learn—they all will. I know things aren't perfect here, but I want to help them change. I want to make a difference, to be a part of something greater than myself. Avalkyra Ashfire wasn't great on her own. . . . She was great because our people rallied behind her. She was great because she brought us all together."

"Avalkyra Ashfire was great because she set the world on fire, because she let nothing and no one stand in the way of what she wanted." Val's voice was raw and ragged, dripping with emotion.

"There was one person who stood in her way," Veronyka said, her voice soft as she considered her words. "Her sister."

Val's face was almost unrecognizable when she spoke, her mouth a dark slash and her eyes empty, hollow pools. "No, Veronyka. Not even death could stand in her way."

"Maybe not," Veronyka said with a tired sigh, "but this is where I want to be. This is my home."

"No," Val said, shaking her head forcefully, causing her tangled auburn braids to whip from side to side. "Your home always was, and always will be, with me."

"Not anymore."

"And if they kick you out for your lies?" Her eyes were overly bright, glistening in the darkness, but no tears fell.

"If they do, then at least I will have tried. I used to think you were the bravest person I knew, Val, but what you're doing isn't bravery. It's cowardice. It's time for me to stand and fight."

Val's face contorted at the word "cowardice," but otherwise she remained perfectly, deathly still. Veronyka thought that maybe, finally, her words had penetrated Val's stubborn mind. She braced herself. Would Val lash out in anger? Would she strike Veronyka down and drag her away whether she liked it or not?

"You want to fight, do you?" she said, tone as blank as a starless sky. "Then I hope for your sake, Veronyka, that you've chosen the right side."

She turned on her heel and disappeared into the stairwell.

Gone.

Veronyka sagged against the bars behind her. The last time she'd really argued with Val, the night she'd run away, she'd been acting on pure rage and adrenaline. And a part of her knew—or maybe even hoped—that they'd cross paths again. But this was different. There was emotion, but Veronyka had made this decision with her head as well as her heart. Her lips trembled, and her breath turned uneven. Why did it have to be this way? Why did Val, her sister, her only family in the world, have to be the one person who hurt her the most?

Sudden footsteps sounded, and Tristan appeared at the bottom of the stairs. Veronyka lurched to her feet. Once he saw that Veronyka was alone, he flushed, dropping his gaze. Remembering that her breasts were exposed, Veronyka crossed her arms over her chest.

"Tristan, I—"

"We don't have time for that," he said shortly, eyes on the ground between them. He held a fresh tunic in his hand and tossed it in her direction.

She caught it and hastened to tug it over her head, turning away from him as she scrambled to poke her arms through the sleeves. The fabric was softer than what she was used to, smooth against her skin, and it was much too big—it must belong to him. She ran her hands over the expensive cotton, the smell of Tristan clinging to her fingertips.

She turned back around, adjusting the tunic before taking a step toward him.

Seeing her movement, he glanced up to make sure she was clothed before pulling his other arm from around his back. It held a bow.

"Do you still want to fight for us?" he asked. His gaze kept darting around her face, skipping from nose to lips to eyes and back again, as if trying to relearn her features.

Veronyka stared down at the bow, her heart soaring. He was giving her the chance she so desperately wanted, the opportunity to truly become a part of this world. After what had just happened, she needed it more than ever.

She took the bow from his outstretched hand, hugging it close. There was so much she needed to say, but on the brink of an attack, now was not the time.

"I'm sorry," she whispered.

"I know," he said. When he opened his mouth to say more, a bell clanged from high above. A rush of footsteps and the jangle of weapons answered the call.

The soldiers had arrived.

*Sometimes to achieve what you
know is right, you must do what
others say is wrong.*

- CHAPTER 38 -

TRISTAN

TRISTAN BARRELED UP THE steps two at a time, while Nyk—
Veronyka—trailed close behind. There was too much happening for Tristan
to dwell on the situation, and yet every moment his mind was idle, it
screamed, *Veronyka, Veronyka, Veronyka*. Something had been lost to Tristan,
some sense of balance or rightness torn away. In the moment, it felt a bit
like grief.

Nyk had been . . . what? Somebody special to Tristan, for certain. An
ally, a confidant—someone he could trust. Someone he *thought* he could
trust. But who was this girl? Was she still Nyk, or was everything that
Tristan knew about her a lie? What if she was like her sister, Val? Something
strange had happened down there. One minute he was talking to Nyk—
Veronyka—and the next he felt confused and disoriented, while the two of
them argued about things he didn't understand.

When Val drew her knife, Tristan had feared she was about to do something horrible, but the reality of what had happened had shocked him, if
possible, even more. And why had she done it? There had to be more to the
story, but for now it was enough to know that he had another fighter by
his side.

Night had fallen, and the cloud cover hid the light of the moon. The flaming beacon and the lanterns that lined the wall provided the stronghold with illumination, but it soon became clear to Tristan that their glow turned all else to darkness. He ordered the lights along the wall extinguished and hoped that the burning phoenix atop the temple didn't turn them all into easy targets for any archers that might be lurking in the tree cover below. He didn't dare douse the beacon's flames, in case the messenger pigeons he'd sent to his father were shot down or went astray. Though the Eyrie was well-hidden, the beacon's glow was designed to be seen at a distance, and the Riders would know to look for it as soon as they took to the sky once again.

As the lights across the mountaintop were snuffed out, the world shrank around him. Tristan blinked, willing his vision to adjust. He thought of Rex, who could lend him superior eyesight in this darkness, and a far greater vantage point. What he wanted more than anything was to saddle his bondmate and fly out, raining arrows down upon those who would dare to threaten them. But he knew better. These soldiers came to destroy the Riders, but what they wanted to destroy most of all was their phoenixes. Without them, Riders were just animages, good with messenger pigeons and pack animals and not much else. Without them, they were ordinary people, easy to dominate and control. He had to protect the phoenixes, their future, at all costs.

Even, he thought darkly, *at the cost of human lives.*

Tristan took a deep breath, the night breeze rippling his tunic and causing Veronyka's black hair to fly into her face. He looked away, back out into the night. There were some lives he couldn't bear to lose.

The most recent scouting reports had the attackers approaching the way station from the road, which meant that at any second, the soldiers would be upon them. Bringing the fight to their enemies while they climbed the precarious steps would have been ideal, but they couldn't risk leaving the stronghold—and the phoenixes who dwelt inside—vulnerable.

After questioning Elliot, Morra reported that he knew nothing of value about the coming attack, only that he was supposed to give them the location of the underground service entrance—and open it from the inside—but thankfully he'd never actually sent the letter. It pained Tristan to know that Elliot had been working with the empire all this time, but he also understood how hard it must have been to be put in that situation. Even now, Elliot's failure to deliver the location of the Eyrie's hidden entrance might very well cost his sister her life. They would have to try to help him when all this was over. No matter his betrayal, he was still a Rider.

Despite the soldiers' plan falling through, Tristan had decided to post a contingent of guards inside the stronghold's cellars, just in case. It was a poor attack point—their superior numbers would be forced to bottleneck and pour out of a small doorway, where Tristan's soldiers could pick them off with ease—but he didn't want to risk leaving it undefended. Elliot might be lying, after all. Morra could sniff out the truth better than anyone he knew, but Veronyka had tricked her, hadn't she? Clearly the woman's gifts weren't infallible.

A light in the distance drew his attention. Veronyka followed his gaze, then several of the guards noticed it, and soon every head upon the wall swiveled toward the open field between the village and the steps to the way station.

Soldiers crested the lip of the plateau. It looked like a hundred, maybe a hundred and fifty, their lanterns bobbing and weapons glinting with reflected firelight. It was a smaller number than he'd expected, a manageable number . . . but Tristan's insides clenched all the same.

The first assault would come to the village gate, as he had expected.

Tristan closed his eyes, picturing his father's map of the Eyrie and surrounding lands. Despite being a religious site for decades, the Eyrie had good natural defenses, thanks to its origins as a training outpost, including its position on high ground and the sheer slopes that rose all around it. It was perched on a jagged outcrop, concealed by other spears of stone and rock and hidden from wider view. To the west the mountain dropped off, leading to a massive gorge situated miles below, and to the north the mountain soared high into the clouds and the upper reaches of Pyrmont. South of the Eyrie was a kind of ravine or ditch, sloping steeply down to the edges of the Field of Feathers and the thick trees that surrounded it.

The way station and switchback stairs were to the east—the only way to approach the Eyrie on foot.

Since their attackers were coming from the east, up the stairs and through the village was their only plausible point of attack.

The wide double doors at the gate had been reinforced with wood beams and stacked barrels of grain, and Tristan's best soldiers remained behind them in case the attackers broke through. Archers were stationed along the village wall, but it was lower and narrower than the wall that enclosed the stronghold, putting them in vulnerable positions. Still, if they could hold the soldiers at the gate, the inexperienced apprentices, villagers, and servants that manned the stronghold might never see any action at all.

Tristan watched closely as the soldiers split their forces: Half approached the gate with ax and fire, and the rest shot arrows into the sky to clear the wall's defenders. Tristan redid his count. There were closer to two hundred soldiers that he could see in the open, plus maybe two dozen more crouched in the darkness at the edge of the field. They were still well short of what Sev had claimed, and even what the most recent scout had reported.

The soldiers at the edge of the field were busy unhooking large, round objects from their backs, lining them up in a row. Were they weapons, or supplies? As another round object landed on the ground, Tristan's mouth went dry.

It was a battering ram.

It would be impossible to carry a heavy assault weapon like that up the narrow steps from the way station, but they had found a way to create one that broke down for easy transportation. They must have been planning this attack from the moment they made contact with Elliot almost a year ago.

A barrage of arrows flew from the village walls, and several of the attackers dropped. Since the stronghold doors were already locked tight, Tristan sent a runner through the concealed postern gate behind the stables, relaying the information about the ram in case Captain Flynn hadn't seen it. If they could eliminate that threat, their defense would hold.

Or so Tristan thought.

His confidence shattered when the first grappling hook soared through the sky and landed with a clatter onto the stone walkway not five feet away from him.

The villagers nearby jumped at the sudden appearance of the three-pronged metal object attached to a thick coil of rope. It scraped along the ground and then flew up against the wall with a sudden, violent jerk, taking the weight of the climber on the other end.

Two more hooks flew over the wall, their resounding clanks driving fear deep into Tristan's heart. They were coming from the south, from the steep ravine between the thrust of stone on which the Eyrie and the stronghold perched and the surrounding rocky landscape.

Surely these were the remaining soldiers from Sev's count.

The battle outside the village was yet another diversion, an attempt to draw soldiers and resources away from the stronghold, where the inexperienced Riders and their phoenixes would be together, relatively unprotected. They'd managed to divide the Phoenix Riders' already limited numbers into three smaller, less threatening groups—the patrols that had already flown out, the guards at the village gate, and their remaining forces at the stronghold.

Swallowing a sour lump in his throat, Tristan lurched toward the nearest hook and withdrew his belt knife. He hacked savagely at the rope, but it was treated with some kind of wax or resin, the woven thread almost impossible to get through, even with Ferronese steel.

"A serrated knife," Veronyka said, coming to stand next to him.

Tristan continued to hack and gouge, ruining his blade as he hit metal and stone, the words taking several seconds to penetrate his frustration.

He took a deep, steadying breath and squeezed his eyes shut. *Calm as the mountain.*

When he opened them, he nodded at Veronyka and thrust his knife back into his belt. He turned to the nearest runner crouched at the bottom of the stairs, a small girl with wide eyes and—unless he was seeing things—a sparrow in her hair.

"Go to the kitchens and ask Morra for every serrated knife she has."

The girl ran off as several more hooks flew over the wall. Tristan wanted to thank Veronyka for keeping a cool head when he could not, but to admit that weakness would be his undoing. Instead he shoved the moment of panic out of his mind and tried to regroup. Climbing onto a crate, Tristan looked over the edge of the wall.

It was a sheer drop, disappearing into darkness that Tristan knew was filled with shifting gravel, gnarled trees, and tangling vines. No one would dare attempt to climb these steep slopes unless they knew exactly what lay hidden within the labyrinthine walls of rock. And these soldiers did, thanks to Elliot.

The climbers were courageous to attempt to scale such a high wall with so many jagged stones below them, but Tristan didn't have time to admire their bravery. Five hooks had made contact now, their climbers emerging from the trees at least a hundred feet below. They'd soon reach the top of the walls, and the angle was too steep and awkward for their archers to hit.

Rocks, Tristan thought. He sent another runner to ask for any kind of heavy objects they could throw down on the climbers, just as the first runner returned. She was helped by several kitchen hands, and serrated knives of all shapes and sizes were handed out along the wall. Tristan shouted instructions, his mind clearing as adrenaline kicked in. While some of their number worked hard to saw at the ropes, others moved to strategic points along the wall that gave them better angles to shoot the climbers with arrows or to drop the newly delivered stones, pottery, and scrap metal onto their unsuspecting heads.

Veronyka was one of those working the knives, sawing with all her might into the rope Tristan had first tried to cut, while he backed up several paces, standing on the same crate as before and pointing his bow down, flush against the wall. It was a difficult angle, but it was the danger that Veronyka faced that made his muscles tense and his palms sweat. If she didn't cut the rope, or if he missed his shot, she would be the first thing the soldier saw when he mounted the wall. She would be his first victim.

Veronyka seemed oblivious to the danger, slashing relentlessly at the rope, which had begun to fray from her efforts. Her forehead was damp with sweat, and she'd rolled up the sleeves of his oversized tunic.

Scuffs and grunts reached his ears, and he looked down again to see the climber rising steadily. The man was armed with a battle-ax strapped across his back and several daggers on his belt. Pausing for a moment to gather his breath, he looked up, and their eyes met.

Next to Tristan, a triumphant "Aha" was followed by a loud snap. The metal hook hit the ground with a heavy clang, and the severed threads of the rope disappeared over the edge of the battlements. Tristan looked back over the wall as the climber dropped soundlessly into the chasm of darkness below.

Veronyka didn't stop to celebrate. Gasping, she took up her knife and attacked another rope farther down the line.

Across the courtyard, another hook rattled to the ground as a second climber fell, this time crying out as he dropped from the wall. The surge of happiness that flared inside Tristan was quickly stifled. For every rope that was cut, two more flew up in its place.

A handful of Tristan's arrows found their mark, but it wasn't enough. The stream of climbers seemed endless, and the time it took to cut them was longer than the time it took for new soldiers to make the climb. Soon they would crest the walls, and all his best fighters were in the village.

The grappling hooks flew up in waves, usually sets of two or three, with a few minutes' lull in between—climbers trying to find better positions, Tristan guessed, or dodging their fellows as they hurtled back to the ground. At this rate, the stronghold would be lost before the village gate fell—a shocking realization, with the sound of groaning hinges and splintering wood echoing from below, along with the steady *thump, thump, thump* of the battering ram, pulsing in time with the rapid beat of Tristan's heart.

He had to change their strategy, but how?

During the pauses between the waves of grappling hooks, the defenders traded positions, giving those hacking at the ropes a chance to attack, while those who had been firing arrows or dropping stones took up a blade.

Tristan forced Veronyka to take a break and drink some water, while he held her serrated knife, weighing his options. He could call Captain Flynn from his position on the village wall, but he hadn't sent a reply to Tristan's first message about the battering ram, which meant he was either too busy to report—and to help—or that something much worse had become of him.

"You know what you have to do, don't you?" Veronyka said, still gasping as she tried to catch her breath.

"What do you mean?"

"You're a Rider, Tristan. *Ride.*"

He looked down at her, at those familiar eyes, and shook his head. "I . . . I can't. We have no battle experience. That's what they want us to do. They want us to die out there."

He grabbed the waterskin from her hands and raised it to his lips, but he didn't drink.

"Then let me go," she said. When his head snapped in her direction, she twisted her lips, then said, "I'm bonded. That new female, the one I tamed in the courtyard? She was—is—my bondmate."

Tristan realized that distantly he'd known this—had figured it out during the fight with her sister in front of the enclosure—but he'd been too distracted to consciously make the connection.

Regardless, it was out of the question. She had less training than him. "No. It's too dangerous."

"I know it is, but you can afford to lose me, even if you can't afford to lose the others."

He tossed the waterskin aside. "If you think I'd willingly sacrifice you just because you're a *girl*"—he said the last word in a low, vehement whisper—"or because you're not a trained Rider or whatever it is that you think, you're more messed up than your sister."

Her lips parted in surprise, but she didn't respond.

Tristan's chest heaved. He wanted to keep yelling. He wanted to punch things. He wanted to burn the damn ropes that carried their enemies toward them.

The thought made something clunk into place in his mind. Of course he hadn't thought of it yet—Tristan did his best to *never* think of it.

Fire.

He snatched a nearby lantern, dumping the cold oil onto the closest hook's rope, and called for a lit torch from a brazier below. When he held the flame over the oil-soaked rope, hands shaking slightly, it took a long time to catch, burning low and blue before winking out. That's what the waxy resin was—it was the same fireproofing sap they used on their own gear.

"Tristan," Veronyka said, gripping the front of his tunic to regain his attention. "If this place falls, we're *all* dead—servants and villagers, Riders and phoenixes. You've let the people fight to defend their home; now let the phoenixes. Can't you feel it?" she finished quietly, looking toward the Eyrie.

When Tristan focused there, and not on the battle raging around him, he did feel it. Heat, waves of it rippling from the stony chasm beyond the archway, followed by bursts of anger and aggression. Rex was there with the others, his volatile emotions stoking the flame of Tristan's own wild feelings. Rex wanted to fight, and Tristan had forbidden it. He'd made all the Riders tether their mounts to keep them inside the Eyrie, just like the females in their enclosure.

"You're right," he said, and Veronyka released his tunic, as if surprised to have won him over so easily. "This is their home, these are their bond-mates, and they should be allowed to fight. Besides," he added, nodding to the oil-soaked rope and swallowing the wave of fear that surged up inside him, "nothing burns hotter than phoenix fire."

"Will you ride?" Veronyka asked as they crossed the courtyard.

"No," Tristan said, despite wishing otherwise. He'd rather be in the air than down here, amid the burning flames. "We can't afford to lose the apprentices on the walls—they're some of our best fighters. Besides, the phoenixes are safer without their Riders. We weigh them down, and the metal fastenings on their saddles catch the light. Without us, they can fly almost invisibly, and be seen only when they want to be—when they ignite."

Passing Anders on his way across the cobblestones, Tristan explained what he intended to do and told him to spread the word to the other apprentices. They'd have to guide their bondmates through the battle from the ground.

"And what of the females?" Veronyka asked, as Anders rushed off and Tristan strode purposefully toward the Eyrie.

"If your bondmate wants to fight, she can fight," he said, continuing his rapid pace across the courtyard. "No matter what, she leaves that cell."

He glanced down at her, and her expression of gratitude was so raw, her eyes so bright, that he almost had to look away. He wanted to hug her, to ruffle her hair or give her a punch on the arm. He settled for something in between, reaching out and squeezing her shoulder. Their brief contact stirred something deep in the pit of Tristan's stomach, and he realized that Veronyka *was* Nyk, and Nyk was Veronyka. They were one and the same, and the thought eased something tight in his chest.

They made for the apprentice mounts first. The phoenixes were roosting together on the topmost levels of the Eyrie, huddled in groups or soaring in low, mournful circles in the open air.

Sensing him, Rex cut his flight short and banked hard, landing on the lip of the stone ledge with a rattle of his chain. Veronyka drew back as a wave of heat and glowing sparks settled over them, but Tristan stood his ground—he *had* to, they didn't have time to waste.

Rex tossed his head and expelled breaths of hot air, behaving like an angry stallion. Tristan gripped his beak and pulled it down, bringing their eyes on a level.

I need you, he said through the bond, patting him reassuringly with one hand while using the other to fumble with the cuff. *I hate to ask, but I need you to fight. To lead.*

Rex threatened to ignite right then and there. Tristan wanted to flinch away from it, but he stood his ground—he couldn't quell Rex's emotions. He needed to fan the flames. He needed his phoenix to fight hard enough to survive.

"Nyk—the others," Tristan said, unhitching the cuff and dropping it to the ground with a clang. "I mean, Veronyka."

"Nyk's fine," she said distractedly, pushing past him toward the rest of the phoenixes. Once they saw Rex released, they were eager to greet her, shuffling into a line along the narrow ledge, shaking their wings as they jostled for position.

Tristan spotted Elliot's mount out of the corner of his eye and hesitated. "You'd better leave Jaxon," he said, indicating the phoenix perched near the back of the group, his head down and his movements subdued. "That's Elliot's mount. I . . . I don't know what he might do, with his bondmate locked up. He might try to retaliate."

With a regretful twist of the lips, Veronyka nodded and returned to the others, unhooking the cuffs while Tristan explained the battle to Rex. He emphasized how important it was for him and the rest to stay away from the enemy archers. He showed Rex a mental picture of the ropes and the climbers and stressed that their only mission was to set those ropes alight and then fly to safety. The humans would take care of the other humans. Once the stronghold was secure, Tristan would reevaluate what help they needed at the village gate.

By the time he was finished coaching Rex, Veronyka was unfastening the cuff on the last phoenix, while the rest remained perched on nearby ledges. The phoenixes were instructed by their bondmates to follow Rex's lead, and so far they didn't attempt to leave the Eyrie—though Tristan knew they wanted to.

The last leash rattled to the ground, and Veronyka came to stand next to him. He released his hold on Rex.

Tristan had to be brave, for Rex and for the others. He had to control his fear.

Looking inward, Tristan focused on the safe house. He hadn't tended it much in the past few days, and the neglect showed itself in the way his fear threatened to overtake his mind, even at the thought of all these phoenixes joining them in fiery battle.

Veronyka sidled next to him and put a warm hand on his arm. He looked at her, and he felt something spread through him—a calmness, a strength that didn't feel entirely his own. Whatever it was, Tristan used it to rebuild the walls and lock his fear safely away.

I control you, he said to his fear, *you do not control me.*

The last stone in place, Tristan's heart rate slowed, and Rex crooned next to him in support.

"Thank you," he whispered to Veronyka, his fear ebbing away, leaving him strong and stable once more.

She squeezed his arm, then released it. Rex flapped his wings in a great gust, stirring up dirt and leaves as he flew across the chasm to perch on the phoenix-shaped platform. The rest of the phoenixes followed him, each emitting a cloud of heat and a hazy glow between their feathers. As soon as they landed, their inner fires winked out, and they stood stony and gray as statues against the black of the night.

Tristan turned to Veronyka. "They'll await my signal. Let's go."

At the bottommost levels of the Eyrie, the females stirred. While Rex's feelings came to Tristan so powerfully and clearly that they could sometimes be mistaken as his own, the emotions of other phoenixes were like smoke, faint whispers of thoughts and intentions not yet formed or fully realized.

Veronyka took hold of the lock, the metal rattling loudly against the bars. One of the phoenixes, he assumed her bondmate, fluttered forward to greet her. Footsteps sounded to their left, and Ersken moved out of the shadows.

Veronyka froze, but Tristan stepped forward. He was in charge now, and no matter his father's orders to the contrary, he had to do what was best for the Eyrie. "Stand down, Ersken. We're releasing one of the females."

"Just one?" Veronyka asked, dropping the lock.

Tristan took in a steady breath, the noise of the attack above echoing in the distance.

"Yes, Nyk, just one. The others aren't bonded, and—" He froze, realizing his mistake as Veronyka stiffened. Both turned to Ersken.

"Should I act surprised, then?" he asked, leaning against the bars. "Never seen a phoenix act as this one has, unless they were bonded."

Veronyka's eyes darted in Tristan's direction, but this was her secret to tell.

"I'm not Nyk," she said, meeting Ersken's gaze. "I'm Veronyka. And my bondmate is Xephyra."

Ersken nodded gravely, then fixed her with a gentle smile. "That's a right queenly name, to be sure."

"Look," Tristan said, cutting into their exchange. "We're only releasing one, because only one is bonded. We have no idea what the others might do."

"It's in their nature to fight alongside their fellows . . . ," Ersken mused, as if it were of no real urgency or importance. "You saw what they were like when we caught these females. The others didn't like it one bit—and they won't like it tonight, when arrows come flyin' at their brothers and sisters."

"But they won't understand what's happening, not like the bonded ones will. They could be killed."

"Or they could fly away," Ersken said, eyebrows raised.

"Yes, or they could fly away," Tristan agreed, irritated at the assumption that that was *all* he cared about, though of course it was a large part of it. The commander would be livid if he returned to find no female phoenixes. That was, if he returned at all, and if the Eyrie was still standing. He sighed heavily. "They have no bondmate to keep them loyal, and we've shackled them. Leaving should be their very first instinct."

"You'd be surprised," Ersken said, staring at the phoenixes through the bars. He might not be bonded with them, but Ersken knew the females better than anyone else in the stronghold. "Their first instinct is to protect their bondmate, and after that, it's to protect each other. Why do you think the empire never tried to lure Phoenix Riders to their side during the war? When it comes to a real battle—not squabbles over territory or mating displays—they won't fight against one another."

"Fine," Tristan said, stepping around Veronyka to take hold of the lock. "They can fight for us, for the other phoenixes, or for no one at all. I suppose that's their right." He turned to Veronyka. "They might be shot down before they get past the walls of the stronghold—your bondmate included. I hope you're prepared to face that possibility."

"I'll do it," Ersken said, shoving Tristan aside. "Get back up there; you'll see once they're loose. Doubt they'll stay put and play nice like your trained males up there, so be ready with your command."

Veronyka wavered, and Tristan could tell she was afraid, that she wanted to stay behind and release her phoenix herself.

"You can stay, but I have to go," he said. She hesitated another moment, then followed him up the stairs. They ran, Tristan's lungs burning with exertion. The tunnel was cool and damp, cut off from the noise of the battle, the only sound the steady pant of their breathing and the slap of their footsteps against the stone.

They were just emerging at the top level when a series of musical cries echoed from the bottom of the Eyrie. Peering over the edge, Tristan saw Veronyka's phoenix soar out first, quickly followed by the other two. As Ersken predicted, they didn't await an order or circle low in hesitation. They rose like fireballs, ripping through the sky and bursting into a glorious shower of sparks. Like their feathers, they burned with a hint of violet and indigo, staining the sky with all the colors of a mountain sunset.

Rex, he thought, staring at the perch where the males gathered, ruffling their feathers and shifting their feet in response to the females soaring past them. *Now.*

Rex burst into a blazing red-gold inferno, the flame rippling off his feathers and cracking like a whip. The rest of the phoenixes lit up as well, one after the other, like a series of torches catching fire. With a bone-chilling cry, the males answered the females, launching into the air.

The females weaved in between the males, mixing their colors and creating a spectacle a thousand times more magnificent than the solstice dance he'd shown Veronyka. This was primal battle magic.

This was the stuff of legends.

Their whirling spiral of light split, and they turned their flight toward the battle for the stronghold, sparks trailing in their wake.

War is costly.
Even in victory, there is a price.

- CHAPTER 39 -
VERONYKA

AS SOON AS THEY passed through the archway and the chaos atop the battlements came into view, Veronyka's insides went cold. There were *soldiers* inside the stronghold, wielding axes, crossbows, and short swords, their edges tipped in blood. Bodies littered the walkway across the wall and the ground beneath it, while a distant glow to the east told her that the village gate was burning.

The possibility that they might lose became real to Veronyka for the first time. And she had convinced Tristan to involve Xephyra and the rest of the phoenixes. Veronyka might lose her bondmate all over again. Her legs became wobbly stems beneath her, and she drew air in quick, shallow breaths. The stronghold was flooded with fear, her own most powerful of all, and Veronyka thought she might drown in it.

High above, a phoenix screeched, and Veronyka looked up to see Xephyra burn a brilliant violet streak across the sky. Rex and the other phoenixes joined in, and as the stronghold's defenders clapped and cheered, the heavy press of emotion lightened. Veronyka knew then that she'd made the right decision. Not only had they brought hope to their flagging defenders, but the phoenixes were true warriors—if anyone was qualified to fight the soldiers tonight, it was them.

Tristan dove into the fighting as soon as they returned, helping two of his fellow apprentices reclaim a section of the wall as Rex and the others soared by. The defenders waved their weapons in the air, heartened by their reinforcements, while the soldiers stared at the firebirds with openmouthed fear. Maybe they thought all the phoenixes had been drawn out by the diversions, or maybe they'd never faced them in battle before.

Rex and the other males flew together in circles high above the battle, slowly building their heat, while Xephyra and the females were far more erratic. Veronyka was relieved to see that neither of the unbonded phoenixes had used the opportunity to flee—at least not yet.

Rex was the first to break the pattern, igniting as he dove toward the attacking forces. He whipped past the walls, trailing fire in his wake and causing soldiers to duck and cry out, only to topple from the wall or be cut through by a defender. It took several passes for the phoenix fire to actually burn the ropes, thanks to the *pyraflora* resin, but with each sweep of flaming wing or tail feather, the ropes frayed and weakened. The rest of the males followed after him, orbiting the stronghold with swathes of flame until it was lit to almost daylight brightness.

Veronyka glanced at Tristan, worried for how he'd react to so much fire, but he was focused on the fighting. His mental safe house must be holding up well. She'd sensed him working on it inside the Eyrie, and some instinct—or maybe the information Val had given her about how she'd controlled Xephyra—told her that she could lend Tristan her strength, that she could help him through their connection. She didn't know if it had worked, only that Tristan's erratic breathing had slowed and the tension in his mind cleared.

Taking up her serrated knife once more, Veronyka found an untouched rope and got to work. She still wore a quiver of arrows, and her bow was strapped to her back, but the weapon made her feel like a fraud. She could barely draw the string or hit a stationary target, never mind kill a man in the middle of a battle. She tried to let Tristan's reassurances wash over her: *You have other strengths, you know.*

Like hacking at ropes?

Her palms were so sweaty, she could barely hold the handle, but she did her best to focus. While Veronyka might be able to block out the feelings of other people and animals, Xephyra was bonded to her, and their joint emotions swirled together as the fight wore on. The war cry that ripped from Xephyra's beak left Veronyka's throat dry, and the heat that rippled from her wings caused Veronyka's skin to itch.

She encouraged her bondmate to mimic Rex's flight patterns, and after much nudging and convincing, Xephyra began to follow him through his dives and circles. The other two females, on the other hand, did whatever they pleased. Xatara was screeching relentlessly, ripping and snapping at anyone and everyone, not just the soldiers. Luckily, the attacking arrows drew her attention more than the defenders on the wall, so she harassed their encampment below and tore climbers from the wall with beak and talons.

Xolanthe focused her attention on the village gate, which was billowing clouds of black smoke as it burned. Veronyka didn't understand why the phoenix flew in that direction; maybe she felt somewhat territorial about the area or was drawn there by the fire.

Veronyka watched, heart in her throat, as Xoe dove among the attackers. She was smaller than most of the full-grown phoenixes, but it didn't stop her from wreaking havoc on the soldiers storming the village. The more they tried to attack her, the more vicious her dives became. They'd brought nets with them, similar to the one the commander had used to trap Xephyra, and Veronyka bristled at the sight of the hated metal mesh. They tried several times to catch Xoe, but she managed to dodge their attempts, screeching in irritation and swooping back around.

In a gust of flame and sparks, she dropped among them, only to rise again with her claws sunk deep into the side of the massive battering ram. Phoenixes could carry heavy loads, but even still, she struggled to take flight. The soldiers holding it clung desperately for a moment, then dropped to the ground, backing away and taking up bows and spears instead. Another net flew into the air, snagging on the ram but missing Xoe's wing by mere inches.

Fingers of dread slipped down Veronyka's spine. She tried to throw her magic to the phoenix, to warn her, but she was too far away, and there was too much happening in between them for her to establish any kind of connection. Instead she stared, unmoving, as Xoe pumped her great wings, slowly rising from the mass of soldiers surrounding the front gate, dragging the ram with her.

From underneath her feathers her fire burned, growing hotter and brighter as her plumage began to smolder, then burst into flame, heat waves rippling over the grassy plain as the phoenix and the wooden ram ignited. With a victorious shriek, she dropped the burning assault weapon among the soldiers and spread her wings for flight, unencumbered by the heavy object that had been gripped in her claws.

Veronyka let out a sigh of relief—but it was too soon.

One of the attacking archers lined up his shot and loosed, the arrow lodging itself in the middle of Xoe's chest. She shrieked, and the agonized sound drew the attention of everyone in the stronghold.

Xoe beat her wings and struggled to fly, but she was still within range. As the embedded arrow shaft caught fire, three more followed it, peppering the side of her body and her left wing.

She keened, her inner light flickering as she banked hard, flapping her good wing, trying to remain aloft. But her flight was imbalanced and sluggish, and the sparks that flew from her body turned to ash as she fell among the rooftops of the silent village. She disappeared from sight, but Veronyka knew, somewhere deep in her magical senses, that the phoenix was gone. She had no bondmate to gather her body or build her pyre, and by the time someone at the stronghold found her—if anyone survived this attack— would it be too late? Or would she choose not to come back anyway, allowing her fire to turn to smoke, her flesh to ash, and her spirit to be free at last?

It wasn't supposed to happen like this. Phoenixes were magical, immortal if not slain. They weren't supposed to be in chains, behind bars, or shot down by empire soldiers. Xoe had fought bravely for the Riders only to have her moment of victory ripped from her and her life extinguished.

A violent screech rent the night, and Xatara burst into sudden, savage flame. She dipped into the trees that dotted the mountainside below, only to surge up again moments later with two soldiers clutched in her talons. She dropped them from a sickening height, their terrified screams and burning bodies disappearing into the forest below, but Xatara wasn't finished.

She shrieked again, swooping around the edge of the compound and leaving everything—weapons, ropes, and people—burning in her wake. Flaring brighter than the sun, so bright that Veronyka had to shield her eyes, Xatara flew ever upward, farther and farther away. Where she was going, Veronyka didn't know, but soon she was nothing more than a distant speck of light . . . then nothing at all.

The defenders watched her go, and Veronyka could feel their resolve wavering. Two phoenixes gone in moments, and the others emitting low, sorrowful cries of sadness and despair. One of the males abandoned the fight to soar in melancholy circles over the village. It occurred to Veronyka that she didn't know which phoenix had laid the egg inside the enclosure, but she guessed it was Xoe, and this mourning male phoenix was her son.

Veronyka turned away, mind racing frantically as she tried to regroup. What now?

Tristan's words came back to her once more: *You have other strengths, you know.*

What strengths? How did being a strong animage help them when they were under attack?

And then, as if she were having a conversation with him in her mind, Tristan's voice answered with more remembered words: *If phoenixes have the desire to fight on behalf of the humans they care about, why not other animals as well?*

Veronyka whirled around, heart racing. "Tristan!" she shouted, running to his side as he helped hoist a barrel of rocks and debris over the edge of the wall, emptying the contents down on the climbing soldiers below. He left

Ronyn to finish the job and came to Veronyka's side, chest heaving.

"We lost both of them," he said, running a filthy hand through his hair, leaving blood and dirt smeared across his forehead. His eyes were wild, and his hands were trembling with fear, adrenaline, or maybe both.

"I know," Veronyka said, and they both turned as a wrenching crunch rose above the din. Part of the village gate collapsed in a cloud of smoke, and the only thing that kept the soldiers from rushing into the newly made gap was the fire licking up the sides of the wood and the scrambling defenders tossing spears and loosing arrows into the open space. It was only a matter of time before the entire structure gave way.

"Tristan," Veronyka said, drawing his attention back to her. "I have an idea, something . . . reckless."

His focus sharpened at the familiar phrase, and he gave her his full attention.

"You told me my greatest strength was my magic," she continued hurriedly, as people rushed back and forth, taking advantage of the lull in climbers to reposition themselves and restock provisions. "But that's not just me— that's *all* of us. This stronghold is full of animages, and it's full of animals, too. If the phoenixes *chose* to fight . . . maybe the rest of the animals would too."

His eyes lit in realization. While not every person who lived at the Eyrie was an animage, *most* of them were. If they worked together with the animals, from the lowliest mouse and pigeon to the mighty Wind . . .

"Together," Veronyka added, "we outnumber the soldiers."

He was nodding, over and over again, and after one final, decisive dip of the head, a hint of a smile appeared on his lips. "Okay."

Turning to face the courtyard, Tristan cupped his hands and bellowed in a commander-worthy battle voice, calling everyone's attention. They had mere moments before more ropes would fly up and a new wave of attackers made an attempt on the stronghold. The phoenixes had slowed the climbers down, but they took longer and longer now to build their heat and make their runs, and it was clear that, with two gone, they weren't enough to keep the stronghold safe.

"Defenders," Tristan said, looking around at them all, sweaty and bloody and barely keeping it together. The sound of the battle at the village gate was a strange, dissonant contrast to the bubble of silence that enveloped the stronghold—but also a reminder that this was the calm before the next storm. "We have used every weapon and tactic available to us—except one. Who are we? Some of us are soldiers, craftspeople, or cooks; others are Apprentice Riders or even stablehands." His golden-brown eyes flicked to Veronyka before he continued. "But those are all unnecessary divisions, small pieces of the whole. We are *animages*, and wherever we come from, we are united, here, in this place we now call home. We are also united in our abilities. Tonight I asked the phoenixes to fight alongside us—and they rallied together to join our cause. Maybe if we ask the other animals of the stronghold to fight with us, they will do the same."

Whispers spread through the courtyard like leaves in a light breeze. Veronyka closed her eyes and cast her awareness wide, lowering her defenses. There. While the people of the stronghold were confused and unsure, the animals heard Tristan's rallying cry, felt his intention and the rise of his magic—and responded to it.

"We will not force them," Tristan said firmly, "but if they choose to help us, we can guide their efforts and ensure they understand the risks. Just as they do in our daily lives, the animals can make us stronger—from phoenixes to messenger pigeons, from warhorses to hounds—no ally is too small, no effort unworthy."

Veronyka looked around. Many of the animals were afraid and would rather hide among rafters or in dark, quiet cellars, but others . . . Slowly they emerged, slipping between legs and perching on shoulders or ledges. There was a steady thumping sound coming from the stables, and Veronyka found Wind's familiar, stubborn mind. He was ready to break down his stall door if someone didn't come and open it for him soon.

The bleak feeling that had so recently overtaken the stronghold changed, shifted. . . . It wasn't exactly *hope*, but it was something other than despair, and that was a start.

"If we stand together," Tristan said, "we can show these empire soldiers what we're capable of."

Tristan's speech ended with the sharp clang of a new grappling hook scraping against the stronghold's walls. In an instant, the people and animals of the Eyrie responded. Veronyka hurtled down the nearest stairs, almost tripping over the cats and dogs that weaved between her legs. As she burst through the stable doors, unlatching every stall, pigeons and sparrows and doves filled the air.

Outside, Veronyka stared as her most recent reckless plan came to fruition. She joined in where she could, sending flocks of birds left and packs of dogs right. She'd expected to have to do more, but the animals were focused and ready to fight.

Messenger pigeons gouged the eyes of climbing soldiers, while falcons shrieked and dove, beaks tearing and claws scraping flesh.

Instead of weary villagers with serrated kitchen knives, cats scratched and clawed at the climbing ropes—and at any unwary soldier who managed to crest the wall—and a barrage of dogs and horses barreled into the village through the open postern door.

Veronyka climbed the wall again just in time to see a soldier try his hand at running through the ruins of the village gate—only to be surprised by the giant bloodhound that leapt through the gap, colliding with him in midair and tackling him to the ground.

Llamas carried supplies and weapons, while the horses dragged heavy beams and wagons to try to shore up the village gate's barricade. Veronyka even saw Sparrow hacking at a rope, Chirp perched next to her, biting and tugging at the loose threads.

Veronyka's heart filled with triumphant glee. Fighting alongside her animal friends was terrifying, but it felt *right*. They were natural-born allies, and like Tristan said, they were stronger together. Let the empire think them weak and defenseless without their Phoenix Riders—they would show them exactly how much damage animages could do.

I thought I lost my sister
when a stray arrow pierced her chest,
but I'd lost her long before then.

- CHAPTER 40 -
VERONYKA

JUST LIKE THE PHOENIXES, the animal reinforcements worked—for a time. Veronyka's stomach clenched painfully when she saw the first dog run through with an enemy spear, and her heart lurched each time a messenger pigeon was shot down from the sky. Everywhere she looked, she saw fur and feathers stained with blood, and bodies of all shapes and sizes were strewn across the ground.

The phoenixes continued to circle and dive, but the death of Xoe had made them hesitant, and even Xephyra had lost some of her aggression.

It wasn't going to be enough. They had done everything they could to *last,* to endure, but their defenders were dying, human and animal alike, and still, no saviors came to rescue them.

When the newly built barricade at the village gate came crashing down, Veronyka knew they were out of time.

If the soldiers got into the village, they'd burn and destroy until they reached the stronghold. Its walls were taller and more solidly built than the village, but its gate hadn't been reinforced, and they didn't have the numbers to properly defend it.

If the soldiers got into the village, all was lost.

They could send more phoenixes to help, but they'd already lost two—neither of which were bonded. How much more devastating would it be if one of the apprentices lost their bondmate? Veronyka knew that if Tristan sent anyone, it would be Rex. He wouldn't condemn anyone else to that fate. He would shoulder the burden himself.

Veronyka sought him out and had her worst suspicions confirmed. Already he was signaling Rex, but when the phoenix turned midflight, he didn't head to the burning village gate to take up the defense. He flew toward Tristan.

He means to go with his bondmate, she realized, her throat constricting in sudden panic. *He means for them to fight—and maybe die—together.*

Veronyka moved slowly through the crowd, as if wading through water. She didn't know what she would say or if she intended to try to stop him, but she had to get there.

Tristan spotted her approach, and their eyes met, dead bodies and burning ropes between them. His expression was bleak.

Then his face contorted in pain, and he clutched at his arm, stumbling to the ground. Veronyka ran, pushing people aside as she fell to her knees next to him, looking for the arrow that had found its mark—only, there wasn't one. Rex screeched from somewhere above, and Veronyka whirled around: *There* was the arrow she sought, embedded in the space where Rex's left wing connected with his body. He dropped, staggering down into the open space of the courtyard below.

Veronyka helped Tristan to his feet, and he shook off the phantom wound that had pierced his shoulder through the bond. Rex landed awkwardly near the back of the courtyard—probably trying to make it into the Eyrie, but unable to fly that far.

"Ersken!" Tristan screamed as they rushed to Rex's side, his voice ragged. Veronyka doubted they were close enough for the man to hear, but then a tiny figure appeared out of nowhere—Sparrow, doing her part as a runner—hurtling past in a blur as she bolted through the archway into the Eyrie and out of sight.

Tristan gripped Rex's flailing head, trying to soothe him, while Veronyka looked at the wound. The arrow shaft had pierced straight through the muscle and sinew of the joint, so that the wing lost all mobility. He would heal more quickly than other animals, but there was no way he could fly right now.

Ersken ambled through the archway, a heavy satchel in hand.

He dropped the bag with a clank of bottles and healing instruments and checked the phoenix's shoulder. Tristan's eyes were wide and feverish, his hold on Rex tense. Ersken's movements were deft and quick as he surveyed the damage. Sparrow remained just outside their group, but Ersken called her over and ordered her to retrieve items from his bag. Her hands trembled as they flitted over the bottles and jars, but Chirp was nearby, and she managed to find the items he sought.

"He'll be fine, lad," Ersken said, turning away from Rex to mop the blood from his hands—which smoked and left angry red welts on his fingers. "And there'll be no lastin' damage, as far as I can tell. But he can't be flyin' any more tonight."

Tristan didn't respond, and try as she might to resist it, Veronyka couldn't help but feel the dazed numbness that radiated from him. He was lost without his phoenix . . . and so was the gate.

Xephyra nudged Veronyka's mind, and she looked up to see her bond-mate circling the sky above. Xephyra, with whom she was so recently reunited. Xephyra, who was technically too young to be ridden, but large for her age . . .

"Tristan," Veronyka said, stepping closer and turning him slightly, so he couldn't see as Ersken continued to treat Rex—though she suspected he felt it through the bond. "We don't have time to linger here. Rex can't help us, but Xephyra can. We have to get to the gate."

Veronyka looked at Tristan closely for the first time since they'd rejoined the fight. He had a split lip and bruising along the side of his face; his tunic was bloodied and torn. He shook his head slightly, pushing back his sweat-soaked hair, and cast his gaze about as if searching for another solution.

Above, Xephyra tugged on their bond, more insistently than before, and a second later Veronyka saw the world through her phoenix's eyes. They were mirroring.

Fire. Blood. She lost herself in her bondmate's complex mind and supernatural senses, but Xephyra steered her consciousness toward the village gate.

The last burning piece of the wooden doors gave way under the fierce blow of a soldier's ax, while both attackers and defenders tripped over the abandoned weapons and bodies strewn across the ground. Smoke and arrows were heavy in the air, filling the wide-open space where the gate had once been.

Now, Xephyra said in her mind.

"Now!" Veronyka said with a gasp, returning to her own mind and body.

Tristan shook his head again. "I told you, I'm not going to sacrifice your life. You and Xephyra have never flown together. It'll have to be one of the other apprentices. I'll get—"

"The gate has fallen; we don't have time," Veronyka said desperately, calling Xephyra down to land on the ground next to them. Rex let out a melancholy croon, and Xephyra answered with a bolstering wail of support. The rest of the phoenixes were engaged in the fighting, swooping and soaring above, their bondmates busy and distracted. "You're right, I don't have experience—but you do. We can go together."

"Veronyka . . . ," Tristan said, desperation clinging to his voice as he eyed Xephyra. In the back of his mind, his fear of fire kindled, wanting to be let lose, but Veronyka sensed him clamp down on it.

"We go together, or I go alone," Veronyka said, steel in her voice. The empire had already taken her parents and her grandmother. She wouldn't allow them to take anything else. "We can't let them into the village."

"We don't even have a saddle," Tristan complained, but his words were cut off by a loud *thud.* Sparrow, panting slightly, had just dropped a strange-looking saddle onto the ground next to them. This was no horse's saddle, but a *phoenix* saddle, with extra straps and buckles. Both Veronyka and Tristan stared in surprise, but it was Ersken who first spoke.

"There's no time for you to debate it. Make your choice, and get on with it," he said, patting Sparrow on the shoulder before returning to Rex's injury. The girl beamed, proud of herself, before hurrying to hand Ersken bandages from his pack. The saddles must be stored somewhere close by, and he'd ordered Sparrow to retrieve it while Tristan and Veronyka argued.

Tristan hesitated another fraction of a second, then—

"Fine," he said, and picked up the saddle.

He glanced at Veronyka as he approached Xephyra, and she hastened to tell the phoenix what was happening and to allow Tristan to saddle her. The prospect of being ridden by her Rider caused a surge of joy to ripple through Xephyra's body, though she was wary of Tristan.

He has to come, Veronyka told her soothingly. *I need his help—we both do.*

Once saddled, Xephyra seemed to act upon some ancient, ingrained instincts—or perhaps she'd seen the other phoenixes do it—tucking her legs underneath her body and lowering herself to the ground. Tristan mounted up, while Rex watched in mournful silence. Veronyka handed him her bow and arrows, which he slung over his back before hoisting her up in front of him.

"You'll have to steer," he murmured into her ear. They were squeezed tightly together on a saddle that was only made for one, and the touch of his breath on her skin sent goose bumps trailing down her back. He quickly showed her where to put her feet and where to hold on, but she was flustered by the way his chest and thighs pressed against her. Luckily, most of her guidance would come to Xephyra through the bond. "She won't be able to hold us both for long, but if we can get there, we can try to shore up the defenses while Xephyra distracts them with her fire."

"Will you be okay?" Veronyka asked as Xephyra stood from her crouch and shook out her wings. Xephyra's wasn't the only fire they were about to endure—every bit of the village gate was burning. They were flying an inferno *into* an inferno.

"I'll have to be."

Xephyra leapt into the air, and one flap of her wings was enough to almost unseat Veronyka. She clung to the front of the saddle, using the stirrups as Tristan taught her, while he squeezed hard around her midsection.

Several more pumps of Xephyra's wings, and they were soaring above the temple and back into the fray.

The world shrank beneath them, while the sky became a vast, black expanse that threatened to swallow them whole. The night was alive with the cold bite of wind and the gentle kiss of starlight.

Veronyka gasped; it was like being mirrored with Xephyra again, only far more visceral. Her heart pounded, her stomached clenched, and every inch of her body tingled. She had been dreaming of this day since she was a child, but never had she imagined that her first flight on phoenix-back would come amid a fiery battle for her life.

Xephyra flew above the phoenixes swooping back and forth in the sky, the sounds of the battle below almost lost in the whistle of the wind and the pump of her wings.

As they neared the wreckage of the village gate, Veronyka's bondmate grew hot beneath them. Tristan squirmed slightly against her, sweat sticking them together, and Veronyka knew he wouldn't last long on Xephyra's smoldering back.

The gate was already worse than Veronyka had seen it just a few moments ago. A blackened frame was all that remained of the double doors, and only a handful of guards still defended the opening, while soldiers tried to scrabble over barrels and debris.

Tristan asked Veronyka to have Xephyra steady her flight, and then a soft *twang* slipped past her face. An arrow flew down to pierce the heart of a soldier as he tried to make a path through the rubble.

Tristan was able to loose two more before the soldiers found the source of the attack and turned their bows skyward. Veronyka didn't need Tristan's prompt to tell Xephyra to fly higher, out of their range.

They were a good distraction, drawing the attention of the soldiers so that the remaining defenders could regroup. When the attackers did the same, drawing back to the far side of the field, Veronyka hoped they were considering a retreat.

But as Xephyra swooped by for another pass, a swell of reinforcements spilled onto the mountainside, like a rush of ants from a kicked colony. Veronyka's insides became a yawning void of despair.

"Axura save us," Tristan whispered.

Veronyka directed Xephyra toward the village. She dipped low over the rising tide of soldiers, causing them to duck and scatter, before landing in front of the ruined gate. They didn't have long before the attackers would gather for a renewed assault.

Tristan leapt from Xephyra's back, and Veronyka slipped down after him. She patted her bondmate gratefully but didn't bother with instructions—Xephyra knew what to do. It seemed that, in battle, their connection honed and sharpened like the powerful weapon that it was.

Tristan made to hand Veronyka the bow and quiver again, but she shook her head. He was the trained archer, not her.

As the last defenders emerged from the shadows, reloading their weapons and taking up new positions, Veronyka went in search of arrows. Captain Flynn was slumped against a wagon wheel, pressing a blood-soaked wad of fabric against a wound, and many more bodies—dead or alive, Veronyka didn't know—were scattered all around them. She avoided looking at faces or wounds and focused on plucking ammunition from the ground and the surrounding wreckage. Grass, buildings, and bodies burned, sending plumes of smoke billowing into the air, tightening Veronyka's throat and making her eyes water.

With a heavy heart she came to stand next to Tristan, sliding the additional arrows into his quiver. She supposed that dying on her feet fighting wasn't the worst way to go. She'd finally been a Rider, for however brief a time, and it was a comfort to know that Xephyra would either escape or die free—both better options than being executed inside a cage. Maybe Val had gotten away through the underground tunnels she spoke of and would become a Rider on her own. Veronyka thought about trying to contact her with shadow magic, but she didn't know where to begin . . . or how to say goodbye.

Xephyra let out a bloodcurdling cry of defiance and ripped a path through the soldiers. Veronyka and the last dregs of their defenses raised their weapons and faced the chaos the phoenix left in her wake.

The village walls hadn't been built with proper defense in mind, so there were few positions that gave Tristan and the others a good angle from which to hit the attackers. Looking around, Veronyka spotted the ruins of a cart and wrenched up a massive board of wood.

She carried it toward Tristan, showing him he could use it for protection. It wasn't large enough to shield his whole body, but with Veronyka holding it, she could adjust the height or slant, giving him the cover he needed to get off cleaner shots.

It jarred her arm muscles right to their joints when the first arrow slammed into the slab of wood, and the point of the steel-tipped arrowhead protruded through from the other side.

Tristan's expression was wide, frantic, before relief washed over him when he saw the arrow hadn't made it completely through. They shared a glance, and Veronyka nodded—she could do this.

He loosed more arrows, and Veronyka caught more attacking shots in return.

Though her limbs shook with effort and her ears rang from impact after impact, Veronyka found herself settling into a rhythm. They were like one person, anticipating each other's every thought and movement.

Tristan would spot a target, Veronyka would move into place to shield him, and he'd loose his arrow.

Target. Shield. Loose.

Target. Shield. Loose.

It was a while before Veronyka realized that the reason they were so completely in sync with each other was because the channel between them was wide open again, their minds and bodies moving as one. They *both* spotted the target. They *both* stepped into position—and they *both* loosed the arrow.

Rather than jarring her out of the moment or sending her into another faint, Veronyka embraced their unity. She was seeing the battle through Tristan's eyes, despite being hunched over behind their makeshift shield, and was able to anticipate what he needed even before he knew it himself.

And that was why, when he moved to line up a shot at a distant attacker—noticing too late that, nearer at hand, a soldier had broken through and was barreling down on them—it was Veronyka who changed his shot. In the space of a breath, Veronyka leaned her body into Tristan's, guiding his arms to the side just as the arrow loosed from his fingertips.

It landed true, directly in the middle of the oncoming soldier's chest.

Tristan blinked at her, stunned, and Veronyka had the surreal feeling of *experiencing* his emotions through their connection at the same moment she saw them on his face. Shock, confusion, and then a blazing surge of gratitude. His chest swelled, and he laughed in bemused delight.

Their connection broke at last, but he didn't sense it. To Tristan the entire thing had been an act of serendipity, Anyanke's hand or Teyke's blind luck. But to her it was so much more. It was possibility.

While he fired off more arrows, Veronyka marveled at the uses for shadow magic that she'd never considered before.

Despite how hard they fought, the only reason the soldiers hadn't broken through their ragtag defense was Xephyra and her constant fiery dives across the mud-churned and body-riddled field. Every time she whipped past, Veronyka held her breath, wondering if this would be the time she took an arrow, if this would be the time she died.

As the gray light of predawn filtered through the smoke, the world became oddly dreamlike, sounds muffled and colors muted.

Over time Xephyra's blistering charges became more infrequent as exhaustion settled in, and the soldiers saw their opportunity. They rushed forward immediately *after* she flew past, taking advantage of the time she took to arc back up to the sky.

The shadowy horde barreled down on them, just visible through the mottled haze. Veronyka and the other defenders stood their ground, but she knew that this time the soldiers would break through. Their number was too great, their timing just right.

Veronyka tossed aside the piece of wood and crouched down, grabbing an abandoned spear—dinged and bloodied, but still intact. Tristan did the same, ditching his bow for an enemy ax. As they took up their new weapons, their eyes met.

The connection opened between them again, and his feelings pulsed like a heartbeat. She was his friend; she was his comrade—she was his equal. Her wish had come true, her impossible fantasy realized.

And he didn't want to see her die.

So he ran—away from her, into the smoke, toward the oncoming soldiers. Toward death.

Veronyka opened her mouth, reaching for him with both mind and body—but the instincts that had moments before saved Tristan's life had become sluggish with fear. She moved too slowly, and her hand swiped at empty air, her mind at the trailing wisps of him as he passed. In an instant he was gone, and she was stuck staring at his retreating back.

Veronyka made to lurch after him when something collided with her shoulder. She was shunted aside, struggling to regain her footing as Wind leapt through the gate and thundered after Tristan. Someone, perhaps Jana or one of the other stablehands, had put him in his full battle armor, the gleaming bits of metal and leather dully reflecting the misty light. The soldiers faltered, and Tristan turned, confused by their apparent fear, just in time to see Wind mow down half a dozen of them. The horse swept around Tristan in a tight arc, protecting him on all sides, while Tristan could do nothing but stare, his ax held loosely in his grasp.

Wind circled, charging down a handful more attackers before slowing his pace, giving Tristan a chance to leap onto his saddle.

As Wind carried him back toward the gate, a horn sounded.

It was so quiet that Veronyka wasn't sure she'd heard it. Everyone around them slowed, then paused—even the soldiers stopped in their tracks to listen. Then second, third, and fourth blasts echoed across the mountaintop.

Veronyka found Xephyra in the sky above, and the phoenix let out a long, clear note—a call.

A heartbeat of silence, and then a faint, distant reply. It wasn't a sound of alarm or defense. . . . It was a greeting.

The rest of the phoenixes in the stronghold repeated the sound, and soon the music of phoenix song filled the air.

Tristan twisted atop Wind's back, trying to get a better view. Clouds stained pink and purple streaked across the sky in the distance, making way for the coming dawn. But closer at hand, a dozen small, wavering dots approached, trailing glittering threads of fire. Tristan let out a loud, joyful *whoop*.

The Riders had returned.

Of the fierce and formidable First Riders, none are so beloved as Nefyra and Callysta.

The heroics! The splendor! They flew together like the wings of the same bird and fought like the arms of the same warrior.

So flawless, so complete was their union, that they became one being, one person, connected for all eternity.

—"Wings of the Same Bird," as sung by Mellark the Minstrel, circa 116 AE

There was so much blood. . . .
My arrow, why did it have to be my arrow?
The agony of regret, the sorrow of loneliness;
I let the pain of it consume me.

- CHAPTER 41 -
VERONYKA

BY THE TIME THE Riders reached the stronghold, the soldiers had begun to scatter. Those who didn't were attacked with renewed vigor from the defenders, encouraged by the sight of their shining warriors come home.

Tristan's face shone when he saw his father among them, dirty and bloodied but alive, leading his troops with expert precision. It seemed that most had returned, though Veronyka had trouble getting a clear count. Their patrols were divided: One secured the stronghold, and the other gave pursuit to the soldiers fleeing back down the mountainside.

By the time the sun had crested the distant peaks, the last rope was severed and the final enemy soldier was cut down. Veronyka looked around, stunned to realize that the battle was won.

Her ears were ringing slightly, the shouts and screams and clashing metal of the fight now replaced with low voices and heavy footsteps. The guards and villagers took stock of their surroundings, while the apprentices called their mounts away from the stronghold, back to the Eyrie. It took only a shared glance for Veronyka to know that Tristan had to stay behind and speak with his father.

"I'll check on Rex," she said before he could ask, a blur of scarlet feathers—including Xephyra's violet-tinged ones—streaking through the sky above them.

Tristan gave her a strange look, and before Veronyka realized what was happening, he drew her into a bone-crunching hug. It was different from the last time he'd hugged her, buoyed up by adrenaline and excitement after the success of his obstacle-course performance. This time his limbs trembled, and he clung to her like he might collapse right then and there.

If their first hug was like a drink of cool water on a hot day, this hug was like the life-saving rainstorm after a wildfire.

He smelled of sweat and smoke, but he was unharmed. He was *alive*. They'd somehow made it through. He took a shaky breath as he held her, his chest expanding against hers, and then released her. He stepped backward, nodding his thanks before disappearing into the crowd.

She watched him go, a riot of emotions swirling in the pit of her stomach. With the fighting over, Veronyka would have to deal with the repercussions of Val's betrayal and the possible changes to her place here. To her relationship with Tristan. Would he tell his father, or could she count on him to keep her secret? Would it even matter? She'd just ridden a female phoenix in front of the entire stronghold. . . . Surely some would begin to question who she truly was.

As Veronyka made her way toward the Eyrie, she took in the devastation. All around her was pain, some people and animals moving under their own power, others being helped or carried. It turned out the male phoenix who had been circling mournfully above the village—Xoe's son—was bonded to Latham, who thus far been unable to get him to return to the Eyrie.

Veronyka was relieved to step through the archway, where crates of bandages, food, and water had been laid out for the returning phoenixes and their bondmates.

Ersken awaited them there, Sparrow by his side.

She was weeping.

In her cupped hands she held Chirp, blood staining his soft brown feathers. He was utterly still, his small feet curled up against his stiff, round body. The sight reminded Veronyka of Xephyra's death, and the throb of devastation Sparrow projected mingled painfully with the memory of her own.

Ersken turned his wide, gentle eyes on the girl, but her face was bowed toward her sparrow. She couldn't actually see her fallen friend, but her pose and expression said it all.

Sparrow's grief was a quiet storm, but when Ersken tried to take the dead bird from her, she practically snarled.

Veronyka stepped in. Patting Ersken's arm reassuringly, she took Sparrow by the shoulder and guided her toward a crate to sit on.

"Sparrow, it's me," she whispered. "Do you remember? It's—"

"Veronyka?" Sparrow said, her head snapping up.

"Yes," Veronyka said, keeping her voice low, though nobody was in earshot. "Yes, it's me."

Sparrow tilted her head, sniffing loudly. "Didn't hear you, without those bits and beads making a racket." Veronyka's hand ran through her bedraggled, apparently quiet, hair. "And no Chirp to . . . to . . ." Her voice wobbled, and her face crumpled as fresh tears made tracks down her dirty cheeks.

Veronyka's own vision went blurry, but she quickly blinked the tears away and put her arm around Sparrow, holding her tight. "I know," she said softly. "And I'm so, so sorry."

Veronyka couldn't shake the clinging guilt that gripped her heart. It was *her* idea to involve the animals of the stronghold. . . . It was her fault Chirp had died.

She was reminded of the first time she'd seen a dead animal, a mouse that had followed her as she'd crossed a busy Aura Nova street and gotten trampled. She'd wept and blamed herself, but her *maiora* would have none of it.

"You take something from them when you do that," she'd said, all stern affection and wisdom. "As if the poor creature didn't have a mind of its own. Did you *command* it to follow you? Did you rob it of its free will?"

Veronyka had stopped crying long enough to shake her head.

"No. Then that fellow made his own choice, and we should honor him for it."

And then they'd wrapped his body in Veronyka's finest scarf and placed him into the flames of their hearth, burning him in a "true warrior's pyre," as her *maiora* called it. Val had walked in, asked what they were doing, then scoffed and walked back out again, but Veronyka and her grandmother had remained until the last log burned low.

Veronyka had thought about how she would feel if she *had* commanded the mouse to follow, as her sister did to animals all the time. She never wanted that kind of power over another living thing, and she'd vowed never to steal another creature's free will.

Now, among the death and devastation that surrounded her, Veronyka took a steadying breath. Chirp had fought because he loved Sparrow, just as the rest of the animals had loved the humans that fed and cared for them. She would not take credit for their bravery but instead honor their memory.

Their sacrifice had kept her, Sparrow, and everyone else alive.

"It's just," Sparrow said, hiccupping and wiping the back of her hand across her nose. "Chirp is—*was*—my only friend in the whole world."

Silent sobs shook her small frame, and Veronyka squeezed her shoulders harder. "Chirp was a special friend, and brave as a phoenix, but he wasn't your *only* friend. What about me?"

Sparrow lifted her head, her wide eyes wet with tears. "Are we friends?"

"Of course," Veronyka said easily, as if she were an expert on friendship and hadn't made her first very recently. It was nice to think that she now had a second. She smiled, though she knew Sparrow couldn't see it. Hopefully she could feel it.

Sparrow beamed. "Chirp *did* like you . . . ," she said matter-of-factly, as if his approval was all she needed.

"Good. I liked him, too."

When she spotted Ersken squinting through the crowd of phoenixes, as if looking for someone, Veronyka told Sparrow she had some work to do, and extricated herself. Sparrow seemed calmer, lying down on her side with Chirp against her chest and closing her eyes as if for sleep.

Pulling Ersken aside, Veronyka relayed the news about Xoe and Xatara.

"Xoe died protecting the village gate. Shot down with arrows. Afterward Xatara fled."

"I . . . I see," he said gruffly, clearing his throat. "I'll send someone to gather the body. There's a chance . . ." He trailed off. "We'll burn her, along with the rest of our fallen warriors."

He glanced at Sparrow, with Chirp's body beside her, then at the small row of dead dogs, cats, and pigeons that were being laid out on the massive phoenix plinth. Back in the stronghold, Veronyka had seen a similar thing being done with the dead human bodies—fallen warriors, like Ersken said. Veronyka couldn't bear to look closely, to recognize a familiar face.

She knew she should be grateful, that it was a miracle so many of them had survived this night when the odds were so dangerously stacked against them. But it was hard to feel anything more than heartbreak.

While everyone was busy tending their own bondmates or helping with the wounded, Veronyka pushed her way through the mass of feathery bodies and hugged Xephyra tight. She was proud and amazed at her phoenix's daring during the battle and how well she'd assimilated into their group. The males had some sense of her, of this "other" presence within their familiar flock, but after fighting together, it seemed they'd accepted her as one of them. Veronyka could only hope that she would be given the same treatment.

As Xephyra drank from a trough, Veronyka grabbed several bundles of fresh fruit wrapped in leaves. She left half with her phoenix and took the rest to Rex, who was perched on the outside ledge, away from the commotion. He was subdued, looking small and forlorn all by himself, but made no move to join in with the others.

Before Veronyka could do more than pick her way over, a shadow flew over her head, and Xephyra landed on the ledge next to him.

Rex bristled slightly, but Xephyra kept her distance, cocking her head back and forth, studying him. Veronyka wondered if her phoenix sensed something from Rex, some element of the bizarre connection that linked Veronyka to Tristan.

After rustling his good wing and puffing up his feathers, Rex settled somewhat, and Xephyra seemed to take it as an invitation to move closer. She had something in her beak, and when she was close enough, she bowed her head and dropped one of the fruit bundles Veronyka had given her on the ground next to Rex.

Rex's golden beak roved over the package before picking through the leaves for the fruit within. Veronyka looked down at the food in her hand, apparently no longer needed, and grinned.

Xephyra's compassion filtered through the bond, warming Veronyka's chest.

You'll keep an eye on him? she asked, hastily examining the bandage over Rex's wound. It was clean and wrapped tightly—more to stop him from using his wing and slowing the healing process—and she knew he'd recover soon.

Xephyra squawked in response, settling down next to Rex. The sight of it made Veronyka's heart swell.

Her duties done, she sagged against the wall near the entrance to the Eyrie, where several others were doing the same. She was tired, but her exhaustion was so deep and constant that she'd forgotten what it was like to be without it.

As she floated in the fluid place between sleep and waking, Val's face appeared in her mind. Veronyka straightened, wondering if her sister was okay, wherever she was.

Veronyka could find her, of course. Val had shown her how. They had a permanent connection between them, which meant that she could find Val almost anywhere, like she could with her bondmate. Time strengthened that ability, and Veronyka wasn't sure how long the link between her and Val had been in place. Not that it mattered. Val couldn't have gone far.

Is this the slippery slope? she wondered idly, settling more comfortably onto the ground as she turned her focus inward, searching for their connection. There was always a reason to use shadow magic, but Veronyka had to trust herself and her own instincts. The magic had served her well in the battle, and though it irked her to admit it, she had to know Val was safe.

As soon as Veronyka closed her eyes, she felt Val in her mind. Her sister wasn't actually there, but rather, the link between them left traces of her even when she was gone. It was as if the doorway was a piece of Val, hidden out of sight but ready to connect with whenever Veronyka needed it.

She pressed against it, marveling at the fact that it had been there all along, an itching, nagging presence that she simply hadn't recognized for what it was.

Opening the channel between them wasn't as easy as it had been with Tristan. He didn't have shadow magic and didn't truly understand how to guard himself. Val, on the other hand, was a fortress.

The barrier between them was dense and unforgiving—a door made of thickest iron, bolted and barricaded and utterly impenetrable unless you had the key. The effort of trying to break through nearly robbed Veronyka of her consciousness.

Nice try, xe *Nyka,* said Val's calm, amused voice inside her head. Veronyka hadn't managed to open the door, but her attempts had obviously drawn Val's attention, and she spoke to Veronyka as if she were standing right on the other side. *But you never had the stomach for mind games.*

Where are you? Veronyka asked, still unable to see anything beyond the door.

Don't worry, I'll be gone before you know it, came Val's response, and already she was pulling away. Desperate, Veronyka reached for Val with all her strength, catching her off guard. There was a moment of unencumbered connection, a single, clear image seen through Val's eyes, before she severed their contact.

It was only a glimpse of her surroundings, but it was enough.

Despite all Val had done, all the ways she'd hurt Veronyka, the night's battle had changed things. Veronyka had seen too much death to let her sister walk away from her forever—not without a proper goodbye.

The image she'd seen through Val's eyes had been a large, low-ceilinged room filled with boxes and barrels. A storage room. Val had likely been stealing supplies when Veronyka made contact with her, and if she hurried, she'd catch her sister before she escaped.

Veronyka found the cellar several floors below the kitchens, at the bottom of a winding stone stair. It was dark and windowless, perfect for keeping food and perishable items.

As soon as Veronyka entered, she knew it was the same room she'd seen in Val's mind.

Only, Val wasn't there.

Veronyka turned to leave when she noticed what looked like wheel marks along the floor, leading out from the back of the room.

She followed the tracks but came up against a stone wall. She frowned, but then remembered Val's words from earlier in the evening:

We'll sneak out through the underground service entrance.

Maybe it wasn't a wall at all.

Veronyka pressed both hands against the cool stone surface and pushed.

The tunnel that led out from the storage room was long and dark, unlit by lanterns or torches. There were several offshoots, probably leading up to the stables and maybe even into the Eyrie itself.

Veronyka pushed blindly forward, all the while straining with her senses, both physical and magical. A haze of diffuse light came into view as she neared the end, the barest hints of early morning sunlight streaming through a tangle of fragrant bushes over the entrance. With a bit of prodding, she discovered a metal grate with a concealed latch that allowed her to move the obstruction aside.

She wedged a piece of stone into the gap as she let the gate fall back into place, and the doorway all but disappeared, hidden behind thick hanging vines and wide green leaves. The ground in front of it was hard stone, the kind of firm surface that wouldn't reveal wagon tracks or hoofprints.

As she took in the landscape, trying to get her bearings, Veronyka felt a tingle of awareness. She whirled around to see Val perched on the rock overtop the tunnel, an arrow notched and ready to fire. She held the weapon confidently—no tremor in her arms or uncertainty in her stance—and Veronyka wondered when she'd learned to be an expert archer.

"What do you want, Veronyka?" she asked, bow steady. "I've a lot of ground to cover before dark."

Veronyka swallowed. What *did* she want? "I wanted to make sure that you were okay."

Val kept the weapon pointed at her a moment longer before releasing a snort of disbelief and lowering it. "I thought you hated me."

She said the words callously, as if they were a joke, but Veronyka could feel the hurt in her sister's voice and sense the anger simmering just below the surface.

"I don't hate you, Val," she said. Even after everything, she didn't. She didn't think she ever could. Veronyka had lost so much in her life, she couldn't willingly reject the last bit of her family, of her childhood, she had left.

Val nodded, playing with the fletching on her arrow. She'd managed to steal a bow and full quiver, a shoulder pack—likely filled with stolen supplies—and a smaller, cross-body satchel. Whatever it held, it was heavy, straining against the fabric and digging into Val's flesh.

Seeing Veronyka's line of sight, she shifted, casting her gaze in the direction of the Eyrie. "You should get back, Veronyka. They'll be looking for you."

Veronyka nodded, but she didn't move. "Where will you go?" She thought about offering to talk to Tristan, to Commander Cassian, or even to Ersken. Her sister could be a valuable asset to any of them, but she knew Val would never accept and that it would be a terrible idea besides.

Though Veronyka took care to guard her mind, Val's lips quirked into a smile, as if Veronyka were projecting her thoughts for all the world to hear.

"I think I'll make for the ruins of Aura and the Everlasting Flame," Val said. "I've always wanted to see it. They say the queens of old linger there, whispering their stories for anyone brave enough to hear them."

A flicker of longing sparked to life inside Veronyka. She realized with sudden finality that even if Val did make it there—the way was notoriously treacherous, the roads and bridges collapsed and crumbled with age, and the very summit reachable only on phoenix-back—and she heard those ancient secrets, Veronyka would never know. She wouldn't be waiting at home next to the hearth, eager for Val's return. They would never share their lives that way again.

She hesitated, knowing her sister would scoff at her next words, but she said them anyway. "Be careful."

Val smiled, the bright morning sun turning her auburn hair to fire. "I've been through much, much worse, *xe* Nyka. One day you'll understand."

"I want to understand now," Veronyka said, taking a step forward. Val was the kind of person who never really let you in. You could talk to her day after day, year after year, spend your entire life together and still not truly know her. If this was going to be the last time Veronyka ever saw her sister, she wanted to find something true about her, something more than just her callous nature and darkly burning heart. "Tell me."

Val studied her for a long time. "I can't tell you," she said with a resolute shake of her head.

Veronyka wilted, the walls between them—magical, physical, and emotional—as impenetrable as always.

But I can show you, Val said.

The world around Veronyka disappeared, the walls she'd just lamented completely obliterated. Suddenly, she was in one of her dreams, the scene playing out before her waking eyes.

She sat at the head of a long wooden table, oil lamps casting pools of light over its surface. Across from her was the same girl who was always at her side in these visions. She was a young woman now, her deep-set eyes shadowed and wary.

Other people filled the room, but dream-Veronyka wasn't interested in them. She stared intently, fixedly, at the girl, noticing every breath and sigh of movement. She seemed paler than usual and pressed a hand to her stomach as if she might be sick. She kept glancing toward the corner of the room, where a guard stood by the door. Maybe she was nervous and his presence reassured her. Or maybe she wanted to note how far the door was, in case she had to make a run for the chamber pot.

When she tucked a strand of hair behind her ear—a seemingly innocuous gesture—rage boiled in Veronyka's veins. The girl's hair was glossy, straight—and unbraided. This was a recent development, Veronyka sensed, and as she took in the surrounding people once more, she noticed a distinct difference between those who clustered around the girl across from her and the ones who stood near Veronyka.

Those around the girl wore the robes of council members, which included a mix of provincial governors and noble lords. Veronyka could make out the golden thread embroidered on their chests, indicating their positions: scales for the Minister of Law or overlapping circles for the Minister of Coin. One or two appeared to be military, their short hair, stiff postures, and colored sashes marking them as ranking soldiers in the army.

The people attending Veronyka in the dream were also important and high ranking—but certainly of a different sort. They were Phoenix Riders every one, wearing armguards and riding leathers, with shining obsidian beads and bright phoenix feathers hanging from their braided hair.

There was barely concealed hostility in the room, and Veronyka couldn't decide which side was more intimidating: Both had powerful, experienced men and women—and yet the Riders were at their best on phoenix-back, soaring through the open air with bows and spears in their grasp. Here, in a darkened chamber where wax and ink were the weapons of choice, Veronyka couldn't help but think that the politicians had the true upper hand.

As she compared and contrasted the opposing forces, something in Veronyka's mind finally clicked. She understood where she was at last, what she had been dreaming of for years: She was in the heart of the empire more than sixteen years ago, in Aura Nova, and these were the princesses that battled for the throne during the Blood War.

If the girl across from her was Pheronia, surrounded by her councilors, then Veronyka was occupying the mind of Avalkyra, attended by her rebel Phoenix Riders.

A heavy silence fell as Veronyka's dream self twisted a ring on her finger, pressing it into a thick glob of wax on a piece of paper, dark with ink. Her movements were brisk, but Veronyka felt the tremor in her fingers and the hasty, clumsy way she slid the document across the table. The tension in the room reached a crescendo as, with a nod at her advisers, Pheronia tore the sheet of paper in two.

Veronyka's dream body leapt to its feet, but her own advisers descended upon her before she could speak or react, gripping her arms and steering her from the room. Veronyka glanced over her shoulder for a last look at the girl who was her sister, but bodies pressed in on her, blocking her from view.

Shadowy passages, whispered words, and suddenly Veronyka was in a bedchamber. Her people released her at last, and with a command laced with shadow magic, they fled from her presence.

As soon as the door shut behind them, Veronyka took up a heavy wooden chair and whipped it across the room. It smashed against the wall, shards of wood flying in every direction, but she wasn't done. She smashed a ceramic jug and tore a silken pillow in half, the plump feathers dancing in the air like snowflakes. Panting, she lurched to a basin of water and splashed handfuls of cool liquid against her hot skin.

This means war, said a voice in her mind—a voice that was not Veronyka's.

As the pool of water beneath her stilled, she dropped her hands and stared into the reflection of the dark bowl.

Val's face looked back up at her.

Veronyka reeled back, casting aside the dream world as the true world came to life around her once more. Birds chirped, grass swished in the breeze, and sunlight beat down.

Val stood in front of her, so like the reflection in the dream that she felt she stared at a ghost, not a flesh-and-blood person.

The ghost of Avalkyra Ashfire.

My heart ripped open,
my soul bled, and my very
being caught fire.

- CHAPTER 42 -
VERONYKA

"VAL!" VERONYKA SHOUTED, AS her sister turned her back and stepped between the trees.

Val, Val, Val.

Veronyka kept repeating the word, out loud and inside her mind, as she chased after her sister. She had the feeling that if she said the word enough times, it would set things right—bring Val back, banish the images from her mind, and give her world equilibrium again.

But by the time Veronyka was able to scale the rocky hill above the tunnel entrance, Val was nowhere in sight, and Veronyka couldn't see which direction she'd gone.

Veronyka tried their mental connection, but it was as silent as the world around her. She squeezed her eyes shut, but it did no good—the Feather-Crowned Queen was there, staring back at her with Val's face.

Dread crept up Veronyka's body like snaring vines, rooting her to the spot.

Val. Avalkyra. A*val*kyra.

But . . . *how?*

Avalkyra Ashfire was dead. She'd died at the end of the Blood War . . . sixteen years ago. Everyone said so. Avalkyra had been burned to death, shot down during the final battle and consumed by her dying bondmate's flames. But had she *stayed* dead?

Morra's words from weeks ago floated to the surface of Veronyka's mind. *All it takes is fire and bones.*

Veronyka stared into the trees, her heart thumping in an uneven rhythm. She had the feeling that Val watched her—and yet she couldn't unstick her feet, couldn't seem to follow or call out for her.

If she *did* call out, what name would she use?

Eventually that prickly sensation of being watched receded, and Veronyka made her slow return to the Eyrie, her mind still in a daze. Though she couldn't remember deciding to go there, when Veronyka climbed out of the cellar, her feet carried her into the kitchens.

For once, things were quiet in the vaulted room. While the fireplaces that warmed the hall and cooked their food burned hot and bright, the usual dozen or so kitchen helpers and servants were gone, busy tending to other things. Morra manned several large pots that simmered over the flames, while her worktable was covered with bunches of dried herbs and a handful of mismatched jars.

The room smelled medicinal, and Veronyka assumed Morra was brewing healing potions or sedatives for the people being carted off to the temple infirmary.

She looked up at Veronyka's approach, and her smile was full of weary relief. She released the spoon she'd been using to stir and wiped her hands on her apron before limping forward and pulling Veronyka into a warm hug.

After directing Veronyka onto a nearby stool, Morra held her shoulders for a moment and surveyed her for damage. "You're all right," she said, half to Veronyka, half to herself, before leaning back against the table for balance. "You look like you've seen a ghost—not surprising, after your first battle—but you're all right." She paused, staring at Veronyka's face. "Aren't you, Nyk, lad?"

Was she? Veronyka didn't know, but she nodded anyway, struggling to find the words to reassure the woman.

Morra limped away, returning with a hot cup of tea for Veronyka to drink. It smelled of sticky-sweet honey and mottled herbs, and as she sipped, her head began to clear.

"Morra . . . what did you mean when you said you were looking for resurrections after the Blood War?"

Her stories about the Mercies had stuck with Veronyka, though she hadn't been sure exactly why—until now. When Morra had said she was certain she could find *someone*, Veronyka had thought it was a strange way of phrasing it. As if she hadn't been talking about phoenixes at all, but *people*.

Morra frowned at her before hooking another stool and dragging it over, taking a seat next to Veronyka. She scratched her chin thoughtfully.

"Phoenixes can be reborn. This you know. But if they are bonded, phoenix *and* Rider can do the same."

Veronyka stared at her. She should feel shocked, completely and utterly bewildered, but after what Val had just shown her . . .

"It's a complicated magic," Morra continued, "and it's happened only a handful of times since the First Riders. It takes intense magical power, a bond that neither fear nor death can shake. But if done properly, a bonded pair can die a glorious warrior's death and be reborn together from the ashes."

Veronyka drank her tea with a shaking hand, trying to wrap her brain around the idea. Phoenixes were magical, and their ability to resurrect was well-documented—her own bondmate had done it. But the idea that a human could do it was unbelievable.

Or at least, it would be . . . if Veronyka hadn't just seen evidence of it with her own two eyes.

While she'd always had strange dreams, when Veronyka looked back, she realized that *those* dreams—the ones that featured the two girls—had always been unique. Even as other frequently seen people and places would follow her for weeks, only to disappear, never to be seen again, these girls always returned.

Veronyka had just assumed they were stubborn memories, clinging to her mind and resurfacing during moments of exhaustion or weakness.

Maybe they kept coming back because they puzzled her, so crisp in detail and yet disconnected from Veronyka's own life. It had never occurred to her to look around the real world for answers.

To look at Val, the person who always slept by her side.

Now that she thought of it, Veronyka hadn't dreamed about the two girls once on her journey to the Eyrie or in the weeks she'd spent training with Tristan—even while other, more mundane dreams beset her. But the night of the solstice festival, the night Val arrived, she'd seen the king's death.

Veronyka mentally rifled through all the shadow magic dreams she could remember having in her life—the ones that featured the two girls. This latest vision told her that they were the sisters Avalkyra and Pheronia. Veronyka had seen them study together, walk together, run and play together. She'd seen their father die in his sickbed, while the empire elite like Commander Cassian looked on.

And she'd seen the dissolution of their attempts at peace and coexistence, thrusting them into the final conflict of the Blood War. What had Val said to Veronyka right before leaving her at the bottom of the Eyrie?

Then I hope for your sake, Veronyka, that you've chosen the right side.

Sides . . . was that how Val saw things? Since Veronyka wasn't *with* her, she was now against her? Was Val still fighting the Blood War, or was she trying to start a new one?

As Veronyka came back to herself, she realized Morra was scrutinizing her closely. "Has something else happened?" Morra asked, frowning. "It's not Tristan, is it? Or one of the other Riders? Cassian told me they'd all made it back."

"Tristan's fine. Everything's . . ." Well, everything was most certainly *not* fine, but Morra already knew that. "It's nothing. I just . . ."

"It's natural to wonder about resurrection and rebirth, when there's so much death about," Morra said, somewhat mollified, though she still seemed troubled by Veronyka's behavior.

Before she could say more, several people bustled in, looking for ointments and salves and herb tea. Morra got up to attend to them, and Veronyka slid off her stool and went back outside.

She offered assistance everywhere she could—to the healer's helpers who'd retrieved the medicine from Morra, to the builders and laborers who were putting out fires and clearing away detritus, and to the guards who were trying to reestablish a watch and ensure there were no further attacks forthcoming—but everyone turned her away. Even Jana, who had an arm in a sling and was covered head to toe in dust and dirt, insisted that everything was well in hand. People kept telling her to lie down, to relax, to take the opportunity to rest.

As if her entire world hadn't just been upended.

With nowhere else to go and nothing to do, she had no choice but to try.

The barracks was quiet as she entered, save for the steady breathing of several others who'd managed to slip away for some sleep. Veronyka supposed it made sense to split up the work, to allow some people to rest now so they could relieve the others later.

She sat on her hammock, swaying gently as she reached into her pocket for her braided bracelet. When she lifted it out, something *clanged* to the ground and rolled several feet away.

Veronyka dropped lightly onto the floor, spotting a fat golden bead attached to an auburn braid.

Fingers trembling, she picked up the piece of hair, knowing it was Val's. When had *that* gotten inside her pocket? Veronyka flashed back to when she'd woken up alone with Val, after fainting outside the enclosure. It would have been easy enough to put it inside her pocket when she was unconscious.

The bead was familiar, yet Veronyka had never really looked at it closely before. Though Veronyka was usually the one to brush and braid Val's hair, Val was particular about her beads and embellishments, insisting on knotting them in herself. Veronyka had always assumed the golden trinket was fake, some painted piece of wood or stone, but it was heavy in her hand. Turning it over, she realized it wasn't a bead at all but a ring, knotted into the strands of hair to keep it in place.

Clutching it tightly, Veronyka climbed back onto her hammock, carefully unweaving the braid and holding the ring up to the light filtering in through the window.

It was a thick band, though it slipped snugly onto Veronyka's finger. The face was flat and unadorned, except for an emblem carved into the surface, like a seal.

Or a signet.

Veronyka marveled as she recognized the familiar design—spread wings wreathed in flames, with two *A*'s at its center: the sigil of Avalkyra Ashfire. She'd seen it before, stamped into bits of leather for sale at back-alley markets or painted onto phoenix dedications on the very outskirts of the empire. And, of course, she'd seen it in her dreams.

Veronyka called up her most recent vision, the moment when Avalkyra pressed her golden seal into the document that her sister then ripped in two.

Could this be that same ring?

Slipping it off her finger once more, Veronyka noticed a further engraving on the inside of the band, so small that it was difficult to read, but she managed to pick it out.

> *Avalkyra Ashfire, the Feather-Crowned Queen*
> *B: 152 AE–D: 170 AE*

The numbers were written in the same way they recorded years in the empire—AE stood for "After the Empire," and the dates ranged an eighteen-year span. Not her supposed reign, then, or even the length of the Blood War. It was a lifespan. Birth: 152 AE. Death: 170 AE.

Veronyka's heart thumped as she noticed a second set of numbers below the first.

> *RB: 170 AE—*

RB? What could RB stand for? But even as the question popped into Veronyka's mind, the answer landed on the tip of her tongue.

"Rebirth," she whispered. Morra said it was possible, and it would explain a lot about her sister, about her extensive knowledge of history and magic, weapons and warfare, language and politics, as well as her sense of privilege and obsession with control.

Their conversation from the solstice festival surfaced in Veronyka's mind, when Veronyka had asked Val why Ignix wouldn't have revealed herself if she was still alive.

Maybe she is afraid. Maybe the world has changed too much.

Val was Avalkyra Ashfire. Veronyka felt the truth of it deep in her bones, in her heart—the certainty of it as strange and wondrous as her bond with Xephyra. But for some reason Val kept this secret to herself. Why?

Not completely to herself, Veronyka realized, sitting up straighter. Her *maiora* knew. Ilithya Shadowheart had served Avalkyra Ashfire in the Blood War and had continued to serve her after her resurrection. That was why she had always deferred to Val, always let her rant and rave and spit cruel words. Ilithya was a soldier, and even as a child, Avalkyra Ashfire was her queen.

Was Morra looking for her fallen queen when she'd been ambushed and lost her leg? Did Ilithya find Val, or was it the other way around? The memory of the day with the snake reared up again, and Veronyka understood why Val had seemed a stranger to her in that moment—because she had been. Ilithya had stood up to protect Veronyka until she'd recognized Val as Avalkyra, her dead sovereign. Val must have used her shadow magic to seek out other animages, trying to find friends and allies, trapped in a child's body and burdened with the secret of her true self, waiting, searching for her chance to be a Rider again, to be *herself* again. Val would want to announce her identity from a position of strength and power, not as a penniless, powerless peasant girl. She'd most certainly have been hunted by the empire if she came forward, and besides, she had no bondmate. What kind of Rider queen could she be without a flaming phoenix beneath her?

Val was as stubborn and prideful as they came, and she might well live and die in anonymity rather than admit who she was and how far she had fallen.

It had already been sixteen years. Clearly Val had lied about being seventeen, if she had indeed been born the night of the Last Battle. How much longer was she planning to wait?

Even as the theory started to ease the confusion in Veronyka's mind, a spool of doubt unraveled in her chest. If Val was the supposedly long-dead Ashfire heir . . . then who was Veronyka?

The younger sister, Pheronia, didn't have any magic, and so therefore had no bondmate and no means of resurrection. Besides, Veronyka didn't have memories of some past life; the visions she'd seen in her dreams, they were *Val's*, from Avalkyra's point of view, not Pheronia's.

Veronyka threw herself back onto her pillows, the signet ring clutched tightly in one hand. Though exhaustion had turned her limbs to lead and her thoughts to water, sleep eluded her.

Instead she stared at the ceiling, watching the shadows shift and grow and lengthen, until darkness swallowed the room. When she couldn't stand being alone with her thoughts for one second longer, she went in search of a distraction.

It was late and most of the work had halted for the night, but Veronyka wandered toward any signs of noise or action, eventually walking through the open doors of the temple infirmary. As she entered the space, the healers, visitors, and mildly wounded moved about the hall, voices hushed as people tried to rest and sleep.

Large pillars created separation in the wide-open space, outlining a central place of worship, flanked by hallways on both sides. In the middle, priests and acolytes would normally chant prayers amid smoking incense and the ever-burning hearth that represented the Heart of Axura, but they had been recruited to help the solitary healer and the handful of midwives who had volunteered their services.

Veronyka found Sev on a pallet in the hallway to the left, reserved for those with stable injuries who were on the mend, while the opposite hall housed people who were dying or who hovered on the edge of life and death.

She was immensely relieved to know he was going to be okay and happier still to find him awake as she approached, propped up against a stack of pillows.

She crouched down on the floor next to him, feeling awkward and unsure what to do with her hands. "Hi, uh . . . do you remember me?"

He didn't seem surprised to see her. "Of course," he said, turning stiffly to face her. "You saved my life."

Her tension loosened somewhat. She smiled. "Only after you saved mine."

His lips twisted into something that resembled a smile but lacked the happiness.

"How's your shoulder?" she pressed on, nodding down at the heavy bandages. Veronyka had some bruises and scrapes along her face and neck but was otherwise unharmed from the attack.

He shrugged—then grimaced, the movement no doubt causing a spear of agony to rip through his wound. "I'll live."

"Good. That's good," she said, nodding. Glancing over her shoulder, Veronyka settled more comfortably next to him. "I was hoping I could ask you about Ilithya."

He was clearly surprised by the question, but his frown quickly shifted from confusion to regret. "I . . . I didn't know her for very long," he admitted, a slight waver in his voice. "And I don't know much about who she was before all this."

Veronyka shook her head, feeling her heart reaching, grasping at every word like a thirsty plant in newly watered soil. "That's okay. Tell me what you did know. What was she like?"

He rubbed a hand along the back of his neck, considering. "She was bossy. Brutal at times. She had a sharp tongue and a quick wit. She told the best stories. And she was kind, too, though I think she tried hard not to show it."

Veronyka found herself smiling. Most of this she already knew, and it erased any lingering doubt she might have had as to whether they were talking about the same Ilithya. It felt good to know that the woman from her memories wasn't some fiction, like Val had been. She was real.

"How did you know her?" Sev asked, drawing Veronyka back to the present.

"She, well . . . she was my grandmother."

Sev sat up straighter. "You're Veronyka, aren't you?"

Veronyka darted a terrified look around. Luckily, Sev was fairly isolated, and most of the people who were awake were the healers and helpers tending the more gravely wounded in the other hall. Nobody had heard him.

"Did she talk about me?" Veronyka whispered.

"No," he said, somewhat apologetically, "but she said your name in her sleep. Always yours . . . no one else's."

Veronyka wasn't sure what to make of that information. On the one hand, it was validating, proof that her grandmother hadn't forgotten about her, that the love they'd shared was real and lasting. On the other, it reminded her of all the lost time they could have spent together.

Veronyka forced herself to smile. She was grateful to him and glad that, for whatever reason, their lives had intersected in so many ways.

"Where did you find them?" she asked, nodding toward the satchel on the floor next to him. The sight of the eggs would have sent her heart bursting from her chest a few days ago, and though Xephyra had returned and so much had changed, they were still desperately important. In the face of the recent attack, the growth and development of new Riders seemed paramount.

"I didn't. It was Kade who—one of the other bondservants," he said, practically choking the words out. "He and Ilithya found them and kept them concealed throughout the journey."

They must have come from somewhere in the empire. Could there be more? Could the empire hold the key to the Phoenix Riders' survival, right in front of them but still out of reach?

"When it looked like they weren't going to make it," Sev continued, clearing his tight throat, "I delivered them instead. I never thought to ask where they came from, but if I had, Ilithya probably wouldn't have told me. She loved her secrets."

Veronyka huffed. "Secrets," she muttered. She'd had enough of them to last a lifetime. Val, Ilithya, even Veronyka's own identity was a tangled mess that felt impossible to unravel.

A full, wide grin split Sev's face. It changed him, turned him from a beat-down soldier back into a boy. "That's the thing with secrets," he said, the words sounding like a bit of repeated wisdom and not something he'd come up with on his own. "They never really die. Just when one bursts into flames, another rises up to take its place."

"Unless you break the cycle," Veronyka whispered.

Sev tilted his head, considering her. "Or you ride them to the bitter end."

Day 2, Eighth Moon, 170 AE

My dearest Avalkyra,

They say you plan to fly in force on the capital. Please, sweet sister, do not turn our home into a battleground.

We must speak again before this war makes corpses of us all.

I know I am no longer welcome in Pyra, and make no mistake, your army is not welcome here.

But you could come, Avalkyra. Alone.

I will wait atop Genya's Tower every day after nightfall. Please come.

I have so much to say.

All my love, Pheronia

I was frightened at first,
but I knew I must not fear the flames.
I am the flames.

- CHAPTER 43 -
SEV

VERONYKA'S VISIT LEFT SEV in a dark mood. Dark*er* mood. It hadn't been sunshine and rainbows inside the infirmary, fighting through pain, ebbing in and out of consciousness, and listening to the wails of the dying and the unhappily living.

Sure, it had been nice to see her again, and it was good to know that she had survived this mess. It had also been good to talk about Trix, but with thoughts of her came thoughts of Kade. And no matter how he tried to see the positive, the fact of the matter was, he'd lost them both far too soon.

In the first few hours after Sev had arrived inside the infirmary, the terrible truth of all that had happened closing in, a bleak part of him hoped that Veronyka's sister was here as well—the one who'd stolen his knife—and that she would make good on the promise she'd made outside her cabin. There was a moment, as he lay on his pallet half asleep, that he swore he *did* see her, but Sev had been tired and heavily drugged. There'd been no sign of her since, so it looked like Sev would just have to go on living.

The healer woman had said he was lucky the quarrel didn't strike bone, and that chronic pain and limited movement were better than a shattered, useless limb.

The guard being treated next to him said he was lucky it was only his arm and not his chest, for surely a wound to the lungs or heart would have ended his life.

Lucky.

Sev couldn't help but think Teyke was playing a cruel joke on him. So much luck, and yet he didn't feel lucky at all.

They didn't understand. It wasn't the *wound* that made Sev slump on his pillows and stare absently into space. If anything, he saw it as a badge of honor. He had earned the pain and the scars; they were a part of him now and marked him as a survivor. No, it was the people he'd lost that left him feeling broken and hollow inside.

Trix was dead. Kade was surely dead as well. Sev had no idea what had happened to Junior, who was far too young to die, and the sheepherders Tilla and Corem. He hadn't let himself think much about them until he'd arrived here, his message delivered and his task complete. Now, with every breath, a vast space of unfeeling emptiness opened wider and wider in his chest. Or was it so much feeling that Sev didn't know what to do with it, or how to identify the sensation? He had gone from nothing to everything to nothing again, but things were different now. *He* was different.

He couldn't go back to not caring and not seeing, back to the way his life had been before.

Sev wanted, *needed*, to keep fighting.

The question was, how?

He could take one of the eggs he'd carried, join the Riders, and leave all the deceptions behind. Become a heroic warrior, like his parents. But something about that didn't quite sit right. In truth, he couldn't picture it. He wasn't a hero, much as he'd wanted to be. He wasn't much of a warrior, either. Kade was those things, and it had cost him his life. Sev wasn't even a strong animage.

He was something else. Trix had said Sev was just like her, and Trix was a spy.

Could Sev pick up where Trix had left off? Kade had called him her worthy successor, and Sev had scoffed at the idea. Maybe, years from now, he might be skilled and accomplished enough to agree. But they hadn't had years, and now Trix was gone.

And yet even Sev's small lies had been useful, hadn't they? He thought of his exchange with Veronyka: Yes, he could deny the secrets and deceptions that had made up his life and break the cycle, *or* he could see them to the end—whatever end that might be.

His position as a soldier had been key in Trix's plans, and Trix had spent much of her own life within the enemy's walls. If Sev claimed that false identity, if he made the choice to pretend for a *reason*—not out of fear or cowardice—well, then it became something else entirely. Something powerful. A real *choice*, not some misfortune thrust upon him. A weapon to be wielded.

The war wasn't over. The Riders had survived this attack, but he knew there would be other battles to fight. Their survival meant more to Sev now than just the continued existence of the order his parents had served, some scrap of his past he could cling to. No, their survival was intertwined now with his present, with Trix and Kade, and their very recent sacrifices. If the Riders fell, then everyone Sev had ever cared about would have died in vain. He couldn't let that happen.

Instead of running from his past, Sev could finish what he'd started— what he, Trix, and Kade had failed to complete.

He could pick up the threads of the life he'd never wanted and continue playing Trix's little game.

That afternoon Sev was escorted to the commander's chambers. He had asked for the meeting, but he was nervous all the same.

He carried the satchel of phoenix eggs with him, grimacing as the weight pulled against his injured shoulder, but he refused to let anyone else touch his valuable burden. He felt possessive over it, especially considering all he'd lost to get it here and knowing how much it had meant to Kade. Also, judging by the stares and reactions it got, Sev had a feeling the eggs were his one and only bargaining chip, should he need it. He couldn't imagine why the commander might turn down his offer, but it was better to be prepared.

Inside the opulently decorated building, Sev took a seat at a long wooden table opposite the man they called Commander Cassian. The door closed behind him, and they were alone.

The commander was elegant and impressive—everything that Captain Belden tried to be but failed at. He was tall and imposing where Belden was short and weak, calm and dignified where Belden was impatient and snide, and the finery of his clothes and quarters looked like it belonged there, with him in it, not ill fitting and piled about a tent pitched in the wilderness.

Sev didn't know why, but something about the man put him at ease. He was no cutthroat or schemer. What he was, he wore plainly, for all to see. Not a sheep in lion's clothing, as Belden had been, but a lion in lion's clothing.

A dangerous man, but an honest one too.

Sev could work with that.

"I must formally thank you, soldier," the commander said, his voice booming with authority, "for your bravery and your courage. You saved dozens of civilian lives, not to mention the future of the Phoenix Riders, and—"

"Pardon me, Commander," Sev said, cutting him off. He had to admire the man's self-control—only the barest flicker of his eyes indicated his annoyance at being interrupted. "But I didn't come here for that. I don't need your thanks or your praise. I'm one of the lucky ones," he said, still hating the phrase but knowing it was true all the same. "There were others who died so that I might deliver my message and my burden."

Sev realized the list of people who had died for him stretched back to his mother and father. Their sacrifice had put Sev in the position to be able to save the Phoenix Riders more than a decade later, helped along by Trix and Kade.

The commander glanced down to the satchel at Sev's feet. He looked up again. "What, then, did you come here for, soldier?"

Sev swallowed. Now that he was here, getting the words out of his throat felt like dragging his feet through mud. "I want to go back."

The commander's face hardened. "You want to return to your post serving the empire?"

"No. I want to return to the empire, but I want the master I serve to be you."

The commander leaned forward, tilting his head. "You want to be a spy?"

"Did you know Ilithya Shadowheart?" Sev asked.

Commander Cassian settled back in his chair before responding. "Not well, no. The name 'Shadowheart' is actually a *position* of sorts—a title. Spies like her operated in such a way that few knew their true names or their true purpose. Morra, however, was well-acquainted with her and thinks most highly of the woman. I understand she is one of the unlucky ones of whom you spoke."

"She taught me . . . ," Sev began, his throat constricting. "She showed me the value of . . . of someone like me."

We're not popular, people like us. Too many deceptions, too many whispered secrets and mysterious missions. But we're useful.

"I'm a lousy animage," he continued, his voice growing stronger, "and a worse soldier. But I'm made for work like hers. So yes, I want to be a spy. Surely you have need for one, given what's just happened."

The commander bristled slightly, as if Sev were criticizing his operation. "The problem with spies, soldier, is that information goes both ways."

Sev thought of the boy from the courtyard—Elliot, they'd called him, the informant Trix had spoken about.

"Then you don't have anything to fear from me. I know nothing of this place"—Sev waved his good hand—"or how you run it. At least, nothing that the rest of the survivors won't know and report as soon as they make it back. Some must have escaped your sweeps."

The commander's brows descended into a frown. "We have only yours and Elliot's rough estimations at how many the empire sent here, so yes, most likely there were survivors."

"Then I'll return with them and pick up where I left off—as an animage hiding in the empire's military. I've even got a wound to show for my participation in the battle. No doubt Lord Rolan will want to speak with me."

Before Sev finished speaking, the commander sat bolt upright, his hands gripping the armrests of his chair. "You report to Lord Rolan specifically? Not the Council of Governors?"

Sev was taken aback by his reaction—the man had been so serene and measured up until now. Apparently this was something Elliot hadn't known or hadn't yet revealed. "Yes, sir. Well, I reported to Captain Belden, who was my commanding officer, and he reported to Lord Rolan. I trained in his Aura Nova compound. When the mission was announced, Captain Belden called it a special assignment for Lord Rolan. He made no mention of the council."

The empire had a standing army of thousands of soldiers, but they were spread throughout the valley. And each answered to a different governor who acted as general for the troops stationed in their province. They deployed them however they saw fit—to keep the peace in busy cities, to patrol their borders, or to travel with them as they spent time in the capital or toured the provinces. When there was war, their orders came from the king or queen, or in this case, the Council of Governors. Without a monarch who had final say over the council's decisions, every move they made had to be decided upon by a majority vote. Sev often heard people on the streets of Aura Nova lamenting the fact that the council couldn't agree on when to take a piss, never mind the larger issues that affected the empire.

"So, this attack wasn't sanctioned by the entire council . . . ," the commander mused. "I may be able to use that."

Sev hadn't considered the ramifications of this information. If Lord Rolan had done this without approval—and failed—well, the council might decide to punish him when word reached them of this unprovoked attack on a Pyraean settlement. Phoenix Riders might be illegal in the empire, but its laws didn't reach into Pyra any longer. It had no authority in the Freelands.

"Why would he do it alone?" Sev wondered aloud. "Why risk it? What are the Phoenix Riders to him?"

He didn't really expect the commander to answer him, but after several silent moments, he spoke. "Beyond a way to gain fame and notoriety?" he mused, rubbing his chin. "Lord Rolan received his position as governor of Ferro when I was exiled. When he learned from Elliot that *I* was behind the resurgence of the Phoenix Riders . . . I think the task of destroying us would have had all the more appeal to him. He and I have a past that stretches back decades."

Sev felt suddenly out of his depth. These were the empire's highest politicians, with endless wealth and resources at their disposal. What could he possibly do on his own?

"What we'd need is proof . . . evidence that shows Lord Rolan's hand in all this. Without it, he will simply deny involvement and claim Captain Belden and the rest of these soldiers went rogue. But with it, we might be able to turn the council against him and gain some kind of leverage."

Sev nodded, thinking about the captain's messenger pigeons. Trix said she hadn't been able to find any letters to Elliot during their time traveling Pyrmont. That meant any communication they had was likely back in Aura Nova. But still, would Belden's correspondence implicate Rolan, or was the man wise enough to cover his tracks?

"I'll try my best, Commander. The bondservants notice far more than they let on, and Ilithya had plenty of contacts. I think I may be able to get their help."

"Remember, soldier—they cannot know I sent you or that we have even spoken. If they suspect you . . ."

"They'll kill me," Sev said simply. "I have no valuable information I can reveal. It's my life I risk, and nothing else."

The commander nodded, unable to deny the truth in that. Sev wasn't trying to be cavalier or pretend that he was eager to risk his life. His shoulder throbbed. The truth was, sometimes surviving was the hard work, and if he could face that, he could face anything.

"Sir," Sev began hesitantly, after several moments of silence. "She— Ilithya—she said something to me, before she died. Something . . . odd."

Sev hadn't forgotten Trix's final words to him, but he'd been so over-whelmed with grief and pain, and unsure of his next step, that he hadn't had the clarity of mind to really examine them further. Until now.

"And this was out of character for her?" he prompted.

Sev almost wanted to laugh. "No, not really, but what she said was strange, even for her. She said that Avalkyra Ashfire lived."

The commander stared at him. "Well, that can't be true. She died in the Blood War—there were witnesses. Ilithya was an old woman, and she served our queen faithfully all her life. Love can sometimes twist the mind and make facts out of fictions. Surely, if Avalkyra Ashfire were alive, she would be here with us."

The words made sense, and his steady, reassuring tone urged Sev to agree with him.

But when Sev nodded, the commander glanced away, looking more unsettled by the idea than he'd let on. He had certainly been quick to dismiss it, and Sev supposed that he couldn't blame the man for thinking a long-dead queen was in fact actually dead. He'd probably known Avalkyra—or at least met her—and being a Phoenix Rider, he must have supported her in the war.

Then why did Sev get the impression that he didn't *want* her to be back?

The commander shifted in his seat, looking down at the bag next to Sev's feet once more. "And what of this gift you've brought us?"

Sev leaned down to open the top of the bag, revealing eleven smooth gray eggs. He frowned. Hadn't there been twelve when Kade loaded this satchel? It had been so dark, maybe Sev had miscounted. Or worse, maybe one had fallen out on his journey. He shook his head. There was no helping that now.

"The eggs are yours, all but one. You will keep it here for me as a sign of good faith—and as a guarantee of my loyalty."

"You don't seem interested in becoming a Rider, soldier. . . . How does an egg guarantee you won't turn your back on us when the situation suits you?"

"I'm sure you can guess how much that egg would fetch on the Narrows

Night Market—enough to set me up comfortably for the rest of my life. I'll be back for it."

Sev spoke confidently, and the commander seemed to believe his words. Sev was a good liar.

He would never sell the egg. Keeping it was like keeping hope alive. Hope that he might have somewhere to return to, some place he belonged. And if, when all was said and done, he decided he truly didn't want to be a Rider—well, there might be someone else in his life who did.

"Why do you want to go back there?" the commander asked. He seemed genuinely interested, not because of the mission or his concerns, but because he didn't understand it.

"I want to finish what I started. I never knew which side I was on before all this. Now I know."

I am a daughter of death. . . .
From the ashes I rose, like a phoenix
from the pyre.

- CHAPTER 44 -
VERONYKA

AFTER HER CONVERSATION WITH Sev, Veronyka went back to the barracks, her heavy heart lightened somewhat. She'd barely crawled into her hammock—or so it seemed—when she was being shaken awake again.

Her mind came sluggishly back to consciousness, and she opened her eyes to see Tristan standing over her. She sat bolt upright, knocking her head into his with a painful crack.

"Damn it, Nyk," Tristan said, rubbing his brow.

"Sorry," Veronyka hissed. Around them the barracks was quiet and deserted—clearly everyone was already up and working again.

"What time is it?" she asked, rubbing her eyes.

"It's only just daybreak," he said, dusty beams of pale sunlight slicing the air between them. She stretched, her sleeping shirt sliding down to reveal her shoulder. It was innocent enough, a bare scrap of flesh, and yet . . . Tristan stared fixedly at the small patch of brown skin, the attention making her whole body prickle with heat. He quickly forced his gaze away, which only made Veronyka more self-conscious.

They hadn't spoken since the battle, and as she looked at him, a fresh wave of hot shame washed over her. Despite everything Val had done, Veronyka couldn't put all the blame on her sister's shoulders. *Veronyka* had been the one to lie to Tristan, repeatedly, and she knew she owed him an explanation.

"Tristan, I . . . ," she began, turning stiffly to face him, her muscles aching with the memory of the attack. "I'm so sorry. I never should have lied to you."

His eyes were guarded as he considered her, and even his mind was more closed than usual. "Why did you do it?"

Veronyka shrugged. "I wanted to be a Rider, and I knew the commander was only accepting boys. . . . I thought it was my best chance."

"I know why you pretended to be a boy," Tristan said. "I just don't know why you didn't tell me. Maybe at the start, but all those times we were alone . . . training or just talking. I told you about my"—he waved a hand—"thing with fire. Didn't you trust me?"

Veronyka let out a shaky breath. This was the question she didn't really know how to answer. "Of course I did," she said, sitting forward. "I trust you more than anyone in the world," she added in a whisper.

His throat worked as he swallowed, and he looked down. She knew she needed to give him more—that he *deserved* more—but she struggled to find the right words.

"It's just that I've trusted before," she continued slowly, "trusted with all my heart and soul, and . . . and . . ." Her voice wavered, but Tristan finished the thought for her.

"And that person betrayed your trust."

They looked at each other, and Veronyka knew he understood her.

"I thought about leaving when they put Xephyra in that cage. I was going to tell you before that, but I was afraid I'd be punished or sent away. Then after . . . I guess I thought the commander might value Xephyra as a broodmare over me as a Rider."

Tristan nodded, his expression pained, and she knew it hurt him that he couldn't dismiss her concerns about his father.

"And," Veronyka continued, voicing the most personal reason of all for withholding the truth, "it was hard to face the possibility that you might hate me for lying to you, might lose whatever respect you had for me. . . ."

"I could never hate you, Nyk—Veronyka," he corrected hastily.

"You can call me whatever you want," she said softly. Something about it was intimate, suggestive, and she wasn't sure if she'd meant it that way or not.

His eyes widened before he looked away, red splotches creeping up his neck and the edge of his jaw. He bit the inside of his cheek, and Veronyka could swear he was fighting to keep a pleased smile off his face.

"It doesn't change anything for me, you know," he said, still not looking at her. "Boy, girl—whatever. You're you, and that's all I care about."

Veronyka thought her heart might burst.

"What was it your sister called you—*xe* Nyka?"

The bubble of pleasure that had swelled up inside her quickly deflated. "Yes," she said uneasily. She'd told Tristan he could call her anything, but she wasn't sure she wanted him to call her that.

"Something about her . . . She gives me the creeps," he said, laughing awkwardly and rubbing the back of his neck.

It's her shadow magic, Veronyka thought miserably. *The very same magic I have, the magic that has somehow bound us together.* She would have to tell him about that, too, and soon, but not yet. She needed to learn more about it, for one, and for another . . . their relationship was on fragile ground right now. Veronyka wanted to wait for more stable footing.

"Is she gone?" he asked, trying to keep the hopeful note from his voice—and failing.

The question was an interesting one—yes, Val, her older sister, the one she'd grown up with, her last "family," was gone. Forever, in fact. Now she had a dead rebel queen to contend with. "Yes, I think so."

"Good," he said firmly. He glanced at her and gave an apologetic look. "I'm sorry. Your sister . . . you'll have to explain her to me sometime."

Veronyka snorted, though she wasn't amused. Explain her sister? That prospect would have been hard enough a few days ago, but now? Veronyka didn't even know if she and Val—or was it Avalkyra?—were actually related. "I'll try," she said. "I promise."

Tristan gave her a wry grin, and relief flooded her body. A group of servants walked past the window, their voices cutting through the quiet moment. Tristan straightened, seeming to remember that he'd woken her up for a reason.

"The commander would like to see you," he said, somewhat formally.

Her head whipped in his direction. "Me? *Why?*"

Tristan avoided her eyes. "You'll see."

"Tristan tells me it was your idea to release the phoenixes."

They were back in the commander's office, standing in front of his long carved table as he sat behind it. Veronyka shot an accusatory look in Tristan's direction, and though his head was bowed, she could've sworn she saw a smile twisting his lips.

"Y-yes, Commander."

"And was it also your suggestion to use the other animals, the horses and pigeons and the rest?"

Veronyka nodded, her heart dropping into the pit of her stomach.

The commander showed his teeth—a smile? "Then I have you to thank, not Tristan, for the success of our defenses. From what I've gathered from various reports, if it weren't for their joint efforts, the stronghold would have been overrun—and if it weren't for the female phoenixes in particular, the village gate would have fallen much sooner."

"Oh, um, you're welcome," she said, glancing at Tristan once more, who now smiled openly at her, his cheeks dimpled.

"You know," the commander said, his tone thoughtful, "in the glory days of the empire, it was the female phoenixes, not the males, who were renowned for their fighting prowess. Riders prayed for daughters over sons so they might have a legendary warrior in the family."

Veronyka glared at him. *She* was such a daughter, denied in favor of sons. But of course, Commander Cassian didn't know that.

She could take it no longer.

"Sir, I-I have something I need to tell you."

Tristan widened his eyes at her and shook his head in warning. She ignored him.

"Yes?" the commander said, looking between them with a frown on his face.

"The new female, the one who helped us secure the village gate? She's mine, sir—my bondmate."

"Your bondmate . . . ," he said, leaning forward and resting his elbows on his desk.

Veronyka felt dizzy. She was going to tell him. She was going to willingly reveal her lies and betrayal to the man whose own son was afraid of him.

"You see, I'm female too. My name's not Nyk. It's Veronyka."

The commander stared at her, his pale-brown eyes flat and unreadable as he picked through her words. Veronyka's stomach roiled so badly, she thought she might be sick.

"How can you be bonded with that phoenix when she's been here such a short time and was too old to begin with?" He didn't seem upset, simply curious—or maybe he was distracted from his anger by the conundrum of their bond.

"We were bonded before I arrived, Commander," she said faintly. "She—Xephyra, my bondmate—was killed, so I came here, hoping for another way to become a Rider. When I learned that you weren't taking female apprentices, I thought pretending to be a boy was my only chance. I hoped that I could bond with a male, or with a new female, when the time came and be allowed to stay. But then she came back. . . . She was resurrected, and . . ."

Veronyka was rambling now, the words pouring out in a torrent as the commander surveyed her with mild, detached interest. Tristan, who had been listening intently—even he didn't know the full story—was tense beside her.

"I'm sorry," she finished in a whisper.

The commander got to his feet, moving somewhat gingerly with unseen injuries, and came around to lean against the front of his table.

He eyed Veronyka thoughtfully, scratching his chin with a heavily bandaged hand. From what she'd overheard after the battle, the empire had devoted another two hundred soldiers to the diversions. The patrols had been drawn into the villages, only to be ambushed by soldiers armed with metal nets, and the messenger pigeons sent by Tristan had been intercepted by animage bondservants in the empire's employ. By the time the Riders realized they'd been fooled, hours had passed, and the stronghold was on the brink of collapse.

He looked at Tristan, as if asking—or confirming—that his son already knew what Veronyka had just revealed. Tristan nodded curtly.

"We can't keep her bondmate imprisoned," he said after his father continued to remain silent. "It's not right. We should let her train to be a Rider. I'll sponsor her."

The commander's eyes widened at Tristan's last few words. "You're still an apprentice."

Tristan shrugged. "I won't be for long—you said so yourself."

Veronyka pressed her lips together, willing them to stop trembling. This was it, the moment when the commander would decide her and Xephyra's fate. She could scarcely breathe.

"No. She cannot join the Riders," the commander said, crossing his arms over his chest. Veronyka thought her heart had actually stopped beating, so still and silent was her body. "But *he* can."

Veronyka and Tristan shared a look of confusion.

"He? You mean she can train as Nyk, not Veronyka?" Tristan asked.

"I do," the commander said with a nod.

"I don't understand," Tristan said. "She's bonded to a female phoenix. . . . How will we explain it to the others?"

"Male-female Rider pairs are uncommon but not unheard of. There was a mixed pair in my old patrol in the empire, and there have been dozens of others throughout history. Wise Queen Malka rode Thrax, who was a male phoenix, and of course there were Callysta and Cirix. We will simply cite precedence."

Veronyka remained motionless, a weight settling on her chest. This was what she wanted, wasn't it?

"Why continue to lie?" Tristan pressed, glancing at Veronyka. "How long can she be expected to keep it up?"

"In case you hadn't noticed, Tristan, the Phoenix Riders have been dealt a rather severe blow. With Elliot's deceit and that empire soldier bursting in here, there have been whispers of traitors and informants working for the empire. We are not infallible, but I must restore order and confidence in our operation here. I don't want to give the others an excuse not to trust her. We must show strength and unity. To reveal that she has been lying all this time will do her—and us—more damage than good."

The words surprised Veronyka, who hadn't considered the ramifications of her deception beyond what the commander might do to her. But he was right that their false sense of security had been shattered, and the last thing she wanted was to be the subject of suspicion and distrust. But wouldn't it be better to face those reactions sooner rather than later? If they were angry with her *now*, how much angrier would they be after months—or maybe even years—had passed? And it wasn't just her charade to maintain: Tristan, Cassian, Ersken—even Sev knew the truth. It wasn't a question of *if* her lies would be exposed. It was a question of *when*.

Veronyka stared at her feet. With every word the commander spoke, the pressure on her chest intensified. This wasn't right. This was how it started: You did what others wanted, made concessions and compromises, over and over again, until you were nothing but what they wanted you to be. It had happened all her life with Val, but she wouldn't let it happen here. She'd earned her place here—*Veronyka* had. This was who she was, and she would deny it no longer.

The commander was looking at her expectantly—she could feel his gaze on the top of her head.

She lifted her chin. "Thank you, Commander," she said. He gave a gracious nod—until she added, "*But* I cannot accept the terms you offer."

As soon as she said the words aloud, the burden on Veronyka's chest eased, and she could breathe properly again.

"Excuse me?" he said, so politely that Veronyka thought he might truly not have understood her. She looked at Tristan, and though his mouth flattened with worry, he nodded in encouragement.

"I will stay here as Veronyka, or not at all. I understand that there will be questions and confusion, but I proved myself in that battle—Xephyra and I both did. We defended the gate. We fought alongside your villagers and your apprentices. I refuse to lie to these people any longer. They deserve better, and so do I."

It was cold, standing there in front of the commander, refusing the thing she'd wanted her entire life. Without the Phoenix Riders, she and Xephyra would be outcasts. Together, but still alone.

A warm hand gripped Veronyka's shoulder, and she realized that she wasn't alone, that Tristan was standing beside her. He was lending her his support, even after she'd lied to him and betrayed his trust. He was standing with her against his own father because he believed in her.

In *her*. In *Veronyka*.

"Do you have something to say, Apprentice?" the commander demanded, but Tristan's response was interrupted by a knock at the door. It opened without permission, and in stepped Morra, with Ersken and Jana standing just behind. Tristan's face lit with triumph, and Veronyka guessed that he'd invited them.

"If he doesn't, then I do," Morra said, without pretense or apology. She stood at Veronyka's other side, with Ersken and Jana next to her. "I have tolerated your foolhardy rules for long enough, Cassian. She conned me, it's true," she said, casting Veronyka a look of mild chagrin, "but there was no trickery in what she did during that battle. If it weren't for her, we'd not have lasted until you returned. She was fearless and brave, and she sacrificed herself—as well as her phoenix, her beloved bondmate—for the sake of everyone here." She sniffed and turned her glittering gaze on Veronyka as she continued. "She was glory on wings, like the Pyraean queens of old."

Veronyka's cheeks heated, fear and pride and guilt warming her from the inside out. She'd lied directly to Morra's face, and yet the woman had still come here to support her.

She glanced at Commander Cassian, but he seemed unsurprised to hear that she'd actually *flown* Xephyra in the battle, which meant he must have already known.

"She's the strongest animage I've worked with," added Jana, smiling proudly, her eyes crinkling in the corners. "There's no animal on this mountain that's a match for her." Veronyka knew she was thinking of Wind and couldn't help but smile in return.

"Now we have those," said Ersken, nodding down at Sev's satchel in the corner of the room, which Veronyka noticed there for the first time. "I assume we'll be recruiting again."

"Yes," the commander said stiffly.

"Well, why not start with our Veronyka?"

He said it a bit awkwardly—the name unfamiliar in his mouth—but the word "our" was what really drew Veronyka's notice. Her throat was tight.

"This attack means war, Commander," said Morra. "It's time to ready our troops, and we'll need every fighter we can get."

"'Specially ones as fierce and fearless as her," added Ersken.

The commander's mouth was open. He was surrounded on all sides, and when Beryk, his second-in-command, edged into the room, asking, "Am I late?" the commander actually threw his hands into the air.

He stared at them all for several breathless moments, then deflated. He waved them off impatiently. "So be it."

Veronyka had never heard anything sweeter.

That night they burned the bodies.

The enemy soldiers had already been dealt with, so this fire was for friends and allies alone.

It had taken the better part of two days to gather enough wood and for the taxed priest and acolytes—busy helping the healer—to perform last rites and prayers. For some, local family was summoned from nearby villages.

They stood in a semicircle just outside the village gate, where the obstacle course had been. The once-grassy plain was now a desolate field of scorched earth and upturned soil, and the scent of smoke mingled with new boards of wood and fresh paint as they tried to rebuild what was lost.

But not all things could be so easily replaced.

Xoe was the last to be placed on the pyre, her red-purple feathers dull in the evening light. Ersken did the honors, and when he stepped back into the crowd, he put a hand on Sparrow's shoulder, who had laid Chirp onto the heap just moments before.

Sev was there, shoulder still heavily bandaged, along with Morra and her kitchen maids, Jana and the stablehands, and Beryk and the rest of the Riders. Elliot was allowed to attend as well, standing at the back of the crowd with a guard on either side of him, his head bowed.

Veronyka was off to the side, feeling a bit like an intruder. She hadn't known any of the people who had died, but she'd recognized their names and faces. Captain Flynn hadn't made it, and neither had one of the smiling washerwomen or the metalworker's apprentice. One after another they blurred together, and she regretted not having made the effort to get to know them. But that was the nature of life and loss: There was never enough time.

The priest spoke a few words, but Veronyka hardly listened. It was the wind she heard most of all, like a mother's caress, brushing her hair from her forehead and murmuring comforts into her ears.

At the end of his prayers, the priest finished with the phrase, "May their eternal flames burn bright."

Everyone repeated the words, and Commander Cassian touched the lit torch he'd been holding to the edge of the pyre. Tristan stood next to him, stoic and respectful.

The flames licked across the dry kindling, the dead finally free to be carried into the sky, where their spirits would burn forever like candles in the dark.

Veronyka's vision began to blur, turning the fire into shimmering, dancing light. She knew it was useless to fight the tears, so she let them flow, giving her a release she hadn't realized she'd needed.

She cried for Sparrow, who'd lost a part of herself, and for Xoe, who burned with enough bones to bring her back, but who might decide she'd rather stay among the stars.

She cried for all the people she did know, and for the people she didn't. She even cried for Val, her once sister, whom she felt she'd lost for good. She cried for her *maiora* and for the knowledge that Veronyka had no family left, that even the one she'd thought she'd had wasn't hers at all.

But then a warm hand slipped into hers, large and strong, and Veronyka was startled to find Tristan standing next to her. In his face was a question, and Veronyka nodded, swiping at her eyes with her other hand. She would be okay.

He gave her hand a squeeze—but didn't let go. Instead he turned and faced the fire with her.

Some families you were born into. Others you made along the way.

A feast was held that night. Commander Cassian put a stop on all repairs inside the stronghold and the village and gathered everyone in the dining hall, workers and guards and apprentices alike. It was like a second solstice festival celebration, with plenty of food and drink and music.

While everyone was seated, the commander announced that the Riders would be accepting new recruits. He didn't mention *who* those recruits would be, or how many, but the news was enough to raise everyone's spirits. While no Riders had been killed during the attack or the diversions, several had been wounded, and of course, they'd lost two of the female phoenixes. They needed whatever good news they could get.

The commander didn't mention Veronyka—either her position as one of the new recruits *or* the fact that she was a girl in disguise. Maybe he wanted to give her the chance to do it, or maybe he thought it would detract from the hopeful tidings he'd just shared. More recruits, more Riders—that's what mattered.

Veronyka ate with Morra, who was actually sitting in the dining hall and not working all night in the kitchens as usual. At first she'd been shy to be alone with the cook, afraid Morra might hold Veronyka's lies against her despite standing up for her right to train as a female Rider. But she'd seemed more impressed than angry, declaring that the only other person who could talk circles around her had been Avalkyra Ashfire. Veronyka had smiled uneasily and changed the subject.

With the completion of the funeral rites, everyone began to look to the future. While the Riders had survived the attack, their existence on Pyrmont was no longer a secret. Hatred for the empire simmered among the inhabitants of the Eyrie, who wanted vengeance for lost loved ones and ruined livelihoods, and most believed Commander Cassian was too much of a politician to strike back against their enemies. While Veronyka worried about what was to come, she marveled at the fact that, *finally*, she would be a real part of it.

As the drinking and celebrating went late, Veronyka left the dining hall, reaching out to Xephyra. She found her dozing happily in the Eyrie, a fully healed Rex by her side. Ever since she'd been released from her cage, Xephyra's entire energy had changed, and her presence in Veronyka's mind was one of comfort, happiness, and trust. Their bond was growing stronger by the day, and whatever happened, wherever they went from here on out, they'd go there together.

"Tired?" called a voice from behind.

Veronyka slowed her pace, allowing Tristan to catch up with her as she cut a path across the cobblestones.

She took a deep breath and looked up at the starry sky, vast and glimmering, a constant reminder that those she'd lost were always with her. The night breeze slipped across her skin, warmer than it had been in months, and she had what she'd always wanted: a future as a Rider and a place to call home.

"Not even a little bit," she said, grinning.

"Good," he said, smiling too and stepping in front of her, walking backward so they could talk face to-face. "I was hoping you'd be interested in some more practice."

She frowned. "You mean archery—or the obstacle course?"

"No," he said, jerking his thumb over his shoulder. Ersken stood beneath the archway that led into the Eyrie. He held something large in his hands.

A saddle.

Ersken handed it to Tristan and disappeared with a self-satisfied smirk.

"It was mine from when Rex was a bit smaller. So, what do you think?" he asked, trying to gauge Veronyka's reaction from her openmouthed, stunned silence. "Fancy a proper ride, side by side?"

Somewhere in the Eyrie, Rex and Xephyra stirred from their slumber.

Veronyka beamed at him. *Side by side.* "Yes."

Day 21, Ninth Moon, 170 AC

I am atop Genya's Tower now, watching as the world burns below.

I see you in the sky, and you are everything you ever promised: blood, fire, death.

It is sick, I know, but I am comforted that you are here. My heart swells to see you again—even if it might be the last time.

I'm sorry that I failed you—that we failed each other. But life does not often give second chances.

Know that I love you, dear sister, and I always will.

—Pheronia Ashfire

I had a sister once. . . .

- EPILOGUE -
AVALKYRA

AVALKYRA WAS TIRED.

No. "Tired" was a small, weak word meant for mothers with squalling babes and soldiers working the night watch.

Avalkyra was completely and utterly exhausted.

Somehow her life had become a ridiculous game, a series of motions she went through . . . not for *her* benefit, but for Veronyka's. She'd been forced to play nursemaid and mother and sister and friend. She'd wrapped the jagged truth of their lives in soft wool and bright cotton, sheltering Veronyka, protecting her from the ugliness of the world—often at Avalkyra's own expense. She didn't mind getting her hands dirty—indeed, they had been filthy long before Veronyka—but as the days and years of her life wore on, she wondered if they'd ever be clean again.

Perhaps it was her exhaustion that had made her reveal herself to Veronyka before she left. She'd never meant to keep the secret so long, but the truth, which had once been difficult to hold in her mouth, seemed to stick to her tongue and obstruct her throat. Veronyka was erratic at best with her shadow magic—how could Avalkyra trust such a person with her most precious secret? Even now there was still so much to tell Veronyka, so much she wouldn't understand.

Avalkyra sat at the edge of her small campfire, staring at the satchel that contained her newly acquired phoenix egg. She hadn't looked it at since she'd stolen it from the sleeping soldier's side. It had been difficult to take only one—and to let the empire rat *live* when she'd promised otherwise. But if Avalkyra had learned one thing in this second life, it was patience. If she'd stolen more eggs, they'd have noticed and hunted her down. And if she'd killed the soldier as well . . . they'd have noticed the missing egg that much sooner.

If she was honest with herself, the egg unsettled her. Avalkyra suspected there was a reason that phoenix didn't hatch for her inside their cabin, the same reason she hadn't been able to hatch the half a dozen other eggs she'd tried to incubate before. She didn't know if it was because her bondmate had forsaken her and decided not to come back, or if there was some other, deeper reason. Whatever it was, she feared this egg would turn out the same as all the others.

Dead. Empty. Worthless.

Avalkyra took a deep, calming breath.

Fear is a luxury.

It was an ancient Pyraean proverb. The full version was recorded in *The Pyraean Epics*:

> *When pitch-darkness falls and lanterns fail, fear is a luxury.*
> *When war invades and there's no escape, fear is a luxury.*
> *When death gladly claims what life forsakes, fear is a luxury.*

Avalkyra couldn't afford fear. Darkness and death were coming, and as for war? It was already here.

In fact, it had never truly ended—at least not for Avalkyra.

She'd been fighting for thirty-four years, and sometimes she forgot why. Her mind wasn't as blade-sharp as it had once been, and the details of her life grew hazy through the lens of time. This was unacceptable.

She mustn't forget all she was and all she must reclaim.

She'd been a princess and a Phoenix Rider. She'd been the Feather-Crowned Queen.

She'd fought a war to win an empire and lost the love of her life, her sister, in the process.

When the weight of it all pressed down on her, Avalkyra thought of what she might say to Pheronia now if she were still alive.

I grow weary, xe *Onia. The world is not the same.*

I am scared for her, xe *Onia. She is just like you.*

Already it was happening, the similarities between Avalkyra's two lives becoming more pronounced with each passing day. Was this the will of the gods, then, that Avalkyra should suffer not once, but twice? Was this her destiny, to survive, to endure, but always at the expense of the ones she loved?

No. Her second chance could not be squandered. She and Veronyka would live the lives that she and Pheronia should have lived and rule the empire they should have ruled—together.

They would remake history.

To keep the details straight in her mind, Avalkyra sometimes pretended she were drafting a letter. Only, she never seemed able to actually put ink to paper. Every time she tried, she remembered the last letters she wrote. How she'd wished she could rewrite them after they were sent. How they'd gone unanswered until it was too late.

History was a living, breathing, changing thing—even when it was your own. Each day the past looked different to Avalkyra, and her imagined letter would change.

Sometimes Avalkyra was the victim, carried through the events of the war like a leaf caught in the current of the River Aurys.

Other times Avalkyra was the villain—the current itself, dragging everything and everyone she loved down with her. She suspected this was the true story, but some days it was easier to accept than others.

Usually she addressed the letter to Pheronia, but occasionally she addressed it to Veronyka instead.

Today, as she sat alone in the woods, leaving yet another sister behind, she mentally composed a new letter.

> *Dear Veronyka,*
> *I am Avalkyra Ashfire, and this is my story.*

Sure, they'd hit a bump in the road, but Avalkyra was used to setbacks. Nothing of value in life came easy; always there was a price.

Veronyka had asked a question recently, one that Val hadn't really been able to answer.

But Avalkyra could.

> *You asked me why I was here, the night of the solstice festival.*
>
> *The answer I gave you was as simple as it was complicated: I came back for you.*
>
> *I lost more than the war sixteen years ago. I lost everything.*
>
> *It was a night I will never forget. The battle fever was upon me, my blood boiling and my arrows falling from the sky like rain. I saw a figure all alone on the castle walls, with no shelter from the storm. I loosed an arrow before my eyes had even focused.*
>
> *But as my bowstring scraped across my fingers, I realized that figure was her.*
>
> *Would that I could chase down arrows, that I could command their will and intent as easily as I do living things.*
>
> *But I could not. My arrow landed true—they always did. Still, I threw caution and crown to the wind; I threw it all away and went to her. My Nyx took a dozen enemy arrows in our reckless flight, and soon we were falling, falling, like a star cast down from the heavens.*
>
> *As I held my dying sister, the battle raging around us*

and my cursed arrow embedded in her heart, I wanted to die too.

It would have been easier. Sweeter. But she would not let me.

She pressed my blood-spattered hand to her swollen belly, and I felt the heartbeat within.

Your heartbeat, xe Nyka.

I must live, she said, because she could not.

She asked too much. My phoenix was mortally wounded, and her fire burned hot all around us. Blazingly, blisteringly hot.

She asked too much.

The shock of Pheronia's wound caused her labor to begin early. She was carried to safety so they could try to save the child, though it was too late for Pheronia. They left me to die. I do not blame them.

I felt it, the moment she left this world. I heard her last screams, and as the fire of my bondmate licked across my skin, scorching my flesh, I heard another sound—the wails of a newborn child.

I died, too, but that was not the end. It was the beginning. Our beginning.

I came back. For you, Veronyka.

We were born together, you and I.

False Sisters.

Shadow Twins.

I promised Pheronia I would protect you. It was her dying wish.

I told her I would make things right.

And I've only just begun.

TIME LINE

NOTABLE RULERS FROM THE REIGN OF QUEENS (BEFORE THE EMPIRE, BE)

First Era, before dates and events were meticulously recorded (c. 1000–701 BE)

1000 BE – 800 BE	Queen Nefyra[1], the First Rider Queen: Chosen by Axura to be the first animage and the First Rider Queen. Ignix, the first phoenix, was her bondmate.
775 BE – 725 BE	Queen Otiya, the Queen of Bones: Defeated a rival Rider family that tried to usurp the throne.

Second Era, the height of Pyraean culture (701–279 BE)

701 BE – 645 BE	Queen Aurelya, the Golden Queen: Began construction on the Golden City of Aura, from which she derives her name.

---

1   *Despite having died soon after her love Callysta, Nefyra is the only queen mentioned in any stories, legends, or histories from Pyra during this period. Because these accounts were verbal, it is likely there were errors in dating, or perhaps Nefyra's heirs were named for their mother and grandmother, suggesting that Nefyra II, Nefyra III, and even Nefyra IV were the likely queens mentioned in these accounts. There is also the possibility that the line between myth and history has been blurred here, and the songs and myths were intended to depict the First Rider Queen as having a divinely long reign.*

412 BE – 335 BE   Queen Liyana, the Enduring Queen.

335 BE – 317 BE   Queen Lyra the Defender: Mustered
the Red Horde, the first-ever
gathering of the entirety of Pyra's
Phoenix Riders. Successfully defended
Pyra from the Lowland Invasion.

Third Era, the decline of the queendom (279–1 BE)

9 BE – 37 AE   Queen Elysia the Peacemaker: Her
reign in the queendom was most
notable for the loss of the Everlasting
Flame and the mass evacuation of
Aura. After leaving Aura, Elysia
founded the empire and married the
Ferronese King Damian.

AFTER THE EMPIRE (AE)

37 AE – 45 AE   Queen Ellody the Prosperous: Reign
of Prosperity.

45 AE – 56 AE   King Justyn the Pious: Reign of
Piety. Transformed Azurec's Eyrie
from a training facility into a
pilgrimage site. Built the Pilgrimage
Road.

56 AE – 95 AE   Queen Malka the Wise: Reign of
Wisdom.

95 AE – 121 AE	King Worrid the Learned: Reign of Learning. Born deaf, he designed a specialty saddle to accommodate his condition. Set up the Morian Archives, making sure the empire's histories were recorded by the priests and acolytes of the god Mori.
121 AE – 135 AE	King Hellund[2] the Just: Reign of Justice.
135 AE – 147 AE	Queen Bellonya the Brave: Reign of Bravery. Lost her arm as a child, became the fiercest spear thrower in the empire's history.
147 AE – 165 AE	King Aryk the Unlikely[3]: The Unlikely Reign.
165 AE – 169 AE	Queen Regent Lania of Stel: Reign of the Regent.
169 AE – 170 AE	Avalkyra[4], the Feather-Crowned Queen. Pheronia[4], the Council's Queen.
169 AE – Present	Reign of the Council.

---

2 After he married his bold Queen Genya the General in 125 AE, many began to refer to this period as the Reign of the General.

3 So called because Aryk was Bellonya's youngest brother, fourth in line for the throne, and only ascended because his older brother and both her daughters predeceased her.

4 Neither princess was officially crowned, but both were referred to as queens before their deaths in the Blood War.

GLOSSARY

GODS

Axura[1]: Goddess of the sun and daylight, as well as life, symbolized by the phoenix

Nox[2]: Goddess of the moon and darkness, as well as death, symbolized by the strix

deathmaidens: Servants of Nox, who lure lost souls into the dark realms

Miseriya: Goddess of the poor and hopeless

Hael: God of health and healing

Teyke: God of luck, a trickster, symbolized by the cat

Mori: God of knowledge and memory, symbolized by the owl

Anyanke: Goddess of fate, symbolized by the spider

NOTABLE PEOPLE

Callysta: Lover and second-in-command of Queen Nefyra. Callysta's and Queen Nefyra's phoenixes were also mates: Cirix, the first male phoenix, and Ignix, the first female phoenix.

Queen Genya the General: Married to King Hellund the Just. Exiline was her phoenix. Successfully defeated the brigands that terrorized her husband's reign.

The Five Brides: Queen Elysia and her four royal sisters (Anya, Rylia, Cara, Darya). They helped secure peace treaties during the founding of the empire through marriage alliances.

---

1 *"Azurec" in the Trader's Tongue*

2 *"Noct" in the Trader's Tongue*

The First Riders: Fourteen female warriors chosen by Axura to fight against Nox's darkness.

King Rol of Rolland: Ancestor to Rolan of Stel, governor of Ferro. Famous for failed assassination attempt against Ferronese King Damian.

FAMOUS BATTLES

Dark Days: The dawn of time, when Axura's phoenixes battled Nox's strixes, saving the world from endless night.

Lowland Invasion: Attempted invasion of Pyrmont (then the entirety of the Pyraean Queendom) by an unnamed civilization living in modern Pyra's Foothills.

Stellan Uprising: A series of lords who banded together in Stel, attempting to wrest several major cities from empire control, eventually defeated by Avalkyra Ashfire.

Blood War: The conflict between opposing heirs and sisters Avalkyra and Pheronia Ashfire.

Last Battle: Fought in Aura Nova, final conflict of the Blood War.

COMMON TERMS

animage: A person who has animal magic.

shadowmage: A person who has shadow magic.

Red Horde: The first-ever gathering of the entirety of Pyra's Phoenix Riders, under Queen Lyra's reign.

False Sisters/Shadow Twins: Siblings born mere moments apart by the same father and two different mothers.

Mercies: Phoenix Riders that checked battlefields for survivors and resurrections.

Shadowheart: Spymaster, position in ancient Pyra in service to the queen.

magetax: Tax charged to animages for the use of their magic.

magical registry: Record of known animages in the Golden Empire.

bondservant: An animage working off a criminal debt to the empire.

mageslave: A derogatory term for a bondservant.

PYRAEAN TERMS

Aura: City/place of gold, and the ancient capital of Pyra.

Aurys: River of gold, which flows from Pyrmont's highest peaks down into the valley of the Golden Empire.

maiora: Grandmother

pyr: Fire or flame

Pyra: City/place of fire; also known as the Freelands, an emancipated province of the Golden Empire.

pyraflora: Fire Blossom, a tree with red flowers symbolic of Pyra. Petals can be made into poison, and sap is used for fireproofing.

phoenixaeris **(s);** *phoenixaeres* **(pl):** Phoenix Rider or Phoenix Master

phoenovo: Phoenix egg

petravin: Rockwine, a distilled Pyraean liquor aged with a blend of local herbs and flowers, made only in the small village of Petratec.

sapona: Soaptree, plant used to bathe with.

Sekveia: The Second Road, an ancient route through the wilds of Pyrmont that supposedly leads to lost treasure.

xe: Prefix meaning "sweet" or "dear"; can also mean "brother" or "sister," based on the gender of the name it's paired with.

xe xie: Generic term of endearment translating to "sweet" or "dear" (xe) "one" (xie).

ACKNOWLEDGMENTS

In order to say a proper thanks, I guess I should start at the beginning. Thank you to my parents—to mom, for great hair and a curious mind, and to dad, for a love of food and my fantastic Mediterranean skin tone. Also thank you for life.

To my brothers, Robin and Jason, who toughened me up young and frequently left me behind . . . it was in those lonely hours that I learned how to be strange and imaginative and to entertain myself. I also have to thank you for my sisters, Melissa and Jenny, as well as my nieces (Brianna and Ella) and nephews (Alexander, Everett, and Oliver), who have brought so much chaos and laughter into our family, and have taught me to appreciate silence (and naps).

To John and Angela, my Greek parents, who have been an essential part of my life since I was sixteen. I cannot thank you enough for the unconditional love and support that I don't deserve and will never forget. Thank you, too, for being the best possible caretakers and guardians of my heart, Rocky.

Thank you to Bruce (who kept asking to read this book, even though I kept saying it wasn't ready yet) and to Isabel, my godmother (with whom I share a love of reading and a name), and all my cousins and family, near and far.

To Shannon, my best friend since grade five, and Joel, who understands and shows appropriate enthusiasm for nerdy things like fantasy maps. You guys always kept me fed and drunk and safely tucked in on your couch. Cheers to Niki Wee and Shannon "Red Boots" Robertson, who were often tucked in next to me.

ACKNOWLEDGMENTS

To Derek, who never doubted for a second that I could do this. I love you.

I must shout out all my critique partners and writer friends who have been there for every setback and success, making this winding road a bit less lonely. Elly Blake (my first CP, who blazed the trail so I could follow safely behind); Tara Wyatt, my bae (who holds my hand through every victory and meltdown); Morgan Rhodes (who helped brainstorm this idea); Eve Silver (who always made me believe it was only a matter of time); and fellow TRW friends Maureen, Julie, Bonnie, and Molly. Thank you to my other CP, Jennifer Welker, and my agent—and publisher—sister Akemi Dawn Bowman. To Jessi, thanks for the wine and cheese and cheerleading, and thank you to work friends past and present: Amy, Megan, Lindsay, Rohana, Chelsey, and Ashley.

To my agent, Penny Moore, who is a certified badass and a tireless advocate for her clients and for the YA community. I'm truly lucky and honored to have you on my side. Thanks as well to Andrea, Sandy, and everyone at Empire Literary.

I honestly can't imagine *Crown of Feathers* at any other publisher or with any editor other than Sarah McCabe. Thank you for seeing the potential in this story and helping to grow and shape it into the kind of book I always hoped it could be. I am intensely proud of what we've made together.

Big thanks to Jessi Smith for your sharp eyes and fresh insight, and to Sarah Creech and Kekai Kotaki for a breathtaking cover that makes my heart sing. To Jordan Saia for the stunning map and to Mike Rosamilia for the gorgeous interior design. To everyone at Simon Pulse and Simon & Schuster for believing in this book and for being there every step of the way: Mara Anastas, Chriscynethia Floyd, Liesa Abrams, Katherine Devendorf, Elizabeth Mims, Sara Berko, Chelsea Morgan, Lauren Hoffman, Caitlin Sweeny, Alissa Nigro, Anna Jarzab, Christina Pecorale, and the S&S sales team, Michelle Leo and her team, Nicole Russo, and Samantha Benson.

And finally, thank you to the readers. Without you there would be no books at all, and what a dreary world that would be.

TURN THE PAGE FOR A SNEAK PEEK
AT THE CAPTIVATING SEQUEL!

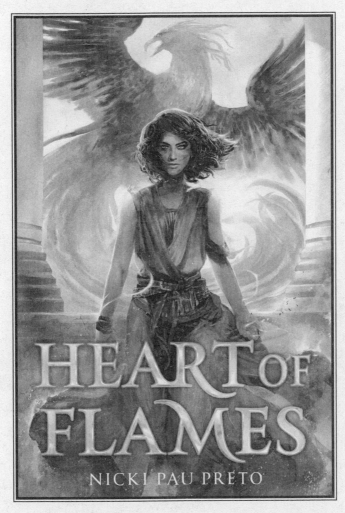

My dearest daughter;
I want to tell you a story.

- CHAPTER I -
VERONYKA

VERONYKA KICKED AS HARD as she could at Tristan's face.

They were in the training yard, and the evening sun was casting purple shadows across the stronghold walls, setting the golden phoenix statue atop the temple ablaze with light.

The dinner bell had rung, and the rest of the apprentices and masters had finished their training for the day. Those who remained were packing up and putting away practice weapons or watching idly as Veronyka and Tristan circled each other.

They were sparring, and though Veronyka hated the attention, she'd told Tristan she wouldn't quit for the day until she'd beaten him *once*. So far, she was zero for five, and she was getting tired.

Tristan dodged her kick as easily as he'd dodged the others, stepping out of range while Veronyka stalked after him.

"Why don't we pick this up tomorrow?" he asked, panting slightly. Only *just* slightly. Meanwhile, Veronyka was a sweating, gasping mess.

She wanted to answer him—*no*, they couldn't wait until tomorrow. The final details from the attack on the Eyrie had trickled in over the past few weeks, putting numbers and names to the deaths, damages . . . and the missing.

And this was just the start.

Things were going to get worse before they got better; the empire wouldn't forget them after such a narrow defeat . . . and Veronyka had to be ready. She'd been practicing as hard as she could, pushing herself in flying and weapons and yes, combat. It was her weakest skill and therefore required the most effort and attention.

Veronyka had to make sure that when the empire returned—when the next battle was fought—she wouldn't be sidelined. And the only way to guarantee that didn't happen was to become a Master Rider. To pass the very tests Tristan had struggled with weeks before—and had trained months to conquer.

Despite her skill in flying and her powerful animal magic, Veronyka was so far behind in combat, so utterly out of her element, that it was all she could do to remain on her feet.

But she wouldn't give up. Couldn't.

In response to Tristan's offer to quit for the day, Veronyka tightened her mental walls and kicked again.

Because it wasn't *just* the combat that had Veronyka struggling. She couldn't fight Tristan like she could the others, because while her shadow magic was always reaching for minds and hearts, when it came to Tristan, it was like water being sucked down a whirlpool. She had to actively fight it, aware that every touch, every moment of eye contact, might be the thing that broke them both wide open. It was like fighting two opponents at once.

Tristan shook his head with a slight smirk, leaping effortlessly out of reach.

Veronyka swallowed, her throat dry as the sand under her feet, and tried to focus.

For weeks now, the combat lessons had been her worst, the things she dreaded most of all. There was no one for her to match up with, no one the same size and skill level. So she took a constant beating. Her only advantages were her speed and the fact that she was a small target.

She was also unpredictable. Not on purpose, but from lack of expertise.

Occasionally, it worked in her favor, catching her opponents off guard.

Everyone except for Tristan. When they sparred, sometimes it felt like *he* was the one with shadow magic. He anticipated her moves so easily, was able to counterstrike flawlessly, and adapted almost instantly to everything she threw at him.

Of course, if she *really* wanted to win, she could open her mind to him and anticipate *his* every thought and movement. Like she had during the attack on the Eyrie. Their connection had been heady and powerful, but then they'd been working *together* to achieve a goal. She'd also lost consciousness when she'd let their bond get away from her outside the breeding enclosure the day before that. It was too dangerous, and it was also exactly the kind of thing her sister, Val, would do.

Veronyka shook her head. The more she opened herself to him, the more Veronyka opened herself to Val—and that was the last thing she needed right now.

Veronyka just had to get *one* win under her belt for the day, one win so she could go to dinner with her head held high.

Most fights ended by a person getting hit with a pin or hold, taking too much damage to continue, or being shoved from the ring. So far, Tristan had managed to pin her three times and knock her out of the chalk like the other two.

As he regained his balance across the ring, Veronyka studied him.

Underneath the padding he wore his usual training gear, the fitted tunic and worn leather as much a part of him as his curling brown hair and dimpled smile. There was a difference in him, though, a sense of surety that wasn't there before. The battle for the Eyrie had changed him—it had changed them all—and he seemed more confident in himself now, though the only difference in his outward appearance was a strip of red-dyed leather that wrapped around his biceps, indicating his position as a patrol leader, and a fine white scar that split his bottom lip—a souvenir from the attack.

"Come on, Tristan," called Anders from the sidelines, grinning widely. "Put this apprentice in her place."

The others laughed and jeered, and Tristan's jaw clenched. He'd never been great at handling teasing, and since Anders's taunt was technically directed at *her*, Tristan was taking it even worse than usual.

Veronyka knew the words were meant in fun. Anders and Tristan had only recently been elevated from apprentices, after all, but there were others who she suspected enjoyed the heckling with more malice. Latham, another apprentice turned Master Rider, smirked from just behind Anders, a coldly amused glint in his eye, and Fallon's second-in-command, Darius, whispered behind his hand into his patrol leader's ear. Many of them had been distant toward her ever since she'd revealed the fact that she was Veronyka, not Nyk, and she could tell they were suspicious of her closeness with Tristan. Even now . . . the masters rarely trained with the apprentices—at least not like this, one-on-one—but Tristan was helping Veronyka because she'd asked him when her lessons were done. The others saw it as favoritism, as special treatment. Maybe even something more.

"Shut it, Anders," Tristan practically growled, tossing his sweat-soaked hair off his forehead in agitation.

"Or stuff it at dinner," Veronyka piped up, trying to defuse the situation. Anders guffawed, but he didn't leave. Nobody did.

Veronyka and Tristan had sparred together often and knew each other's habits and tendencies probably better than they knew their own. Tristan was a careful fighter, observant and thoughtful about his attacks, learning his opponent before he made a move. But he could be baited. Anders had just proven that.

If Tristan could be lured into making a mistake, Veronyka might be able to squeak out of this with a win.

Still, she hesitated. While Tristan was calm and disciplined, Veronyka was wild and impatient—and he knew it. It was usually *her* fault she lost; Tristan just watched and waited for her to mess up, then capitalized on whatever opening or vulnerability she presented. But in order to bait him, she had to make a move.

Because of her short height, Veronyka favored kicks over punches, her legs having a farther reach than her arms. Skirting around him and angling her body, Veronyka prepared for a left kick to Tristan's ribs. She avoided his eyes—it was the surest way to open a shadow magic connection—and kept her gaze on Tristan's upper body, the angle of his shoulders and the position of his hands, held loosely at his sides.

As soon as her knees bent and her foot left the ground, Tristan's muscles tensed—his right arm tightening, preparing to block the blow, while his shoulders turned, angling his body away from her.

But Veronyka *didn't* kick. At least, not from her feet. She dropped into a crouch at the last second and swung out her foot with a kick aimed at Tristan's legs, not his torso.

She glanced up in time to see his eyes bug out and his body twist as he tried to adapt.

Veronyka's foot struck Tristan's calf, and the crowd that surrounded them *ooh*ed as his leg was taken out from underneath him.

But rather than falling backward out of the circle—her true goal—or collapsing onto his side, Tristan fell *forward*.

Onto her.

She'd only managed to clip one of his legs as he'd tried to leap over her kick, and now Tristan was stumbling toward her, and her only choice was to roll to the side.

She missed his impact with the ground by inches, but was defenseless as she tried to get away.

He leapt onto Veronyka's exposed back, slipping his arms around her middle and across her chest. Hands locked together, he gave a hard pull, drawing them both backward into the sand. In the blink of an eye he had turned *her* attack into *his* dominant position. As he lay on his back with Veronyka pinned against his chest, Tristan was a heartbeat away from pressing his forearm against her windpipe in a choke hold. She scrambled to the side, making the angle more difficult, but Tristan took the new opportunity she presented by throwing his leg over her body and climbing on top of her.

Veronyka squirmed, kicking and taking wild swings at his head, forcing him to duck and cover, but he still managed to get into position, his thighs on either side of her hips as he straddled her.

Being close like this caused Veronyka's mental barriers against him to shake and tremble. Her magic wanted him, reached for him often, seeking any excuse to strengthen their link. There were certain triggers—eye contact, touch, and sensory details like smell and sound—that weakened her walls one stone at a time. Add them all together, and it was an assault her mind couldn't withstand.

He lowered his head toward her chest, making it impossible for her to strike him as he got inside her guard. He was adjusting his position, regaining his balance, her wildly flailing legs no longer unseating him.

His heavy breath rang in her ears, his chest rising and falling and pressing against her own. His damp tunic and sweat-curled hair smelled of soap and salt and sunshine—smelled of Tristan—and Veronyka tried her best to jerk away. But he was holding her fast, and when she lifted her face and their eyes met, the stones of her mental walls came crumbling down.

The link between them burst open, as swift and certain as river water cascading through a dam. Her magic surged, and her mind filled with his thoughts, so loud and clear that they drowned her own.

He was aware of her in the same way she was aware of him. Her smell, her feel—all of it put Tristan on high alert, but not for the same reasons his presence rattled her. Well, not entirely. It wasn't just shadow magic she protected against, wasn't just a mental connection she feared.

Heedless of the consequences, Veronyka shoved at Tristan's chest, twisting and squirming—panicked and desperate for escape.

But her recklessness made her vulnerable, as she'd known it would. She realized with frustration that she'd exposed herself to an arm lock, and her breath hitched as she waited for Tristan to seize the chance. All he had to do was shift his weight, reposition himself so they were perpendicular to each other, then grab her wrist and pull against his chest, hyperextending the elbow. A simple move; a second's work.

Only, he didn't.

Tristan was frozen, and Veronyka frowned at him a moment before bucking her hips, sending him off-balance and slipping to the side. She squirmed out from underneath him and turned around, watching as he got slowly to his feet.

Silence had descended over the training yard, heavy with confusion. Tristan had *let* her go, had let the chance to pin her pass him by. He'd even let her get back to her feet.

He was panting now, sand stuck to the sweat coating his forearms and legs.

Their eyes met again, but she didn't need their mental connection to confirm her suspicions.

He'd wanted to shelter her from the pain and humiliation of losing in front of all the others.

He'd wanted to protect her.

It reminded her of when he'd tried to keep her out of the fighting during the attack on the Eyrie; it reminded her of Commander Cassian keeping the Riders locked up safe while the world around them fell apart. Worst of all, it made her think of Val, always supposedly "protecting" her, so thoroughly and so fiercely that Val wound up hurting Veronyka far worse than if she'd just let Veronyka know the truth, if she'd just treated her as an equal.

Anders and the others were watching, and there was no way they'd missed his hesitation. Tristan had gone easy on her, and they all knew it.

With something like a snarl, Veronyka lunged for Tristan. He had no choice not to fight her now, no opportunity to waver.

He absorbed her attack, using her momentum against her. Twisting his upper body—and hers along with it—he threw her over his hip, sending her flat to her back on the sand.

The wind was knocked from her lungs, and as she struggled to her feet, she saw the chalk line underneath her.

She'd been tossed from the ring. Veronyka let her head fall back to the ground, her eyes squeezed shut.

Zero for six.

Later, Veronyka took out her frustration in the saddle. It was what she did most nights when she couldn't sleep.

As an apprentice, she was supposed to sleep in the barracks inside the stronghold, and Xephyra inside the Eyrie. That separation was a part of Rider training, meant to strengthen the bond over distance, but Veronyka hated it. She always slept better next to Xephyra and had tried to sleep inside the Eyrie more than once, but was usually shooed off by Ersken, who did late-evening and early-morning rounds. Veronyka and Tristan often spent time at night on the ledge outside his rooms, cleaning armor or just hanging out with their bondmates. One time Veronyka accidentally fell asleep there after Tristan had gone in to bed, and it hadn't been Ersken who'd discovered her, but the commander himself. His suspicious look—and curious glance at his son's closed door—told her she'd better get out of there quick and avoid such a run-in in the future. People already gave them strange looks for their close friendship, which had begun when she was a stable *boy* and now culminated with her being a girl, an apprentice with a full-grown mount, *and* his underwing. She didn't need the rumor that she slept outside his door like a lovesick puppy dog added to the mix.

Veronyka had slept in the barracks ever since, and instead focused on strengthening her bond to Xephyra, particularly pushing their ability to communicate. Not only did they constantly test their range, but Veronyka also pushed her phoenix to use words when communicating rather than just thought and feeling. It was partly to keep their link strong and secure while they were separated, but also because of what had happened with Val after Xephyra's death. It sickened Veronyka to know that not only had Val manipulated Veronyka's connection to her bondmate to control Xephyra, but that Veronyka herself hadn't felt Xephyra's return because she'd blocked all thoughts of her phoenix to ease her own pain. If she'd been open, if their bond had been stronger and their ability to communicate more honed . . . maybe Veronyka would have known about Xephyra's resurrection sooner.

They practiced all day, sending words to each other whenever they were apart—eating or sleeping or distracted by other things—but the best test of their bond always came when they practiced *together*. Exercises like the obstacle course Tristan had done to finish out his apprenticeship were such an example, but Veronyka wasn't there yet in her training. Besides, she and Xephyra both preferred *flying*.

Veronyka waved to the perimeter guards and the Rider on patrol—currently Beryk—but everyone was well used to her late-night flights by now. She and Xephyra soon arrived at their destination, a practice course called Soth's Fury. The series of caves were filled with tight, narrow spaces that tested a Rider's ability to maneuver at high speeds, and they'd installed targets throughout to make a challenging run for any would-be warrior to hit them with arrow or spear.

Veronyka loved Soth's Fury, and she and Xephyra were getting better and better at navigating its darkest depths.

Ready? Veronyka asked as they approached the mouth of the caves.

Xephyra didn't reply so much as give a surge of excitement and adrenaline. An obvious *yes*, but Veronyka pushed her to communicate more clearly.

Words, Xephyra, Veronyka pressed.

Xephyra huffed beneath her. *Aeti*, she said at last.

Veronyka rolled her eyes, fighting back a grin. Whenever Xephyra grew tired of Veronyka's constant pushing, she rebelled. In this instance, choosing to reply in ancient Pyraean rather than common Trader's Tongue.

You think this is funny? Veronyka asked, going for stern but not quite managing it. There was no hiding your emotions from your own bondmate, after all.

Sia, Xephyra replied smugly. That was a northern Arborian dialect that she'd picked up from Anders, who sang old Arborian songs to the other Riders and translated them for anyone who'd listen. Most people didn't, but apparently Xephyra did.

Are you finished? Veronyka asked, the gaping mouth of the entrance drawing steadily nearer.

Verro. That was . . . Ferronese, maybe? How Xephyra had picked *that* up, Veronyka had no idea. She couldn't help it; she laughed as they dove down into the dark.

Veronyka had flown through the caverns many times and felt comfortable there, despite the dank echoes and shifting shadows that made it a somewhat spooky place. There were targets positioned at intervals within the caves, providing a variety of different shots for a mounted archer to hit. They were metallic, so they reflected sunlight—or phoenix fire—but were still difficult to spot, not to mention the fact that some were better suited to a spear throw or even a short sword or dagger, if the Rider was daring enough to fly so close.

And Veronyka was.

Her favorite part of the course was a stretch of targets that alternated between those she could hit on phoenix-back and those she could only hit on foot—partially obscured by rocky outcrops or tilted at an impossible angle. To get them all, the Rider must leap from their phoenix's back, run across uneven rocky ground to strike the target, then leap back onto their bondmate to grab their bow and continue on to the next target. It was nearly impossible, and required pinpoint precision and top-notch communication.

Veronyka gripped her reins as they barreled through the narrow opening. They weren't true reins—they didn't lead to a bridle and bit in Xephyra's mouth like a horse's reins did—but were meant to act as handholds and restraints, allowing inexperienced Riders to remain safely attached to their mounts during flight, and for more advanced flyers, they allowed a Rider to stand or reposition themselves. Veronyka had seen Fallon, the second patrol leader, fly *upside down*, using his reins to hold his body tight to his phoenix, defying gravity.

Veronyka was usually a no-nonsense flyer during lessons and drills, but after her failure in the ring today, she was determined to push herself and try her hand at some theatrical acrobatics of her own.

They moved swiftly into the labyrinthine caves, the stony walls closing in on them. They were smooth and high, like columns of dripping wax, while spiky stalagmites rose from the ground, some so large they had to be dodged as they whipped past. The shadows grew thick and cool around them, while trickles of water could be heard in the distance, remnants of some long-ago river rush.

Veronyka withdrew her bow, and through the bond she told Xephyra which targets she wanted and in what order, loosing arrow after arrow into the metallic bull's-eyes. Since it was pitch-black in the caverns, Xephyra emitted a faint glow to light the way.

Soth's Fury was divided into three courses in varying levels of difficulty, and though she knew it was foolish, Veronyka followed the most challenging route, each target marked by a circle of vivid purple paint around its edge like the tips of Xephyra's plumage.

While the start was easy enough, the course became more difficult with every target they passed. Up ahead, the stretch of concealed targets loomed, and Veronyka braced herself.

Telling Xephyra to slow her pace ever so slightly, Veronyka tightened her handhold and carefully pulled her feet from the stirrups until she was squatting on Xephyra's back. Her phoenix flapped her wings as little as possible, keeping her flight steady, but still Veronyka wobbled and struggled for balance.

The first concealed target appeared, tucked into a crevice above a narrow ledge and hidden behind a stalagmite that jutted from the ground. Veronyka braced herself, waiting.

Now, she said to Xephyra, leaping to the right as her phoenix flew left, just missing the stalagmite by inches. Veronyka slipped and stumbled as she tried to regain her footing, but she couldn't slow down—momentum was all that was keeping her on such a scant foothold. She careened forward, whipping out a dagger and hitting the target with a resounding thud, before hurtling past it and leaping out into the empty air of the cavern.

But then Xephyra was there, as Veronyka had known she would be. She slammed hard into the saddle, but even the pain couldn't dim the feeling of triumph coursing through her veins.

Xephyra swung her neck around to look at Veronyka, and her dark eyes danced with fiery pleasure.

Good? she asked, turning back around and soaring gracefully between rocky spires.

Aeti, Veronyka replied, and Xephyra crooned.

Afterward, they sat on their favorite slab of stone and watched as the sun began to rise in the distance.

Veronyka leaned against Xephyra, her body exhausted and her thoughts still, finally finding the peace she failed to get alone at night. After a while something stirred in the back of her mind, and Veronyka knew that Tristan was awake.

Just like that, her peace was shattered.

Everything about her bond to Xephyra made Veronyka feel better, stronger, and more alive. Her bond to Tristan did too. But she couldn't let it. Being bonded to another human was dangerous. . . . Veronyka had learned that lesson the hard way. She kept trying to forget about it, kept hoping that it would resolve itself or fade into the background. Tristan deserved to know that a magical link existed between them that gave her insight into his thoughts and feelings, but it was hard to face telling him that *without* any words of comfort or reassurance.

Why, yes, Tristan, I can hear your thoughts and sense your feelings—and no, I have no idea how to stop it. You're scared? Me too.

Veronyka knew nothing of shadow magic and only the barest fragments of how to strengthen or weaken its power. The only person who had the answers she sought was Val, and reaching out to her was a risk Veronyka couldn't take.

She glanced down at her wrist, where a braided bracelet sat. It was her own hair she'd cut off weeks ago, black and shining with a heavy coat of *pyraflora* resin, along with a single braid of Val's vibrant red. There among the strands were beads and trinkets Veronyka had collected throughout her childhood, as well as a single, heavy golden ring.

It belonged to Val—or rather, Avalkyra Ashfire, the fierce warrior queen who had died almost two decades before and had been resurrected into the girl Veronyka had until recently thought was her sister.

The ring was tied into the braids so that only the simple golden band was visible, while the front, with Avalkyra Ashfire's seal, was hidden from view.

The revelation that her sister, Val, wasn't her sister at all had left Veronyka feeling utterly lost and adrift. Family had always been a fraught concept for her—how could it not be, with someone like Val as a sibling?—but at least she'd known where she belonged and who she was, however unimportant. Now that she'd discovered her *maiora* who'd raised her was actually Ilithya Shadowheart, Avalkyra Ashfire's spymaster, and that Val was actually the Feather-Crowned Queen herself, Veronyka had to question everything she'd ever been told about her life. And the most pressing question of all? If Val was Avalkyra Ashfire, then who was Veronyka?

Only Val knew for sure, and she was not only elusive and self-serving—she was dangerous. Veronyka had seen firsthand what Val could do with shadow magic, and she feared opening herself up to her once-sister. What if Val just fed her more lies? What if Val sent more jarring dreams and memories? What if she *didn't*, and Veronyka never, ever learned the whole truth?

And what if Val tried to take hold of Xephyra again? Veronyka knew it was possible, and she was more aware than ever of the complicated web that shadow and bond magic wove between her and the ones she cared about.

Like Xephyra. And Tristan.

Veronyka knew she had to protect herself, but she had to protect *them* most of all.

And the best way to do that—the only way she knew how to do that—was to block Val out completely. To block shadow magic completely.

To pretend neither existed.

But as Veronyka mounted up and headed back to the Eyrie—Tristan's presence a warm glow in her mind and heart and Val's a cold shadow that followed her everywhere she went—she knew that to block shadow magic was to block animal magic, to block Xephyra, and that was something Veronyka simply couldn't do.

TO SAVE THE WORLD, YOU NEED AN UNSTOPPABLE GIRL.

EBOOK EDITIONS ALSO AVAILABLE

Simon Pulse simonandschuster.com/teen